ADVENTURERS
WANTED

The Adventurers Wanted series by M. L. Forman

BOOK ONE
SLATHBOG'S GOLD

BOOK TWO
THE HORN OF MORAN

BOOK THREE
ALBREK'S TOMB

BOOK FOUR
SANDS OF NEZZA

BOOK FIVE
THE AXE OF SUNDERING

BOOK FIVE

ADVENTURERS
WANTED

THE AXE OF
SUNDERING

M. L. FORMAN

SHADOW
MOUNTAIN

© 2017 Mark L. Forman

This book is a work of fiction. The characters, places, and incidents in it are the product of the author's imagination or are represented fictitiously.

Visit us at ShadowMountain.com

Library of Congress Cataloging-in-Publication Data

CIP data on file
ISBN 978-1-60907-934-5

Printed in the United States of America
LSC Communications, Crawfordsville, IN

10   9   8   7   6   5   4   3   2   1

For all the fans who waited so patiently without complaint.
Thank you.

INVICTUS

BY WILLIAM ERNEST HENLEY

Out of the night that covers me,
　　Black as the pit from pole to pole,
I thank whatever gods may be
　　For my unconquerable soul.

In the fell clutch of circumstance
　　I have not winced nor cried aloud.
Under the bludgeonings of chance
　　My head is bloody, but unbowed.

Beyond this place of wrath and tears
　　Looms but the Horror of the shade,
And yet the menace of the years
　　Finds and shall find me unafraid.

It matters not how strait the gate,
　　How charged with punishments the scroll,
I am the master of my fate,
　　I am the captain of my soul.

CONTENTS

CONTENTS

CONTENTS

ACKNOWLEDGMENTS

Ah, acknowledgements. This is possibly one of the hardest parts of writing. There are so many people who make a book possible, many of whom I don't even know. How can I thank them, you all? All I can say is thank you, and I hope you all know how much your work means to me. Thank you, thank you.

Special thanks to the Shadow Mountain crew—Chris, Heidi, Derk, Sarah, Richard, and Malina—who have waited without complaint for this book to be finished. Sorry about the wait and thank you for not grumbling—or at least not grumbling where I could hear you.

A very special thanks to my editor, Lisa Mangum, once again. Lisa makes me look good, because I really don't know much about writing. I tell a story; Lisa makes it readable for all of you. In this case, Lisa also managed to push me along when I really didn't want to be pushed. In short, this book is only here because Lisa kept things moving forward.

Thanks once again to Brandon Dorman, the illustrator for his amazing cover art.

Last but certainly not least, thanks to you, the readers. None of this would really matter without all of you. Thank you, and keep reading.

Prologue

Alex woke in darkness. He knew that he was awake because of the pain. It felt as if he'd fallen down a long flight of stairs, hitting every step on his way down. He tried to sit up but the pain was too much, and he slumped back to the ground once more.

Where am I? he thought. *How did I get here?*

Even thinking hurt, but now that the questions had started there was no way to stop them. He tried again to get up and failed. All at once his body moved without his even thinking about it. He scrambled to his knees, looking around wildly. He knew he was trying to find someone, but who?

"Vankin," Alex said softly.

Yes, Whalen Vankin should have been close by, but why? Who was Whalen Vankin? Why should he be close? Alex tried and failed to find a face in his mind, the face that went with the name Whalen Vankin. His failure troubled him. His mind wondered for a time, going completely blank, and then a new question came: an important, urgent question that he had to answer.

Who am I?

For a moment the question didn't make sense. He thought

about the answer for a long time, slowly forming the words in his mind before speaking.

"I am Alexander Taylor, adventurer, wizard, dragon lord, and . . ."

"Say it again," a voice inside his head demanded.

"I am Alexander Taylor, adventurer, wizard, dragon lord . . ."

"Again, louder," said the voice.

"I am," Alex started but stopped as a new pain ripped through his brain.

"Again," the voice demanded.

"I am Alexander Taylor, adventurer, wizard, and dragon . . ."

"Again, again, again," the voice screamed over the growing pain.

"I am Alexander Taylor, adventurer and, and . . ."

The words came slower and the pain in his head pounded like a giant hammer every time he spoke them. Alex didn't know why, but he had to keep repeating the words.

"I am Alexander Taylor, adventurer, wizard, dragon . . ."

Each time he said the words the pain grew. It felt like pieces of his brain were being torn away, and he put his hands on his head to try and protect himself from the pain. He continued to try to say the words, all of the words, but with each attempt he knew that something was forgotten, something was lost.

"I am Alexander Taylor . . . I am Alexander . . . I am Alex . . . I am . . ."

His mouth continued to move but there was no more sound coming out. The pain was so bad that he hardly noticed when he fell back to the ground and curled himself into a ball. Darkness closed in around him once more. When he woke again all of this would be forgotten, but there would still be one question to answer.

———•••———

Out of the darkness came light, and with the light came pain. The pain was terrible, but it seemed to be fading. He moved slowly, unsure of himself and unsure of everything around him. His eyes felt out of focus, and the small lights above him were dim and seemed to be winking off and on. He reached out for them, trying to touch them or capture them in his hand, but he could not. His pain wasn't as bad when he put his arms down, and it was easier to breathe as well. For a long time, he stood looking up at the little lights, trying to remember what they were and why they were there, but he couldn't remember.

Eventually he noticed that the strange little lights above him were going out and staying out, but things were becoming clearer. He looked around and faced a blindingly bright light that appeared from nowhere. It confused and comforted him at the same time. He struggled toward this new light, and it grew brighter as he moved. He thought he must be getting closer to the light, because it was getting warmer. Everything he could see had changed, from darkness to gray and then to brilliant colors. The colors all had names, but he couldn't remember what they were.

Staggering forward, too weak and worn to worry about forgotten names, he watched the bright light climb into the sky. It was warm, and it would have filled him with hope, but he had forgotten what hope was. All that he knew was he had to keep moving, moving to where the light had come from. He tried to think of why he needed to move but there was no answer, there was only a desperate need to keep going.

As the light moved higher into the sky he stopped looking at it. He touched his side once, trying to force more air into his lungs. The searing pain forced him to his knees, and it was a long while before he could get up and move forward once more. He avoided touching his side as much as he could after that, holding his arm across his chest to prevent it bumping him and bringing back the pain.

As the bright light was sinking behind him he rested for a moment, looking into the bag he was carrying. It was empty, but he felt that there should be something there, if only he could remember what it was. This bag was important, but he couldn't remember why. The bag didn't matter. It was light enough to carry, and its straps helped him to keep his arm from bumping his side.

Times of darkness and light passed almost unnoticed. His only thought was to keep moving; moving to where the bright light had first appeared. The dark times were worse than when the bright light was above him. There were noises in the darkness, noises of things moving around him that he could not see. They were like ghosts in his mind, reminding him of things he had forgotten and could not remember.

Finally, after what felt like forever, he reached his end. Unable to struggle forward another step, he leaned against a large object that grew out of the ground. He was finished, and whatever force had driven him to move forward for so long was gone. There was nothing now, nothing but to sit and wait for darkness to cover him. Perhaps the darkness would take away his pain, and he could finally rest.

CHAPTER ONE

THE BEGINNING

One year earlier

A lex gazed into the flickering fire. He was restless and impatient, and he was angry with himself for feeling that way. Waiting was hard for him, but he knew there was nothing else that he could do. His friend Whalen Vankin had asked him to wait; wait for a message that might not come. Why Whalen wanted him to wait he did not know, and that's what made waiting so hard. Whalen had not explained what he was doing or where he was going. The old wizard had said that he had to check on something, and had asked Alex to wait for him to send word, because he might need help.

Dozing off in front of the fire, Alex suddenly jerked awake. His eyes scanned the room as he got to his feet. Powerful magic had just been used somewhere close, powerful magic that Alex recognized as coming from Whalen. He started toward the door, but had only taken a single step when an urgent tapping started. Alex almost jumped to the door, only just lifting the latch before Whalen pushed his way into the house, forcing Alex to take several steps backwards.

Whalen spun around, looking back into the darkness outside, and then slammed the door shut and threw the bolt to lock it. Alex stood in stunned amazement. His friend looked terrible. Whalen's clothes were dirty, his hair was a confused mess, and it looked like he hadn't eaten for days. Alex could tell that Whalen was nervous, possibly even afraid, but he didn't know why.

"Whalen, what's happening?" Alex asked.

"Who are you?" Whalen demanded, turning to look at Alex.

"What? You know who I am. What's going on?" Alex asked again.

"Tell me who you are," Whalen demanded, his eyes ablaze with power. "Tell me as if this is the first time we've ever met."

Alex took a step back, surprised by Whalen's question and the sudden gathering of power—power that he was prepared to use. For a moment Alex considered how he could defend himself, but that thought slipped away as he saw the desperate look on Whalen's face.

"I am Alexander Taylor, adventurer, wizard, and dragon lord," Alex said in as calm a voice as he could manage.

"Is it safe here?" Whalen asked. "Have you seen any strangers in the area? Have you felt any magic or had any feeling that you were being watched?"

"We are perfectly safe here," said Alex, confused by the questions. "I haven't seen anyone at all in a month, and I'm sure that nobody is watching me or my house."

"In your second true form, what do you become?" Whalen asked, his staff rising slightly.

"I am a dragon," Alex said. "A dragon of true silver."

"Indeed you are," Whalen said, his entire body relaxing. "I'm sorry, Alex, I had to be sure that you are you."

"Why? What has happened to make you so afraid?" Alex asked, terrible ideas filling his mind. "And how would my telling you who I am convince you that I am who I say I am?"

"Oh, there's no need to worry—not yet, at least," Whalen said, moving into Alex's house. "Nothing terrible has happened. Well, at least not anything I know about. As for my believing that you are who you say you are, that's a silly question. You know very well that all words have power. Anyone saying that they were you would not be as convincing as you are. Besides, who else would know about your second true form?"

"Not many people," Alex answered. "But what has happened to you, Whalen? You look terrible, and your sudden entrance was a bit alarming to say the least."

Alex returned to his chair in front of the fire and motioned to Whalen to take the chair next to it. He watched his friend with concern, noticing how tired and worn he looked. He wanted answers, but he knew that Whalen would explain things in his own good time.

"It appears that I've stirred up a hornet's nest," Whalen said, after getting comfortable in the chair. "The last time we talked, I told you that I needed to check on some things. It seems that there are people who aren't happy about my checking."

9

"What things?" Alex asked. "What have you been doing since you left me here waiting for you?"

"Yes, it is time that I explained everything to you," said Whalen, and then fell silent once more.

For what seemed like a long time Whalen said nothing, and Alex knew that his friend was trying to gather his thoughts. There seemed to be some great sorrow in Whalen, a sorrow that Alex had never seen before.

"There is a dark wizard," Whalen said at last, not looking at Alex. "He is moving slowly, carefully, but I know where he is. More importantly I know who he is—or at least who he *was*."

"Do you want to capture him? Is that why you said you might need my help?"

"Capture is not an option," said Whalen, closing his eyes and leaning back in his chair. "This wizard must be destroyed—completely. That is why I asked you to wait. That is why I need your help, Alex."

"But you can destroy him, can't you?" Alex asked.

"Do you remember, not so long ago, I told you how many wizards I have trained?" Whalen asked without answering.

"Yes, you said that two of your students had taken staffs."

"You are one. The evil that I am now after—he is the other."

"But how? I don't understand," said Alex, shaken by Whalen's words. "If he took the oath as a true wizard, how could he have turned to evil?"

"He was always evil, but I did not see it," Whalen said, his voice shaking slightly with emotion. "I chose not to believe what I knew to be true, and trained him against my own better judgment."

"But why?"

"Because he . . . he is part of my family," said Whalen, his voice dry and cracking. "He is, or was, a great-great-great-grandson of my brother. Oh, there are too many generations to count them all."

"In all those generations you stayed in touch with your family?" Alex asked.

"Yes, though they did not know who I was," answered Whalen. "It would not have mattered anyway. From the moment I saw this boy, I knew him. He looked so much like my brother. . . for that reason alone I agreed to train him as a wizard."

"Now he's turned to evil, and you must destroy him," said Alex, feeling truly sorry for Whalen.

"I must try," said Whalen. "The trouble is that he will know when I am near, just as you know when I am near. I have no hope of sneaking up on him, and even if I could get close, I'm not sure that I am powerful enough to destroy him."

Alex thought about what Whalen was saying for a few seconds before speaking. He understood why Whalen had asked him to wait, why his friend needed his help. Destroying a wizard would not be easy, but the idea of destroying a member of Whalen's family troubled Alex. If there was any way to reclaim him, to turn him back to good, he had to try. After several more seconds of thought, Alex said the words that he had never dreamed of saying.

"You want me to destroy him for you."

"It is the only path I can see that might lead to success," Whalen said. "Though if I must, I will face him alone. It is, after all, my responsibility. I will not ask you to follow this path with me if you feel that you cannot."

Whalen's words hit Alex like a slap in the face. Whalen was offering him a way out. Whalen would not demand his help; he would only ask for help, help that Alex could see he desperately needed.

"I will not desert you," Alex said firmly. "Will you tell me his story? The story of how he came to be what he is? I would like to know as much as I can before I face him."

"It will be some time before you face him," said Whalen, sounding both relieved and grateful that Alex had agreed to help. "He is gathering his power in the castle of Conmar, on the western edge of the western land of Jarro."

"Conmar Castle?" Alex asked.

"An ancient place," Whalen said, his voice soft. "There are many legends in Jarro about the castle of Conmar. It was once a center of power and it is believed that many wizards lived there over the ages. Some stories say that the lords of Conmar were wizards and pirates, and that they had dealings with dragons and sea serpents. Other stories say that the wealth of Conmar came from lands to the west, lands that no one else in Jarro has ever discovered."

"As interesting as the legends are, I would like to know the story of your nephew," Alex said.

"Jabez," Whalen said. "He has the same name as my long-dead brother."

"I'm sorry, Whalen. I know this can't be easy for you, but I need to know all you can tell me about him," Alex said.

"A short story, though the telling may be long," Whalen replied, but he did not go on.

For several minutes Whalen said nothing. When he did begin to talk his voice was little more than a whisper. Whalen's story was a sad one, and at first Alex wondered how much of it he would have to relive in his own lifetime. Whalen had become a wizard while still a young man, and had often returned to his home after adventures. He had seen his family die of old age, their children grow and have children of their own. After the first few generations he had not gone home as often. It was hard for him to visit the places of his youth, hard to remember those who had been close to him and were now gone.

Whalen kept track of his family over the years, however, though he seldom visited after the first hundred years. He would from time to time return to his old home, but he never told anyone who he was. He would go as a traveler or a merchant—anything but a wizard. His family remembered that there had once been a wizard in their family, and they were proud of that fact.

After more than three hundred years of being a wizard, Whalen had gone home to see how his family was getting on. When he had visited in the past he had always made sure his family was taken care of. He would sometimes use his magic and sometimes spend some of the treasure he had won on adventures to help them. It was important to him that his family always had enough, and never went without. Alex understood this, but he found it odd that Whalen had kept returning home for so long.

On this particular visit, Whalen had met his nephew, though many generations separated the two of them. The young Vankin's name was Jabez. Not only did he bear the same name as Whalen's brother, he also looked like Whalen's brother. More important to Whalen was the fact that Jabez had magical abilities, and it didn't take Whalen long to see that Jabez had the makings of a wizard.

So Whalen took Jabez as his apprentice and taught him the ways of magic. More than once he had reason to worry about what Jabez would do with his training. Whalen's love of his long dead brother allowed him to overlook anything Jabez did wrong, or that might be considered evil. He thought his nephew would grow out of his cruel ways and give up the small evils that were part of his life.

After years of training, Whalen had asked Jabez to take the wizard's oath and become a true wizard. Jabez agreed to this, as it fit in well with his own plans. Whalen didn't know anything about Jabez's secret plans, so he was happy to see his nephew become a true wizard.

"At first he did many good deeds," Whalen said, his voice heavy with sorrow. "He was kind and generous, and I thought he had become the man that I had always hoped he would be."

Jabez had gone on adventures, traveled to many lands, and done a great deal of good in all the lands he visited. Whalen had never suspected that anything was wrong, and he never would have known that Jabez had turned to evil—except now Jabez had returned from the dead.

"He faked his own death in Barkia. For over two hundred years I've thought him dead, but now . . . now I know that he is alive."

"How did you find out?"

"Dreams, emotions, thoughts coming into my mind that I didn't understand. Do you remember when we last met, the thought that came into your mind? The thought that was not your own, and you didn't know where it came from?"

"Yes, I remember," Alex said, thinking back to that day.

"It came because I was close to you, and that thought came into *my* mind. We are linked by magic, you and I. Just as I am linked to Jabez. His anger and his evil sometimes enter my mind, and it is all I can do to push those thoughts out."

"Do my thoughts and feelings enter your mind?"

"Not often," Whalen said with a weak smile. "Your mind is more closed to me than Jabez's. Mostly because of the way you were trained as a wizard, and partly, I believe, because of what you are. Jabez was trained as a normal apprentice, and so our minds grew much closer together than yours and mine are."

"Was my training so very different?" Alex asked without thinking.

"You know it was, Alex. Most apprentices spend years with their masters," said Whalen. "You and I spent how long to-gether? A day? Two? You learned almost everything on your own, which is an impressive thing. It has been brought up more than once in the council of wizards, though no conclu-sions about your remarkable abilities have been made."

"But you are still my master. Our minds are still linked by magic."

"Yes and no. In name I am your master, but I think in reality you are your own master. But we're getting off the subject."

"Of course," Alex said, not wanting to press Whalen for answers to his own questions.

"Jabez has returned, and he has turned away from the path of a true wizard. At first he hid his mind from me, but now he doesn't seem to care. If anything, he has let me feel his thoughts as a kind of challenge. It almost seems that he is daring me to come and find him," Whalen said, his voice trailing off as he finished.

"I take it from your story that you've been in Barkia. You had to find the place where he was supposed to have died."

"Yes, I was in Barkia. That's where I stirred up the hornet's nest."

"What do you mean by hornet's nest?" Alex asked.

"I foolishly went to Barkia as myself," Whalen answered. "I didn't think anyone would notice, or if they did notice me they wouldn't know why I was there. Unfortunately, someone did notice me, and they were curious enough about why I was there to keep an eye on me. I suppose you can guess who it was keeping their eyes on me, following me, and even trying to ambush me more than once."

"The Brotherhood," Alex said without having to think about it.

"Yes, our enemies in the Brotherhood. I'm certain that Jabez is a member of the Brotherhood. He may even have been part of them when he faked his death and vanished."

"That was more than two hundred years ago. It's hard to believe the Brotherhood has gone unnoticed for so long."

"Oh? I don't think it's hard to believe. Consider your last adventure. Nezza had been a divided land for five hundred years or more. We know the Brotherhood was at work there. Who knows how long they've been plotting and working evil?"

"Yes, I suppose that's true. I never really thought about how long they've been around."

"Neither had I. In any event, I discovered that there are a great many more people working for the Brotherhood than you might think. Most don't know they are working for them, I'm sure of that. Still, there are a fair number of magical people working either with or for the Brotherhood. I had a close call with half a dozen warlocks before I managed to get out of Barkia."

"Warlocks? What exactly do you mean by warlocks?"

"I mean the worst version of a warlock that you can think of. Powerful magical people trained in the darkest magic. Oh, they aren't dark wizards, not even close, but warlocks work together when they can. Six warlocks working together are a dangerous enemy, even for me."

"But you managed to escape them."

"Yes, I escaped, and led them on a wild chase. I didn't think they would follow me, but they did. For the last eleven days I've been on the run, trying to put them on a false trail before coming here."

"I'm sure you've lost them," Alex said.

"For now," Whalen said. "Sooner or later they will show up here in Alusia—I'm sure of that. They know I live here, after all, and they probably know that you live here as well."

"Do we need to worry about being attacked?"

"No, not yet at least . . . but we're getting off-topic again."

Alex didn't say anything for a time as he thought about what a group of warlocks might do if they turned up outside his house. A direct attack on him would not be their first idea, they would try to ambush him, or perhaps . . .

"Yes," Whalen said. "They would attack the innocent and try to draw you into a trap."

"I'm sorry," Alex said. "I was just thinking about the danger that might come."

"You should consider the danger, but I think it would be less if you are not here when they come looking," Whalen said.

"Of course, but Whalen, if Jabez is at the castle of Conmar, there's no real need for both of us to go there. I mean, I can take my dragon form, fly to Conmar, and destroy him."

"If only it were as simple as that," Whalen said, shaking his head. "You see, there's more to the story than I have told you. There are things I've learned about Jabez recently, things that make this task more dangerous and difficult than I would have thought possible."

"Tell me, what have Jabez and his friends in the Brotherhood done to make things so difficult?"

"We cannot simply destroy Jabez. He has used some very old magic to protect himself from any attempt I might make. If we were to destroy him as he is, he would simply vanish for a time and reappear in another land. It would buy us time, but it would not put an end to his evil."

"What magic has he used? How can he be destroyed and not destroyed at the same time? Death is final, Whalen, there's no coming back," Alex said.

"The magic Jabez has used links his life force to every person he has ever done good for," Whalen explained. "I told you, when he was first a wizard he did many good things. Now he has perverted his good deeds into twisted evil. His life force is bound to the people he helped, and to their children, and their children's children. To destroy Jabez completely, we would have to kill every living thing his magic has touched, or . . ."

"Or?"

"Or we must find a way to cut the magical link between Jabez and his victims."

"Is there a way to break the link?"

"We—and when I say 'we,' I mean you—must use the Axe of Sundering. Only the Axe has the power to break the spell that Jabez has placed on himself and send him to the shadowlands forever."

"Where is this Axe of Sundering?" Alex asked, afraid that he already knew the answer.

"Jabez has it, protected inside of Conmar," Whalen said. "How it is guarded I do not know, but I am sure that he has protected it well." Whalen reached into his bag and pulled out several books bound in black leather.

"What are those?" Alex asked.

Whalen tapped the cover of the book on top of the stack. "Journals. I think they might be helpful to us."

"Did you write them?" Alex asked.

"Yes, and so did Jabez. While I was training Jabez, I asked him to keep a journal. It is a common practice for apprenticing wizards, a way for their teacher to check up on them."

"Should I have been keeping a journal?" Alex had written

down some of his adventures, and he knew some details about his adventures were recorded in Mr. Clutter's shop, but he had not kept a personal journal.

"No—I did not ask you to keep a journal because your power was growing so fast. And all the letters you and I have exchanged over the years probably count, wouldn't you say?"

"Do you think Jabez's journals can help us find the Axe of Sundering?" Alex asked.

"I doubt that, but they might give you some clues about how and where he has hidden it. The journals can do something else to help you," Whalen answered. "Memories are often lost or grow distorted over time, as I'm sure you know. These journals, however, hold the truth of what really happened at the time it happened. I am sure that what Jabez and I wrote in these journals will be far more accurate than anything I might remember now."

"I'm sure they will help me understand Jabez, but we really need to know what his plans are right now. We need to know what he is going to do next, not read about what he's already done."

"Yes, but looking at his past will help us guess at his future plans," Whalen said. "All writers reveal something about themselves, whether they mean to or not." Whalen handed the journals to Alex. "Read them. Study them. I believe they will help us with our task."

"You mean our task of sneaking into the castle of Conmar, finding the Axe of Sundering, stealing it, finding your nephew, and using the Axe on him?" Alex said.

"I know, I know. It is, perhaps, an impossible task," Whalen said, shaking his head.

"While we think about doing the impossible, might I suggest a bath and a hot meal for you," Alex said.

"An excellent suggestion, and most welcome," Whalen said, smiling for the first time since he'd arrived. "Keep an eye on the big picture, but deal with the problems at hand first."

Alex laughed at Whalen's comment, and went to fix something for his friend to eat. His mind was already working on the problems that had arisen with Whalen's quest. There were really too many problems to think about at one time. Getting inside the castle of Conmar and finding the Axe of Sundering would be almost impossible, but there was a long way to go before they had to worry about that.

Traveling to Jarro was the first step, but that was going to be more difficult than normal as well. The Brotherhood had been following Whalen, and Whalen seemed to think that they were still looking for him. Traveling through the great arch could be dangerous, as the Brotherhood would probably have someone watching it. Once they made their way into Jarro, then what? Alex didn't know much about the land of Jarro, so as Whalen's meal started to cook he took out his magic bag.

Alex had maps of all twenty-seven known lands, as well as maps of many lesser-known lands. His map of Jarro was a good one, better than most, and he unfolded it on his kitchen table so that he could study it as he cooked. Jarro, unlike the other lands Alex had visited, was not one land. Most of Jarro was made up of three massive islands: Eastland, Midland, and Westland. Alex found the great arch marked near the center of

Eastland, and on the far side of the map there was also a mark for what had once been the city of Conmar.

"Ah, good, you have a map," said Whalen, as he walked into the kitchen still drying his hair.

"A good map, but I don't see that it will help us much," Alex said.

"Well at least it will give us some idea of where we are going, and how we are going to get there," Whalen said, helping himself to the food Alex had prepared.

"I'm guessing that Jabez will want to take over all of Jarro at some point. Since he's based in Conmar Castle, he must plan on starting in Westland."

"Yes, I'm sure that's his plan. I don't know how far along his plans are, but I think it would be safe to assume he has control of at least part of Westland already."

"At least the area around Conmar."

"It wouldn't be wise for us to suddenly turn up in Westland. Jabez will have more than one escape plan, and if we both turn up in Westland he may simply vanish before we have a chance to get the Axe."

"So where do you think we should turn up?" Alex asked.

"I don't think we should turn up at all," Whalen said. "That is, we shouldn't turn up together."

"What, then?" Alex asked.

"I have a plan, or at least the beginning of a plan," said Whalen.

Alex listened while Whalen explained what he thought they should do. Alex thought that Whalen was being overcautious and that his plan would take too long. He thought they should move as fast as possible toward Conmar Castle and attack Jabez. If Jabez ran away, well, at least the land of Jarro would be safe.

"I know this isn't the way you'd like to do things," Whalen said. "The thing is, Alex, I know Jabez. I know what he is looking for and what he is most likely to do when we get close. I believe we *can* get close, maybe close enough to destroy him— if we follow this plan."

"This is your adventure, Whalen," Alex answered after some thought. "I'll do what you think is best."

CHAPTER TWO

DETAILS

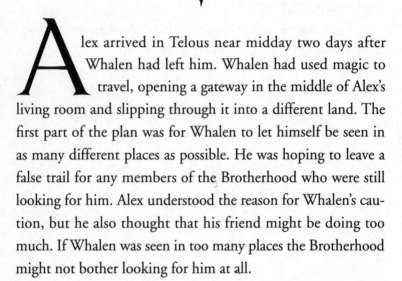

Alex arrived in Telous near midday two days after Whalen had left him. Whalen had used magic to travel, opening a gateway in the middle of Alex's living room and slipping through it into a different land. The first part of the plan was for Whalen to let himself be seen in as many different places as possible. He was hoping to leave a false trail for any members of the Brotherhood who were still looking for him. Alex understood the reason for Whalen's caution, but he also thought that his friend might be doing too much. If Whalen was seen in too many places the Brotherhood might not bother looking for him at all.

"Details," Whalen had said. "If you want to make people believe that you are doing something that you are not doing, you need to pay attention to the details."

Alex wasn't sure he agreed with Whalen's comment. He thought that too many details would give the truth away. Still, Whalen had been a wizard far longer than Alex had, and he seemed to know what he was doing.

Walking to the Golden Swan, the finest tavern in Telous, Alex was surprised to find the lobby crowded. It looked like several adventures were getting underway, and most of them appeared to be starting at the Swan. It took Alex some time to get a table and something to eat, and he kept his eyes open for old friends. He didn't see anyone he knew, however, and the adventurers he did see didn't pay any attention to him. Some of these adventurers might guess who or at least what he was, but none of them let their interest show.

"Details," Whalen's voice said in the back of his mind.

Alex being seen in Telous was another part of Whalen's plan. He thought it would be a good idea for people to think Alex was off on some new adventure and not suspect that he was really traveling with Whalen. Alex wasn't worried about what people thought, he was only worried about what the Brotherhood might think. There were old wizards in the Brotherhood, and they would know as much as Whalen did about leaving false clues.

After eating his meal, Alex made his way to Blackburn's smithy. Whalen had made the point that he couldn't carry his magic sword as he traveled—it was too well known. But even if nobody recognized his magic sword, it was too fine a weapon for an apprentice merchant to carry.

Apprentice merchant, Alexander Kessler, Alex thought. *That is who I will become when I get to Jarro. I'm in a hurry to catch up with my uncle, Barak Kessler, in the city of Shinmar.*

Alex had all afternoon before he had to go to Mr. Clutter's shop so that he could vanish from view, and Blackburn's was a place worth spending time and treasure in. He wanted to make sure he found a good sword to take the place of his magic sword, and perhaps a dagger to go with it. Alex also knew that

Mr. Blackburn was not a man to rush when it came to choosing a weapon.

"Perhaps an axe since that is what you'll be using when you face Jabez," Alex's O'Gash commented in the back of his mind. *"A little extra practice with an axe might help."*

"Ah, Master Taylor," Mr. Blackburn said as Alex entered the shop. "Good to see you again, good to see you."

"Mr. Blackburn," Alex replied, bowing slightly. "I'm in need of a good sword, something that looks common, but is the finest quality."

"Looks common?" Mr. Blackburn asked.

"Something that a merchant might carry," Alex explained. "Nothing too grand, but the blade should be made of the finest steel."

"Aye, I understand what you're looking for," Mr. Blackburn said with a nod. "Let me see, I have several good swords that might do for you. Now wait a moment, yes, that might be the best."

Without saying anything more Mr. Blackburn hurried off into the back of the shop. Alex could hear him moving things about, and the search made Alex curious. What kind of sword would Mr. Blackburn show him? Alex didn't doubt that Mr. Blackburn would bring a good sword, but it seemed odd that he would have to search for the sword he wanted.

"Here we are, then," said Mr. Blackburn as he returned several minutes later, a large black box under his arm. "This is something special I made a few years back. The merchant who ordered it never collected it, so I won't feel bad about selling it to you."

The box was made from a dark wood that Alex had never seen before, with a fine silver lock on it. Mr. Blackburn produced a small silver key from his shirt pocket, and after opening the box, turned it so Alex could see inside. The gently curving scimitar in the box was plain to look at, but there was something about it that Alex liked. There was also a dagger in the box, which was a miniature copy of the sword. The metal in both blades had a wavelike pattern, though the black leather handles had no design at all.

"The steel in those blades has been folded over six hundred times," Mr. Blackburn said with pride. "It's as strong as or maybe stronger than any I've ever made."

"It is a fine piece of work," said Alex, lifting the sword from the box. "It is well balanced and comfortable to hold."

"Aye, I'd have to say that it's the best pure sword as I've ever made, though a bit plain for most people," Mr. Blackburn replied.

"What price would you ask for such a sword?" Alex checked the scabbard as he spoke.

"It won't be cheap," Mr. Blackburn said, his eyes on the sword. "I'd not sell it to just anyone, but seeing as it's you . . ."

"I understand. I believe that I also need an axe."

"An axe? You'll excuse me for saying, but a sword and an axe seems like a lot of weaponry for a wizard to be carrying."

"True enough," Alex said with a smile. "I know, however, that I shouldn't always count on magic to get me out of trouble. I'm sure you'll remember, when you measured me for my first weapon, that you found I could use a sword, an axe, or a staff."

"Oh aye, I remember that."

"I thought it would be wise to at least learn how to use an axe, even if I don't plan on carrying one all the time."

"Aye, there's wisdom in that. What type of axe were you thinking of?"

"Type?"

"Well, axes are a bit different than swords," Mr. Blackburn chuckled. "You could get, say, a poleaxe, which could be as long as seven or eight feet, or a small one-handed fighting axe. You might prefer a throwing axe, or a two-handed battle-axe. There are a lot to choose from."

"Yes, of course," Alex said.

Alex had no idea what type of axe the Axe of Sundering might be, and that worried him. It could be a massive two-handed battle-axe, or it could be something much smaller. He thought about it for a moment, and decided that something in the middle would be best.

"I think something like a dwarf axe," Alex said at last. "Something that I can use with either one or two hands, depending on what needs doing."

"Of course," Mr. Blackburn said. "A good choice, I think. Poleaxes can be more dangerous to the user than the enemy if the user doesn't know what they're doing. The small one-handed axes are also more of a specialized weapon. Now, let me see . . ."

Mr. Blackburn showed Alex a number of fine axes, letting Alex hold each of them in turn. While Alex had never used an axe in combat, he did know something about how to use them. He had several dwarf friends who carried axes, and when he'd asked about how to use them in battle his friends had been happy to show him the basics.

Alex had also practiced fighting with an axe and other weapons on his own. He had used magic to conjure up opponents to fight, and an axe or any other kind of weapon to fight with. The conjured warriors couldn't do any real damage to him, just as his magically created weapons couldn't do any damage to anything he might hit with them. It was a kind of game, a game that he thought might be useful to him now.

If I have time for such training games, he thought.

"And if you can use that magic in Jarro without Jabez or Whalen noticing," his O'Gash added.

After trying several of the axes, Alex chose one that felt comfortable in his hands. It was a fair-sized axe that he could use with both hands if he wanted to. It was also light enough that he could easily hold and swing it with just one hand. The axe was plain looking, its metal left unpolished except for the razor-sharp edge.

"A good choice," Mr. Blackburn said. "You don't need no fancy work on it. I mean you're not going to be trying to impress anyone with it, are you?"

"No, I don't need to impress anyone with it," Alex agreed. "So, how much do I owe you for these three fine weapons?"

"Well, the axe isn't much. It's a fine weapon, I'll stand by that, but it is rather plain. I normally leave axes that way so the buyer can custom order any design they want," Mr. Blackburn said. "The sword and knife, I can't sell too cheap, even to you."

"Name your price, my friend—these are exactly what I'm looking for," Alex said.

"Well, I'll not haggle with a wizard, so I'll make it plain. I'll take three hundred gold for the sword and knife, and say eighty for the axe. So, three hundred and eighty for the lot, and a bargain at that price."

"A bargain indeed," Alex said, reaching for his magic bag. "I'd not rob you of such fine weapons. I'll give you four hundred and fifty for all three."

"Done. And I hope these weapons serve you well."

After paying for his new weapons and thanking Mr. Blackburn for his help, Alex left the smithy and made his way back into town. He was ready to go, ready to face whatever it was that Whalen had planned for him.

"I hope we're ready for whatever Whalen has planned," Alex's O'Gash whispered.

Alex didn't reply to his O'Gash—or sixth sense, as some people called it. He didn't normally talk to this magical voice in his head, but he always listened to it. His O'Gash had saved him more than once in the past, and he wondered now, for the first time, if every wizard's O'Gash was as talkative as his was.

He didn't need anything in town, but he had to spend the rest of the day doing something. Whalen had suggested that he visit as many shops as possible, just in case someone was looking for him. Whalen wanted him to be seen in Telous, and if possible, seen going to Mr. Clutter's shop as well.

"Details," his O'Gash said, sounding amused.

Alex spent his time wandering through the different shops in Telous. He bought a few things without really thinking about it. There were a few books from the bookstore that looked interesting, some extra blankets, and some new clothes and boots. As the afternoon wore on he returned to the Golden Swan and ordered a large dinner for himself. He continued to keep his eyes open for any adventurers he might know, but he didn't see anyone.

As Alex finished his meal he was a little on edge, excited, and worried. He wanted to get moving, and he worried about what he would face once he was moving. The Brotherhood came into his mind once more. They were a dangerous group, and there was no telling what they might have planned. They had already tried to ambush Whalen more than once, and if they discovered that he was going after Jabez . . . well, Alex didn't dare guess what they might do.

Jabez was another problem. Alex believed what Whalen had told him about Jabez turning to evil. He believed that Jabez was part of the Brotherhood, but he was also part of Whalen's family. Knowing that Jabez was related to Whalen troubled Alex. He had once been a good and kind wizard, and that made Alex think—how had he turned to evil? How had he lost the path of a true wizard? Could he be turned back to good? Alex had stored Jabez's journals in his magic bag's library. So far he didn't have any answers, but the questions continued to nag at him just the same.

With dark thoughts about the Brotherhood trying to take over the known lands, Alex made his way to Mr. Clutter's back door. He didn't know enough about the Brotherhood— that much was clear. He didn't know how many members the Brotherhood had, or how powerful those members might be. What little he did know about the Brotherhood and what they had done was bad enough.

"Ah, Master Taylor," Mr. Clutter said as soon as his magical back door opened. "Master Vankin said you might be stopping by."

"Mr. Clutter," Alex said, bowing slightly and making sure the back door closed behind him. "Did Whalen happen to mention *why* I would be stopping by?"

"Oh, yes, yes. No details of course, but he said you would be needing a large room for the night."

"If it won't inconvenience you."

"No trouble, no trouble at all. Happy to help when I can. I think I have the perfect room ready for you."

Mr. Clutter turned and started to move out of his office without saying anything more. Alex wondered what Whalen had said to Mr. Clutter, because the adventure salesman was not normally so businesslike.

"It's one of the basement rooms," Mr. Clutter said over his shoulder as Alex followed him. "Not much furniture or comfort, I'm afraid, but Master Vankin said you simply needed a large room."

"Yes, fairly large, I think."

"Well, this should work fine, then."

Mr. Clutter paused to light a lamp, and then led Alex down a long set of stairs. Alex had never been in Mr. Clutter's basement before, and he was surprised by what he found there. The basement appeared to be a tangle of rooms with no real hallways at all. Each of the rooms was packed with something different: furniture, books, boxes of all different sizes and colors, cages of various sizes, lamps, clothes—even shoes. Everything Alex could think of seemed to have a room, and each room had only a narrow space in it that allowed Mr. Clutter and Alex to move to the next room.

"I'm sorry for the mess," Mr. Clutter said. "Had to do a bit of rearranging down here after I heard from Master Vankin."

"I hope we aren't causing you too much trouble," Alex said.

"No, no, it was time to shift things around a bit anyway," said Mr. Clutter, leading Alex through a room full of dinner plates, pots, pans, and glasses. "I should know to keep one of these rooms empty. This isn't the first time Master Vankin has needed a large space for something."

"He's done something like this before?" Alex asked.

"Oh, I couldn't say," Mr. Clutter answered. "Don't know what the two of you are doing this time, so I don't know if it's anything like what he did the last time, do I?"

"No, I suppose not."

"Ah, here we are, then."

They'd entered a large, mostly empty room. There was a single table with a lamp on it, two chairs, and a couch next to one wall. The room was about thirty feet wide and maybe fifty feet long, with no openings except the one Alex had just come through. What really surprised Alex was that the ceiling of the room was at least twelve feet high.

"Enough space?" Mr. Clutter asked with a smile.

"I'm sure it will be," Alex said.

"Well then, can I get you anything else? Something to eat or drink perhaps?" Mr. Clutter asked as he lit the lamp on the table.

"No, thank you," Alex said, his mind already thinking about the gateway magic he was going to use.

"Well then, I will wish you a good night," Mr. Clutter said, turning to leave.

"Mr. Clutter, how long have you known Whalen?" Alex asked before he could stop himself.

"Oh my, that's hard to say. At least four hundred years, a bit longer than that really, truth be told. Master Vankin helped me get set up in the adventure business, you know."

"No, I didn't know that. To tell the truth, I was just thinking about how little I really know about Whalen."

"I'm not surprised." Mr. Clutter chuckled. "Master Vankin keeps himself very much to himself. Never talks much about what he's done or where he's been. Never shares his worries or troubles with anyone, as far as I know. Still, well . . . perhaps I shouldn't say anything."

"What?"

"Well, as it's you I'm talking to, I don't suppose it will hurt. When Whalen was here, telling me to expect you and all, well . . ."

"Yes?"

"Well, I've never known him to show his emotions. When he was here I could tell he was worried, though. I might even say he was afraid. He seemed like a man walking toward his own grave, if you'll excuse the expression. He wouldn't say what he was planning, but I for one was happy to hear that you were going with him."

"Well, let's hope we don't need to worry about any graves."

"No, no graves. I will ask you to keep an eye on the old man, though I'm sure you'll do that without my asking. Seeing him that way, well, it shook me a bit. I'll just say that I'd take it as a great personal favor if you bring him back from, well, wherever it is the two of you are going."

"I will do all that I can to keep him safe," Alex promised, troubled by Mr. Clutter's words.

"Then I will also wish you good luck with whatever it is you and Vankin are doing," Mr. Clutter said, bowing to Alex and turning away.

"Thank you," Alex managed to say before Mr. Clutter was gone.

Alex walked to the table and then turned to look back at the entrance to the room. He was surprised by what Mr. Clutter had told him, and by the request to watch out for Whalen. Mr. Clutter seemed sincere. He really seemed to care about Whalen, and that made sense, as he'd known Whalen for so long. Still, something in the back of Alex's mind started to ask questions.

Could he know? Alex asked himself. *Could he know what Whalen and I are going to try to do?*

Sitting down at the table, Alex's eyes returned to the entrance of the room. A darker thought entered his mind, and he suddenly felt uncomfortable looking into the darkness on the far side of the room.

Could Clutter be part of the Brotherhood? Alex thought.

The idea seemed crazy. Clutter was a trusted seller of adventures, not some evil spy for a secret society that was trying to take over the known lands. Still, the Brotherhood had spies, and Clutter would be a good spy to have. Clutter knew about most adventures going on in the known lands—and who was on those adventures. If the Brotherhood had Clutter as their spy, they could learn much without any real danger of revealing themselves.

"No," Alex said softly. "I don't believe it."

Alex shook off his suspicions about Mr. Clutter being a spy, and then sat for a time doing nothing. He moved to the couch and lay down, thinking a nap might be a good idea. He was too eager to sleep, however—and there were still hours to go before he needed to open the gateway. He got up, walked around the room several times, and then drew his new sword and took some practice swings with it. Finally, he went back to the table and reached for his magic bag.

Taking out his map of Jarro, Alex spread it on the table and sat looking at it. He ran the few details he knew over and over in his mind. The plan was basic. Whalen wanted to start their adventure in Eastland, the furthest place away from Conmar and his nephew Jabez. Alex didn't see the need to start so far away, but he'd agreed to do what Whalen wanted. It wouldn't matter much anyway, as they would be sailing for Midland after less than a week in Eastland. But then what?

Alex took his new axe out of his magic bag and practiced what his dwarf friends had taught him. He was extra careful as he swung the axe, making sure to not accidently hit himself with it. Slowly he began to feel more confident as the axe spun around him, but he knew he needed more practice.

Returning to the table, Alex laid down his axe. He took out his new sword and knife as well, and started working a bit of magic into all of them. He knew that the weapons were strong, but he thought a little extra strength and maybe a spell to keep the blades sharp couldn't hurt.

One part of Whalen's plan troubled Alex more than anything else. Whalen had told him not to use magic unless he absolutely had to. It seemed a bit strange, not using any magic, but Alex knew Whalen had his reasons. Whalen had also said that if he didn't turn up in the city of Shinmar—the port they planned to sail from—that Alex should not wait for more than a day or two.

"If I'm not there by then, find a ship that will take you to Midland," Whalen had said. "I will catch up with you there."

"And if you don't catch up?" Alex asked.

"Then I will depend on you to take care of our problem," Whalen answered, not commenting on what his not turning up would mean.

The thing that stood out most in Alex's mind was the fact that Whalen had asked for his help. Alex tried to remember all the stories he'd heard or read about Whalen, and one thing was clear in all of those stories. Whalen had gone into dangerous places, he had fought great evils, and he had always done those things alone. Never, in any of the stories Alex could think of, had Whalen Vankin ever asked for help. Things were different now, it seemed, and Alex didn't know what that might mean.

Eventually Alex returned his map and axe to his magic bag. He stood up and prepared himself to work the magic that would open a gateway into the land of Jarro. Pausing for a moment, he looked at his magic bag. A lot of people knew what magic bags looked like, and carrying a magic bag would mark him as something more than an apprentice merchant. He'd been foolish not to think of it before, but at least the answer was obvious. Working some simple magic, Alex disguised his magic bag, making it look like a common rucksack. With that final detail taken care of, he moved to the center of the room and started to work the gateway magic.

Alex recalled the instructions Whalen gave him before they parted ways. "You need to focus your thoughts on the place you want to go. It will be difficult the first time, as the gateway may not appear exactly where you think it should. I don't mean just where you are going, but also where you are. You'll need some space when working the magic, at least at first, just in case the entrance of the gateway appears further away from you than you want it to."

Mr. Clutter had provided the space, and now Alex focused on the memory that Whalen had magically given to him. He could see a massive white stone to his left, trees in the distance, and open land all around him. The open land was covered with small white stones. The stones didn't make a road or a path—but there was a pattern. Alex wasn't sure what larger pattern they made, but he could see them clearly.

What are those stones? Alex thought as the magical gateway opened a few feet in front of him.

Without hesitating, Alex stepped through the gateway and into the land of Jarro.

CHAPTER THREE
THE GRAVEYARD

A lex arrived in complete darkness. He instantly realized the mistake he'd made, and he felt foolish for
not thinking things through. It was nighttime
here in Jarro, as he knew it would be. The problem was that
his eyes were used to the lamplight in Mr. Clutter's basement
room, and there was no light here at all. He looked up at the
sky as he turned to break the spell that held his gateway open.
The moon was hidden behind clouds, but it looked like the
clouds were breaking up and moving away.

Closing his magical gateway, Alex closed his eyes as well,
hoping to improve his night vision as quickly as possible.
Taking several deep breaths, he waited. He could smell rain,
wet grass, and mud. He opened his eyes and looked around,
searching for the massive white stone landmark from Whalen's
memory. It was visible a few yards to his left, and he knew that
his gateway had opened exactly where he'd wanted it to.

Orienting himself by checking the cloud-hidden moon
once more, Alex started to walk toward the main road. He'd
only taken a few steps, however, when his left shin slammed
into something that was both hard and solid. He tried to keep

his balance as he also tried to rub away the pain in his shin, but he couldn't manage it. He hit the wet ground hard, and continued to rub his aching shin. When he finally sat up, Alex tried to see what he'd walked into. The moonlight broke free of the clouds to help him, and he wasn't happy about what he found.

"A gravestone?" Alex said in a lowered voice.

Looking around in the moonlight, Alex realized where he was. He almost started to laugh, but he stopped himself and just shook his head instead. Now he understood what all the white stones in Whalen's memory were, and why they made a pattern.

Honestly, Whalen. You could have told me I'd be walking into a graveyard, Alex thought.

Getting back to his feet, Alex checked the placement of gravestones. Most of them were at just the right height to slam into his shins if he wasn't paying attention, and he didn't want to repeat that experience. He checked his direction once more, and then started forward at a slower, more cautious speed. He had two or three miles to travel before reaching the main road, and he wanted to get there before the sun came up if he could.

As Alex made his way through the graveyard, he had to wonder why Whalen would choose this place for him to enter Jarro. It made sense when he thought about it. Most people didn't like graveyards, and very few would ever enter a graveyard after dark. Alex wasn't worried about running into anything dangerous or evil. Graveyards weren't normally the scary places most people thought they were, not even after dark. He didn't think he would run into anything at all, except maybe some wild animals. It was at that moment, however, that he heard a noise he recognized.

Someone was digging, and not too far away from where Alex was standing. The shovel made more noise than normal as it cut through the wet, gravely ground. There was only one reason for someone to be digging in a graveyard at night, and Alex knew what that reason was and it didn't make him happy.

Grave robbers, Alex thought.

The idea of people robbing graves troubled him, but it wasn't any of his business. He was here to help Whalen and to stop Jabez, but still . . . in all the lands Alex had visited, robbing graves was a serious crime. Walking away and letting whoever was digging in this graveyard went against his sense of honor as an adventurer. He had to stop this crime, even if stopping it was far more dangerous for him simply because he wasn't supposed to use magic.

Alex moved toward the sound of the shoveling. He crouched down, hoping to use the small gravestones to hide his approach. The noise grew louder, and it was soon clear that two shovels were being used. It made sense that two or maybe three people would be doing the work. Graves were deep, and digging them up would take a fair amount of time and effort.

The gravestones Alex passed were getting larger, and he guessed that he was moving toward the center of the cemetery. Soon the gravestones were as large as life-size statues, and he didn't need to crouch any more. A glint of light caught his eye, and as silently as he could he moved toward it.

"Why we digging up this grave?" a voice said in the darkness.

"'Cause, Cobb, this is the grave we're being paid to dig up," a second voice answered.

"Least it stopped raining," said a third.

"Shut up, Dixon, that's not what I mean," Cobb said. "What I want to know is, why *this* grave? There's hundreds of graves here, so why's this one so special?"

"I told you, the gent what's paying us wants the bones out of this grave," the second voice answered.

"How's he gonna know what grave we get the bones out of?" Dixon asked. "We could dig up any old grave and get bones. I told you, Flynn, something closer to the main road woulda been easier."

"Better than being way out here in the middle of this cemetery, that's for sure," Cobb agreed.

"What, afraid of ghosts and such?" Flynn asked. "After all the years we been doing this, you started getting spooked, have ya?"

Alex was about to jump out from behind a gravestone. His plan was to yell and shriek, like some kind of monster, hoping to frighten the grave robbers away. Then Flynn said something that stopped him.

"The gent what's paying for this job will know if we got the right bones. He's got more than a bit of magic in him, or I'm an honest man."

"Magic," Dixon said. "Don't like working for them magic folk."

"You just keep diggin'," Flynn answered. "He's paying enough for this job, and more."

"Paying enough maybe," Cobb said. "But if there's magic

involved you can bet there's something dangerous in this here grave. I say we fill it in and get going."

"Keep diggin'!" Flynn demanded. "Ain't nothin' down there but bones. This here grave is more than two hundred years old. Even if it is a wizard's grave, his magic ain't still hanging about after two hundred years."

A two-hundred-year-old wizard's grave? A magical person who wanted the wizard's bones? Alex didn't like what he was hearing, and it was clear to him that this was more than just a normal grave robbery. Whalen had told him not to use magic, but Whalen couldn't have guessed that something like this would happen. Alex knew that wizard's bones were only used for the darkest of magic. Only some great evil like Jabez or the Brotherhood would be looking for wizard bones.

Taking a chance, Alex peeked around the gravestones to see the grave robbers. One was standing at the foot of the grave, holding a lantern so the other two could see what they were doing. Only the heads of the other two were visible, and it was clear they'd been digging for some time. They all looked lean, underfed, and dirty. Alex considered what to do to them. Changing them into bats or rats might be a fitting punishment for their crimes, but a loud *thunk* broke Alex's train of thought.

"That's the casket," Cobb said from the grave.

"Pry it open and let's get busy," Flynn said, angling the lantern to get a better look.

The sound of wood breaking and nails being pulled filled the air. These grave robbers didn't hesitate now that they were so close to their prize. Alex made up his mind in an instant.

Lifting his left hand, he worked some magic, and a cold wind came howling through the graveyard.

"What's that then?" Dixon asked, also from the grave.

"Just the wind," Flynn answered as he looked around nervously. "Here, take the bag. Let's get what we're after and then get out of here."

"What, we're not gonna fill the grave in again?" Cobb asked.

Alex worked a little more magic and a fog started to rise from the earth. In the distance the sound of a screech owl echoed in the darkness.

"You want to hang around filling in an empty grave, that's your business," Dixon said. "I say we get what we came for and quick step it out of here."

"What's this?" Cobb said, lifting something toward the light. "Looks like a book of some kind."

"Here, give me that," Flynn said. "Maybe our employer will pay something extra for it."

Alex worked more magic, and a more powerful and colder wind came screaming through the gravestones. The fog lifted and spun wildly around the graveyard, filled with tiny sparks of green and yellow light. The sparks weren't really noticeable, but they added light to the graveyard, a pale ghostly light. Slowly, figures began to appear in the mist, figures of armored men holding weapons. The warriors Alex created were moving slowly and silently, marching toward the grave that had just been unearthed.

At first, Flynn didn't notice anything. He lifted his lantern and glanced around once, as if he'd heard something, and then turned his attention back to the grave. Alex thought for only a second, and then added weight to his soldiers. The footsteps weren't very loud, at least not at first, but Flynn looked up suddenly, swinging the lantern in a wide circle as he tried to see what was moving in the darkness. A loud creaking sound came from the grave, and Flynn jumped.

"This old coffin is solid," Cobb said. "I've seen coffins in the ground less than a week that aren't as solid as this."

"Quality bit of work when it was put here," Dixon said.

Flynn didn't say anything; he was too busy looking around the graveyard. Alex's soldiers were close, close enough for the grave robber to see them moving. His mouth fell open, but no sound came out of it. It looked as if he had been turned to stone as the blood drained from his face. His mouth moved up and down a few times, but still no sound came out. Finally, he let out a terrified, high-pitched scream, dropped the lantern and the book he was holding, and ran wildly into the darkness.

Cobb and Dixon looked up when Flynn screamed. They looked around, unsure of what they were looking for or what to do, and then they saw the ghostly warriors. Cobb looked like he was about to faint. He clutched at Dixon's jacket, his eyes bulging out of his face. Dixon desperately tried to pull Cobb's hands away from his jacket, finally breaking free by ripping his jacket in half, scrambling out of the grave, and running away as fast as he could. Cobb, realizing that he was alone, opened his mouth in a silent scream and after some frantic attempts to exit the grave, ran headlong after his companions.

Alex waited for a moment, and then broke the spell that created the ghostly warriors. He walked to the grave and looked down into it. The empty sack of the grave robbers was lying across the chest of the skeleton like a blanket. He felt sorry for this long dead man, wizard or not, and he realized that there was a bigger problem that he hadn't seen until now.

Scaring away the grave robbers had saved the bones for the time being, but some magical person wanted these bones. They would find other grave robbers willing to come and dig this grave up again. Even if this first set of thieves told the story of what they'd seen, not everyone would believe it, or be afraid.

Alex magically resealed the coffin as he thought about what to do. He looked at the gravestone, hoping to find a name to go with the bones. Whalen might know something about this person, if they were a wizard, but the stone was unmarked. Keeping these bones safe wasn't his job—he didn't even know if they truly were the bones of a wizard. He had already broken Whalen's instructions about using magic, however, so he thought that a little more magic couldn't hurt. He focused his mind on what he wanted to do, combined his wizard and his dragon magic, and slowly pushed the dirt from the grave back onto the coffin.

It took a long time to fill the grave with dirt, which was part of Alex's magic. The coffin would remain in the grave, but the grave was now much deeper than it had been. Alex's magic would allow the coffin to go deeper and deeper into the earth if someone tried to dig it up. Grave robbers could dig as deep as the lid of the coffin, but if they tried to touch the coffin it would sink under them. They could dig and dig, and no matter how deep they went, the coffin would always remain just out of reach.

Well, that's safe, and no real harm done, Alex thought, and then his eyes fell on the book.

He hadn't thought about the book while working his magic, and he didn't think it was really worth worrying about. An old dried-out book that was buried with this person could be anything. He stepped around the grave and picked it up. He brushed the dirt off the cover, and turned it toward the moonlight. The lantern the grave robbers had used had broken and gone out when it was dropped, so it was no help. The cover of the book was blank, as was the spine, telling him nothing. Alex carefully lifted the front cover, hoping to discover what this book might be, and was stunned by what happened.

The front cover of the book tore away from the rest of the book as he lifted it. The corner that he held in his fingers turned to dust, and the rest of the cover fell to the ground and shattered like glass. Alex didn't understand. The cover had felt solid in his hands. The grave robber had held the book and dropped it, and there hadn't been any damage done. He turned slightly and lifted the book closer to his face. It would be almost impossible to read anything in the moonlight, but he tried anyway.

A spark of magic jumped from the page, and Alex jerked his head back instinctively. Some of the words on the page shone like fire in the moonlight, burning themselves into his mind. The magic wasn't strong, and Alex knew that he could break it, but the words were important. Only a dozen or so words burned in the moonlight, and then the book crumbled to dust in his hands.

Alex wiped his hands and looked down at the pile of dust

at his feet. This was unexpected, and he wasn't sure what to make of it. He thought about the words he'd seen, and tried to fit them together. All of the words had been written in the common language, but none of the words were common.

"*Darloch est messer,*" Alex said softly in the darkness.

The hair on the back of his neck stood up. These words were from the language of the dragons, and Alex had to think about what they might mean. Depending on how the writer had meant to use them, they could mean *master of dragons.* If the writer had meant something different, the words could be translated as *destroyer of dragons.* Alex couldn't be sure. He needed to see what was written before and after these three words or they simply didn't make any sense.

As he started to leave the graveyard once more, Alex thought about the other words he'd seen. Something about an unnamed dragon—no, it was a dragon without a name. What in the world could that mean? Dragons *always* had names; they often had many names. Alex also knew that all dragons had one special name that they kept hidden. Every dragon had a true name, the name that made them what they were. A dragon without a name made less sense to Alex than a master or destroyer of dragons did.

A problem for another time, Alex thought.

"*Make sure you have time. This is important,*" his O'Gash commented.

Alex smiled at the comment. He would remember what he'd seen, even if he didn't understand what it was about. Perhaps Whalen would know. Whalen knew all kinds of myths and legends, and if he didn't know about this *darloch est messer*, he might know someone else who did.

While his thoughts about a nameless dragon continued to bounce around his mind, Alex focused on his next set of problems. First, he had to get to the city of Shinmar, hopefully without running into any more trouble. Second, he had to hope that Whalen would already be in Shinmar when he got there. If Whalen wasn't there, and if he didn't turn up within a day or two of Alex's arrival, then Alex knew he'd be in real trouble.

Whalen had said that if he didn't turn up that Alex should go on to Midland, and he would catch up. If Whalen didn't catch up, however, then it would be up to Alex to take care of Jabez. Alex knew that Whalen trusted him to take care of this problem alone, if he had to; but he also knew it would be a far more difficult task if Whalen wasn't there to help.

One step at a time, Alex told himself. *I'll face that problem if and when I must.*

CHAPTER FOUR
THE ROAD TO SHINMAR

Alex found the main road about an hour after the sun came up. The grave robbers had slowed him down, but not by much. He checked the road to make sure nobody was in sight before leaving the woods that he'd been traveling through. Pausing at the edge of the road he looked for any signs of travelers. There were no tracks to be seen, and he guessed that the rain of the previous night had washed all signs of travelers away. He tested the surface of the road with his finger, and discovered that it was much harder than he'd thought it would be. He didn't want anybody to know that he'd been near, or that he'd even come from the direction of the graveyard. Stories had a way of spreading after all, and he didn't want any connection to the stories the grave robbers would certainly be telling.

Having discovered that he could walk on the road without leaving tracks, Alex started off to the west. The city of Shinmar was at least three days away, but he wanted to hurry. He didn't have any fears to drive him, but there was one thing that troubled him. The sky was cloudy and the clouds were growing darker. Alex had no doubt that there was rain in his future, and the idea of walking in the rain or worse—spending a night outdoors in the rain—was something he hoped to avoid.

Alex felt like he was making good time as he walked down the well-made road. At first he spent time looking at the land around him, but the dark clouds made it hard to see very much. He could see the outlines of low rolling hills, what appeared to be a thick forest, and now and then a small river. The weather made everything look dark and old, even unwelcoming. Alex wasn't worried about the way things looked, but one thing did stick out—there didn't seem to be any people around. There were no houses or buildings to be seen along the road, and Alex thought this was strange.

There must be farms and villages somewhere, Alex said to himself as he walked, but if there were, he didn't see them.

Alex paused when he thought it was close to midday, though with the weather it was hard to tell. He was thinking about getting something to eat, as it had been a long night and he was hungry. Looking around for a dry spot to sit and eat, Alex saw something that made his heart sink. A wall of rain was slowly moving across the land toward him.

"Looks like I'm going to get wet before I get anything to eat," Alex said with a sigh.

He looked ahead, hoping to see a tree that was large enough for him to get some shelter. The only things he could see growing near the road, however, were thick bushes and weeds. He didn't see any options. He was going to get wet, so he might as well keep walking until either the rain stopped or he found someplace where he could get out of the rain.

Swinging his disguised magic bag around, he was just

pulling a heavy, waterproof cloak out of it when he noticed something. What had looked like a small grass-covered hill to his left was not a hill at all, but a small moss-covered building. Quickly putting on his cloak, Alex trotted off toward the shelter he'd hoped for.

A deafening roar of thunder shook the ground under Alex's feet just as he reached the building's doorway. He stepped into the building as the rain came crashing down behind him. The rain seemed almost angry that he'd escaped it, and Alex had to smile at the idea. His smile froze, however, when he heard the sound of a sword being drawn behind him. Instinctively, his right hand moved toward his own sword, but stopped before it got there.

"I wouldn't," a voice said from the darkness. "Not unless you're looking for trouble."

"It seems that trouble has already found me," Alex replied, turning slowly toward the sound of the voice.

"No, stay where you are," the voice commanded, "until I decide whether you're friend or foe."

"If you're looking for money you'll be disappointed," Alex said. "I have very little, but you are welcome to it."

"Humph. I'm no thief. What you have is your own, and I'll not take it from you. Are you alone?"

"I, ah . . . well, yes, I am completely alone," Alex answered, surprised by the question.

"Well, you look like a good and honest fellow, so I suppose I'll let you stay. Not the kind of weather to be out in anyway."

"No, it's not."

"You can turn around now if you want. I'll do you no harm."

"And I'll do you none," Alex replied as he turned to look at the stranger.

Alex was surprised by what he saw. The man looked young, no more than twenty-five, but his voice had sounded much older. It took Alex a second to understand, and when he did, a look of surprise must have shown on his face.

"I've always looked much younger than I am," said the stranger.

"You do look younger than you sound," said Alex, smiling slightly.

Alex could see more than most people, and it wasn't hard for him to understand why this stranger looked so young but sounded so old. There was elf blood in this man, though not very much. He didn't have any magic in him, but he was related, probably several generations away, to the elves. It wasn't just the relation to the elves that had surprised Alex—there was something more. Alex's magic allowed him to see this man's aura, the energy that often gathered around a person. The energy was strong and bright, and while there was no magic in the man, there was certainly some kind of magic connected to him.

"I am Alexander Kessler," Alex said, remembering the name that Whalen had told him to use. "My friends call me Alex."

"Judging by the fine sword you carry, I will hope to call you a friend," the stranger answered. "My name is Joshua, and I am a traveler from Westland."

"You are a long way from home. What brings you so far to the east? If you don't mind me asking, that is."

"A quest of sorts," Joshua said. He waved his hand at the building around them. "I am visiting the ancient shrines of Jarro. It is something of a family tradition."

Alex knew that Joshua was only telling him part of the truth, but he didn't ask any questions. Joshua was already suspicious of strangers, and Alex didn't want to put him on guard. Alex's mind continued to try to figure out what other magic was involved with Joshua, but the answer remained just out of reach.

"Well, I was just looking for a dry spot where I could have something to eat," Alex said, changing the subject. "If you are willing to share your shelter, I am willing to share my food. You are welcome to join me if you like."

"I was just thinking about going to find something to eat. If you have enough for both of us, I will gladly join you."

Alex laughed at the reply and pulled off his cloak. Swinging his magic bag off his shoulders, he pretended to rummage around inside it to find some food. He was careful not to let Joshua get a good look at the disguised magic bag, just in case. In less than a minute Alex and his new friend Joshua were sitting on the floor of the ancient shrine, eating a meal of bread, cheese, and dried fruit that Alex had provided. Joshua ate hungrily, as if he hadn't had anything to eat for several days. Alex didn't say anything, but it did make him wonder. Joshua was nervous of strangers, careful, and didn't appear to be eating as often as he might. There were many possible reasons why Joshua was this way, but Alex knew that it wasn't the time to ask.

Alex and Joshua didn't talk as they ate. Alex had many questions that he wanted to ask, but most of them would make him sound like a stranger to this land. He didn't want anyone to know that he wasn't from Jarro, so he kept his questions to himself.

"I'm traveling to Shinmar," Alex finally said as he was finishing his meal. "I hope to meet my uncle there, and then sail to Midland."

"Why are you traveling to Midland?"

"My uncle is a cloth and fur merchant. He's training me as his apprentice, and he has business in Midland."

Joshua didn't say anything for a time, but he looked as if he was considering what Alex said. Alex wondered if Joshua might suspect that he wasn't really an apprentice cloth merchant, but he really couldn't tell.

"I was planning on going to Shinmar as well," Joshua finally said. "I'm on my way home, and Shinmar is one of the largest ports here in Eastland. I doubt, however, that I will find a ship that will take me all the way to Westland."

"Well, if not all the way to Westland, perhaps we can travel together to Midland. I know we've only just met, but I think I would like to get to know you better."

"You may regret it," Joshua said more to himself than to Alex.

Alex gave Joshua a hard look, but didn't say anything. Joshua simply acted like he hadn't said anything at all. He got up, brushed the crumbs off his pants, and walked to the doorway.

"The rain is letting up," Joshua said. "Give it a few more minutes and we'll be able to travel without getting too wet."

Alex put away what was left of the food, folded his heavy

cloak, added it to his bag, and then slipped the knapsack over his shoulders. He walked to the doorway as well, watching Joshua as he moved. There was a sad look on Joshua's face, a look of some great trouble or loss. Alex didn't know why exactly, but he felt in his heart that he needed to help Joshua.

"Help him?" the voice in the back of Alex's mind asked. *"You know nothing about him or his troubles, and you have your own business to deal with in this land."*

Alex ignored his O'Gash, and simply stood watching the land as the clouds parted and the afternoon sun broke through. Without a word Joshua and Alex started off, and Alex wondered how much he could learn about Joshua if he remained as tight-lipped as he had been so far.

"I've not traveled this road before," Alex said after several minutes of walking. "Do you know how far the next town is?"

"Six, maybe seven miles," Joshua answered. "We should get there before it gets too dark."

"It would be good to spend the night indoors, if possible," Alex said, trying to get a conversation going.

"Indoors is not always better than out," Joshua said and fell silent once more.

It was clear that Joshua was reluctant to talk, and Alex was willing to live with the silence. His mind, however, went back to the question of why—why was Joshua being secretive? Why had he drawn his sword when he had first appeared, and why did he make sure Alex was alone before putting his sword away? Alex could see that Joshua was troubled, maybe even afraid, but he couldn't see any reason why. Still, his O'Gash was right. He knew almost nothing about Joshua, and until

Joshua chose to tell him more, there was nothing Alex could do to help him.

Joshua walked fast, as if some great need pressed him forward. Alex was able to keep up without any trouble, but this was one more thing that made him wonder about his companion. They came to a small town before the sun had gone down, and it didn't take long for them to find a tavern to spend the night. Once the arrangements had been made, Joshua went right to his room.

"I'll be leaving at first light," Joshua said as he turned to close the door of his room. "If you are up and ready to go we can travel together. If you prefer to sleep later, then I will thank you now for your kindness and wish you luck in your travels."

"Kindness?" Alex asked.

"You shared your meal with me, and I thank you."

"A small enough kindness. I'll be ready at first light."

Joshua didn't say anything more. He closed the door to his room behind him, and before Alex could even open to door to his own room he heard Joshua wedge a chair under the doorknob.

A strange thing to do, Alex thought as he closed his own door. He really must be afraid of something.

"Or someone," his O'Gash added.

———•◦•———

The next morning, Alex was waiting just outside the tavern when Joshua turned up. Joshua looked surprised to see him there, but he flashed a smile and nodded. They started off without a word, but before they had left the town Alex handed a small bag and a leather flask to Joshua.

"What is this?" Joshua asked, looking into the bag.

"You didn't take time to eat anything, and I thought you might be hungry," Alex said.

"Are you always so kind to strangers?" Joshua asked, taking a bun out of the bag Alex had given him.

"No, not always. Only to those who I can see need the help."

"You think I need help."

"I think you've had a hard time here in Eastland, and you don't want to talk about it. I don't know what your troubles are, and if you don't want to talk about them, that is your business. That doesn't mean, however, that I can't lend a helping hand, or offer a little kindness."

"You're a good man, Alex Kessler, and I hope you won't have to pay for it."

"Pay for it?"

"An old saying from Westland. 'Good men always pay for their kindnesses.' I hope it proves untrue for you."

Joshua was more willing to talk as they walked that morning. He was still guarded in what he would talk about, however, saying very little about himself or his home. He was willing to talk about his travels and the places he had been since starting his quest.

"Midland is an interesting place," Joshua said as they went along. "They have great caravans there that travel all around the land. It is said that some people live their whole lives as part of a caravan, always traveling and never having a fixed place to call home."

"I've heard something of the caravans," Alex said.

"They aren't what you think, and maybe exactly what you think at the same time. There are traders and merchants of all kinds, but there is so much more. They have actors and acrobats, magicians and fortune tellers, even exotic animals that most people never hear about, and fewer still ever get a chance to see."

"It sounds exciting. I would like to—"

"Stop and be recognized," a voice broke in before Alex could finish.

Alex and Joshua both stopped in their tracks. Five men on horseback moved out of a small wooded area to the right of the road, and barred their path. Joshua looked worried but determined. Alex wasn't sure what to think, as Whalen hadn't warned him that he might be stopped in the road by what looked like soldiers.

"Don't reach for your weapons," the man who had first spoken said. "We don't want any trouble, but we are ready for it if you try anything."

Alex looked at Joshua and then back at the men in the road. Joshua's worry had turned to fear, and Alex didn't know what he was going to do. Deciding that he'd better do something himself, Alex took a deep breath and called back to the men in front of him.

"Who are you? What do you mean by stopping travelers on the common road? By whose authority do you stop us?"

"We mean no harm," came the answer. "We need only

learn your names, nothing more. As for authority, well, we out-number you so that should be authority enough."

"Bandits?" Alex whispered to Joshua.

"No—worse than bandits," Joshua answered.

"I think I can take the three on the left, if you can deal with the two on the right," Alex said, his eyes studying the men in front of him.

"A good plan, if there were only five of them," Joshua said, jerking his head toward the road behind them.

Alex took a quick glance, and found that six more men had appeared behind them. There were too many to fight, at least too many to fight without using magic. He thought about what he could do, what he might have to do. Joshua's fear was growing, and Alex could see that he was desperate not to be questioned by these men. He had to do something, and he had to do it now.

"We run," Alex whispered. "The gully to the left of the path, just ahead. You go first, I'll be right behind."

"What? I . . ." Joshua seemed lost, but then he understood what Alex was saying.

With a half-smile and a slight nod, Joshua broke into a dead run. Alex was less than a step behind him, and they both jumped over a low fence beside the road that had clearly been put there to keep people from falling into the gully.

"Stop! After them!" the leader of the group shouted.

As he fell into the gully, Alex let loose the smallest bit of magic. The horses of his pursuers all reared and turned sud-denly, as if spooked by something in the brush. The sudden confusion gave Alex and Joshua a few seconds' head start, but

Alex knew it wouldn't be enough. Instead of running, Alex had another idea. As soon as he and Joshua were in the gully and out of sight, he grabbed Joshua from behind and dragged him down into a series of thick bushes and small trees.

"What? Why? What are you doing?" Joshua stammered.

"Quiet," Alex commanded. "Don't speak and stay as still as you can."

The noise of horses crashing through the trees and bushes was soon all around them. Alex and Joshua didn't make a sound or move a muscle. Alex, however, realizing the trouble they might be in, worked a little more magic. He sent his thoughts along the gully, kicking a rock here and there, snapping a branch, making noises that these men would have to follow. It wasn't long before the noise around them faded, and Alex got on his knees and took a quick look around.

"We should give them a few minutes before we move back to the road," he whispered.

"Back to the road? Are you mad?" Joshua whispered back.

"They are off in the trees looking for us," Alex said. "We can move faster on the road than we can off it, so while they're busy looking, we'll get away."

"Maybe," Joshua said more thoughtfully. "So long as there aren't more of them on the road, waiting."

"We'll be more careful. Now, while we let them get a bit of distance, why don't you tell me who they are?"

"How should I know?" Joshua asked, but the look on his face gave him away.

"It was all too clear that you were afraid of them. You were willing to fight them if there was any chance of winning. You know who they are. Don't bother pretending that you don't."

"Yes, I know who they are," Joshua admitted after a moment of unhappy silence. "Or at least I know who they serve."

"Tell me."

"They are the servants of the lord of Conmar. I should say, the so-called lord of Conmar."

"And who is that?" Alex asked, even though he suspected he knew who Joshua was talking about.

"An evil man who has taken control of the ancient castle and taken the title as his own. He wants to take control of Westland, but he doesn't want to fight unless he has to. Instead of having an open battle, he takes hostages. He takes the relatives of those in power, and threatens to do them harm if the powerful don't do as he says."

"And you are related to someone in power?"

"My uncle is Lord Darthon, ruler of the southern kingdom of Westland. He is a brave and true-hearted man, and he would never bow down before this evil man, wizard or not."

"Wizard? The lord of Conmar is a wizard?"

"There are some who say he is, or that he at least has some magic. My uncle will not bow to him, but—"

"But if the lord of Conmar has you in his power, your uncle might be forced to do his bidding," Alex finished for him.

"My father went missing when I was young, and my uncle has raised me as his own son," Joshua explained. "My aunt and uncle have no children of their own, and I am an only child. It would break their hearts if some harm came to me, and this despicable man knows it. It was to keep me out of Jabez's hands that my uncle sent me on this quest."

"Jabez?" Alex asked, pretending he did not already know the name.

"The lord of Conmar, though not many people even dare to say his name out loud. He would use me to control my uncle and to enslave my people. I would rather die than let that happen."

"Well, I can see there is a great deal of trouble in Westland."

"It won't stay in Westland, not if Jabez gets his way. He'll take Westland first, but he won't stop until he rules all of Jarro."

"Let's hope that it doesn't come to that," Alex said, getting to his feet. "For now, we should be going."

Joshua got up, but he caught Alex's arm as he turned to go. "Thank you, Alex. Thank you for helping me."

"My uncle taught me to always help those I met along the road. He says you never know when you might be the one who needs help, so it's a good habit to be in."

"Your uncle is a wise man," Joshua said.

"Yes, he is very wise, indeed," Alex said with a grin.

"Please give him my thanks when you see him again."

"I will," Alex said. He hoped Whalen would be in Shinmar as they had planned. Until then, traveling with Joshua and trying to keep him out of trouble seemed like a good idea.

CHAPTER FIVE

SHINMAR

It was nearly midday three days later when Alex and Joshua reached the city of Shinmar. They had avoided the towns and villages they came to along the road, and they had been careful not to run into any more of Jabez's soldiers. Caution had cost them time, and Alex was worried that Whalen might have already sailed for Midland. The extra day of travel couldn't be helped, as Alex was unwilling to leave Joshua to an unknown fate.

"We won't need to worry about soldiers from Conmar here," Joshua commented as they passed through the city gates. "In the country, ten or twelve men can do what they like and there's nobody to interfere, but here there are plenty of soldiers and citizens to stop them."

"I wouldn't relax too much," Alex replied. "You may not need to worry about a group of soldiers looking for you, but . . ."

"But?"

"I think that here in the city, two or three men could drug you or knock you unconscious and spirit you away," said Alex. "They might have a ship waiting already, or they could just hide you someplace until a ship from Conmar arrives."

"You have a devious mind," Joshua laughed, but he glanced around nervously just the same.

"I was just thinking of how I would go about capturing someone. I also think it might be a good idea for you to sail to Midland and not try to find a ship going directly to Westland."

"And why is that?"

"Because if I was trying to catch you, I'd make sure all the ship captains that sail to and from Westland knew what you look like. I could either make up a reason why you are wanted or simply offer a reward for your capture," said Alex. "I suppose you know at least some of the ships that sail to and from Westland."

"I know many of them, though most of them only sail between Midland and Westland."

"It might be best for you to find a ship in Midland to take you home. A ship captain you know you can trust."

"Yes, that might be best. I hadn't thought things through as much as you have. I suppose I am lucky to have met you, and I hope that you are never the one trying to catch me."

"And I hope you won't have anyone trying to catch you in the near future. Now, my uncle said he would be staying at a tavern called the White Stag. I hope he hasn't sailed to Midland without me."

Alex and Joshua found the White Stag without any trouble, as it was one of the largest taverns in the city. The owner of the Stag seemed to recognize Alex as soon as he saw him, which was a surprise to Alex.

"Master Kessler told me he was expecting you," the owner

said. "He's been a bit worried that you wouldn't get here in time to sail with him. He's down at the docks now, making sure all your goods have been properly loaded."

"Do you know which ship he has chosen?" Alex asked.

"The *Dawn Star*," the owner answered. "Sails at first light tomorrow."

After thanking the tavern owner, and arranging for a room for Joshua, Alex and Joshua left the tavern and made their way to the docks. Alex wasn't sure how Whalen would react to Joshua, but he hoped it wouldn't be a problem. Now that he thought of it, Alex wasn't even sure what Whalen would look like. He was certain to be wearing some disguise, because he couldn't travel openly.

The *Dawn Star* was a large ship, with three masts and nearly a hundred members in her crew. Alex didn't have any trouble spotting Whalen, disguise and all. He was shorter now, with dark, messy hair, dark eyes, and a stomach that, while not fat, was certainly much larger than Whalen's.

"Ah, nephew," Whalen called out as soon as he saw Alex. "Thought you might miss the ship and have to wait here in Eastland until I got back."

"I'm sorry I'm late," Alex answered. "I've had a bit of an adventure getting here."

"Oh? And who's your friend here?" Whalen asked.

"This is Joshua. We met along the road," Alex said. "He's looking for a ship to take him to Midland."

"Plenty of ships going that way at this time of year," Whalen replied distractedly. "Might even find a place on the

Dawn Star here, if you're lucky. We leave at first light, and I have a lot to do before then."

"Anything I can help you with, uncle?"

"No, no, not just now. Take your friend and talk to the captain, see if there's a place for him on the ship. Oh, I know you've got stories to tell about your journey, but they will have to wait until tonight."

Without another word Whalen walked away to check on some cargo that was sitting on the dock. Alex gave Joshua a look that plainly said, "Yes, he's always like that," and the two of them went off to find the captain of the *Dawn Star*.

Alex was happy to learn that there was room on the ship for Joshua to join them, and arrangements were quickly made. With that matter settled, Alex and Joshua walked back to the White Stag and had their lunch. They remained in the tavern all afternoon, as Joshua seemed to take Alex's warnings about someone snatching him from the city seriously. It was well after dark before Whalen joined them, looking worn out after a hard day's work.

The three of them ate their dinner together, but Whalen seemed distracted by other matters. He didn't ask Alex any questions, and the only question he asked Joshua was whether or not he'd found a place on the *Dawn Star* for the voyage. After dinner, Joshua excused himself and went to his room, and Alex and Whalen went to a suite of rooms that Whalen had taken for them.

"Well," Whalen said as he took a seat in front of the fire. "You'd better tell me everything that's happened."

"More than you might imagine in so short a time."

Alex took his own chair and told Whalen everything from the beginning, starting with his adventure in the graveyard and the magic he had used to keep the bones of the suspected wizard safe. When Alex mentioned the strange book that had crumbled in his hand, Whalen interrupted Alex's story.

"I don't think that grave belongs to a wizard," Whalen said. "I don't recall there being any wizards here in Jarro for a long time, longer than the two hundred years since this fellow was buried."

"Perhaps. Still, somebody wants those bones, and there was that strange book in the grave."

"Yes, and you were right to protect the bones. Wizard or not, he should rest in peace. As for the book, I wish you'd been able to read more of it."

"It crumbled to dust almost before I realized there was any magic in it."

"Hmm," Whalen said, his eyes fixed on the fire. "It seems to me I've heard something about a dragon with no name, something very old. I don't remember what it was about, and this 'darloch est messer' business means nothing to me at all."

"I'm sure it's important, though I don't have any idea why. I'm also sure that darloch est messer and the dragon with no name are connected somehow."

"Possibly, possibly . . . but I don't see that we can do anything about that right now. I'll ponder on it. Like I said, I'm sure I once heard or read about a nameless dragon, but it might have to wait until our business here in Jarro is finished."

"So long as you promise to think about it."

"And now, tell me about Joshua. Why have you brought him here with you? I mean, apart from the obvious, that is."

"The obvious?"

"Oh, I can see his aura as plainly as you do," Whalen said with a chuckle. "I, however, have been around long enough to know what it means. I also can see that he is somehow related to the elves, so he's probably from Westland and related to the sea elves. A strange coincidence since we are traveling to Westland."

"Sea elves?"

"I will tell you of them later. Right now, I must ask if you have ever seen an aura like Joshua's around anyone else?"

"Only around people with magic in them. Joshua has no magic in him, but there must be some magical connection to explain his aura."

"I've only seen such an aura, as you say, around a non-magical person a few times. And every time I have, it turns out that there is something special and important about that person. I believe that young Joshua has some important role to play in the future of Jarro. From the brightness and color of his aura, I should say a role for the good."

"I would guess that you're right. As to why I brought him with me, it's because your nephew, Jabez, is trying to capture him."

"What!" Whalen nearly shouted.

Alex laughed at Whalen's shocked surprise, and he quickly explained how he had met Joshua and about their encounter with Jabez's soldiers along the road. Whalen didn't say anything when Alex had finished his story. He sat staring into the fire with a deep look of concentration on his face.

"Well then," Whalen finally said, "Jabez must know that Joshua is special, and he wants to control him if he can. Sending men all the way to Eastland just to capture Joshua is a bold move. Perhaps Jabez is becoming desperate. We might be able to use that to our advantage."

"Jabez will find that Joshua is not easy to control."

"No, no, he won't be, but that won't stop Jabez from trying. You were right to bring Joshua along and to help him out of trouble, but . . ."

"But what?"

"Well, I'm not sure what we can do to help Joshua, as much as I'd like to. I doubt very much that Joshua would agree to travel with us, and I'm not sure that's a good idea anyway. We can't put our own mission at risk. Still, he seems a clever young man, and if he's Darthon's nephew, he should know how to take care of himself."

"There must be something we can do," Alex said, and then paused to consider what Whalen had actually said. "Wait . . . you know his uncle Darthon?"

"Oh, I met Darthon years ago, the last time I was here in Jarro, in fact. He's a good man and devoted to his people. Jabez will hate him of course, and I'm sure he will do everything in his power to either control or destroy Darthon."

"If you know Darthon, we have to do something to help Joshua."

"We can see him safely to Midland. After that, I'm afraid he will have to look after himself."

"If Joshua really is important to the future of Jarro, wouldn't we be risking that future by letting him go his own way?"

"This entire quest is a risk. We're facing a dark wizard, who I know for a fact is extremely powerful. We're also facing the Brotherhood, and you know how dangerous they can be. If Jabez discovers we are here, I don't like to think about how much help he could call on to track us down. Besides, taking Joshua with us could do as much harm as good."

"Jabez is bound to find out that we are in Jarro, sooner or later."

"Later would be better. Still, we have a few things in our favor."

"Like?"

"Like the fact that Jabez will not ask the Brotherhood for help if he thinks he can defeat me on his own. He's never been good at asking for help, and I'm sure he believes that he can deal with me by himself."

"Not asking for help must run in the family," Alex said with a half-smile.

"What do you mean?" Whalen asked.

"I know how hard it was for you to ask for my help," Alex said. "In all the stories I've heard and read about you, you've never asked for any help, even if you should have."

"Stories you hear or read don't always tell you everything that really happened," Whalen answered. "Still, I will admit that I don't like putting other people at risk, not if I can help it. Now, I have worked out our plan for once we reach Midland."

"What is it?" Alex asked.

"Since we are in disguise as a cloth and fur merchant and his apprentice, once we reach Midland, we will join one of the caravans that travel that land and slowly make our way to the west. Now, before you start to argue about wasting time, I've already considered that."

"And you've decided that a slow approach to Westland is better than a fast one."

"If we suddenly turn up in Westland, Jabez may run. If he thinks that he has time to prepare, or to set a cunning trap for me, he will wait."

"How soon do you think he will know that you're in Jarro?"

"He may suspect it already, but I don't think so. He won't *know* I'm here until we are much closer to Conmar. As for you, well, he may not know you are here at all, at least not until it is too late."

"So long as I don't use my magic."

"That is important as well, but not exactly what I meant. When I told you not to use magic, what I meant was don't use magic that will bring notice. The magic you used at the grave-yard won't be a problem, as anyone who hears the story—or goes looking for the wizard's bones—will attribute any magic they may encounter to the dead wizard."

"So what do you mean that Jabez won't know I'm here until it's too late?"

"It's because of what you are, Alex. I haven't mentioned it before, and I don't think you are even aware of it, but it is difficult—even for me—to see you simply as a wizard."

"What do you mean? You know I have magic. You know I'm a wizard."

"Oh, I know what you are, but if I simply look at you . . . well, I can't see your power the way I can every other wizard I've ever met. I think it has something to do with what you are, and maybe who you are. You are part dragon after all, Alex, and dragons are very good at hiding when they want to."

"But I'm not trying to hide, at least not from you."

"No, but you've never really thought about *not* hiding from me either," Whalen chuckled. "It is an interesting advantage, and I think it will be useful."

"Perhaps it will," Alex said. "Still, I don't like the idea of taking so much time to get to Westland. We already know from Joshua that Jabez is on the move and that he wishes to rule all of Jarro. We need to stop him as soon as possible."

"As soon as possible—without risking too much," Whalen answered. "If we rush in, Jabez may flee, but his armies will be left without a leader. With Jabez in control, they will attack Westland and try to take over, but without Jabez they might attack anywhere. Jabez may even send them on a deadly mission that he knows will fail—just to hurt the people of Jarro and to spite us for interfering."

"Yes, I suppose he might do something like that."

"So we will move slowly . . . at least for now. We will travel across Midland—or, more correctly, *around* Midland—and gather as much information as we can. We might even be able to warn the people of Midland of what might be coming. After all, Alex, we could fail. If we do fail, it would be wise to at least give some warning to the people, and perhaps prepare them for the wars that will follow."

"I don't want to think about failing."

"Nobody wants to think about failing. I'm sure that Jabez isn't thinking about failure—and that might also be to our advantage. The thing is, we need to think about what will happen if we fail. Think of it as a motivation to *not* fail if you like, but we need to think about it just the same."

"Alright, I understand. So . . . after we travel around Midland, then what?"

"I'm not sure yet. Things may change as we travel, or everything might work out exactly as we want it to."

"I think it is unlikely that everything will go our way."

"Yes, I think that as well. For now, I think we should plan on sailing to Westland once we reach the western edge of Midland. The people in the north of Westland are friendly enough to strangers, and the mountains that run down the center of the island are not nearly as high. We will find our way over or around the mountains in the north and then move south to Conmar."

"Well, at least we have a plan," said Alex thoughtfully.

"A plan that we can change as we learn more about what Jabez is doing. Have you had a chance to read the journals I gave you?"

Alex shook his head. "A little, but I haven't discovered anything that will help us right now."

Whalen nodded. "Keep reading whenever you have time. Perhaps something will turn up."

"And perhaps you will spend the rest of the evening telling

me about the sea elves you mentioned earlier," Alex said, smiling.

"Ah, the sea elves," Whalen said, leaning back in his chair. "I thought they would interest you. Unfortunately, I can't tell you very much about them. I've never met any sea elves, but I know they are here in Jarro, and I know they are a secretive bunch, more secretive than any other elves I know of, except perhaps for the dark elves. One rumor says that sea elves were once dark elves, who, having lost so much on land, turned to the sea. Another story says that they were once closely connected to the men of Westland."

"Which would explain the elf blood in Joshua," Alex said.

"Yes, that would explain it," Whalen agreed. "I have also heard it said that the sea elves remember their family ties, even though they are now distant. According to some old stories, they are still in contact with some groups in Westland, and take a great interest in their distant relatives."

"That seems odd. I mean, wouldn't any relations of theirs be separated from them by at least hundreds of years and many generations of men?"

"Yes, that is true."

"There must be books, family records. Something more than just stories and myths. Someone must know the truth. Someone must have met them and talked with them."

"Oh, I'm sure they have," Whalen laughed. "But I would guess that anyone they've talked to has agreed to keep their secrets."

"Strange," Alex said. "Strange, and a little sad."

"Sad?"

"Sad that an entire race of elves should be unknown."

"I can only tell you the rumors that I've heard. Perhaps, before we leave this land, we can discover the truth together."

"I would like that. Though we have a great deal to do before we can go looking for answers to old stories and rumors."

"We do indeed," Whalen agreed.

CHAPTER SIX

VOYAGE TO MIDLAND

◆

Morning came sooner than Alex would have liked. The walking they'd done the last few days had left him sore and a little stiff. He wished that he'd been able to bring his horse, Dar Losh, on this journey with him, but that just wasn't possible. Whalen was still sitting next to the fire, where Alex had left him the night before. The fire was now cold, but Whalen didn't seem to notice or to even care.

They found Joshua waiting for them in the inn's common room. He was eager to be going. They all ate a hurried breakfast and then Whalen led the way to the docks. The sky was clear and a soft breeze was blowing across the sea. To Alex, it looked like perfect sailing weather.

"I always enjoy sailing," Joshua said as they walked. "The open water, the wind blowing in your hair, everything about it is wonderful. I've always felt more at home on a ship than on land."

"Then perhaps you should become a sailor," Alex joked. "Or maybe a ship captain would be better."

"I've considered it," Joshua said. "At one time I thought I

would try to become one, but it takes years to learn the trade, and . . ."

"And?" Alex asked.

"My uncle wasn't happy with the idea," Joshua said. "He says that my place is with my people."

"Your uncle speaks truly," Alex said. "Though I can understand your love for the sea."

The *Dawn Star* moved away from the docks before the sun had risen, and by the time the sunlight was on the surface of the water they were moving away from Eastland. Alex, Whalen, and Joshua all stood at the railing on deck, staying out of the way of the working sailors. They didn't talk at all, but watched in silence as the land shrank behind them and the sea grew wider in front of them.

"How long will it take to cross to Midland?" Alex finally asked.

"Only a week or ten days," Joshua answered before Whalen could. "If we have fair winds and the weather holds."

"And if the weather doesn't hold?" Alex asked.

"It's not the time of year for storms," Whalen said. "We may run into some wind and rain, but nothing the *Dawn Star* can't handle."

"She is one of the largest ships that sail this sea," Joshua added. "Most of the trade ships only have one mast, maybe two. A three-master like this will only sail between the larger ports, while the smaller traders will sail to almost every small port they can find."

"Large ships and large cities are good for business," Whalen said. "We are bound for Hafnar, one of the largest cities in

Midland. With a little luck, we should be able to do some good trading while we are there."

They remained on deck for a time but didn't talk much. The sea air and the movement of the ship was relaxing to Alex, and he let his troubled thoughts about the future slip to the back of his mind. Whalen eventually went to his cabin, saying something about checking his inventory logs. Joshua remained with Alex, a dreamy look of happiness on his face.

———•••———

Four days after they set sail it began to rain lightly. The sea remained relatively calm and the wind was light but the captain and crew appeared to be worried. Alex couldn't see any reason to worry—even with the light wind they were making good time. Still, the troubled looks of the crew were hard to miss.

When he had a chance to talk to Whalen alone, he asked about the captain and crew's dark mood.

"They call this 'serpent weather,'" Whalen explained. "This is the kind of weather that sea serpents prefer, so the sailors are afraid."

"Are there many sea serpents here?" Alex asked.

"No, not that many. I've seen a few in my travels here, but I don't think there have ever been that many of them. And the ones I have seen have all been in the larger north and south seas. These smaller seas between lands are too confining for the likes of them."

"Do you think a sea serpent would attack a ship as large as the *Dawn Star*?"

"I've never heard of a ship this size being attacked, but who knows. The serpents I've seen were much too small to attack something this size, but . . ."

"And if we run into something bigger? What are the chances that we'll be attacked?"

"If what you mean to ask is, 'What are the chances that we'll need to use magic to fight off an attack?' then the answer is, 'I'm not sure.'"

"Maybe you haven't heard about a ship this size being attacked because the ships that have been attacked never make it back to port."

"Let's not worry about that unless we have to. We'll use magic if we must. But we can't do what we came here to do if we don't get to Midland first. There's no sense in worrying about it. If we're attacked, *then* we can worry."

The next day the rain was gone but heavy gray fog replaced it. There was no wind at all, and the fog moved about the ship like anxious ghosts. Alex could tell the sailors' fears were growing. Many of them would jump at the slightest sound. Even Joshua seemed nervous when Alex found him standing on the deck.

"This is serpent weather," Joshua said, shaking his head. "I don't like it, even on a ship this size."

"I suppose you've heard tales of sea serpents in your travels," Alex said.

"I've done more than hear tales. I've seen some of the

monsters of the deep—monsters that could toss the *Dawn Star* about like a toy."

"Let's hope we don't run into anything as dangerous as that."

Whalen soon appeared on deck, his eyes moving around the ship, a worried look on his face. The fog made it difficult to see anything, but Whalen kept looking at the sea as he paced back and forth along the deck.

"Your uncle seems troubled," Joshua commented.

"He's worried for the time we are losing," Alex said. "In business, time is money, you know."

"Perhaps it is," Joshua said, his eyes looking up at the slack sails. "But if we run into a monster, time and money won't mean much of anything here on the open sea."

Alex didn't reply, and they fell silent for a long time, looking into the fog and thinking their own thoughts. Alex could tell that Whalen was worried, and that made him worry as well. He thought that he could probably drive away a sea serpent, but not without using his magic, which would reveal him as a wizard to the crew. Right now, he hoped that the wind would start blowing again and the fog would lift.

"Alex," Joshua said after a time. "I want to thank you for everything you've done for me."

"I've done little enough," Alex said.

"No, you've done a great deal. You helped me escape the soldiers of Jabez. I won't forget that. I just want you to know I'm grateful, just in case."

"In case of what?" Alex asked, troubled by Joshua's words.

"In case we don't both make it to Midland," Joshua said.

"Don't talk nonsense," Alex said, patting Joshua on the shoulder. "We'll both get to Midland. Once the wind starts blowing again, we'll be there in no—"

Alex was cut off as the ship suddenly shuddered as if it had run aground. Joshua was thrown to the deck. Alex clutched the ship's railing desperately to keep his feet. Shouts broke out around the ship, but the loudest voice belonged to the captain.

"Get the lines over the side," he bellowed. "Get those men out of the water."

Alex quickly scanned the deck, but the fog was too thick for him to see exactly what was going on. Sailors were running across the deck, ropes were flying around, and the unsettling sound of moving water—a lot of moving water—filled the air.

"Alex, take the bow, I'll take the stern," Whalen, who had appeared out of nowhere, shouted in Alex's ear. "Do whatever you have to do to save the ship."

"But—" Alex started.

"Whatever you have to do," Whalen repeated as he hurried away.

Alex turned toward the bow of the ship, but he hadn't taken a step when the deck swayed wildly under his feet once more. Tripping over one of the sailors, Alex jumped back to his feet and started forward. Dodging between the panicked sailors who were trying frantically to get their friends out of the water, Alex made it as far as the forward mast before the deck moved under his feet again. This time the ship didn't jump—it spun. The sound of something hard moving and cutting into the wooden side of the ship filled the air. Alex looked back toward Whalen, and saw something he didn't understand.

Whalen was hanging over the side of the ship, a grappling hook attached to a long, thin rope in his hands. As Alex watched, Whalen threw the hook over the side, keeping a firm hold on the rope. In a moment the rope pulled tight and started racing through Whalen's hands. For some reason Alex couldn't figure out, Whalen had hooked the sea monster.

As soon as he felt the magic, Alex understood what Whalen was doing. As the rope sped through his hands, Whalen was pouring magic into it. As soon as the last few feet of rope slipped away and vanished over the side of the ship, Whalen let his magic loose. A deafening crash of thunder filled the air, and Alex wondered if the monster could survive so powerful a blast of magic. The answer to his question appeared an instant later. The monster's tail emerged from the water, spun wildly over the ship, and, like a whip, snapped the rear mast of the ship in half. Sails and debris rained down over Whalen, and Alex lost sight of him.

Alex wanted to run toward the stern, but his brain told him that he had to move forward. He turned away from the scene of trouble and continued forward. This sea serpent was larger than he'd imagined, and more powerful than he'd thought possible. His brain raced, trying to think of some way to drive off the beast, but his mind was blank. He'd never faced a creature like this before, and nothing he'd ever read seemed to fit the problem at hand.

Alex didn't have long to think. As he jumped over a fallen sailor, the ship spun again, he staggered, and he found himself looking back at the stern. He had just turned around again when the head of the great serpent broke the water and rose above the bow of the ship. Alex was stunned by the great beauty and power that he saw. The creature was elegant, almost fragile-looking, but what really caught Alex's attention was that this massive sea creature looked familiar—it looked more like a dragon than any creature except a dragon should.

Alex's stunned amazement was broken as Joshua pushed past him, a massive harpoon in his hands. With a natural ability, and more strength than Alex would have thought possible, Joshua heaved the harpoon forward, directly at the beautiful head of the sea serpent.

Alex was unable to speak, but his mind screamed *No!*

Alex lifted his left hand as if he was holding his staff. The harpoon slowed in his mind, and with less than a second to act, Alex magically put a shield between the beast and the weapon. The harpoon bounced harmlessly away from the sea serpent's eye, but the serpent still flinched backward by instinct. Alex could feel the monster's rage as its eyes scanned the deck in search of its attacker.

Let it go, Alex said in his mind, pushing the thought toward the sea serpent. *I have saved you from the blow, now let your anger go.*

The serpent's eyes came to rest on Alex and the creature paused. For a moment it seemed to consider Alex, perhaps judging how dangerous he was. The creature's eyes moved back along the length of the ship, finally pausing on Whalen. There was a sudden silence, the kind of total silence that never happened on the open sea. The sailors stopped shouting, the ship became still, and the waves on the water were frozen in place.

A dragon lord and a wizard together, the sea serpent's words formed in Alex's mind. *What brings such power to this land?*

Our reason for being here is our own, Alex answered. *We need to travel across this sea, and I ask your leave to do so.*

Reasons for one so powerful are never simply your own, the serpent said. *What price will you offer for safe passage?*

Price? Alex asked. *I have saved you from a terrible blow that might have killed you, or at least taken your eye.*

The serpent thought for a moment. *I will accept this act of kindness as the price for safe passage. As for your reasons for being here, they are plain enough for the wise to see. Two men of power, sailing to the west. You come seeking the evil one, the wizard that lives in the castle of Conmar.*

Yes, Alex admitted, *we seek to destroy that evil, or at least to drive it out of this land.*

I will leave you then, and wish you luck, the serpent said.

You have my thanks, Alex said, bowing slightly.

Slowly the monster began to lower itself into the water, but it paused as its head reached Alex's level. It looked at him for a moment, and then it spoke out loud. The serpent spoke the same language as the dragons, a language Alex understood perfectly, though no one else on the ship could. The serpent's words were a warning for Alex.

"Destroy the evil in Conmar if you can, dragon lord. Be warned that he is not alone in the evil he has brought to this land," the sea serpent said. "Be warned also that the wizard you seek has a dragon as a servant as well."

The instant the sea serpent vanished beneath the water, time snapped back into being. Sailors were suddenly shouting, the ship creaked and moaned, and the sound of the waves filled the air once more. Alex turned to check on Whalen to make sure he was alright.

Everything had happened so fast that most of the sailors had not seen any of it. The captain of the *Dawn Star* rushed to Joshua's side and bowed. "We are in your debt, serpent slayer," the captain said. "And in Master Kessler's as well, for bringing you on this voyage."

Whalen came up behind the captain as he was speaking, a strange look on his face. He clearly knew that something had happened, but he didn't know what it was.

"I am not a serpent slayer," Joshua said, his voice shaky and a little weak.

"Perhaps not in name, but I saw your mighty throw of the harpoon," the captain said. "And I saw the sea serpent vanish beneath the waves. Your timely work has saved this ship and all aboard her. You will be rewarded when we reach Hafnar, and if you ever need a fast ship to carry you, the *Dawn Star* is at your service."

"You are most kind," Joshua answered, more than a little confused.

Alex knew that, between things happening so fast and the magic of the serpent, Joshua had no idea that the harpoon he had thrown had been deflected before it reached its target.

The crew gathered around Joshua, and they were all whispering about what the captain said he had seen. Joshua was the hero. He had driven off, maybe even killed, the monster from the deep, and saved them all from certain death. Once the celebration had started there was no stopping it. Joshua accepted their cheers and praise, but he also tried to downplay what he had done. The celebrations continued until the fog started to lift and the wind began to blow once more. Then the sailors happily returned to their work and the captain gave the order to sail for Midland.

It was late that night before Alex and Whalen had a chance to discuss what had happened. Most of the crew was asleep, and the two wizards found a secluded spot near the bow of the ship to talk. Whalen wanted to know everything that had happened, and Alex was happy to tell him. Repeating the details helped him to think things over and decide what exactly they meant.

"What did you do?" Whalen asked, looking over his shoulder to make sure they were alone.

"I blocked the harpoon that Joshua threw," said Alex. "I don't know why, but I couldn't let that harpoon hit its mark. Then I spoke to the serpent, or rather we shared our thoughts."

"I thought as much," said Whalen.

"It knew who—or, I should say—*what*, I am," Alex went on. "It knew I was a dragon lord, and it knew you were a wizard."

"We could hardly avoid that," Whalen said unhappily.

"No one will know. It won't speak of this meeting to anyone."

"Do you think you can trust such a creature?"

"Yes, I do," Alex said, thinking about what the sea serpent had told him.

"And I trust you. Perhaps this story will not reach Jabez and we will still be safe."

"The serpent will keep its word. Not just because it said it would, but because of what it said out loud."

"It spoke out loud?" Whalen asked in surprise. "I've only heard a few stories where sea serpents actually spoke out loud."

"It spoke in the language of the dragons. I should have expected it, because it looks so much like a dragon."

"Yes, I suppose it did. What did it say?" Whalen asked with interest.

"It told me to be careful because the wizard at Conmar has a dragon as a servant," Alex said, looking out over the water. "I got the feeling that there was at least one dragon at Conmar, maybe more."

"That will make things more difficult. I'm sure Jabez will use the dragon to guard his most prized possession—the Axe of Sundering."

"I'm sure you are right, but that's not what troubles me."

"What could trouble you more than having to fight a dragon to get the Axe?"

"What troubles me is why. Why would a dragon serve a dark wizard? I know not all dragons are good. Some—all right, *most*—are evil, but even if an evil dragon did what Jabez wanted, there would still have to be some payment in return. And I doubt any dragon would do everything Jabez wants, although . . ."

"Yes? What is it?"

"It was the way the serpent said it," Alex began, thinking hard to remember the exact words. "The way he used the word *servant*, it made it sound like the dragon *must* do whatever

Jabez commands. It was closer to *slave* than *servant*, and that troubles me, because I don't see how that can be."

"Wouldn't most dragons do as *you* command?"

"They might, but I wouldn't count on it," Alex said with a laugh. "Dragons are independent, and they love their freedom. I don't see a dragon giving up that freedom for any reason."

"Well, you would know more about that than I do," Whalen said, turning to look out across the water as well. "I'm glad you were able to drive the monster away without revealing who or what you really are to the captain or the crew."

"And I'm glad it went," Alex said. "I just wish I understood what it meant about the dragon. As unlikely as it would be for a dragon to be a servant, it's impossible for me to imagine a dragon as a slave. I would think you'd have to kill a dragon before you could make it a slave."

"One more thing to think about and hopefully deal with in the future."

"Well, as long as it's just the one," Alex said with a wry smile.

To Alex's relief, the rest of the voyage to Hafnar was uneventful. The weather remained clear and the wind fair, and the ship moved easily across the open water. Joshua was the most popular person on board, though Alex could tell that all the attention was beginning to bother him.

It was late afternoon on their ninth day at sea when they sailed into the port at Hafnar. The captain called the crew around to announce that the ship would be unloaded the next morning. Before Alex, Whalen, and Joshua could leave and find a place to spend the night, the captain asked them to wait for a moment. With a great deal of cheering from the crew, he presented Joshua with two fair-sized bags of silver coins and a smaller bag full of gold.

"This is a small price to pay for my life, the lives of my crew, and my ship," the captain said. "And I will say again: If ever you need a ship, we are at your service."

"You are most kind," Joshua said, bowing to the captain and crew. "I will not forget your kindness to me."

"A good deed well rewarded," Whalen commented, leading the way up the dock. "I suppose I should also reward you, as you've saved both my nephew and myself. You've also saved our goods by bringing us safely to port."

"No, no," Joshua said. "Between friends, there is no need for rewards."

"Then we shall count ourselves lucky to be called your friends," Whalen replied. "Now, I believe there's a very good inn just up here on the right."

Chapter Seven

The Caravan

The next morning, Joshua and Alex said their good-byes early. Joshua was keen to be on his way, mostly because he was nervous about Jabez's soldiers finding him in the city.

"May fortune follow your path," Alex said as they parted outside the inn.

"May we meet again in happier times," Joshua answered before turning away.

Though Alex had only known Joshua for two weeks, he knew he would miss his friend. He hoped that Joshua would be able to make his way home safely and someday fulfill the promise that Alex knew was waiting for him. Alex stood and watched as Joshua walked down the main road. He hoped that Joshua would be able to avoid any trouble, and most of all he hoped that his friend could avoid falling into Jabez's hands. Alex remained looking down the road long after he'd lost sight of Joshua.

"May fortune follow your path," Alex repeated in a whisper.

Whalen was waiting for Alex in the common room of the inn, and once Alex arrived, he was all business. The *Dawn Star* was to be unloaded that morning, and the cloth and hides that Whalen had bought in Eastland as part of their disguise as merchants would be loaded into wagons. Once their goods were ready, they would meet with the leader of the caravan that Whalen wanted to join. With any luck, the two wizards would be part of the caravan before nightfall and on their way once more.

"The caravans are mostly traveling groups of traders and merchants," Whalen explained. "They travel from city to city and from land to land. The one we're trying to join will travel to the north and west. It will take us at least a month or two, probably longer, to get to the western edge of Midland this way, but I think it will be time well spent."

Alex didn't comment. He wanted to move faster and confront Jabez sooner. He was worried about what Jabez would be doing while he and Whalen traveled around Midland. Jabez was already causing trouble in Westland, and Alex didn't think it would be too long before that trouble got worse.

"Trust me, I'd like to get to Conmar as soon as we can, but this will be the safest way," Whalen said, as if reading Alex's mind. "Jabez will have spies everywhere, and not just spies looking for travelers. If we go racing across Midland and into Westland, we'll be spotted easily."

"Spies that can sense magic?" Alex asked.

"Perhaps," answered Whalen, "but I think it more likely that he'll be looking for anyone who doesn't fit in."

"But we don't fit in, do we?" Alex said with a half-smile.

"No, but that's exactly why he'll miss us."

"I don't understand," Alex said.

"We'll be traveling with a caravan," Whalen answered. "Caravans are full of people who don't fit in for one reason or another. Yes, they are mostly merchants, but even then they don't really fit in when it comes to cities and towns. They prefer the open road to staying in one place. Some caravans even have a few magical people with them as well."

"Won't that be dangerous for us? I mean, won't these magical people start to question what they feel and see when you and I are around them?"

"No, I don't think so. When it comes to the caravan and its members, they act much like a family. Each man's business is his own, but if someone from outside the caravan causes trouble, the caravan is united against the outsider."

"I see," Alex said, thinking things over. "Then I suppose a caravan is the safest place for us to be, even if it takes longer to reach Westland."

"If we can join one. I've sent a letter to the leader of the caravan we're trying to join, but as yet nothing is decided. I suspect they'll want to have a look at us before making a decision. I believe they will accept us, but there is a chance we'll be turned down."

"And then what would we do?"

"Let's see what the caravan leader says before we make any other plans," Whalen said, dodging the difficult question.

Together they headed for the docks. When they arrived, they saw that their goods were already off the ship and loaded into three wagons. Alex wondered why Whalen had bought so much, and how the two of them would be able to drive three wagons. His second question was soon answered as three men approached. Whalen explained that he had hired the men to help drive the wagons, and that all three were members of the caravan they hoped to join.

"And if we are not accepted into the caravan?"

"Then I will pay them for today's work, and that will be the end of it. Now, come along, I have to meet with the leader of the caravan, and it would be best to complete the meeting before the midday meal."

Alex didn't ask any more questions as he walked with Whalen behind the wagons. Even though Whalen didn't seem to be worried that they might not be accepted into the caravan, Alex didn't know what they would do if they were not. Instead of asking questions, he looked at the buildings and houses of Hafnar as they went along. He was surprised when he noticed that the wagon drivers were leading them out of the city.

"The caravan is camped outside the north gate," said Whalen, noticing Alex's glance. "Most caravans do not enter cities because there is never enough room inside a city for the entire caravan in one place."

"Just how large is this caravan?" Alex asked, remembering the size of the main square of Hafnar.

"I believe there are four hundred wagons, and between five and seven hundred people," said Whalen.

"That many?"

"Some merchants bring their families along," said Whalen. "Some don't even own homes in a city or town because the road is their life. Others own homes but only stay there from time to time when they wish to rest from traveling."

Alex nodded but didn't say anything more. He thought back to what Joshua had said about the caravans, how they could be more than he would expect them to be. He hadn't really thought about who would be in the caravan, however, and he decided that it made perfect sense for entire families to be included.

The caravan's camp was large but well organized. The wagons were arranged in an exact order, allowing all the merchants of the same kinds of goods to be close together. The wagons were set up so that a large area to sell goods was created in the center of their camp. It also meant that the caravan was protected from outside attacks. Being next to a city there was little need for protection, but Alex thought it was wise of the caravan to take precautions. There was one large opening that allowed people from the city to enter and exit, and Alex and Whalen headed straight for it.

"Wait here with the wagons while I talk to the leader of the caravan," Whalen said, looking around at the crowds of people. "It shouldn't take long."

Alex simply nodded and walked a little closer to their wagons. He leaned against the side of one wagon and watched Whalen walk away. He was still troubled by what might happen if they were not allowed to join this caravan. Trying to find something else to think about, he looked around the camp, studying the people who belonged to the caravan.

After several minutes of waiting and watching, Alex noticed a group of five young men walking towards him. He studied each of them as they came forward, noticing that they all carried swords and daggers, just as he did. When the five young men were only two or three yards away they stopped, spreading out in a slight half circle and looking at Alex.

"He looks a bit small," the largest of them said.

"Everyone looks small to you," another replied.

"Don't look like he has any magic," a third said.

"Few enough do," the fourth said.

"We were wondering what trade you are in," the fifth young man said, addressing Alex for the first time.

"My uncle and I are cloth and fur merchants," Alex answered.

"Ah, a tailor," the young man said with a smile. "I should have guessed. He wears his sword as a tailor would."

The other young men laughed at this statement, and Alex smiled as well.

"And what trade might you be in?" Alex asked, noting the good humor of the group.

"My family trades in weapons and metals," the young man answered proudly. "As you can plainly see, I carry my sword as a warrior would."

Alex glanced at the way the young man's sword was attached to his belt, noting that it was exactly like his own sword. He smiled, remembering the first time he had ever worn a sword, and how his friends had taught him to attach the scabbard and the straps.

"Yes, I can see you wear your sword in the correct fashion," Alex said. "Though the way a man wears his sword has little to do with how he uses it."

"He speaks wisely," one of the other young men said with a laugh.

"Wisely perhaps," the first one said, taking a step closer as he spoke. "Though what could a tailor know of swords? Or how to use them?"

All of the young men laughed once more, and Alex had to laugh as well. He could see where this was leading, and he thought he would be more than a match for any of the group. His adventures had been an excellent training ground, and he had put in many hours practicing against magically conjured enemies as well. Even without his magic sword, Alex knew he could hold his own against almost anyone, and was a better swordsman than most men would ever be.

"A tailor's work is to cut and shape," Alex said. "What more is there to swordplay?"

"What indeed?" the young man said with a sly smile. "Perhaps you will show us how you cut and shape."

"The lesson may prove a hard one to learn," Alex said, putting his left hand on his sword. "The last man I tried to teach did not learn well, and has given up trying . . . if you know what I mean."

"Oh, then I must be careful," the young man said with a laugh. "Perhaps, if you are willing, we can find something less dangerous for you to teach with."

"A craftsman is only as good as his tools," Alex said.

"Truly said, but still, we don't want anyone to give up trying," the young man replied happily. "Here now, I have just the thing. Eric, do you still have those blunted swords you were carrying earlier? I would not wish to cut a craftsman—even by accident."

The largest of the five produced two swords that he had been carrying behind his back, and Alex had to laugh. It seemed the young men were ready for any reply he might have had, and would only be satisfied by trying his ability to use a sword.

"A fair weapon," Alex said, taking one of the swords and testing its balance. "And a good thing it's blunt. I wouldn't want to harm a warrior with a simple tailor's tools."

The young men all laughed at Alex's comment and moved back a little to give Alex and the other young man room. Alex removed his usual sword, hanging it on a hook on the side of the wagon. The young man who had been talking was pleased to see this, and took the time to remove his own sword as well. They were just preparing to duel when a girl's angry voice broke in.

"Lupo, what do you think you're doing?" she said, her eyes blazing with anger.

Alex looked at her as she hurried up to them, noticing how much she looked like the young man he was facing. She was younger than he was, but she had to be his sister.

"The tailor is going to teach me his craft," Lupo replied with a smile.

"You know what Father said about dueling. He'll break your sword if he catches you," the girl said loudly.

"I'm not using my sword," Lupo answered, unconcerned. "We'll be using the blunted training swords—as I do not wish to damage this young tailor."

"You can't," the young woman almost screamed. "He's a *tailor*. What chance does he have against you?"

"He's accepted my offer, and he claims to have taught others," Lupo said. "I won't do any lasting damage, so where's the trouble?"

The girl gave up on Lupo and turned to Alex. She stepped forward, a troubled and urgent look on her face.

"Please, sir, do not accept this challenge. My brother is one of the finest swordsmen in all of Midland, and he will make you look a fool."

"To look a fool to one of the finest swordsman in Midland . . . that's not so bad," Alex said. "To presume victory before the battle is fought—that is truly foolish."

"Well said," one of the other young men said.

"Please, stand aside," Alex said to the girl. He bowed slightly to Lupo and lifted the blunted sword in salute. "We shall see who the greater fool is here, if only for the fun of it."

"For the fun of it," Lupo replied with a laugh, raising his own sword in reply.

Alex and Lupo approached one another slowly, and Alex noticed that several members of the caravan were gathering around them. They had obviously heard Lupo's sister yelling and wanted to see their champion in action. Alex also thought that Lupo's sister might have been trying to attract her father's attention and put an end to this mock duel before it began.

"When you get tired of teaching, please say so," Lupo said, adjusting his grip.

"And when you get tired of learning, please let me know," Alex replied.

Lupo attacked slowly, testing Alex's ability to deflect his blows. Alex blocked the attacks easily, but he made it look more difficult than it really was. He had learned from his friends on his adventures that not revealing his skills too soon was one key to learning how skilled his opponent was.

Lupo made several lunging attacks, all of which Alex deflected. He could see that Lupo was a good swordsman, but perhaps not as good as he thought he was. He was a little slow to recover from his attacks and he often left himself open for counters. Alex didn't bother to counter just yet, but he watched as Lupo started to become frustrated. After several minutes of blocking Lupo's attacks, Alex knew exactly how good Lupo was, and he knew how best to defeat him. On Lupo's next attack Alex countered, gently tapping Lupo on his left arm. Lupo stepped back in surprise, unsure of how Alex had managed to land the blow.

"Every man is occasionally blessed with luck," Lupo said, lifting his sword in salute once more.

"And some men prefer not to wait for the blessing," Alex said, once again returning the salute.

The attacks came quicker now, and Lupo was a bit more careful. Alex continued to block the attacks, and after another few minutes he countered again, striking Lupo gently on his right side. Once more Lupo stepped back in surprise, and a small cheer went up from the crowd that had gathered.

"It seems you have much to teach," Lupo said, his smile still in place.

"And you my friend, have much to learn," Alex answered.

Lupo laughed happily and attacked once more. Alex was

glad that Lupo was not becoming angry, because he didn't want to make enemies in the caravan that he and Whalen hoped to join. He also thought he should try to end the duel as soon as possible. The crowd was quickly growing around the two of them, and Lupo's father was sure to notice. He didn't want Lupo getting into trouble.

"How much trouble will you be in if we are caught?" Alex asked as he circled and deflected yet another attack.

"If you are winning, not much," Lupo said with a laugh.

"Then I will try to win," Alex answered.

Several more minutes passed, and Alex deflected all of Lupo's attacks. Three more times he gently touched Lupo with the blunted sword, and each time Lupo laughed as if nothing could make him happier. It was clear to Alex why Lupo had a reputation as one of the best swordsman in Midland. Alex wondered if Lupo wished to learn more about swordplay. There were probably few men willing to practice against him—even with blunted swords.

"You know a great deal, tailor," Lupo commented as Alex tapped him yet again. "Yet all your points have all been won by counters. Do you ever attack?"

"I thought I would test your attack before trying your defense," Alex said with a laugh. "If you would prefer to defend for a while, well . . ." Alex saluted Lupo with his sword, and then attacked.

He moved quickly, as he'd been taught to do, watching everything that Lupo did. To attack was to put everything in and force your opponent to expose his own weaknesses. Alex soon landed three more blows, though none of them were very hard, and Lupo stepped back as if stunned.

"Enough," Lupo said, breathing hard and raising his sword. "I see now that I am the fool and that I am far from being one of the greatest swordsmen in Midland."

"You fight well," Alex said, raising his own sword. "I think a little practice and advice would make the match more even."

"And I think I told you not to do any more dueling," a large man with dark hair and a full beard and mustache said, stepping into the open area between Alex and Lupo.

"Father, I . . ." Lupo began, a nervous look on his face.

"You don't need to say anything," the large man said, his stern face changing to a smile. "It's not often that a man gets to see such a duel, and I'm glad you were wise enough to use blunt swords. If this had been a real duel, I would no longer have a son to yell at."

"Father, we must have this man in our company," Lupo said, his worried look disappearing into a smile. "He is the greatest swordsman I have ever encountered."

"So I see," the man said, glancing first at Alex, and then addressing Whalen, who stepped up beside him. "Master Kessler, you did not tell me that your nephew was so great a swordsman."

"He has many talents," Whalen said. "I haven't seen him in several years, and this is our first trip together. I neglected to mention his training with the sword because I didn't know he had learned as much as it appears he has."

"I see," the man said, glancing once more at Alex. "I think I have made a good agreement then, as your nephew's sword may be of great service to us all. We often face bandits in the far north, and every sword is needed."

"I'm sure my nephew will do all he can to defend the company," Whalen replied with a smile.

"Very well. I am Lycan, master of this caravan." He held his hand out to greet Alex. "You will take orders from me as long as you are part of this group."

"As you wish," Alex said, taking Lycan's hand after glancing at Whalen for his approval.

"You've already met my son, Lupo," Lycan said. "And his sister, Jinar, though we call her Jin. You'll meet my wife, Janet, when time allows. Welcome to the caravan and to our company."

There was a general cheer from the crowd at Lycan's words. Alex knew that most of them cheered because he had defeated Lupo and not made him look a fool. Lupo had taken the defeat well, so the cheers didn't trouble Alex.

"And it looks as if you've met some of Lupo's friends," Lycan continued as the crowd broke apart. "Eric is a distant cousin, and my apprentice."

Alex glanced at Eric, the largest of the young men who had approached with Lupo. He had a friendly look about him, though he seemed a little shy. Alex smiled and tossed Eric the blunted sword. Eric caught it easily and returned the smile. He seemed more than a little pleased that Alex had bested Lupo with the blunted swords, and Alex guessed that Eric had often lost to his cousin with the same swords.

"You are part of our company now, so let us eat together,"

Lycan said, leading them away from the wagons and toward the center of the caravan's camp.

Alex paused for a moment to retrieve his sword from its hook and then he hurried after Lycan and Whalen. He saw that Lupo and Jin had both waited for him, and he was glad to see that they both looked happy about his and Whalen's acceptance into the group.

"You fight very well," Lupo said, holding out his hand to Alex.

"As do you," Alex replied, shaking Lupo's hand.

"You defeated me easily," Lupo laughed. "I felt like an untrained child."

"You have skill, but you need more training," Alex said.

"Where did you learn to fight like that?" Jin asked.

"I've had many good teachers," Alex answered, hoping to avoid any more questions.

"I've been hoping to find someone who could help me train," Lupo said, pointing Alex to one of several long tables at the center of the camp. "I have great hopes of becoming an adventurer someday."

"Don't start talking like that," Jin said, a mix of anger and worry in her voice.

"Father promised he would send me to the oracle next year," Lupo replied. "Adventurers do not choose themselves," he explained to Alex as the three of them sat down at a table, "but must be chosen by an oracle or by some other magical means."

"Yes, I've heard the stories," Alex said.

"There is an oracle in the south of Midland, and I've

wanted to go there for some time," Lupo continued. "My father doesn't think I should become an adventurer, as it can be a dangerous life. I told him that traveling in a caravan can also be a dangerous life, and I still want to try."

"So he's made a bargain with you so you won't run off on your own," Alex said with a knowing smile.

"My father told me if I stayed with the caravan for a year and then still wanted to go looking for adventures, he would send me to the oracle," Lupo said, excited about the idea. "I've traveled with the caravan for seven months now, but I've seen little that I would call adventure."

"Your family hasn't always traveled with the caravan?" Alex asked.

"We used to live in Teslor, on the western coast of Midland," Jin said before Lupo could answer. "When Father made his deal with Lupo, Mother and I insisted on coming along."

"It didn't make much sense for them to remain in Teslor," Lupo added. "My older brothers both travel with other caravans. In fact, one of them leads a caravan of his own now."

"But you must still have family and friends in Teslor," Alex said, wondering why an entire family would leave their home and travel with a caravan.

"A large family and many friends," Lupo said with a laugh. "But Mother was tired of staying home while Father traveled, and Jin was old enough to come along."

"The caravans all have rules about bringing children along," Jin said seriously. "Most caravans won't allow anyone younger than fifteen to travel with them."

"That makes sense," Alex commented. A large pot of stew

was being passed along the table and Alex filled up his bowl. "Young children could be a problem while traveling."

"And there's always the chance of being attacked by bandits," Lupo added, helping himself to the stew.

"Are caravans often attacked?" Alex asked.

"Only in the far north," Lupo said as he began to eat. "We've only traveled north once in the last seven months, and we were attacked by a small band."

"They were only trying to steal horses," Jin said, passing Alex a basket of bread. "Father says a real attack would have been much worse."

"I'm sure your father is right," Alex said, remembering his own encounters with bandits. "I hope we don't run into a real attack."

"With you along, the bandits would be the ones in trouble," Lupo laughed.

"One sword could do little against a large group of bandits," Alex said before he began to eat.

Lupo and Jin both seemed unconcerned about bandit attacks, but Alex knew too much not to worry. Bandits, he knew, would seldom attack a large company, but they would try to steal horses if they could. To attack a company as large as this, the bandits would need to be almost an army, and Alex had never heard of a bandit army.

"I've just had a wonderful idea," Lupo said, his spoon halfway to his mouth. "You should ask your uncle to let you come to the oracle with me. Then we could become adventurers together, riding off to distant lands and bringing back bags of treasure."

"I've heard many stories of adventurers," Alex said, smiling at Lupo's suggestion. "It seems that many adventurers are often in great danger and find little reward."

"But when they do find success the rewards can be huge," Lupo said, his eyes alive with excitement.

"And if you don't find success? If you never make it back to Midland?" Jin asked.

"Each must find his own path, and live the life he was made for," Alex said softly, not remembering where he had heard the words before.

"Exactly," Lupo said. "Each must find his own path, and I hope mine is to become an adventurer."

"Then I will hope for you," Alex said. "Though I think my path will lead me further west. My uncle has had thoughts of going to Westland."

"Father will talk him out of it," Jin said confidently. "Westland is full of trouble, and there is little profit for merchants there."

"Trouble?" Alex asked.

Lupo nodded. "Worse than bandits, I hear. A few members of our company came from Westland, and we've heard some stories about what's happening there."

"I'm sure my uncle will want to talk with anyone who has news before making his final decision," Alex said.

They finished their meal, talking of more general things. Alex liked both Lupo and Jin, and he felt uncomfortable not being able to tell them about himself and the fact that he was already an adventurer. He knew he couldn't tell them who or what he was, but it bothered him just the same. He had kept his identity a secret before, but it had never been like this. When he had not told others who or what he was in the past, it was to protect them, not to protect himself. Now it was different, and the more he talked with Lupo and Jin, the more his words felt like lies.

"I don't know if I can keep this up," Alex said to Whalen that night as they prepared to sleep next to their wagons. "I don't like making things up about myself, things that aren't true. I don't like not telling people the truth."

"You don't like living a lie," Whalen said.

"Yes, I suppose that's it."

"It is never easy, even for an old man like me," Whalen said, watching Alex as he spoke. "What you need to remember is the reason behind the lie. We are working for a greater good."

Alex's head snapped up. He had heard those words before. He didn't like the meaning behind those words—either then or now.

"Yes, the same words the Brotherhood uses to make their cause seem noble—the greater good. You don't like what you think those words mean."

"I do not."

"That is because you only see one side. What the Brotherhood means when they say those words is power for the Brotherhood and slavery for everyone else."

"That is exactly what they mean."

"But that is not what I mean. When I say 'the greater good,' I mean freedom. Freedom for the people of the known lands. Freedom to do what they want, and to become what they want."

"Even if they become evil?"

"Yes, even freedom to become evil. This battle between good and evil, between the Brotherhood and the true wizards, is a battle between freedom and slavery. It is a battle we must win."

"I never thought about it like that."

"Now you have something new to think about."

"Yes, I do. But I still don't like hiding who I am."

"I understand. New friends share their hopes and dreams, and you naturally want to help them. You want to give them advice and tell them where you've been and what you've seen. It is a difficult thing to find ourselves trapped between what we *want* to do and what we *have* to do."

"It seems foolish, all this sneaking around," Alex said, looking into the night sky. "Jabez will know when we are close to him, so why bother trying to sneak up on him?"

"He will only know when I get close," Whalen said. "He won't know you for what you are until he sees you, possibly not even then. We've talked about that."

"Yes," Alex said, unsure if Whalen was right or not. "If we remain together, however, he will know when we approach."

Whalen didn't reply, and soon it sounded like he had gone to sleep.

Alex remained gazing up at the sky. His thoughts weren't on the stars, or on the lie that he had to live. His thoughts were far away on a hidden island, where Salinor, the oldest of all dragons, maybe the oldest of all living things, made his home.

Was it the fact that Alex was part dragon that was making it hard for Whalen and perhaps impossible for Jabez to see him for what he was? Was the magic of dragons so different than the magic of wizards? Alex wasn't sure, even though he'd used both wizard and dragon magic. Perhaps Salinor would be able to tell him.

It happened slowly, but eventually Alex's mind seemed to leave the circle of wagons behind, drifting back across the sea to Eastland. He let his thoughts go, knowing where they would lead him, and hoping for an easy answer. His thoughts moved quickly over the water, but not any water in Jarro.

After a time, Alex found himself standing near the secret cave on the Isle of Bones, calling out in his dragon voice to his friend.

"You have traveled far in thought," Salinor said, his giant silver head lifting as he looked at Alex.

"I have questions," Alex said, unsure if he dared ask them.

"Yes, I can see that. I see your mind more clearly than your wizard friend, and I understand it better."

"Then you already know what I would ask."

"Yes," Salinor answered, his voice deep and thoughtful as always. "Dragon magic and wizard magic are both the same and different, though not in the ways you might think."

"Then is there a way? Is there a way I can hide myself and my power from another wizard?"

"You already know the answer is yes," Salinor said, his giant head tilting to one side as he spoke. "You still think with the mind of a man, so you do not see things as clearly as a dragon would. If you thought like a dragon, you would already know the answers to your questions."

"But I don't know how to think like a dragon. All my life I've thought like a human."

"There have been times when you acted without thinking. You knew what to do by instinct alone, and at those times you were very close to thinking as a dragon."

"Yes, I remember. Can you help me? Help me to think like a dragon but remain a man?"

"I can help you, though it will be difficult, as I have never thought like a man," Salinor replied with a booming laugh. "Let us begin."

Chapter Eight

Across Midland

The next morning Alex woke early. He had learned a great deal from Salinor, but he still had a long way to go in his learning. He knew now that there was a way for him to hide himself from another wizard, but it wouldn't be easy. He had to practice thinking like a dragon, letting go the *ifs* and *whens* of human thought, and living more in the moment. Living in the moment was how Alex thought of dragons, but there was more. Dragons lived each moment as if that moment was all that mattered. At the same time, however, dragons looked at the future and the past as they were also part of the moment. Alex had a difficult time thinking of the future and the past as part of the present moment. It became harder still when thinking about what might happen in the future seemed more important to him than what had happened in the past.

There was little time for Alex to practice his dragon thinking. The caravan was preparing to move. He and Whalen ate breakfast with the rest of the company, and then organized their wagons. Alex had been assigned to ride north with Lupo and half a dozen others. They were to scout the road ahead to make sure the path was clear and that there were no bandits that might attack the caravan. This far south, bandits were not a large concern, but Alex kept his eyes open just the same.

By midday they had ridden several miles north of the caravan. There was little to report. The road was good and there were no signs of bandits. Alex and the others stopped to eat in the early afternoon and Lupo asked Alex to tell them one of the stories he'd heard about adventurers. Alex wasn't sure what to say and would have preferred not to tell any story at all. The other members of the scouting group joined Lupo in calling for a story, however, so Alex told them the first part of his own first adventure. He was careful to make sure it sounded like a story he had heard and not something he had actually done.

By the time they had finished their meal, Alex had gotten as far as his first battle with the three-legged troll and the discovery of the troll's cave. Lupo and the others thought the story was a good one, and made Alex promise to tell them the rest when there was time. Alex agreed, but he wasn't happy about it. His feelings about living a lie had not changed, and the story he had just told felt like the biggest lie of all.

"I've been told that trolls often keep large amounts of treasure," Lupo said as they started riding north again.

"The story says there was a fair amount of treasure in the troll's cave," Alex said. "Still, stories often say more than is true."

"And sometimes less," one of the men with them commented.

"You tell the story well," Lupo said, glancing at Alex as

they rode. "You made me feel like I was there with the young adventurer."

"And glad to be here in the warm sun," another of the men joked. "A three-legged troll is nothing to laugh about, not if you've ever seen one."

"Have *you* ever seen one?" Lupo asked, looking over his shoulder at the man.

"I've seen trolls with two legs, and that is more than enough," the man answered. "I have heard that a troll with three legs is both meaner and faster than a troll with two."

"A two-legged troll moves fast enough," another man said with a laugh.

"Are there many trolls in Midland?" Alex asked.

"I've never seen any, but I've heard stories," Lupo said. "Some stories say that the trolls travel in bands, while others claim that they are slaves to the goblins."

"Are there goblins in Midland?" Alex asked, remembering his encounters with the evil creatures.

"Not that I know of," Lupo said, glancing around to see if any of the men knew differently. "The stories about goblins come mostly from Westland, which is one of the reasons there is so much trouble there now."

"I would guess so," Alex said. "Many stories of adventure involve goblins, and from what I've heard, they are a terrible enemy to face."

"Well, we shouldn't have to worry about that," Lupo said. "The worst we are likely to meet are bandits, and I would hope only small numbers of them."

They rode through the afternoon. Now and then two or

three of them would ride to a nearby hill so they could get a
better view of the land around them. About three hours after they had eaten, they started looking for a campsite. Alex
thought this could be difficult, because they had to have space
for all the wagons and horses in the caravan, but it proved easy
to find. They happened upon a large meadow and it was clear
that many caravans had traveled this way before.

The main caravan came into view as the sun was setting.
The movement of the caravan was well planned, and Lupo explained how it worked to Alex as they waited at the campsite.
Each morning riders left the caravan to scout the road ahead. If
there was anything to report or trouble, they would hurry back
to the main body. If there wasn't any trouble to report, they
would wait at the campsite for the rest of the caravan to catch
up. Normally the caravan camped for the night a few miles
from the next city they would stop at. The next morning, the
leader of the caravan would ride with a few others to the city
and get permission for the caravan to set up outside the city's
walls. Once permission was granted, the caravan would move
the last few miles to the city. Once they were set up they would
stay for three days or more, selling their goods and trading for
what they needed.

"Few cities would ever deny permission to a caravan,"
Lupo said. "The trade is important to them, and the cities often profit as much as we do."

It made sense, and Alex could see why most cities would
be happy to have the caravans arrive. They would be able to
obtain things that they could not get anywhere else, and news
from places they might never go. They would be entertained

by the actors and acrobats that traveled with the caravan, and have a chance to see exotic animals that were uncommon in Midland—or everywhere else for that matter. Alex could see that Whalen's decision to join a caravan had been a good one. They could travel in safety, collecting news and rumors from far-off places, and not draw any attention to themselves.

"That story Lupo was trying to tell at dinnertime sounded familiar to me," Whalen said, as he and Alex were preparing for bed.

"Yes, well . . ." Alex replied, unsure if Whalen was upset or just teasing him.

"The part of the young adventurer seems to have grown since the last time I heard the tale," Whalen went on with a slight smile.

"Lupo did add a few things in his telling," Alex said, relieved that Whalen was smiling.

"What brought that story up, if you don't mind my asking?"

"Lupo thinks he would like to be an adventurer. When we stopped for lunch, he asked me to tell him a story about adventurers—you know, something I'd heard. The other men joined in, calling for a story, and well, that one just came out."

"No harm done," Whalen said, sitting down on his blankets. "Still, you might be a little more careful in which stories you decide to tell. Stories about you, even if nobody knows they are about you, can be dangerous."

"How so?"

"Hearing a story about you, or rather, about a young

adventurer who did so much, might bring you to mind. It could make certain people think about you, and who you know, and what you've done in the past. They might not connect you to that young adventurer, but it could make them think."

"I see. I suppose that some people know about my connection to you as well. Some people might suspect that I'm helping you if they were to hear a story about me, that is."

"It's possible. I'm sure our enemies in the Brotherhood know a great deal more about you than you might think. They aren't fools, after all. They would want to know as much as possible about you, just in case."

"I'll keep that in mind if I tell any more stories."

"Now," Whalen said, taking out his pipe, "I need you to tell me a story."

"What story?" Alex asked, surprised.

"I need to know what happened in Nezza, and what, if anything, you've learned about our enemies."

Alex was silent for a few minutes thinking about his last adventure and deciding what was important and what wasn't. Whalen didn't hurry him and didn't ask questions as Alex told him everything. It took him a long time to explain everything that had happened and what he had discovered in Nezza. When he'd finished, Whalen sat with his eyes closed for several minutes, deep in thought.

"It seems you have a dangerous enemy," Whalen finally said. "I don't think we need to worry about Magnus at the moment, but this Gaylan person interests me. We will need to be careful of him, I think."

"I don't think he's in charge of the Brotherhood, but I'm sure he's important . . . in the organization, I mean."

"No, not in charge, but certainly in direct contact with the person who is in charge. If we could find and track Gaylan . . ."

Whalen trailed off, but Alex didn't need him to go on. It was clear. If they could track Gaylan then they could find the head of the Brotherhood. If they could find the head of the Brotherhood, they could put an end to the evil the Brotherhood was causing. Only one person was in charge of the Brotherhood, and that person was powerful enough to control the other members of the group. Other members that were, perhaps, throughout all the known lands.

Alex didn't sleep much that night. His thoughts about the Brotherhood troubled him. When he was finally able to push those thoughts away, he tried to relax his mind and think more like a dragon, but he lay awake for a long time, and it was nearly sunrise before he allowed himself to rest and sleep.

After breakfast, Lycan rode off with a few other members of the caravan to get permission to move closer to the city. Alex watched them ride away and wasn't surprised when Lupo came looking for him.

"We have until midday at least," Lupo said. "I thought we might use some of that time to practice with the blunt swords."

"Will your father be angry?" Alex asked.

"This isn't dueling—this is training," Lupo laughed.

Alex agreed, and was pleased to see that Lupo was not alone in his desire to learn. Several of the young men from the caravan came to watch them practice, and Alex made a point of getting them all involved. While it would have been easier to just teach Lupo, he thought that training them all might be more helpful. If they were attacked on the road they would be better prepared to defend themselves and the caravan.

When Lycan returned to their camp, Alex had several of the young men paired up and practicing with each other. He was walking around the group, observing their skills and making suggestions or demonstrating what they were doing wrong. Lycan sat on his horse watching for several minutes before riding over to them with a smile on his face.

"You could have waited until I could join in," Lycan said with a laugh.

"In the future we will," Alex said.

"No, it is better this way," Lycan said. "I have many things to do and little time to learn new things."

"You should try to join us, Father," Lupo said, walking up beside Alex. "With a few months of this training, we will be ready for any enemy we might meet on the road."

"I doubt we will meet anything we cannot handle now," Lycan said, smiling down at his son. "Still, it is good to be prepared for anything, so I will try to join in when I can."

The afternoon was busy. Setting up tents and getting all of the wagons in place took a lot of work. By the time the evening meal was prepared, the caravan was almost ready to start trading with the city. It had been a long day for Alex, and he had not been able to relax his mind as much as he had hoped he would.

That night Alex spent some more time trying to think like a dragon, trying to understand everything Salinor had told him. Now and then he thought he might be getting close to thinking like a dragon, but he was never sure. He might have been thinking like a dragon for a moment, but something would always distract him just as he was almost there—dogs barking in the night, unknown noises from the city, even the sound of wild animals moving outside the camp. It seemed that the smallest thing would break into his thoughts, and Alex knew that he'd never think like a dragon if he couldn't keep his focus while allowing those things to happen around him.

Everyone was up and moving early the next morning. There was much to be done before they started trading with the people in the city, and everyone had something to do. Alex helped Whalen set up their tables, asking questions about the goods Whalen had brought with them. Whalen explained everything in a low voice so that only Alex would hear what he was saying. Alex was supposed to be his apprentice, after all, and should have already known most of what Whalen was telling him.

The company ate breakfast, and then Lycan gave the order to move some of the wagons. The wagons that were moved were the ones closest to the city gates, and had only been placed there to keep the people of the city out until everything was ready. Alex was surprised by how many people were already waiting outside the circle of wagons, and he guessed that it had been some time since a caravan had come this way.

Alex worked with Whalen all morning, surprised by how good a salesman Whalen turned out to be. Whalen would call out to the people who passed, letting them know exactly what it was he had to sell. It didn't hurt that Whalen sold things at a good price, and would often let people argue his prices down. Alex didn't think that Whalen was going to make any money on this journey, but then again, they hadn't come to Jarro to make money.

They spent four days at this small city, before the caravan prepared to move on. Once again Alex would be riding ahead of the caravan, but this time the next city was two days away instead of one. They were still far south of any likely trouble, but Alex stayed alert for any signs of danger. He wasn't looking just for possible trouble for the caravan; he was looking for anything that might be trouble for Whalen and himself.

So it went as the caravan moved north and a bit west along the ancient roads of Midland. They stopped at every city on the road, and they encountered no trouble. The crowds were always happy to see them, and to Alex's surprise he was able to learn a great deal about what was happening in Midland and in Westland.

It was a happy time for Alex, even as busy as he was. He continued to teach Lupo and the others how to use the sword, and was pleased that they all seemed to be learning quickly. He also continued to practice thinking like a dragon and working his dragon magic. He wouldn't do anything that would be noticed, but using only his dragon magic took more concentration than he'd thought it would. Two things continued to trouble him, however; he had to continue pretending to be something he wasn't—and Whalen.

Whalen was talking less than usual, and he seemed to have something on his mind all the time. The old wizard looked tired, even early in the morning, and Alex wasn't sure that his friend was sleeping at all. Whenever Alex asked him, Whalen would smile and say it was nothing, but Alex knew that wasn't true.

After almost two months of travel, Alex found something else to worry about.

Riding ahead of the caravan, scouting their path as he often did with Lupo and several others, he noticed some unusual tracks. When he first saw them, he felt confused, but after a closer inspection, he was sure of what they were.

"Goblins," Alex said, wiping dirt from his hands. "Ten at least. Maybe as many as twenty, moving west."

"How can you be sure?" Lupo asked.

"These tracks were made by iron shoes," Alex said, following the tracks with his eyes. "Goblin soldiers either wear iron shoes or no shoes at all."

"Ten or twenty goblins won't bother the caravan," one of the men commented from his horse.

"You don't know that," another man said. "Goblins are fierce. They could be a danger to the caravan. Maybe a danger to the nearby cities as well."

"If there really are only ten or twenty goblins, the caravan should be able to handle them," Alex said, climbing back into his saddle. "But this could be a scouting party for a much larger force, or perhaps a small group of raiders."

"You think there are more of them?" Lupo asked.

"I don't know," Alex said, considering what he knew about goblins. "I don't think twenty goblins would be moving in country like this alone."

"But they're moving west, and our path lies to the north," Lupo said nervously.

"They were going west when they crossed the road," Alex corrected. "That was before dawn this morning. Where have they gone now?"

Lupo thought for a moment. "Tonlar, ride back and tell my father what we've found," he said. "Alex, you and I will follow these tracks to see if they change directions or meet others. The rest of you, continue along the road, but be careful."

The men all nodded and Tonlar turned his horse around and headed back to the caravan. Alex smiled at Lupo and started off along the trail the goblins had left. If the tracks continued to the west there would be little to worry about, but if they turned north, there could be trouble.

For most of that afternoon Alex and Lupo followed the goblin tracks, but they continued to move almost due west. No other tracks met the ones they were following, and Alex felt certain that the goblins had not joined with any others. Still, it was strange to see goblin tracks in Midland, and Alex felt unsettled the rest of the day.

Later that night when Whalen and Alex were alone, Whalen asked, "You are certain they were goblins?"

"I know goblin tracks when I see them," Alex said.

"And you followed them west," Whalen said thoughtfully.

"For more than ten miles," Alex said, stretching his legs.

"A pity you didn't track them east as well," Whalen said, sitting down on his own blankets.

"Why? They were moving west."

"*This* group was going west, but I wonder where they came from. I've never heard of goblins in Midland, and this news worries me. Goblins don't often cross seas to reach new lands, so I have to wonder where this group came from."

"You think Jabez has something to do with it?" Alex said, considering the possibilities.

"I'm certain of it. He is moving faster than I thought he would, faster than I hoped he would."

"Moving toward what?"

"Open war, perhaps. I'm not sure what his plans are, but I'm sure he wants to control all of Jarro before he's done."

"You believe the goblins are working for him. I didn't think goblins would serve a human."

"He's not just a human, but a wizard. And not just a wizard, but a dark wizard. They will serve him as long as they see some profit in it."

"Then perhaps we should move faster. I know you want to keep as quiet as you can and stay out of sight, but if Jabez is ready to declare open war . . ."

"Not yet," Whalen said, his voice soft. "He's not ready yet, we still have time."

Alex didn't like Whalen's answer, but he didn't argue. Whalen knew what he was doing, and he had a strong magical connection to Jabez. If Whalen felt that Jabez wasn't ready for open war, then Alex felt certain that Whalen was right. Without saying anything more, Alex rolled into his blankets and went to sleep.

The next day they moved north once more, stopping a few miles from the next city the caravan would visit. There were no more signs of goblins, and Alex hoped that there wouldn't be. He'd dealt with goblins before, and he knew how dangerous they could be. He thought about changing his sword, putting away the fine blade that Mr. Blackburn had sold him and replacing it with Moon Slayer, his own magic sword. He knew the goblins would be afraid of his magic sword, and that fear alone might be enough to save the caravan if they ran into trouble, but he also knew that using Moon Slayer would call unwanted attention to his and Whalen's quest.

Happily for Alex, there was no news of goblins in or around the city they arrived at the next day. The days turned into weeks, and after three weeks and five more cities, Alex had almost forgotten the goblin tracks he had found. The caravan was almost as far north as they would go, approaching the sea. When they came to the sea they would turn due west, and move across the northern part of Midland before starting south once more. Alex knew he and Whalen would be leaving the caravan soon and starting off for Westland. He was sad to leave the caravan. He had enjoyed it more than he'd thought he would. He had made a great many friends in the company, and it would be hard to say good-bye to them all.

Whalen, Alex noticed, was still quiet and unhappy, though he still said that nothing was wrong. Alex knew something was very wrong, and that Whalen was keeping it from him so he wouldn't worry. Alex also noticed that Whalen, apart from just looking worn and tired, now and then seemed a little confused. Whalen had always been alert and full of energy, and the change troubled Alex more and more. He kept a close watch on his friend, hoping that Whalen was just worried about what lay ahead.

CHAPTER NINE
THE EMPTY VILLAGE

The caravan approached the village of Welding. It was a small village, but it was important to all the caravans that traveled this way. Welding was on the coast and also where the main road split. One road went north, and caravans crossing Midland to the north would follow it. Alex and Whalen's caravan would take the other road, called the lower crossing. The lower crossing was considered safer to travel, as it never entered the wilder, bandit-filled lands of the far north.

Welding was different from most other villages for another reason. Every caravan along this route would stop for the night there, even though it was a small village and not really a place for trade. But oftentimes goods were shipped to the harbor at Welding and would be waiting for the caravan to arrive. Occasionally goods from the caravan would be sent by ship south from Welding as well. Lupo told Alex all about Welding, and that there were three other villages just like it, forming a kind of square around what might be called the corners of Midland.

It wasn't yet noon when Alex and the other scouts arrived at the edge of a small wood. Here the road turned toward the sea, dropping down into a shallow valley where the village stood. Alex was in front, leading the group. A quick look at the village in the valley told Alex that something was wrong. He held up his hand so the others would stop before they all rode out of the trees. He didn't know exactly what was wrong, but he thought it best not to have them out in the open where they would be seen.

"What's the matter?" Lupo asked, riding up beside Alex.

"The village," Alex said. "It's not right."

"It looks the same as it did last time we were here," Lupo said without concern.

"I don't see any people," Alex said. "And there's no smoke from cooking fires."

Lupo looked down at the village without saying anything. His face had become stern, and his eyes searched the valley and village for any sign of life. After a more than a minute of looking and not seeing anything at all, Lupo turned to the rest of the scouts.

"Be ready for anything," Lupo said. "Spread out on the road and leave some space between each other. If this is a trap, let's not make it easy for anyone to catch us all."

The others understood what Lupo was saying, and with a nod Lupo and Alex started forward. Alex heard the men behind him checking their weapons, but he wasn't sure weapons would be needed. If this was a trap, the important thing was that at least one of them got away to warn the caravan. He kept his eyes moving, searching for anything that was out of place. His mind started plotting, and he couldn't help thinking that if this was a trap the wooded area they had just ridden through would be the best place for attackers to hide.

There was no movement in the village as they approached, and the only sound was a slight breeze blowing in from the sea. It wasn't until he and Lupo had ridden to the edge of the village that they saw the first sign of trouble. A body was lying in a ditch at the side of the road, and from the look of him Alex guessed the man had been dead for three or four days.

Lupo motioned with his hand, and the other scouts closed in around him. They all saw the body, but they didn't speak. Alex let his magic reach out, looking for any signs of life in the village, hoping that things weren't as bad as he feared. There was nothing for his magic to find, or at least nothing living. The village was empty.

"Gareth, ride back and tell my father what we've found," Lupo ordered. "Jon, Eric—Parlasea is the nearest city along the north road, half a day's hard ride at least. Make the best time you can, and let them know as well. Be careful."

"And the rest of us?" a man named Walsh asked.

"We'll search the village for any survivors," Lupo answered, desperate hope in his voice. "Use caution. If there are survivors they might fear us or even attack us."

"And if there are no survivors?" Walsh asked in a troubled voice.

"Then we'll start digging graves," Lupo answered.

Gareth rode off at top speed, wanting to bring Lycan and the caravan forward as quickly as possible. Jon and Eric moved at a solid gallop, but Alex knew that however fast they reached the city, it would be at least a day before any help came from there. Alex and the rest of the group moved into the village quietly, nervous and afraid of what they might find.

Alex, Lupo, and the three remaining members of their group stayed close together. With a great deal of caution, they searched every building from top to bottom. They found a dozen more bodies, and Alex made a note that all were men, and they all looked to be between the ages of eighteen and maybe forty years old. There were no women, no children, and no old people.

A small hope blossomed in Alex's mind. Perhaps the women and children had somehow escaped. The hope didn't last long as he helped to carry thirteen dead men to the small cemetery just north of the village and realized that if there were no dead women or children it had to be because whoever had done this wanted the women and children alive. Alex's mind started looking for answers, and he didn't like any of the answers his brain came up with. He tried and failed to push the dark thoughts away and started digging.

The work of digging graves didn't force his dark thoughts away, but it did help him to focus his mind. It was possible, he reasoned, that most of the villagers could have escaped. They might have seen this trouble coming and fled, leaving behind only a few men to try to defend their village.

"If that is the case, where are they now?" Alex's O'Gash asked. *"Once the trouble was over, they would have returned to their village. They would have at least buried their own dead."*

Alex didn't have any answers. He turned the problem over in his mind, trying to find some way that the villagers might have escaped. Escaped and not returned to bury their dead. Something evil had happened here, and Alex was already thinking that Jabez was involved. But why Jabez would do something like this, Alex had no idea at all.

"What do *you* think happened here?" Alex finally asked Lupo as they took a break from digging.

"Pirates," Lupo answered without hesitation. "They often raid small villages and towns near the coast. They can get supplies, and sometimes they get a few men who are willing to join them."

"You say this happens often?" Alex asked.

"Well, not *that* often," Lupo said. "Raiding towns and villages can cause trouble, once word gets out. Ships are warned, as are all the other towns and villages along the coast, and at least those nearby will be on guard. This, however, is strange."

"Strange how?" Alex asked, already suspecting the answer.

"So many dead. Pirates don't often kill, at least not when they raid a village or town. They may kill one or two people if they have to, but we've found thirteen bodies. That seems like a lot for a small village like Welding."

"And we've found no survivors."

"Yes, that as well. Pirates will sometimes resort to kidnapping. They will hold a person—or perhaps a family—for ransom if they think they can get a good price for them."

"But an entire village?"

"No, I've never heard of that. If they took the entire village, who would be left to pay the ransom? It doesn't make any kind of sense."

They didn't say any more as they went back to digging. Alex could see that Lupo was as troubled as he was about what they had found—and what they had not found. Alex thought Lupo was right about the ransom idea. If pirates had taken everyone in the village, hoping to get paid for their return, who would pay? If the caravan hadn't been traveling this way, who would even know that the village was missing?

"Someone would find out, sooner or later," Alex's O'Gash said.

Later might be what the attackers hoped for, Alex answered.

Alex paused in his digging to look at the village. The village was mostly made up of houses, and only had two or three public buildings. There were several large warehouses near the harbor, but they were separated from the village by a hundred feet of open ground. Alex guessed that at least a hundred to a hundred and fifty people had lived here. With only thirteen dead, that would leave a minimum of eighty-seven, far too many to take them all away on a single ship.

Alex's thoughts were interrupted by trumpets suddenly sounding from the hill to the north of the village. A large number of armed men on horseback came sweeping into the valley. Alex and the others stopped their work, gathering together once more. Lupo moved forward, holding up his open right hand as a sign of peace.

Most of the riders moved through the village and down to the warehouses and harbor area. A dozen men quickly encircled Lupo and the others. They looked to be soldiers, and their movements were well ordered. They didn't say anything for a minute or more, just looking at Alex and his companions. Finally, the man who appeared to be in command lifted his own right hand as Lupo had done.

"I see our comrades didn't have far to go before they found you," Lupo said.

"Not far," the commander answered. "I am Teamor. Who are you, and why have you come here?"

"I am Lupo. We are scouts for the caravan of my father, Lycan of Tresland. We are traveling north, though we mean to take the lower crossing to the west."

"So your messengers have told us," Teamor said, lowering his hand. "How long before your caravan will arrive?"

"They should be here before the sun sets," Lupo said.

"They will be welcome and considered friends, as are you all," Teamor answered. "In evil times it is good to meet men of honor, like yourselves."

"Our honor is in our deeds, in our words, and in our lives," Lupo said.

Alex looked at Lupo. His words seemed to be memorized; some code or special ceremony that Alex didn't know anything about. It was the right thing to say and it rang true, but Alex was slightly concerned. Whalen hadn't mentioned anything about special words or codes when meeting with soldiers or even armed men. Did Whalen know about this and had simply forgotten to mention it, or was this something Whalen knew nothing about?

The moment passed, and Alex hoped he would have time to ask Lupo about the words he had said. The soldiers took over the work of digging graves, and Alex and his companions were invited to join the commander for the midday meal.

Once things were in order and Alex and the others had taken their places, Teamor told them what had happened in the village, or at least what he knew. The villagers kept watch on the harbor, and they had seen the raiding ship long before it came to their small port. This was not the first time that pirates had come looking for supplies and water. Most of the people from the village had gone into the hills to the north, while thirty of the men had remained behind. It was almost a custom here in Welding for the men to bargain with the pirates, trading with them so they could get what they needed without causing any real trouble for the village.

"Such things have happened so often in the past that the villagers were not troubled or afraid," Teamor said. "I fear that will change in the future."

Things seemed to be going as they should, as they had many times in the past, but then something went wrong. The pirates had suddenly attacked. The people in the hills had seen them when they started killing the men of the village. Fear had filled them, and without waiting to see what the pirates would do, they had fled.

"They came to Parlasea three nights ago, and if things had been ready as they should have—" Teamor shook his head. "We should have been here sooner, and in future we will be."

"This has happened to other villages?" Lupo asked, seeing the look on Teamor's face.

"Not to any nearby," Teamor answered. "But word has come of similar things happening in the far north and the west. We should have expected something to happen close, but it is hard to imagine evils close to home when stories come from far away."

"Nobody wants to believe evil stories, but all too often they're true," Alex said, more to himself than to anyone else.

"Yes," Teamor agreed. "And there are other stories you should hear, stories of dangers on the inland roads. I doubt that a full caravan will find any trouble, but your scouts or anyone wandering too far off might."

"What stories?" Lupo asked, concerned.

"I will speak to your father when he arrives," Teamor answered. "Bandits have long been a problem in the north, as I'm sure you know. It seems that of late they have moved farther south as well."

"I'm sure my father will welcome any information you can share," Lupo said.

The caravan appeared well before sunset. Lycan, hearing the news of what had happened in Welding, had hurried them forward. The men of the caravan were well armed and alert when they came rolling into the valley, but there was no need. Lycan was quick to discover all that had happened, and after only a few minutes of putting the caravan in order, he went off with Teamor to talk privately.

Alex wanted to have a private talk with Whalen, but with all the commotion of the caravan's arrival and getting set up for the night he wasn't able to. Finally, after taking care of his assigned duties, Alex walked toward the harbor alone. He wanted to think. He was looking for answers about what had happened here and why. Most of all, he was worried about the future and the adventure that he and Whalen were on. He was sitting at the end of the dock looking out at the darkening sea when Lupo came looking for him.

"You seem troubled," Lupo said softly. "I understand that what happened here wasn't pleasant, but you seem to be taking it harder than you should."

"And how hard should I take it?" Alex asked.

"Well, I—" Lupo started and stopped. "I just mean that, well . . ."

"What?" Alex asked. "Speak your mind. I won't be offended."

"Today was bad, I know that. Still, it seems to me that you've been in a dark mood for many days now, and the further north we've traveled, the darker your mood seems to get," Lupo said. "It's like you're waiting for something you hope will not come."

"Are my thoughts so open to you?" Alex asked in surprise.

Alex thought that he had been hiding his feelings. He believed that his concerns about the future, about Whalen, and about his eventual meeting with Jabez were known only to himself.

"You don't hide your worries as easily as you think," Lupo answered. "I don't know what your troubles are, but I can see them in your face. I can hear the echo of them in the laughter you use to hide them."

"Today *was* bad, but it is not the cause of my troubles. It is the future that worries me, a future that I cannot see or even guess at."

"Only an oracle can see the future, and even they cannot see all. Don't let the unknown drag you down in worry. Look to the future with hope."

"I have hope. It's just—"

"Just that you're thinking of adventure. I suspect that since I told you of my dream to become an adventurer, you've had some thoughts about your own future as a merchant."

Alex was surprised by Lupo's guess. It wasn't what he had expected his friend to say, and it missed the truth completely. Still, he couldn't tell Lupo what was really bothering him, and the thought of becoming an adventurer was as good a cover story as anything.

"Being a merchant seems a dull life," Alex said. "I wish I had some idea of what my future holds."

"I thought as much. Perhaps I can help you."

"Have you become an oracle, able to predict my fate?" Alex joked.

"Nothing as grand as that. I do, however, know of something that might help. It is a place we will pass as we travel to the west, a place that many people claim is magical."

"What place is that?" Alex asked, interested.

"A cave. There are some who claim that if you sleep in this magical cave you will have visions of your future."

"'Some who claim,'" Alex repeated. "Do *you* make this claim? Have you slept in this cave?"

"I've promised not to name those I know who believe. And I know that the cave doesn't bring visions to everyone."

"You've tried it yourself, haven't you?"

"The last time we passed this way," Lupo admitted. "I had no visions or dreams. Still, those who claim to have seen their future seem happier for it. Perhaps you will have the dreams and find the answers you seek."

"I don't suppose there is any harm in trying," Alex said, his mind catching on a new hope. If such a place as this magical cave was along their path, it might be useful for his current quest. He didn't know if he would find any answers, but there was a chance that he might.

"It's at least ten days before we get there. The cave is hard to find, but I'd be willing to guide you, if you want to try it."

Alex agreed, even though his reasons why were not what Lupo thought. Lupo seemed happy to have helped his friend, and that helped Alex feel happy as well.

Later that night, when most of the caravan had gone to sleep, Alex had a chance to talk with Whalen. At first the old wizard simply listened to what Alex had to say and his thoughts about what had happened at Welding. Alex still thought that Jabez was somehow involved, but he still hadn't determined how.

"It's just a small village, and far away from the land Jabez is trying to control," Alex said. "I don't see why he would care about such a place."

"Of course he cares about this place," Whalen answered, as if it was all perfectly clear. "You're not thinking like an evil wizard, Alex. You're not thinking of how the Brotherhood works and gains power."

"What do you mean?"

"You were in Nezza, and you saw how things were done there. Lies, rumors, mistrust—those are the weapons of the Brotherhood. That is how they divide people, make them afraid, and unsure of who they can trust."

"That's true. Still, the east side of Midland is a long way

from Westland. Why would Jabez already be spreading his lies and rumors here?"

"It's never too soon to spread the seeds of doubt. Never too early to kindle the fires of fear that he will use to his advantage later. I have no doubt that Jabez is behind this trouble—and a great deal more, unless I miss my guess."

"Is there nothing we can do? Can't we at least warn people about what Jabez is up to?"

"Who would we warn? Who would believe us? As you said, Westland is far away, the troubles there are not the troubles of Midland. Few in Midland would believe any such warning of a coming evil, and those who might believe us are not in a position to do anything about it."

"Then I suppose all we can do is go on as we are, and reach Westland as soon as possible," Alex said with a sigh.

"If we achieve that, then we will be able to do more," Whalen said.

CHAPTER TEN
CAVE OF DREAMS

The days passed slowly as the caravan moved away from the village of Welding. There was sadness for what had happened in the village, and fear had touched all of their hearts. If such things could happen in Welding, what other evils might already be spreading over the land? Alex could see that Whalen was right and that this was exactly what Jabez and the Brotherhood wanted. Spreading fear and worry was the whole reason Welding had been attacked, and the plan was working.

"There's nothing we can do about it right now," Whalen said. "But it might be turned to good before the end."

"How could something so evil be turned to good?" Alex asked.

"It will wake people up, make them more aware of the trouble that is coming. Yes, it will make them less trustful of strangers, but it may, I hope, make them more watchful as well."

"And people who are watchful will make it harder for Jabez and his minions to do more harm."

"We can hope so."

Hope. Hope was all Alex had right now. They were still moving slowly toward Westland, and there wasn't much he could actually do to fight the growing darkness. Jabez remained free to act as he wished, a fact that troubled Alex more and more as the days passed. It seemed unfair. Jabez should be afraid—he should be the one taking care and worrying about the future.

He must know that Whalen is on his way, Alex said to himself.

"Perhaps he does not care," Alex's O'Gash answered. *"Perhaps he does not fear Whalen Vankin at all."*

Alex thought about that. It would be incredibly foolish of Jabez to not at least account for Whalen's opposition to his plans. Jabez couldn't be that foolish, and the Brotherhood would not be that foolish, but what did that mean for Alex and Whalen?

"He is taunting you. Trying to draw Whalen out before his plans are ready," his O'Gash said. *"If Jabez can get Whalen to act before he is fully prepared, that would gain him and whoever is with him a great advantage."*

"So Whalen must not act too soon," Alex said softly. "I must help him to wait until we are ready."

Alex knew what he said was true, but he didn't like it. Waiting was always hard for him, and waiting while other people were being hurt was harder still. Whalen seemed ready and willing to wait, but now Alex understood how much this slow approach to Westland troubled his friend. Whalen knew that this was his and Alex's best chance for success, and he was determined to follow it whatever the cost.

Looking at Whalen's face, Alex noticed again how tired his friend looked. It was more than just the long journey. Alex suspected Jabez was constantly trying to find a way into Whalen's mind, to discover where he was and what he was up to. That would have been bad enough, but Whalen's own worries were also written in the lines of his face, worries about what Jabez was doing, what harm would come if he moved too slowly or too quickly, and worries about what the future held. It was almost too much to think about, and Alex's respect for Whalen grew. To carry all of the troubles and worries that he had and still move forward was an incredible act of courage.

Thirteen days after leaving Welding behind, the caravan came to the place where Alex hoped to find some answers. They were in a shallow valley with a small river that ran to the northeast. The land to the north rose slowly to distant mountains, and south of their camp there were several tall hills. Lupo had pointed to the hills when the caravan had stopped, letting Alex know that the cave of dreams was close.

As the sun sank in the west, Lupo and Alex rode away from the camp. Alex was surprised to see half a dozen other men following a short distance behind them. He thought his visit to the cave was a secret, and he turned to Lupo for answers.

"I told my father that you wish to visit the cave," Lupo said. "With all the rumors of trouble on the road, he sent a few extra men to watch, just in case."

Alex nodded and rode on without comment. He knew Lycan and Teamor had spoken together at Welding, and the news was that the bandits of the north were more active than they had been for many years, and many smaller groups had found trouble or simply disappeared as they traveled. Lycan had hinted that something worse than bandits might be lurking within the wild lands between the northern cities, but what this new danger was, no one could say.

"I am grateful your father is allowing us to go to the cave at all," Alex said as he and Lupo started climbing the hill where the cave would be found.

"He is worried, of course," Lupo replied. "But the cave of dreams is well known in our caravan. Many people seek to learn their future here, and he would not stand in your way. He would only stop us from coming if there was a definite threat to the caravan, or if he thought we would be in too much danger."

"Seeking knowledge about the future might be more dangerous than the rumors of bandits."

People feared oracles because of what they might say, and magical places like this cave might be worse. Oracles would try to bring peace of mind with their predictions, but that wasn't true from magical places. If the cave worked, if Alex was lucky enough to have a dream or a vision, it would show him truth, but it might not be easy to understand. An oracle might at least try to explain their predictions, but this cave would explain nothing.

"Here," Lupo said, stopping his horse and climbing out of the saddle. "Here is the path you must follow. I can go no further."

Alex climbed off his horse and looked up the well-used but slightly overgrown path ahead of him. A chill ran through him, and he felt strangely reluctant to follow the path alone. He unsaddled his horse and picked up the bundle he'd prepared to take with him. Most of it was firewood, but there were also a few small tokens he'd gathered from people in the caravan. He'd been told to leave these items at a small shrine in the cave as an offering of thanks or as a wish for luck.

"I suppose I should go," Alex said. "If there's any trouble, call out. I may hear you and be able to help."

"If there's any trouble it will be yours, and I will not be able to help you in any way," Lupo answered.

Alex nodded and started up the path. Lupo was right, of course; Alex was far more likely to find trouble here than Lupo and the others were. His reluctance to follow the path grew stronger as darkness started to close in around him, but he shook it off and continued to climb.

The path was steeper and more difficult that it had looked. Alex climbed for a long time before he suddenly came to a wide flat space on the hillside. Ahead of him was a dark opening, much darker than the night that had fallen around him. He moved forward, pausing to look around at the entrance of the cave, and then conjured a faint weir light to guide him into the darkness.

Whalen might not have approved of the weir light, but Alex didn't think such small magic would be noticed. There was also the fact that he couldn't see anything inside the cave, and he needed some form of light if he didn't want to wander in blindly.

The cave, Alex discovered, was not deep. It went straight into the hillside for eight or nine yards and ended at a small altar with a deep fire pit just in front of it. The altar was covered with small trinkets like the ones Alex had brought with him. The cave and the altar didn't surprise Alex, but the slight tingly feeling he had as he entered did. He mostly felt the tingling in his hands and feet, and he recognized it as the same feeling he'd had the times he had visited an oracle.

Undoing his bundle, Alex started a small fire in the pit and then sat back and looked at the altar in front of him. From the look of some of the tokens he could see, this place had obviously been in use for many, many years. He placed his own small gifts carefully among the others. He added a few sticks of wood to his fire, and then leaned back against the cave wall and waited. He had no idea how the magic of this cave worked, or even if it would work for him.

At first he was eager and hopeful, but nothing seemed to happen. He wondered if he should speak, possibly to call for the magic of this place to help him, but it didn't seem right. After a time, he built up his fire again. He sat and waited and watched the flames of his fire, and slowly, without really noticing, he fell asleep.

A roar and the sudden light of flames filled Alex with fear. He jumped to his feet and rushed forward, and then he realized he was no longer in the cave. It took a minute for his brain to catch up, but he soon knew that he was in a dream. The magic of the cave was working. He looked around, and the darkness melted away.

He was standing on open grassland and it was dark. Howls from wolves were all around him, but no, that wasn't right. It wasn't wolves, exactly, and there was language in those howls, words in some evil, twisted language that Alex did not recognize. The sound of running feet and frightened shouts filled the air, and Alex was no longer alone. The caravan was under attack, and as Alex tried to move to help defend it, he found himself bound and unable to do anything.

Alex closed his eyes for a second and when he opened them again, he was standing in front of a small, young dragon that was golden in color. He was in an enclosed room filled with treasure, and again, things didn't seem right. He thought for a moment that this was the dragon's lair, but the treasure seemed too neatly stacked, and there were lamps and torches lighting the room. Looking at the dragon, Alex felt great sorrow fill his heart, but he didn't know why. The dragon didn't speak, but it motioned with its head as if it wanted Alex to come and look at something.

As he started forward, his vision shifted and suddenly Alex was looking through the eyes of the dragon, which were focused on an old iron box. The lid of the box slowly opened. Alex wasn't sure what he was looking at. There were two egg-shaped stones in the box, but to call them stones was unfair. They glowed like pearls in sunlight, but they were more gray and brown and larger than any pearls Alex had ever seen.

His vision shifted again, and Alex found himself in another room. The light here was dimmer, coming only from low-burning torches. Goblins stood in a group in front of what looked like a stone throne on which sat a man with a staff. The name *Jabez* came into Alex's mind, and a mix of fear and hate filled his heart. A man walked to Jabez's side, leaning toward him and whispering something that Alex could not hear. Jabez seemed pleased by whatever was said, and, getting to his feet, he lifted his staff and said, "Let it begin."

Alex was suddenly outside, wind and rain hitting his face. Armies of goblins and men stood before him, and as horns sounded behind him they began to cheer. The war they had long been waiting for was beginning, and they were happy in the evil they would bring. A massive figure nearby suddenly spread its wings, and Alex recognized it and the others like it as gargoyles that took to the skies and flew over the armies.

The snippets he was seeing began to shift more quickly, and many were harder to see or understand: a ship on a distant sea; an ancient-looking city in the mountains; the drawbridge of a castle; a face he did not recognize; Whalen's face, pale and streaked with blood; a white light reflecting from the sharp edge of an axe. Alex sensed that the vision was moving into the future, a future that may or may not be. The future was never certain, and the visions were less clear the further away from the present they were. Finally, Alex was left in a gray darkness, stunned and confused by the dozens and dozens of images he had only partly seen.

Out of the darkness a single face appeared. Salinor, the great and ancient dragon, was there but Alex could only see his head. The dragon looked at Alex for a long time, not speaking or giving any sign that he even acknowledged Alex was there. Finally, after what felt like days of silence, the dragon spoke, but his words were no more than a whisper.

"Of course there is a way. With magic, there is always a way."

Alex woke with a start. The sun was rising in the east and

shining into the cave. Alex took a few minutes to organize his thoughts and clear his mind. He had seen a great many things in the night, and now he had to sort through them and decide which were most important to his current adventure. He got up, stretched, and made his way out of the cave. As he looked down the hill in the morning light, the words he had read in the magic book in the graveyard came to his mind once more.

"*Darloch est messer*," he said softly.

He still had no idea exactly what it meant, and nothing he had seen in his visions seemed related to those words. He wondered why they had come back to him now, and what they could possibly have to do with the story of a nameless dragon. He scratched his cheek, ran his hand through his hair, and then went down the path to where Lupo was waiting for him.

"Did it work?" Lupo asked as soon as Alex came into view. "Will you be coming with me to visit the oracle when we travel south again, or should I not ask?"

"You should not ask," Alex answered with a smile. "Though I do have more answers today than I had yesterday. As for the oracle, only time will tell."

Lupo returned Alex's smile but did not question him about what he had seen. He seemed happy enough to know that Alex had found some answers, even if he had no idea what Alex's true questions had been. Lupo still dreamed of visiting the oracle and becoming an adventurer, and even though Alex wanted to say something about his dreams, he did not. Whalen had made him promise not to reveal anything about himself, and even though he hated keeping secrets from his friend, Alex kept his word.

They rejoined the caravan just before it got underway. Whalen gave Alex a quick look, asking without words if he had learned anything, and Alex nodded. It was troublesome to have to wait before sharing what he had learned with Whalen, but the time gave Alex a chance to think about things and get them clear in his own mind.

"Jabez is about to start his war," Alex said when he and Whalen were finally alone. "He's built a vast army, and he's ready to set them loose on Westland."

"You know this?" Whalen asked.

"Yes, it was part of the dreams I had," Alex answered.

"That will make things difficult for us, and prevent any help from Midland reaching Westland for some time. I'm sure that is why Jabez is starting now, hoping to control all of Westland before anyone can interfere."

"I don't understand. Why would help from Midland not be able to reach Westland?"

"It's the wrong time of year. In the winter months, strong, cold winds blow mainly from the west to the east. Most ships that sail between Midland and Westland are not as well equipped for such winds. Most are smaller ships, and not made for heavy weather. Even the larger ships would find it difficult to sail to Westland before spring."

"Then how are you planning to get us there?"

"We'll manage, one way or another. Now, what else did you see? Anything at all might help us."

"I don't know if any of it will help, but I did see a lot," Alex answered, and then told Whalen all about his dream.

Whalen sat in silence for a long time after Alex finished

talking. There was much to think about, and many questions that Alex didn't know the answers to. When Whalen finally spoke, his questions were not what Alex expected.

"The stones you saw in the iron chest—did you get any feeling that they were magical?" Whalen asked.

"No, I don't think so," Alex answered.

"You say they were like pearls, but more gray and brown," Whalen went on. "Was there perhaps a hint of green? Just a hint of green, like pale jade?"

Alex thought for a moment, trying to recall in his mind exactly what the stones had looked like. He had no idea why Whalen was so interested, but he realized the stones must be important if they had been in his dreams and Whalen was asking about them.

"Yes," Alex said after a pause. "There was just a hint of green in them, now that I think about it."

Whalen frowned. "And you say you saw two of them in the iron box?" he asked softly.

"Yes. There were two. What are they?" Alex asked, confused.

"Do you know what Orion stones are?" Whalen finally asked.

"No, I've never heard of them before."

"I'm not surprised. For many years I've believed, or at least hoped, that they were all destroyed. It appears that they were not."

"What are Orion stones? Why do they concern you so much?"

"Orion stones are ancient weapons used by magical people. They were created and used by evil people and their servants."

"What do they do?"

Whalen rubbed his forehead. "Let me see . . . how best to explain. Do you remember what I told you about magic—how it can be thought of as a bowl collecting raindrops?"

"And every time I use magic, it's like pouring some of the gathered water out of the bowl," Alex said.

"Yes, exactly," Whalen said, nodding. "Well, Orion stones are like magical sponges, or perhaps leeches would be a better way to describe them. When you use magic against someone who is carrying one of the stones, the stone absorbs your magic until your bowl is left dry."

"But that's not possible," Alex said, shaken by the idea.

"Oh, it is," Whalen said. "What's more, after your magic is gone and you are dead, the holder of the stone can break it and steal your power for himself."

"What if your magic is gone, but you *aren't* dead?" Alex asked, thinking over Whalen's words.

"Then, if you can break the stone, I believe the magic would return to the rightful owner."

"I don't know. I might believe the stones could drain someone's power, but I don't think you could really give that power to someone else. I don't think it would work."

"I hope you are right. Personally, I think it probably refreshes the stone holder's own power. Refills their magical bowl, as it were."

"Yes, I think that is more likely,"

"Well, let's make sure we don't find out what will happen

if the stones are used against us. Whether they will or will not steal a person's magic, I don't think either of us wants to find out firsthand how they work."

"At least we know Jabez has these stones."

"Yes, and if we get the chance, we should take them away from him."

"You mean if *I* get the chance. So after I sneak into the castle and find the Axe of Sundering, then I should also steal these stones?" Alex said, half smiling.

"Well, if the opportunity comes up," Whalen said, returning the smile. "And if you do get the chance to take them, you should keep one for yourself. It would only be fitting if Jabez's own weapon was used against him."

"What if Jabez is carrying the stones when we turn up?" Alex asked.

"If that happens," Whalen said, "then I think the both of us will be in a great deal of trouble."

"Well, as long as we know," Alex said.

CHAPTER ELEVEN
FEAR IN THE DARK

Now that Alex and Whalen knew Jabez was starting his war, the caravan seemed to move at a snail's pace. It was as if extra hours had been added to the daytime, and the nights were filled with waiting and restless sleep. It felt to Alex like the caravan hardly moved at all, even though he knew that the wagons were moving at the same speed they always had.

Everything seemed dull and gray. Alex knew that a great many things were in motion, and that the fate of Jarro hung in the balance. None of that had any effect on the caravan. The days went on, the routines remained the same, the towns and cities they visited looked like towns and cities they had already seen.

Two weeks after Alex's visit to the cave of dreams, something changed, though Alex was slow to notice it. The caravan was settling in for the night, circling the wagons, lighting watch fires, and preparing the evening meal. Alex felt tired after a long day of travel, and then a shiver of fear ran down his back.

Sitting up straight, Alex looked around slowly. He looked

at the caravan that he knew so well, and then at the green valley where they were spending the night. Nothing looked out of place. Nothing looked threatening or dangerous in any way. He tried to focus his mind on what might have caused him to shiver on this warm evening. He could find nothing, no cause, and for some reason, that scared him more than the strange moment of fear had.

For a minute, Alex wasn't sure what to do. Something was wrong, he was sure of it, but he had no idea what it was. He considered using his magic for the first time in a long time. Just a little magic to search the land around the caravan for danger; just a little magic that no one would ever notice. He was about to turn his magic loose, when Whalen suddenly appeared. The look on the old wizard's face was enough to stop Alex cold.

"Do nothing," Whalen said quietly as he walked up to Alex. "Whatever you're thinking, no matter how right it might seem, do nothing."

"You felt it as well, then," Alex said, matching Whalen's quiet tone.

"Oh, yes, I felt it," Whalen said. "I've been around long enough to know it for what it is as well. We'll talk about this after the evening meal."

Whalen walked away, leaving Alex with more questions than he'd had before. He watched his friend go, wanting more than anything to find out what Whalen knew. But instead, he slowly turned and walked to the center of the caravan where the evening meal would be served.

Alex forced himself to eat, though food was the last thing

on his mind. He talked with his friends, laughed at their jokes, and acted as he was expected to act. It was all for show, and all Alex was really thinking about was what had happened, and what might be about to happen. He was sure something important was looming, and Whalen knew or at least guessed what it was.

Again the thought of using his magic came to him. Just a little magic to find out what was happening. Just a little magic that nobody would notice. It might be important. The lives of his friends in the caravan might depend on his knowing what was going on. People could die if he wasn't ready to act.

"*Do nothing,*" Alex's O'Gash repeated. "*Listen to Whalen and do nothing.*"

Alex forced down the desire to use his magic. He tried to focus on his food, on the people around him, anything but the strange sense of fear he'd felt. Whalen said that he knew what it was. If anything dangerous was going to happen, Whalen would be ready to deal with it.

Except Whalen has been distracted, Alex thought. *Could this be some new attempt by Jabez to find Whalen? Some magical attack on Whalen's mind so Jabez can find out where he is?*

Looking down the long table at Whalen, Alex couldn't see any sign of worry or fear. In fact, he couldn't see any sign of anything on Whalen's face. He didn't look distracted. He didn't look as worn or tired as he had before. Somehow, Whalen looked at peace—rested, relaxed, without a care in the world, and certainly no sign that danger was close.

A new thought came to Alex's mind, one that he tried to push away but could not. What if Jabez had broken through

Whalen's defenses? What if Jabez had been able to overcome Whalen? What if Jabez was somehow *controlling* Whalen?

"No," Alex's O'Gash said firmly. *"Whalen is not so easily defeated, and you would know if Jabez was in control. You would know if Whalen had lost this battle."*

"Yes," Alex whispered to the plate in front of him. "Yes, I would know."

It seemed to Alex that the meal lasted for hours. Even after everyone had eaten all they could, nobody wanted to leave the tables. Eventually people began moving away, gathering around the large campfires in groups, unwilling to leave the light and their companions for their beds. Alex stayed near the campfires for a short time as well, but soon slipped away, hoping to find Whalen and answers to his questions.

It took Alex some time to find Whalen. At first he wandered aimlessly around the camp, not really looking. When he realized what he was doing, Alex shook himself. Fear touched him again, but this time he ignored it. He focused on finding Whalen and moved off into the darkness. Strangely the night seemed darker than it should have been. The moon had not come up yet, and though it had been a clear day, no stars could be seen.

Alex paused for a moment, looking up at the night sky. He turned and looked back toward the campfires, noticing how distant they seemed to be. It felt like he was looking down a long tunnel, and the campfire at the end of it was so very small.

"That's not right," Alex said softly, rubbing his eyes.

"No, it is not right," Whalen answered, stepping out of the

shadows. "It's not right at all, and I'm afraid there is nothing we can do about it."

"What do you mean?" Alex asked. "You said you knew what this was, and now you say we can't do anything about it. Whalen, what's going on?"

"A test," Whalen answered with a sigh. "An evil test that we must not fail, no matter the consequences."

"I don't understand. Explain what is happening," Alex demanded.

"This is the work of evil men," Whalen said. "Of warlocks. Clearly they are working for Jabez and for the Brotherhood that he serves. They have filled this valley with their spells, with fear and doubt. Their magic is at work all around us. You see how the members of the caravan huddle together near the fires, afraid to leave one another, afraid to go alone into the night."

"Yes, but—" Alex started.

"No," Whalen cut him off. "You are thinking we can break the spells of fear, that we can drive off any warlocks that might be near or destroy them. Normally I would agree with you, Alex. Normally I would say yes, but tonight we must not. Tonight we must let things be, and hope for the best."

"What?" Alex asked. "Why? Why should we let evil reign tonight? Why shouldn't we break this magic with our own?" Alex paused, then shook his head in understanding. "Oh."

"Yes," Whalen said, nodding his head slowly. "You see the answer even as you speak. This evil is trying to draw us out, to find us. They want us to break their spells with our magic. They want us to protect those we travel with. But if we do, we will be revealed to them, and we cannot let that happen."

"What do you think will happen?" Alex asked, knowing that Whalen was right and they must do nothing.

"I don't know," Whalen answered. "Perhaps nothing except for a fearful night with little or no sleep for our friends. If we are lucky, that's the only price we'll pay."

"But you don't believe that," Alex said.

"No, I don't. I think we have more to fear than simple spells and darkness," said Whalen. "These warlocks will have something more than just this planned. Something they think will draw me out, force me to show my magic." Whalen's voice had grown soft and distant, as if he were studying something in the distance, and not really thinking about what he was saying.

"Whalen?"

"Promise me, Alex," Whalen said urgently. "Promise me that you will only use magic to save yourself. No other reason. Only to save yourself, if you must."

"Whalen, I don't think—"

"Promise!"

"I promise. Only to save myself, if I must. No other reason," Alex said reluctantly.

Whalen relaxed visibly. "You must think all of this is only the foolishness of a worried old man."

"I don't think you are foolish," Alex said, trying to sound reassuring.

"Well, we'll soon find out," Whalen said, his eyes searching the darkness around the camp. "As I said, maybe nothing will happen. Maybe it will just be a hard night for the caravan, and tomorrow we can move away from this evil place."

After watching the darkness with Whalen for a time, Alex walked back to the campfire. Most of the members of the caravan had gone to bed, but a few remained, sitting up late with the assigned watchers. He could see that they were troubled, but they did not know why.

As the moon finally began to rise, Alex left the fire and went to find his bed. Something was coming, something was going to happen, he was sure of that, but sitting by the fire and waiting for it was difficult. Looking into the worried faces of his friends tore at him, and knowing that he had promised not to use his magic to help made him angry.

Alex had fallen into a half sleep when the attack finally came. He could hear sudden shouts that were full of fear, but his body was slow to move. His mind was in some other place, but he didn't know where, and he didn't remember what he had been thinking.

With great effort, Alex got to his feet. He shook his head to clear the darkness that had filled his mind. He looked around the camp, but what he saw only confused him. The watch fires that were kept burning all night had gone out. The only light came from the moon, and even that light seemed reluctant to fall on the camp.

Alex could hear people running, shouting for fire and light, screaming in fear. He started forward, going in the direction where most of the yelling was coming from. He bumped into several people as he went, unable to see them in the darkness. It sounded like the entire camp was running around in the dark, afraid of something they could not see.

"Get the fires going again!" Alex heard Lycan yell. "Whatever you need to do, do it. We need light."

"Attackers on the north side!" an unknown voice called.

"Bows are useless in this darkness."

"We have wounded men on the north!"

"Can anyone get some light?"

Confusion was all around him. Shouting voices, screams of rage, cries for help. Alex spun around and around, unable to tell which direction was north, unable to help those who needed him. For an instant he considered letting loose his magic, relighting the fires, and breaking the magic that was being used against the caravan. Then the instant passed and he did nothing. His promise to Whalen held him, bound him to do nothing.

"It's what the enemy wants, you know," Alex's O'Gash whispered. *"They want you to use your magic to show your power, and then they will have you."*

"Magic is not my only weapon," Alex answered.

He turned slowly, listening to every sound, and then moved in the direction where he thought he heard fighting. He may not be able to use his magic, but he still had a sword, and he was more than willing to use that.

The darkness seemed to lift as he moved, or at least Alex could see more than he had before. He dodged running men and women, scanned the camp for trouble, and finally found what he was looking for. The attackers were in front of him, only a few dozen yards away, but Alex froze in his tracks when he saw them.

They were as tall as a man, but their bodies were covered in long dark hair. They had sharp, bloody claws instead of hands, and their eyes glowed red in wolflike heads. Alex had never seen creatures like this before.

One of the foul creatures had knocked someone to his knees and was lifting its clawed hand to finish him off. Through the darkness, Alex could see the man on his knees was Lupo. Blood flowed from a deep cut on his cheek.

Alex ran. Forgetting to draw the sword at his side, he slammed into the creature at full speed.

It felt to Alex as if he'd hit a tree. He tumbled through the dirt for several yards, scrambled to his knees, and looked up into the face of the wolf creature he'd hit. The creature was faster than Alex. It was still on its feet—Alex didn't know if he'd knocked it down or not. A low growl came from the creature, and the back of its hand slammed into Alex's jaw. Alex felt himself lift off the ground, spin head over heels in the air, and slam back into the dirt.

For a moment Alex was dizzy. He was afraid he might pass out, which would be the worst thing that could happen. He had to save his friend. He tried to get up, but his mind wasn't sure which direction was up. He tried to see where his enemy was, but everything was blurred. He knew he was in trouble. The creature was too fast and too strong. He'd been a fool to run at it the way he had, and now he was helpless. His foolishness might have just cost him his life—and Lupo's.

"No!" a harsh and powerful voice echoed in Alex's mind.

Suddenly Alex found himself standing upright, facing the wolf creature in front of him. His skin seemed to ripple under his clothes, hardening into armor. The darkness around him melted away, and he could see as clearly as if it were midday. He looked down at his hands, but they were not hands, now they were the miniature claws of a dragon.

Alex looked back to the enemy in front of him, prepared for battle.

The wolf creature was frozen, its nose lifted as if sniffing the air. Suddenly it let out a whine of both fear and pain, its eyes dimmed and grew wide, its muscles went stiff.

Alex set his feet, expecting an attack.

Then the creature dropped to all fours and ran away.

Surprised, Alex looked around for more of the creatures, but they were all running away now. Somewhere in the distance he thought he heard a low whistle, but he couldn't be sure. He watched as the last of the creatures disappeared into the night, and then he looked back to the claws that were where his hands should be. Slowly the claws turned back into hands as he watched. He felt his skin soften, and though he didn't know what had happened to him, he knew that he was his human self again.

He looked at Lupo, who was still kneeling on the ground. His eyes were glazed over and he looked confused.

"Alex?" Lupo asked. "Where did you come from?"

"I came to help you," Alex said, hoping Lupo had not seen his strange transformation. "I'm glad you're safe. Here, let's get you back to your wagon."

Alex slipped his arm around Lupo's shoulders and helped him stand up. As they turned toward the caravan wagons, firelight suddenly broke the darkness as dozens of torches spread out around the camp.

Alex looked up at the sky. The moon and stars shone brightly now, and he could tell it was only a few hours before dawn. He let his gaze fall to the ground, and his heart went cold inside of him. There were bloody, wounded people all around. Not just men who had been trying to defend the caravan, but women and even a few children were lying on the ground.

Alex did what he could to help Lupo and the others without using his magic or giving himself away. Fortunately, the caravan had several healers and vendors of herbs and potions traveling with them. It was long after sunrise before all the wounded were taken care of, but Alex was sure they were all in good hands. What troubled him most was the fact that seven people were missing. There was no sign of them anywhere in the camp. Remembering how quickly the wolflike creatures had attacked, Alex was sure the people had not simply vanished.

A fire of rage began to burn inside Alex. He felt hate, raw and hard. He hated the creatures that had attacked the caravan. He hated the warlocks that had used their magic to spread fear and darkness. He hated the Brotherhood that was the root of all this evil, but more than anything he hated Jabez. Jabez, the would-be ruler of Jarro and powerful dark wizard of the Brotherhood.

Alex walked away from the camp in the late morning. Lycan had decided they would remain where they were for another day, at least until the wounded, including Lupo, were a little stronger. Some of the caravan members looked doubtful when he'd said this, and it was clear they feared another attack.

No one complained, however, and they went about the daily business as well as they could.

For a time, Alex followed the tracks the wolf creatures had left, but he saw no sign of humans among them. He already knew in his heart that the seven missing people were dead. He also knew that three or four more of the wounded would be joining them before the caravan started moving once more. Lost in his troubled thoughts, he hardly noticed when Whalen walked up beside him.

"You are angry with me," Whalen said—it was not a question.

"Yes," was Alex's only reply.

"You have a great deal of hate in you at the moment. You should let it go."

Alex didn't say anything. He refused to look at Whalen, letting his eyes follow the trail his enemies had left behind instead.

"Go ahead and say it," Whalen said after a long time. "Tell me what you are thinking. Tell me how this is all my fault. Tell me how you could have saved your friends if I had not made you promise to hide your magic."

"I could have saved them all," Alex almost shouted in a tone that was angrier than he would have liked. "I could have broken the spell of darkness and fear. I could have brought light and fire to the camp. I could have destroyed those creatures and their warlock masters before they could have hurt anyone."

"Yes, I imagine that you could have done all that and more, but then where would you be?" Whalen asked.

"My friends would be alive," Alex answered, looking at Whalen for the first time.

He looked tired and pale, almost fragile. This wasn't the Whalen Vankin Alex knew, this wasn't the powerful wizard of story and song. This was a tired, sad old man, who only went on because he could not and would not lay down and stop. This was a man who would never, ever give up.

"Your friends would be alive, yes, but you would be stuck with the caravan for who knows how long," Whalen said. "Jabez would attack again—you know he would. He'd send more warlocks, more dark creatures, maybe an entire army to destroy you."

"That doesn't matter now, does it?" Alex replied, angry with Whalen for being right and with himself for being foolish.

"It's a hard lesson to learn, and it never gets any easier, I'm afraid," Whalen almost whispered.

"What lesson can be learned from this madness?"

"That you can't save everyone," Whalen answered. He put his hand on Alex's arm. "You saved Lupo. You should be happy about that."

Alex stood in silence for a long time. He knew that Whalen was right. He'd learned this lesson before, and he knew that he would have to learn it again. He couldn't save everyone no matter how much he wanted to, and for some reason that felt incredibly unfair to Alex.

"Perhaps," Whalen started after a long pause. "Perhaps I should not have asked you to come with me on this adventure."

"Whalen, I don't—"

"Or perhaps I should have sent you alone," Whalen interrupted. "I really don't know anymore. It seems as if all my choices, at least the ones where Jabez is involved, go astray."

"I'm glad to help, Whalen," Alex said as Whalen remained silent. "I'm just tired of all this sneaking around, hiding and pretending to be someone I'm not. It would be so much easier if we could just get to Conmar, deal with Jabez, and put an end to the Brotherhood."

"We will," Whalen replied. "Soon we will reach the east coast of Midland, and then we will make our way to Westland. The time for sneaking and hiding is almost over."

"What if Jabez already knows where we are?" Alex asked.

"How could he know that?" Whalen replied. "Neither of us used magic, and we managed to drive the creatures away."

"I'm not so sure about that."

"What happened?"

"During the attack, I somehow changed into a dragon. Not my true dragon form, but something different, something in between. My skin turned to armor and I had talons. I don't know how I did it, or why it happened."

Whalen thought for a moment before speaking. "I don't know how you did it either, but I know I would have felt it if you had used your wizard's magic. This must be something else. Did anyone see you change?"

"I don't think so. Lupo was nearby, but he was injured and it was dark."

Whalen nodded. "It could be that because you are the only

wizard who is also a dragon, the change may have happened because your dragon side was protecting you."

"Perhaps that is the answer. And perhaps that is also why the creatures ran away."

"Yes, if the beasts from last night caught scent of a dragon, it would explain why they ran. Almost all creatures fear dragons."

Alex looked to the west, a grim smile on his face. "Then let us hope Jabez fears dragons as much as his evil creatures do."

CHAPTER TWELVE

ON TO WESTLAND

The caravan ended up staying in the valley for three days. There were no more attacks, but they did have to bury five members of the caravan who had been wounded by the wolf creatures. Lycan sent a large group with Alex to search for the missing people. They followed the wolf tracks for ten or twelve miles, but then they simply vanished. Alex remembered hearing a whistle during the attack and suspected it came from one of the warlocks. If so, then perhaps that same warlock had opened a magical gateway for the creatures to escape through. He kept his thoughts to himself. If it had been a warlock, there wasn't anything anyone from the caravan could do about it.

When the caravan finally began to move on the fourth day, spirits rose a little. Everyone was glad to be leaving the valley behind—and the trouble they had experienced there. Whalen was clearly in better spirits, even though Alex could see he was still troubled. Alex felt sure it had something to do with Jabez.

As they moved from the lonely north of Midland to the more populated west, the caravan stopped more frequently. Alex grew more irritated with each delay, but there was nothing to be done. Jabez had started his war, and he was already moving and trying to take control of all of Jarro. Alex felt a great need to hurry, to stop Jabez before his armies grew too strong, but he had to wait. Alex knew that he and Whalen could not simply race off to Westland now that they were so close, but the delays and waiting were almost too much.

"Ten days or maybe two weeks, and we'll be in sight of the sea," Whalen said one night.

"How long after that will we leave the caravan?" Alex asked.

"Not long. We'll wait until we reach Denmar. About three weeks, I would guess."

"Three weeks," Alex said, annoyed.

"It could be worse. I had planned to travel down the coast with the caravan for several more weeks. It is the wrong time of year to sail to Westland, at least from this far north. We'll need to go south before we can even think about finding a ship that will take us."

"Then why leave the caravan?"

"Because, like you, I feel the need to hurry. Jabez is moving much sooner than I thought he would. He must think he will have the advantage, because help from Midland cannot easily reach the north of Westland. We need to move faster, that much is clear. I think if we are lucky, we can find a boat to take us down the cost. If not, we will buy a small boat and sail it ourselves."

"Jabez will have spies watching the ports."

"I'm sure he will. Still, since it's the wrong time of year for easy sailing, they may not be as watchful as they should be."

"Somehow, I think Jabez's servants are always watchful."

"You may be right," Whalen chuckled. "Jabez would not be understanding if any of his servants made a mistake. I'm sure all of his servants have seen his anger, even if he didn't want them to."

Alex didn't ask any questions. He had read both Whalen's journals and Jabez's journals multiple times and felt he knew what kind of person Jabez was. Whalen may not have seen it when he was training his nephew, but he had written enough for Alex to understand. Jabez did not stand for other people making mistakes—and he was quick to point out those mistakes. He could never accept that he had made a mistake, so the blame always fell on someone else.

As the days went by, Alex tried to spend as much time as he could with his friends in the caravan. He knew that he would miss his traveling companions and their simple ways. Life in the caravan had been a good experience for Alex—and a lot of fun as well. One evening as he sat by the fire, Lupo sat down beside him.

"Why so glum?" Lupo asked, breaking into Alex's thoughts.

"What?" Alex asked, turning to look at his friend.

"Just now. You were staring into the distance with a vacant look on your face, and you sighed in a very sad way."

"Did I? I was just thinking about the adventures I've had traveling with the caravan."

Lupo nodded. "I still think you should come with me to visit the oracle. If you thought traveling with the caravan was an adventure, just imagine what could be waiting for us in another land."

"Thank you for your offer, but my future is with my uncle, and I think our path will lead us a different way." Alex nodded to the scar on Lupo's cheek. "At least you have a good story to tell your friends: 'Lupo and the Battle of the Wolfmen.'"

Lupo touched his cheek and laughed. "Honestly, I don't remember much of that night. Just that when you appeared, the creatures ran away. I think you were the real hero of the battle."

Alex waved off the compliment. "A true friend is a true hero, and I count you as one of my truest friends." He slapped Lupo on the shoulder. "Now, tell me about Denmar. It's our next stop, isn't it?"

"Ah, Denmar," Lupo said. "A city with a bit of everything, where rare goods from the west are common, and the mysteries of the world are revealed. They say that Denmar is one of the few places in Midland where the sea elves will land, though I've never seen one."

"I thought sea elves were just rumors and stories."

"Oh, no. There are far too many stories for the sea elves to not be real. I do know there is more magic in Denmar than there is in any other city of Midland. There is an ancient library there with magic books in it, or so they say. Many people travel to Denmar looking for magic of one kind or another, though few talk about it openly."

"I wonder how many of those looking for magic find it in Denmar."

"I couldn't guess. There are wise people in the city, or at least close to the city. They dress as monks, and almost never speak."

"If they do not speak, how do you know they are wise?"

"Simple," Lupo answered with a smile. "They are wise enough to hold their own tongues."

"Ah, wisdom indeed," Alex laughed.

Alex and Lupo went off to the evening meal together. Lupo was happy to share all the information he had about Denmar. Most of the stories seemed too fantastic to be real, and some were just too silly to be true. Lupo, however, was especially keen to tell the many stories he'd heard about the sea elves. His eyes lit up with excitement as he told the stories to Alex, and even as doubtful as he was, Alex enjoyed the stories.

That night, Alex lay in his blankets and looked up at the stars, his mind filled with the stories Lupo had told him. Sea elves—even the name seemed strange. Where did they live? Could they possibly live on the open sea all the time? They must visit land occasionally, or how else would they get wood to build or fix their ships? Alex soon slipped into dreams about the sea elves, happy dreams that he couldn't quite remember when he woke up.

The days went by both too slow and too fast for Alex. The need to move forward was always in his mind, so each day felt like it was twice as long as it should be. At the same time, Alex was desperately trying to spend as much time with his friends as he could, trying to remember all the people and the fun that he'd had while traveling with the caravan. It was strange, having both too much and not enough time.

It wasn't long before the western sea was in view, and the caravan turned due south. Whalen, planning for their departure, told Lycan he was expecting a shipment from Westland. If the shipment was waiting at Denmar, they would continue south with the caravan, but if it was delayed, he and Alex would have to wait in Denmar. Alex knew that there was no shipment—it was just a way for Whalen and himself to leave the caravan without questions. It was a good plan, but like the rest of his made-up life, the lie troubled Alex.

The night before the caravan opened for business at Denmar, Alex and Lupo sat up late with some of the other young men. They looked at the city and talked about what their futures might hold.

"Denmar," Lupo said when he and Alex were finally alone. "A city of hopes and dreams. I wouldn't mind spending some time here."

"Your father might mind if you try to get out of work," Alex replied.

"I could talk to him. Maybe I could stay with you and your uncle until your shipment arrives. Then we could catch up to the caravan," Lupo suggested.

"If the shipment hasn't already arrived, there's no way of knowing how long we'll have to wait," Alex replied.

He felt a sudden fear. What if Lupo really did want to stay with them? Lycan might allow it if he believed their shipment would be coming soon. If Lupo remained, it would be almost impossible for Alex and Whalen to move on to Westland.

"I know it's not possible," Lupo said after a pause. "Father would never agree, now that we're on the final leg of our journey."

"Your home is south of here, isn't it?" Alex said, hiding his relief.

"Yes, it's eight, maybe ten more weeks of traveling," Lupo answered. "The caravan will grow smaller as we go south. By the time we reach home, there won't be much of it left."

"Until next year, when you start out again."

"And by then I may be on my way to find an oracle. I must admit, the idea of what the oracle might say scares me a little."

"They say that the only thing to fear from an oracle is finding out the truth about yourself."

"Reason enough to fear then, as finding out about myself might mean the end of all my hopes and dreams."

Alex didn't answer. He understood Lupo's fear, because he felt a little of it himself. He was also going on a journey that would teach him about himself. Only it wasn't a kindly oracle he was searching for, but a great evil, a darkness that he had to overcome or else his own hopes and dreams would come to a sudden and violent end.

For the first time Alex thought about what failure might mean. He wasn't thinking about the cost to Jarro, its people, or all the other known lands if Jabez and the Brotherhood won. He thought only of himself. Failing meant that he would die— or perhaps something worse. He was risking everything to face an unknown power. Why should he risk his life? Why should he risk his own future and happiness for the nameless masses of Jarro? Why should he risk it all—even for Whalen?

A sudden chill ran through him and Alex shook himself.

The questions slipped away, and Alex felt a shadow of darkness move across him. The dark magic went almost unnoticed . . . almost. Alex could see now that the doubts came from the west. Jabez was working some magic to spread doubt through all of this land, and his spells had taken Alex almost unaware. Alex looked at Lupo, and he could see the doubt clinging to him like a dark mist. Lupo seemed unaware of anything—even of Alex—as fear and doubt clouded his mind.

"I will risk everything because of who I am and what I am," Alex said softly. "Evil and darkness will not last forever. Doubts, real or imagined, will not stop me from doing what must be done."

Alex moved his hand slightly and reached out to touch Lupo's arm. Lupo started, as if suddenly shaken awake.

"I . . . I must have dozed off for a moment," Lupo said, rubbing his eyes.

"It's late, and tomorrow will be a long day," Alex said, getting to his feet.

"Yes, it will be," Lupo agreed. "And for now at least, the future still holds hope."

"The future always holds hope," Alex replied, and wished his friend a good night.

The following morning was gray. Heavy, dark clouds filled the sky, and it looked as if a storm was brewing. The business of the caravan went on as normal, and Alex spent most of the day helping Whalen sell the goods they'd carried across Midland. Alex noticed immediately that Whalen's bargaining skills had changed. He had always sold their goods at a fair price, and sometimes let people talk him down in price, but now things were different. His prices were lower than they had ever been, and he rarely put up a fuss when someone asked for a discount.

"It's just a game," Whalen said softly to Alex. "We need to get rid of as much as possible before we leave for Westland. I don't fancy paying someone to store these things while we're away. Especially since I don't think we'll be needing them again."

On the caravan's second day in Denmar, Whalen left Alex in charge of their things and went into the city alone. The story was that he was going to check on the expected shipment from Westland, but Alex knew he was looking for a ship to take them further down the coast. When he returned late that afternoon, Whalen was clearly troubled.

"The shipment hasn't arrived yet," Whalen said loudly, walking up to the tables where their goods were spread out. Once he was closer, though, he lowered his voice so only Alex could hear him. "This isn't good. No ships have come in from Westland for weeks, which is odd considering the time of year."

"You've told me that delays are part of the business," Alex answered.

"We've got to get out of here," Whalen whispered to Alex as he pretended to check their goods.

"Trouble?"

"Jabez's men are in the town, watching. At least one of them is a warlock."

"Did he—"

"No, he didn't recognize me. I didn't give him the chance,

but it will be difficult to remain out of sight if we stay here much longer. At least the caravan only has one more day here. We'll leave after the caravan closes tomorrow night."

As much as Alex didn't like lying about needing to wait for the shipment from Westland, he was glad Whalen had already established the story. They would be able to leave the caravan quickly and quietly now, without any questions.

After the caravan closed the next night, Whalen spoke with Lycan and arranged to trade the few remaining goods they had in exchange for a pair of sturdy horses. Lycan was happy to make the trade, but sad to see Whalen and Alex go.

The next morning, Alex and Whalen prepared to head to Denmar to "wait for their shipment to arrive."

Alex was about to mount his horse when Lupo came running up to them.

"I thought I'd missed you," Lupo said, catching his breath.

"You nearly have," Alex answered with a smile.

"I just wanted to wish you luck," Lupo said. "I will remember you, my friend, and hope to travel with you again."

"And I will remember you," Alex said. "May all your hopes come true when you visit the oracle, my friend."

Lupo smiled, bowed, and then returned to the caravan.

Alex watched him go, and then climbed on his horse and followed Whalen toward the city. They didn't actually enter the city, however. They rode around it, as if heading for the southern gates. Once out of sight of the caravan, they turned due south.

They rode for about two miles before Whalen reined his horse to a stop and climbed off.

Alex stopped as well. "What are you doing?" he asked.

"With Jabez's warlocks looking for us, we clearly can't go to Denmar. Besides, I doubt any new ships have arrived in the city in the past few days. We'll have to find a ship elsewhere."

"But we don't dare go to another city looking for a ship," Alex said. "If Jabez has men watching in Denmar, he'll have men watching all the ports."

"Yes, I'm sure he will. In fact, he'll probably have more men in the cities further south, as we can't sail west until we first move a good deal south. Still, I think we might find a small boat in one of the fishing villages along the coast."

"Small boats aren't made for voyages on the open sea."

"We'll be fine. It's not uncommon for fishermen to make the journey between Midland and Westland when the weather is fair."

Alex looked up at the sky. "From the look of the clouds, I wouldn't count on fair weather."

"We'll be fine," Whalen repeated.

Alex climbed off his horse. "And what about the horses? We can't just leave them here."

Whalen smiled. "Don't worry. I've been around long enough to learn a few tricks that don't even need magic to work. The horses will find their way back to Denmar once we have gone."

Alex realized Whalen had thought of everything, or so it seemed. Whalen spoke to the horses in a strange language that Alex didn't understand, and then Whalen and Alex turned to the south. They made good time, and were soon walking south along the beach.

"We'll stick to the shore," said Whalen. "Less chance of meeting anyone than if we were on the road. Sooner or later we'll come to a village where we might find a boat."

Alex nodded his agreement. While they walked, Alex would look back to the north often, just to make sure they weren't being followed. He couldn't help noticing the dark clouds that hung in the sky, and he worried about the storm he knew was coming.

On the morning of their third day on the coast, the storm arrived. At first it was only a light rain and a little wind, but by midday it had become something much worse. The rain fell hard and fast and the wind stirred the sea into a frenzy. It was hard to see very far ahead because of the rain, but that wasn't their biggest problem. The beach they were on had grown narrow, and the landward side was blocked by high cliffs. Waves came crashing onto the narrow strip of land, bowling Alex and Whalen over as they tried to walk, and then trying to drag them back into the sea before the next wave arrived.

"We need to get off this beach," Alex yelled over the wind. "If we stay here we'll be battered to death against the cliff wall, or dragged out to sea with the waves. Maybe both."

"We'll be lucky not to drown first," Whalen shouted back. "I can see a rocky point, maybe half a mile ahead. If we can get there, we'll see what our options are."

They pressed on, helping each other to stand when the waves hit, and pulling each other back to the land when the waves tried to drag them into the sea. It was hard work, and it felt like hours had passed before they even got close to the rocky point Whalen had seen. It was too high to climb and the rock was too broken to get a good hold. A large mound of broken rocks had fallen from the cliff, forming a barrier that ran into the sea.

Alex and Whalen looked at each other; neither of them willing to say what they both knew had to be done. After resting for a few minutes they went forward carefully, trying to stay as close to the rocks and as far from the sea as possible. It was an impossible task with the wind-tossed waves crashing into them. They would have to wade and hope that the water wasn't too deep and the waves not too large.

Their going was slow. The rocks were slippery and uneven, but the waves were not as bad as Alex had feared. When they reached a place where they could see the beach beyond the rocky point, the sight gave Alex hope. The cliffs were not so high here, and there was a wide stretch of open beach above the waves. The thought that they would soon be out of the waves—even if heavy rain continued to fall—was a relief. Alex managed a tired smile as he pressed forward, and then he heard a roar from behind him. He looked back over his shoulder.

What Alex saw confused him at first. It looked as if the sea had tilted sideways, or that the ground under his feet was strangely sloped. Understanding came quickly, and Alex turned to look at Whalen. The old wizard was too far ahead of him; Alex wouldn't be able to grab him and help him through the massive wave that was coming. Alex sucked in his breath, hoping that he could yell loud enough for Whalen to hear him over the wind. He tried to shout, but the wave crashed down on him before he could make a sound.

Alex felt himself lifted off the submerged rocks, and

tumbled until he didn't know which way was up. The icy water clawed at him, pulling him deeper into the sea. He tried to swim, to fight his way to the surface, but it was no good.

"Don't panic. Relax," Alex's O'Gash whispered. *"Save the air you have. Fighting the sea will only make it worse."*

It wasn't easy, but Alex did as his O'Gash said. He let his body go limp, he didn't fight, he let himself float freely in the sea. His lungs were burning for want of air, his brain was screaming at him to breathe, and finally his head broke the surface of the water. He gulped in as much air as he could, not knowing when the next wave would crash down on him. He looked wildly around, searching for Whalen, looking to see where he was, trying to find the beach that he knew couldn't be far. There was nothing to see but foam and water.

Gulping in another breath, and getting almost as much water as air, Alex tried to get his bearings. The water was cold, draining his body heat away second by second. Swimming in this stormy sea would be hard, but swimming the wrong direction would be fatal. Alex thought for a moment about changing his shape, becoming a seal or a fish to stop the cold water from killing him and to help him find his way.

Before he could work any magic, Alex felt himself being lifted again. He sucked in as much air as he could, and tried not to fight the wave that was carrying him. His body was pulled under the water and tumbled around and around. He didn't fight it; he let the sea have its way. The sudden impact with the rocky shore drove most of the air out of Alex. He tried to get more air and cling to the rocks that were under him, but the retreating wave filled his nose and mouth with water and sand.

When the pull of the wave grew weaker, Alex lifted his head. He was still in the water, but his knees and hands were on rocky ground. Coughing and spitting, he crawled up the beach until he felt that he could go no further. Slowly he rolled over and sat up, again looking for Whalen. He saw nothing at first, but after he wiped the water out of his eyes, he could see what might be a man, fifty or so yards further down the beach.

Stumbling and half crawling, Alex made his way down the beach. As he got closer he could make out Whalen's beard and gray hair—his magical disguise had been washed away. Whalen sat up and started coughing violently before Alex got to him, and when he tried to stand he only flopped back into the water.

"Whalen," Alex called weakly. "Are you alright?"

"I'm getting too old for this kind of thing," Whalen answered, and continued to cough.

"Let's get off the beach for now," Alex said, relieved that Whalen appeared to be alright.

Whalen didn't answer but simply nodded his agreement. Helping each other to stand, they staggered away from the water's edge but only managed to go about a hundred yards before they both fell down and had to rest. Alex rolled onto his hands and knees and vomited up what felt like a gallon of sea water. He was dizzy and cold and he wanted to conjure up a magical fire to warm them.

"If Jabez or his helpers find us in this, then I feel sorry for them," Alex said grimly.

"It's not as bad as that—look there," Whalen said, pointing.

Alex looked but saw nothing. He blinked, shook his head, and then he spotted what looked like a rising trail of smoke further up the shore.

"I think we've found a fishing village, and not a moment too soon," Whalen said.

CHAPTER THIRTEEN
ALONG THE COAST

Alex woke with a start, half rising from the straw pallet where he'd been sleeping. He lowered himself slowly back onto the straw. He'd had a fever for two days, and his stomach had been as unsettled as the storm that raged around the small hut he was in. The storm had passed, and so had Alex's fever. He was still weak from lack of food, but he felt much better than he had.

Turning his head to one side, Alex surveyed the hut. Glowing coals in the fire pit gave a little light, but a brighter light was already growing outside. There was a bucket near his head (which he'd used more than once), a few rough chairs near the fire pit, a small table next to the back wall of the hut, jugs of water, cups, plates, utensils—nothing special. A second straw pallet was on the opposite side of the room, and as he focused his eyes on it Alex saw that it was empty.

"Whalen," Alex said in a weak, hoarse voice.

There was no answer and no movement in the hut. Alex wasn't worried; Whalen would be close. He'd hardly left Alex's side since the two of them had arrived here, and he'd been very concerned about Alex's condition after he'd swallowed so much sea water. Now it seemed the danger had passed, and Whalen was out and about, preparing for the two of them to continue their journey.

Slowly Alex got up. He was hungry after his long fast, but more than anything he was thirsty. He knew that drinking salt water was never a good idea, but he hadn't had much choice when the waves had dragged him into the sea. He tried to stretch the soreness out of his body as he moved to the water jugs for a drink.

"Ah, good, you're up," Whalen's voice said from the doorway. "I was just coming to check on you. I'll need your help today, as I've found us a boat."

"If you've already found a boat, why do you need my help?"

"Well it's an older boat, and it hasn't been used for some time. We'll need to make some repairs to her before she'll be seaworthy. Some of the locals are willing to give us a hand, so it shouldn't be too much trouble."

"Her?"

"Boats and ships are always called *her* or *she*," Whalen said. "Well, almost always."

Alex didn't reply. He took another long drink of water, and then looked around the hut for something to eat. Whalen seemed to read his mind and started to laugh.

"Good, your appetite has returned. The villagers have already had their morning meal, but I'm sure they'll get you something when they see you're up. They've all been worried about you since we arrived."

"Really, why?"

"Mostly because they're good people," Whalen answered,

waving toward the door. "Also because they believe it would be a bad omen if a stranger in need died in their village."

"Well, I'll try not to die," Alex said with a slight smile. "That would be very rude of me."

Whalen led Alex to the far side of the village, where the boat he had found for them was waiting. A half dozen men were already there, checking the sides for gaps and warped boards. Whalen made some quick introductions, but before Alex was allowed to do any work or even to look at the boat more closely, he was being served his morning meal. It was not anything like a normal breakfast, as it consisted of fish stew and bread. Alex was happy just to have something in his stomach, but he paused in his hurried eating to thank the villagers and mention how good the food was.

The day's work was not that hard, but it was tedious, hour after hour of pressing tar-soaked rags into every crack and crevice of the boat, letting them dry, and then brushing a layer of tar on top of the rags. The tar had a strong smell that Alex did not like. Some of the villagers, seeing Alex's wrinkled nose, laughed and told him he would get used to the smell soon enough.

Late in the afternoon, as the final coat of tar was drying, Alex took a walk around the village. He wanted to see how these people lived, but he also wanted to try something he'd been thinking about. He didn't say anything to Whalen because he was sure Whalen would object to it. He would let Whalen know later, once they were on the move again.

With the sun setting behind them and the boat declared seaworthy, the entire village turned out to help Alex and

Whalen push her into the sea. When the small craft slid grace-
fully into the water, the villagers cheered happily. Whalen tied
the boat to one of many large rocks along the shore and left
her for the night. The villagers had planned a feast to celebrate
the boat's return to the sea, and to honor their new friends and
wish them luck in their travels.

The feast was not the grandest Alex had ever been to, but
the food was good and there was plenty for everyone. Everyone
was happy, and the party went well into the night. When Alex
and Whalen finally returned to the small hut they'd been using,
Alex realized how tired he was after the long day.

"It would have been faster and easier to repair the boat
with magic," Alex commented as he dropped onto his pallet.

"Perhaps," Whalen said, turning to look into the darkness
outside the door. "Faster and easier for Jabez to find us as well."

"If he's still looking," Alex said, closing his eyes.

"You know he's still looking," Whalen answered without
moving. "He's watching and waiting, and we have no choice
but to go forward with our plan."

"Don't worry so much, Whalen. It will make you old before your time," Alex said and yawned.

If Whalen answered Alex didn't hear him, as he was already
fast asleep. As he slept a feeling of peace filled him, and he
dreamed of happy places and friends. Some of the faces in his
dreams he did not recognize, but he knew they were his friends
just the same. For some unnamed reason that he could not
even think of when he woke up, Alex was sure that their mission here in Jarro would be a success.

Alex and Whalen were up early the next morning. With

many thanks and calls of good luck and fortune, the two of them sailed out with the other fishing boats from the village. Alex had sailed before, but never in so small a boat. Whalen, however, knew what he was doing, and quickly taught Alex what he needed to know. The morning breeze carried them away from the village, and soon they'd left the other boats behind and were headed due south along the coast.

Whalen seemed happy to remain silent and sail south, and Alex didn't bother him with questions. He was busy thinking his own thoughts and trying to form a plan for the future. They were getting closer to their goal now, but if Whalen had a plan he had not shared it with Alex. At midday Whalen took out some of the provisions he had bought in the fishing village, and divided them between Alex and himself.

"We may want to change course," Alex commented as he accepted the food.

"Change course?" Whalen asked. "To where?"

"I think we should sail farther west than we are now. If we remain in sight of land we could be spotted."

"One small boat moving south will hardly trouble anyone."

"Perhaps not, but I'd like to avoid being seen if we can."

"You're worried because I'm not wearing my disguise. After the storm washed it away I couldn't really conjure it up until we were alone."

"Maybe you shouldn't put it back on at all."

"What, and travel as myself? I may not have spent much time in Jarro, Alex, but I'm still too well known here. I'd be spotted by Jabez's men at any port we come to, and that would mean trouble."

"And that is why I think we should sail farther to the west. If we stay away from Midland, we won't be seen, and you won't need your disguise."

"Do you think Jabez might use this little bit of magic to track us down?"

"No, not exactly. It has been your rule, however, that we not use magic at all here in Jarro."

"Well, yes, but I had to have a disguise, and—"

"I understand. I'm not saying it was wrong to use a little magic, maybe even more than we have been. I don't know all there is to know about magic, and I don't know how Jabez could find us if we used magic, unless it was something extraordinary or one of his people caught us in the act."

"There are ways."

"Yes, I'm sure there are, but that's not my point. What I'm saying is that *you* shouldn't use magic, and I'll tell you why. You have a magical connection to Jabez."

"Yes, we've talked about that," Whalen said, looking puzzled.

"And Jabez has been using that connection to try and pry his way into your mind. I've seen how hard you've been working to block his attacks."

"It is not the easiest of tasks, defending your own mind."

"I'm sure it's not," Alex agreed. "However, I have no connection to Jabez, so I can use magic more freely than you."

"Perhaps you can, but I wouldn't count on my magical connection to Jabez being the only way he can find our magic—or us."

"No, I'm sure it's not the only way he can find us, but this is what I'm thinking: I don't believe Jabez can find my magic at all, so long as I don't do anything out of the ordinary and no one sees me doing it."

"I don't know," Whalen protested.

"Even you have a hard time seeing my magic, and you know who and what I am," Alex said quickly. "If no one sees me doing magic, I don't believe Jabez will even know I'm here."

"Maybe not, but I don't like the idea."

"Let me ask you a question," Alex said before Whalen could continue. "Did you notice anything odd or magical when we were in the fishing village?"

"I'm not sure what you mean. Magical? No, I saw no trace of magic at all while we were there. Why do you ask?"

"Well, don't be angry. I had to test my idea to be sure."

"Test what idea? What have you done, Alex?"

"I used my magic. Yesterday, when I took a walk in the afternoon, I used a few spells."

"*Spells*? More than one?"

"Well, the villagers were so kind and generous to us, and I saw how they wouldn't accept payment from you, so I did a bit of magic."

"What exactly did you do? This is important, Alex, tell me everything."

"I put spells of increase on their fields and herds. I put a spell of bounty on the sea, so they'll have good fishing as long as that lasts, and I put spells of safety on their fishing boats."

Whalen sat in silence for a time. Alex wasn't sorry for what he had done, and tried hard not to smile because of the stunned look on Whalen's face.

"You did all that, and I didn't notice anything," Whalen said finally. "I would have thought that, I mean, I should . . . I should have noticed something."

"I really didn't want you to," Alex said. "I was trying to hide the magic as much as possible, and as you know, dragons are very good at hiding things."

"I'll never doubt that again," Whalen said, shaking his head in disbelief.

"You're not angry?"

"No, I'm not angry," Whalen said with a grudging laugh. "So, you've done all this magic without my noticing, which means there is no way that Jabez would notice either. So what's your plan?"

"Well, first of all, you should not use any magic at all," Alex said.

"And second?" Whalen asked.

"That's a bit trickier."

"What is this idea of yours, Alex? Tell me what you're thinking."

"Yes, well, I've been thinking about this for some time, and I'm almost certain it will work."

"*What* will work?" Whalen pressed.

"I believe that I can hide you from Jabez using my dragon magic. I mean . . . if you, knowing who and what I am, and being close to me . . . Well, what I mean is, if *you* don't see me using magic, and Jabez can't see it either, then maybe I can use that magic to make it impossible for Jabez to see *you*."

"I see," Whalen said thoughtfully. "Do you think it will

work? Do you think you can hide me and block the magical connection between Jabez and myself?"

"Yes, I believe I can," Alex said confidently. "The link between you and Jabez will still be there, and you will have to continue to guard your thoughts, but . . ."

"But what?"

"Well, the connection will be weaker—maybe 'fuzzier' would be a better word. As if you were very far away, in a distant land, and magic was interfering with the link."

"That makes no sense at all, and yet perfect sense at the same time. You don't think Jabez might notice you while you're trying to hide me, do you? If there's any chance of him finding out that you're here, we can't risk it."

"He won't notice me. I'm sure he won't."

"Alright, so if you do all the magic from now on, and I'm hidden from Jabez—then what?"

"Then we stay away from the shores of Midland. I've done some reading on weather-working magic, and I found something called the 'Mage Wind,' which I think will help us sail farther west than the winds of Jarro might allow us to."

"Yes, the mage wind is a simple spell. I've used it myself many times. It is a bit more difficult if you cast that magic on a large ship, but on a boat this size it should work wonderfully."

"Good, then you can explain it to me if I don't get it right. So, we hide you, sail to the south and west across the sea and come to Westland unnoticed. Of course it will mean more time at sea, and we do run the risk of running into another storm, but . . ."

"But nothing. It's a very good plan, and when I do reappear in Westland, Jabez will be taken by surprise."

"Let's hope you don't need to reappear before we get to Conmar Castle."

They finished their meal, and as they ate Whalen explained the mage wind spell to Alex. Hiding Whalen with his magic was really quite simple, so simple that Alex felt bad for not thinking of doing it sooner. Alex's first attempt to raise the mage wind, however, was more than he had planned for. He nearly tore the sail off the mast, and the boat spun around wildly. After a quick magical repair of the sail, Whalen suggested that Alex start slower, and then add more power to his spell as he got a feel for it. By the time the sun was setting, Alex had mastered the spell and their small boat was making good time to the southwest, far from the shores of Midland.

"Well, it seems we have some time to talk," Whalen said as the darkness gathered around them.

"Talk?"

"About our business. For you to ask questions, and for me to try to answer them. We have several days with no one around to hear or interrupt, so we should use them."

"I'm not sure where to begin," Alex said after a moment of thought. "I don't have many questions about Jabez. Your journals answered most of those."

"But you do have questions."

Alex didn't say anything for a time as he sorted things out in his mind. Whalen didn't rush him, and sat quietly gazing out to sea.

"The biggest questions I have don't really have anything to do with the quest we're on," Alex finally said.

"Really? What questions are those?"

"Well, before we started this adventure, you told me that the council of wizards didn't all agree that there is a Brotherhood, or at least they didn't want to believe that something so evil could be happening."

"I may have misspoken. What I meant was that while they don't want to believe in something so evil happening, they really don't want to believe that they aren't *aware* of it happening. There are some very proud wizards on the council, Alex. For something like this to be going on for so long without them noticing . . . well, let's just say that it wouldn't look too good, and it would wound their pride."

"But some of them believed you."

"I've managed to convince two or three of them, yes."

"What are they going to do? If we fail on this quest, or if an attack comes in some other land while we're dealing with Jabez—what will they do?"

"They will do what they can. But I'm afraid it will be too little, too late to prevent a lot of trouble."

"But they are the council of wizards. They could summon all the wizards in the known lands to help them if they wanted to."

"Ah, I see that I've failed in your education," Whalen said with a sigh. "The council of wizards is not as powerful as you seem to think."

"What do you mean? They're the *council*," Alex said. "They fight evil, help train young wizards, and make sure that wizard law is not broken. I swore an oath to obey the wizard laws, Whalen."

"Yes, that is true. And we also settle disputes between wizards from time to time, and try to answer questions about magic," Whalen said. "What we don't do—and can't do—is command other wizards to obey us."

"So the council has no power to command?" Alex asked in surprise.

"We were not elected or appointed to the council, Alex. The nine members of the wizard's council are simply volunteers who want to help. It has been suggested from time to time that we try to gain some power to command other wizards, but I have always been opposed to that idea."

"Why?"

"Because I fear that if the council was given any power to control the actions of other wizards, we would end up becoming like the Brotherhood we are fighting to destroy," Whalen answered. "Power tends to corrupt, and the temptation to use that power, even for good, could cause a great deal of harm."

"Yes, I can see how that could happen," Alex said. "So you think if trouble starts somewhere else, or if we fail here, the council won't be able to stop the Brotherhood."

"They will do all they can. The problem is that they don't all believe, and by the time they do believe, it might be too late."

"Then we must not fail," Alex said.

"Well, we must do our best not to," Whalen agreed. "Now that you understand about the council, what else would you like to know?"

"You've given me a lot to think about already. I'm not sure I'm ready for any more answers tonight."

"Then rest. You can let the mage wind drop. The winds of Jarro will blow us to the south, and we have to go further south before turning west."

Alex moved to the bow of the boat and lay down, but he did not go to sleep. For a time, he thought about what Whalen had told him about the council of wizards. He was worried about how little real power they had to fight the Brotherhood. He could understand Whalen's point about power corrupting, and for a short time he wondered about why the members of the Brotherhood wanted power. Some of them might believe that they were working for a greater good, but the power they desired turned all their good to evil.

As the moon rose in the east, Alex's thoughts turned to Jabez. He had read Whalen's journals, and he felt as if he almost knew Jabez. He had learned a great deal from both Whalen's and Jabez's writings, and he had to wonder how Jabez had gone so wrong. He had not always been evil, but he had always wanted power and the praise of others. That desire had turned him away from Whalen, and away from the path of a true wizard.

A memory of Whalen's voice echoed in Alex's mind—"A wizard should do his work and then be gone."

Alex glanced at Whalen in the moonlight. He was sitting quietly beside the boat's tiller, looking at the stars. Alex smiled to himself and wondered how it was that he had learned so much from his friend in such a short time, and how Jabez had failed to learn the same lessons after so many years. Perhaps it was because Jabez was so familiar with Whalen. Maybe he had failed to take the simple lessons to heart.

As Alex considered all of this, he realized he didn't really have any questions about Jabez that he needed to ask. There were things he wanted to discus with Whalen, a few ideas that he wanted to talk over, but no real questions. He knew Jabez well enough, and while he might understand *how* Jabez had turned to evil, he could not forgive it.

When morning came, Alex was still thinking. The winds of Jarro were hardly blowing, so he raised the mage wind once more to carry them south and a little west. As he and Whalen ate their breakfast, he brought up some of the ideas he'd had during the night. The first thing that came to mind was Jabez's belief that ancient places held magic, and that the magic could be used if you knew how to call it up.

"He may have a point," Whalen admitted. "I've often found that magic tends to gather—or perhaps linger—around ancient places. I've never spent a lot of time in such a place though, so I don't know if such magic could be used by a wizard."

"It would explain why he chose Conmar for his base."

"Yes, it could. We'll have to be careful as we approach. If Jabez has found some way to use the magic of the place, there's no telling what he might do with it."

"What *could* he do with it? I doubt he could use it for just anything, but that doesn't mean he couldn't use it for some things."

"Perhaps. Don't try to overthink it, at least not now. If Jabez can use the magic, well, we will just have to deal with that when it happens."

Alex thought about this ancient magic for a few minutes, and then turned their talk to another topic that had been on his mind.

"What are the people of Westland like?"

"Like most other people, I suppose," Whalen said after a moment of thought. "They want to live their lives in peace, or at least with as little trouble as possible. They are more like warriors than the people of Midland, and they will not give in to Jabez just because he claims to be lord of Conmar, or even because he's a wizard. They go their own way, and they don't like to be told what to do, like most people."

"Joshua told me that Jabez was taking hostages. How do you think that will affect what the people of Westland do?"

"It will keep them from attacking Jabez for a time. Though I think that at some point they will realize that Jabez will never return the hostages he has taken, and when *that* happens, things could go very bad for Jabez."

"By the time they see what he is doing, it may be too late for them to fight. He's holding the hostages to buy himself time. I suppose the real question is, will the people of Westland help us? Or will they at least stand aside and let us pass through their lands to Conmar?"

"Perhaps," Whalen said and fell silent.

Alex let the silence grow as he thought about what was coming. Jabez was already powerful in Westland, and he had started his war of conquest. He was strong enough to send warlocks and monsters into Midland and soldiers into Eastland. He was growing strong quickly, and Alex and Whalen had been slow—perhaps too slow.

"How far south do you plan on going?" Alex finally asked. "We need to hurry, Whalen. Time is running out."

"Time is running out, but then, it is always running out," said Whalen. "I'm not sure how far south we will have to go. To reach Conmar from the west we will have to cross the mountains of Westland. The passes over the mountains are high, and if the winter snows have started to fall, we may need to go a long way south before we can go west."

"Then we should sail more to the west now," said Alex. "Once we have Westland in sight, we can judge the mountain passes. If there's too much snow, we can sail south quickly enough with the mage wind in our sail."

For the next three days, Alex pressed the mage wind into their sail. The small boat almost skipped across the sea, but when they came in sight of Westland, things did not look good.

"The mountaintops are hidden by clouds, but I can plainly see snow far down on the slopes," Whalen commented.

"South then," Alex said. "South as fast as we can. If we must, we could sail around the southern end of Westland and back north to Conmar."

"Those coasts will be dangerous. Jabez is sure to have many watchers along the coast," Whalen said. "I would prefer to come to Conmar by land if we can."

"We'll find a way," Alex said, turning their boat to the south.

They sailed south, staying just in sight of land. For the first few days the weather was fair, and they saw no other boats or ships as they went. On the fourth day of sailing south along the coast, the weather changed. At first it was only a little rain, but slowly the storm grew around them. On the fifth day the rain came harder, and the winds seemed to change direction every few minutes. It was difficult to see the coastline, as great drifts of fog covered the sea around them.

"It's going to get worse before it gets better," Whalen said as the gray evening turned to darkness.

"We'll find a way," Alex said again, and fell silent.

Long before dawn on the sixth day, the storm had come in full force, and it was all they could do to keep their boat afloat. Whalen held the rudder, while Alex bailed water and tried to use the mage wind to keep them going south. There was no time for rest, as waves crashed over them from what seemed like every direction.

"We need to find a harbor," Whalen yelled over the shrieking wind. "This boat wasn't made for such high seas."

"She'll hold together," Alex shouted back.

They sailed in the storm for what felt like hours. Alex added some magic to strengthen the small boat, as the winds and waves seemed determined to break it to pieces. Whalen was right; this boat was not made to sail in high seas. The low sides of the boat allowed almost every wave that hit them to fill it with water; and Alex was only able to keep them from being swamped by using magic.

"To the west!" Whalen yelled. "A light to the west."

Alex looked but saw nothing but waves and fog. A wave crashed over them, nearly knocking Alex down, and for a few minutes there was no time to do anything but keep the boat afloat. When another wave lifted the boat, Alex took a quick look to the west. A beacon could be seen, a bright yellow-orange fire on the shore.

"It's a long way off!" Alex yelled.

"It might be our only chance!" Whalen yelled back.

Whalen held the rudder fast while Alex used the mage wind to fight the wind and sea of Jarro. The timbers of their boat groaned and popped as the storm tried to push them south and east, further from land. Alex redoubled the magic he'd used to hold the boat together, but he could feel the boat tremble like a frightened animal under his feet. Even with his magic, Alex could feel the planks of their boat ripping apart, when suddenly the sea became calm. Surprised, Alex looked around to see what had happened. The rain continued to fall, but the wind had dropped and the waves had been left behind. They had sailed past a headland to the north, and into a wide harbor where many ships were tied to rocky docks.

"We've made it," Whalen said.

"Made it where?" Alex asked.

"I'm not sure. Before we go ashore, change your sword and take out your staff. We will travel as ourselves here. The time for hiding is over."

"Perhaps. But it would be best if *you* remain hidden from Jabez, at least for now."

CHAPTER FOURTEEN

THE DRAGON'S TRAP

I t didn't take long for Alex to retrieve his staff and his magic
sword from his magic bag. He attached the sword to his
belt, and immediately felt more like himself.

"We will declare ourselves openly," Whalen said, "but do
not say more than is needed. Say you are a wizard but not that
you are a dragon lord."

"Will that matter to these people?" Alex asked.

"I doubt it, but it would be best to leave some things hidden," Whalen answered.

Ready for whatever lay ahead, Alex summoned up a light
mage wind and guided their boat toward the docks. Before
they were close enough to call out, Alex could see several men
gathering on one of the docks, and Whalen worked the boat's
rudder to guide them to the group. Alex noted that Whalen
had been right; these men did look more like warriors than any
of the other men he'd seen in Midland. They were alert, and
looked to be ready for anything.

"Well met," a man holding a lantern called as they approached the dock. "I am called Brock. I am the harbormaster
here."

"Well met," Whalen called back. "May we come ashore?"

"We'd hardly put you out in a storm such as this," Brock said. "Yet caution demands we know something about you before we welcome you to our city."

"We will gladly tell you all we can, but perhaps we can find someplace drier to talk," Whalen said.

Brock nodded and caught the rope that Whalen tossed to him. Their boat was quickly secured to the dock, and Alex and Whalen stepped ashore. Alex noticed that the men from the city kept their distance, and that at least three of the men carried crossbows under their cloaks.

"Lucky you made land at all in such a small boat and in such a bad storm," Brock said.

"It was more than luck," Whalen answered in a pleasant voice. "But I do wonder what city we've managed to come to."

"We'll talk indoors," Brock said, waving his lantern and starting off down the dock.

Alex and Whalen followed, and the men from the city followed them. They left the docks behind and went up through the winding roads of the city. They walked in silence for a long time, and Alex guessed they were several hundred feet above the sea and nearly a mile of winding roads from the docks.

"In here," Brock finally said, stopping before a heavy wooden door.

Glancing up, Alex could see that the building was some kind of fortress. The men who had followed them from the docks had fallen behind, but Alex knew they were there and that their numbers had more than doubled. These men were afraid of something, and Alex wondered what kind of trouble he and Whalen had just walked into.

Brock led them through the doorway and down a long hall that had no decorations of any kind. At the end of the hall-way, they entered a large round room with a round table and a dozen chairs around it. Except for the lantern Brock was carry-ing, the room was dark, but Alex knew it was not empty. Brock placed his lantern on the table, motioned for them to sit down, and shuffled to the far side of the room.

"Any trouble?" a soft voice asked.

"No, my lady," another, deeper voice answered.

Alex, listening with his wizard's ear, could hear the low-ered voices plainly. There was trouble here, but he wasn't sure just how much. He took a chair next to Whalen, letting his eyes look beyond the lantern light. He could see a dozen men standing silently near the wall on the far side of the room. Each man held a crossbow pointed at Whalen and himself.

"They have the look of wizards, but I see no magic," the soft voice commented.

"Just men, then?" her companion asked.

"Doubtful, considering how they arrived here. Use cau-tion. There is something about them, but I cannot make it out," the soft voice answered before trailing off.

A large man stepped into the light. "Forgive me, gentle-men, for your long march." His deep voice filled the small room. "You are doubtless tired from your travels, and hungry, I daresay. Food and drink is on the way, and then we will find you a place to rest."

"I think some talk would be more welcome than food or

rest," Whalen said. "When we arrived, I asked what city we had come to, and I've been waiting for an answer for some time now."

"You don't know where you are?" the large man asked.

"It is not so easy to keep track of where you are in the middle of a storm at sea," Whalen said with a slight smile.

"True enough," the man replied, running his hand over his face. "First, however, I will ask who you are, and what your business in Westland might be."

"You reveal nothing," Whalen said thoughtfully. "Very well. I am Whalen Vankin, wizard and member of the council of wizards."

"And you?" the man asked, looking at Alex.

"I don't enjoy speaking while under threat," Alex said, looking past the speaker to the armed men behind him. "However, as you appear to be set on this course, I am Alexander Taylor, wizard and adventurer."

"Threat?" the man asked, looking from side to side as if no one was there. "Clearly there is no threat here for a wizard, and even less for two."

"Little enough," Whalen said, giving Alex a warning look. "Come now, sir, will you not tells us who you are, and what city we have come to?"

"I am Timold, lord of this city, and before I say more I will ask that you both place your staffs on the table in front of you and move back toward the door," he said sternly.

"I had hoped for a friendlier greeting," Whalen commented.

"You will be held under guard until such time as the king's council can decide what to do with you," Timold said.

"We don't have time for this nonsense," Alex said, his dragon's temper starting to rise.

"Lay down your staffs and move back," Timold repeated.

"There is no need for this," Whalen said.

"Lay down your staffs or we will use force," Timold almost shouted.

"Enough of this!" Alex shouted back.

With one quick move, Alex was on his feet, his staff held up and ablaze with a pure white light that filled the room. He magically froze the crossbows, so when the men behind Timold all tried to fire their bolts, they found their crossbows useless. Many of them dropped their crossbows and tried to draw their swords.

"Enough!" Alex repeated, raising his hand and freezing the swords in their scabbards.

"Alex, be calm," Whalen said. "I'm sure we can make Timold see reason. It will just take some time."

"We've wasted too much time already," Alex replied. "I can see Jabez's hand at work here. Fear and mistrust fills this land already. We are not your enemy, Timold. We do not serve the so-called lord of Conmar. We have come to destroy this evil, or at least drive it out of your lands. If you will not aid us in our quest, then stand aside and let us pass."

"You claim not to serve the lord of Conmar, yet you use magic against us," Timold replied, tugging on his frozen sword. "How can we know why you have come here and who you serve?"

Alex could see that his temper was creating a problem instead of helping them find answers. He took a deep breath to calm himself, and considered Timold's question. How could he prove that they didn't serve Conmar?

"Before I answer, tell us what city we have come to?" Alex said. "Knowing where we are might help us to answer your questions."

"I don't see how knowing where you are can help in any way," Timold said. "However, I can't see that it can hurt either. You have come to the city of Valora, capital of the southern kingdom of Westland."

"Valora," Alex repeated. "There is one among you, Joshua by name, nephew of your king. He will know me, and he will speak for me."

"Lord Joshua is not here," Timold said. "He did not return from his quest in the east, and it is rumored that—"

"He has been taken by the lord of Conmar's men," Alex finished for him. "I was afraid this would happen, Whalen. We should have done more for him."

"What more could we have done?" Whalen asked.

"You know Lord Joshua?" Timold asked, his tone softening.

"I met him in Eastland and helped him to escape some men who had come from Conmar," Alex answered. "The three of us traveled together to Midland. He was going to make his way home from there. Whalen and I had made other arrangements for our own travel, and so we parted company nearly eight months ago."

"Your words ring true, and the timing seems right, but . . ." Timold stammered.

"There is a way." A figure in a hooded cloak stepped forward for the first time.

It was the softer voice that Alex had heard when they first entered this room. Alex looked at the figure, and he could see magic around it, strong magic that was trying to hide itself and its owner. Alex smiled slightly, because he knew that the voice was too musical for a human; it was the voice of an elf.

"True wizards cannot lie if they swear by their staff," the elf said. "We know something of Master Vankin, but his fiery young friend is a mystery to us. Still, if they will swear by their staffs that they mean no harm to your people, that they do not serve the evil in Conmar, you may trust what they say."

"Will you so swear?" Timold asked, looking from Alex to Whalen.

"Gladly," Alex and Whalen answered together.

A wizard swearing by his staff was a simple and powerful test, but it required magic. Alex worried that the act of swearing by his staff would reveal Whalen to Jabez, but he didn't try to talk Whalen out of it. So, after swearing by his own staff, Alex turned all his thoughts on Whalen, working to hide him and his magic from Jabez. He hoped that Jabez was not actively looking for Whalen, but then Alex felt a small flicker of Whalen's magic escape from his hiding spell. Even though it was small, it was like a blazing light shooting across Alex's mind, and he knew that if Jabez was looking at all, he would see the same light.

Alex concentrated and with great effort, pushed the flash of magic away from Whalen and out across the stormy sea. Alex hoped that Jabez would think that Whalen was somewhere out at sea and perhaps even believe that Whalen had been lost at sea, but Alex didn't think they would be that lucky.

Alex looked up and saw that the hooded elf was watching everything he did, as if trying to see something that wasn't there. He wondered how much the elf might know, and how much she only guessed at. Alex's own magic had hidden Whalen and himself from Jabez, but he wasn't sure it would hide them from a very magical elf who was looking right at them.

"We will find you a place to rest, and then discuss what we can do to help you in your quest," Timold said.

"Rest can wait. We are farther south than I thought, much farther," Whalen said. "We should talk to your king, Lord Darthon. I'm sure he will have a great interest in our plans."

"That will not be possible," said Timold. "Lord Darthon has fallen ill, stricken by some sickness that we do not recognize or know."

"What are his symptoms?" Alex asked in concern.

"He lies in his bed like a dying man, unable to eat or even speak. His eyes are open but he is unable to see. Our healers have not been able to do anything for him, and they fear for his life," Timold answered in a troubled voice.

"How long has he been this way?" Whalen asked.

"He has been ill for some time. For weeks now, he has been listless and distracted, one might say lost in his own mind. His condition worsened about ten days ago," Timold said.

"Take us to him at once," Whalen said, jumping to his feet. "This sounds like some devilry of Jabez's making. Some magical sickness he sends to weaken your people."

"Devilry to be sure, but, even our friends"—Timold bowed slightly to the elf—"are unable to help him."

"We may be able to help where they cannot," Alex said. "Please, you must let us try."

"I don't think—" Timold started, but the hooded elf interrupted him.

"It is said that wizards see what others cannot. Perhaps they can find what troubles your lord where I cannot."

Timold nodded, and led the group out of the building and into the streets of Valora. A dozen men and the mysterious elf accompanied them through the light rainfall. The sky was lighter now, though the storm at sea would prevent any real sunshine through the clouds.

It seemed that everything in Valora was made of gray stone, which was depressing in the rain. The buildings, while well-made and richly decorated, looked cold and cheerless in the early gray morning light. Even the empty streets were made of crafted stones carefully laid into patterns that Alex couldn't quite make out.

Alex noticed that their path led up the side of a mountain, with switchbacks that wove back and forth several times. At each turning they passed through a wide gate. After passing through five gates, they came to a level path that led them into a massive open square. On the far side of the square was a castle that might have been white in proper sunlight, but under the storm clouds was as gray as all the other buildings.

They paused at the castle gate, where the twelve men who had accompanied Timold fell back and four men in gold and silver armor assumed the role of guards. Timold said a few quick words to the gatekeeper, and then he and the elf led Alex and Whalen into the castle. Alex could see very little of the inside of the castle, as most of its lamps were not lit. His mind was filled with thoughts about Darthon's mystery sickness. Would he and Whalen be able to help? Could they detect whatever dark magic Jabez was using when a magical elf could not?

Finally, they entered a chamber high within the castle's main building. The four guards who had followed them from the gate remained outside with two others who were already stationed there. The lamps were burning low, and Alex felt strangely unsettled.

"Wait here a moment," Timold said, then he and the elf entered another nearby room.

"What do you think this is?" Alex asked Whalen.

"I don't know," Whalen answered. "There are many dark spells that can make men sick, but they don't last this long usually. Dark magic does its work quickly. It may cause great pain for the sufferer, but it is almost always quick—or at least quicker than this."

"Something Jabez learned from the Brotherhood, no doubt."

"I fear so."

Timold returned to the room alone. "Come this way, if you will. The healers fear that Darthon does not have much time left in this world. If you can do anything at all, now would be a good time."

Alex and Whalen followed Timold down a short hallway and toward another dimly lit room. Timold entered first, followed by Whalen.

Inside the room, eight or nine shadowy figures crowded

around a bed. On the bed lay a man, about fifty years old. A woman sat beside him who Alex suspected was his wife. Whalen marched up to the bed and looked down at the man with concern. "We will assist in any way we—" Whalen started to say and stopped.

Alex, still standing in the doorway, froze in place. He took a deep breath and smelled magic in the air. Licking his lips, he could almost taste it, and he knew that this illness was not the work of Jabez or any other wizard.

"Whalen, get them out," Alex said in a deep, growling voice. "It is a trap. Get them all out. I will go for Darthon."

"What? Alex, I don't understand—what do you mean?"

"The dragon," Alex answered. "Please, get them out of here."

Alex didn't wait to see if Whalen understood him or did what he asked. His mind had already moved away from his body and into a magical place that was both real and unreal at the same time. It was a place created by the mind of a dragon, and Darthon had been trapped there for a long time.

Alex blinked a few times to clear his vision and found himself in a wide, shadow-filled valley. Multicolored boulders formed strange shapes like nothing he'd ever seen in the real world. Plants and trees were everywhere, but they were all dead and gray; there was nothing green or living that Alex could see. An empty riverbed snaked through the valley floor, and Alex followed it as he began his search.

Walking was difficult, as the rocks in and along the empty river were large and jagged; clearly, no water had ever flowed past them to smooth their edges. Where there were no rocks, there was sand, so deep and soft it was difficult to walk through. It was hot in the valley, but there was no sun above him, and the sky was just another shade of gray. Alex pressed forward, his own will driving him on.

Minutes or hours passed and nothing really changed. Time and distance were meaningless here, and it was only Alex's will-power and magic that kept him moving in the right direction. Obstacles appeared in his path, and Alex made his way around them or over them. He would not be stopped. It was a kind of maze, a winding path that always looked the same no matter where you looked or how far you walked. Finally, Alex found what he'd been looking for, but what he saw did not make him feel any better.

A golden dragon stood to one side of the dry riverbed, its eyes fixed on the small figure of a man. Alex knew that the figure was Darthon, or at least his mind and spirit, trapped inside the dragon's spell. The figure of Darthon tried to escape, but the beast toyed with him as a cat would a mouse. Every time Darthon darted one way, the dragon blocked his escape. Every time Darthon tried to rest, the dragon would close in and force him to move.

"Hold!" Alex yelled, his voice booming through the valley like thunder.

It was a command that no mortal, not even a wizard, could give to a dragon. But Alex was more than a man, more than a wizard. He was a dragon lord.

The dragon turned to look at Alex, then it rose up on its hind legs and beat the air with its wings. Fire flared from the dragon's mouth, filling the air but touching nothing else.

Alex took a few steps closer and leaned on his staff, watching the dragon.

After a time, the dragon settled down, resting on its haunches, ready to spring, but Alex's command held it where it sat.

Alex focused his mind on the dragon in front of him. When he was certain it could not attack him in any way, he turned his attention to Darthon. He moved slowly forward, gently speaking Darthon's name. Darthon stood as still as stone, his eyes looking into emptiness, seeing nothing. When Alex was close enough, he reached out and touched Darthon's shoulder, speaking his name once more.

"I . . . I am lost," Darthon mumbled. "I have wandered too far, and I can't find my way back again."

"Your people need you," Alex said, watching Darthon's face. "You must return to them and lead them in these troubled times."

"My people. I must return, but I . . . I don't know the way," Darthon answered in a voice that was too tired for words.

"Remember Valora," Alex said. "Remember your family and friends. They are waiting for you. You must go."

". . . must go," Darthon repeated. "And you? Will you come to my kingdom? Will you aid us in our time of need?"

"I am already here, waiting for you," Alex answered. He summoned a weir light, and the small ball hovered at eye level. It was the brightest thing in the entire valley, and the dragon roared in anger.

Darthon turned toward the light like it was the sun.

"Retrace my path," Alex said to the weir light. "Lead Darthon home."

The weir light bobbed and spun, making Alex smile.

"Go now," Alex said to Darthon. "Follow the light. I will be there when you wake."

The weir light began slowly floating back along the dry riverbed.

Darthon didn't say anything, but he managed a weak smile. He lifted one hand, reaching for the light, and started walking. Alex watched him until Darthon and the weir light vanished into the distance. He knew that Darthon was making his way home.

Alex turned to face the dragon. The golden dragon remained ready to attack but sat motionless. For a moment, Alex considered taking his second true form as a great true silver dragon. In this magical place, he could do so easily, and just as easily destroy the enemy in front of him. He looked at the dragon once more, and then moved forward without changing.

"You know what I am," Alex said. "You know what I can do if I choose to."

The dragon did not answer; it simply nodded its head and then looked down at the ground, almost as if ashamed.

Alex had not expected this. He thought the dragon would speak to him. At the very least, he thought the dragon would try to bribe him or convince him that it had done nothing wrong. He let the silence grow between them, and with it his anger began to grow as well.

"You serve the evil of Conmar," Alex said in a cold voice.

"You do the bidding of the evil wizard Jabez. Have you nothing to say? Speak for yourself. I command you to speak."

The dragon lifted itself on its hind legs once more. Flames and smoke issued from its mouth, and it let out a roar of pure rage, mixed with a deep agony. Stamping the ground and flapping its wings, the dragon twisted and twitched as if in great pain, but it said nothing. Finally, the dragon calmed and turned its head away from Alex, unwilling to face him.

"You cannot speak," Alex said, suddenly understanding. "Jabez has stolen your voice. You are truly his slave."

The dragon turned its head back to Alex, nodding slowly in pain and defeat. As Alex looked at the dragon he saw something he had never expected to see. It broke his heart and filled him with an inner rage at the same time. The dragon in front of him was crying.

"I will free you of this curse," Alex said. "I swear by all that I am, I will free you from Jabez's evil."

The dragon might have smiled, but Alex couldn't tell. After swearing his oath to free the dragon, both the valley and the dragon began to vanish like mist under the morning sun. The magic that had trapped Darthon was broken. Alex looked out across the fading emptiness, knowing that the dragon would never reveal to Jabez what had happened. Alex took a deep breath, bowed his head, and spoke one last time before returning to his physical body.

"I will free you and all of Jarro from the evil of Jabez."

"Alex?" Whalen's voice came softly in the darkness. "Alex, are you alright?"

"I am fine," Alex answered slowly. "How long?"

"You have stood motionless since just after dawn, and the sun has already set," Whalen answered. "The healers are afraid. You . . . you mentioned a dragon."

"The dragon of Conmar," Alex said. "The dragon that Jabez keeps as a slave. That trial has passed; Jabez will know nothing of it. Let the healers back in, and I will wake Darthon."

Alex heard Whalen leave, and he slowly opened his eyes. The room was still dimly lit, and Darthon lay resting on his bed. Nothing looked different but many things had changed. Slowly, Alex stretched his stiff body, then took a few steps to the side of the bed. His senses were heightened, so the sound of Whalen and the healers returning seemed incredibly loud to Alex.

"Darthon," Alex said softly once the healers had taken their places. "Darthon, it is time to wake up."

Darthon's eyes fluttered and opened. He tried to sit up but was too weak to manage it. The healers, including three more hooded figures, propped him up on pillows. Another healer gave him something to drink. Darthon took a swallow, coughed, and then finished the drink. Alex watched but did not speak, and Darthon's eyes never left his face. He lifted his hand to Alex, and Alex reached out and took it.

"Praise the ancients you have come," Darthon whispered. "In our darkest hours, you have come."

"Rest," said Alex. "You need food and rest. We can speak later."

Darthon nodded and Alex turned to go. Whalen looked at him with an unasked question on his face. He followed Alex out of the room and down the hallway, where Timold was waiting for them.

"Darthon? He is recovered?" Timold asked.

"He is out of danger and will recover fully soon enough," said Alex.

Timold breathed a sigh of relief. "You have done our people a great service this day, and your names will always be honored here. Come, I will lead you to a place where you can eat and rest."

"Whalen may want food and rest, but I need something else," Alex said. "A quiet place—a garden, perhaps. Someplace I can be alone for a time."

"As you wish," Timold replied, a puzzled look on his face.

"After great acts of magic, a wizard often needs to be alone to clear his mind," Whalen said to Timold. "My friend will recover, but solitude will help him recover more quickly."

"Then it shall be as he wishes," Timold answered. "There is a garden here in the palace, and I will see that you are not disturbed."

Timold led Alex and Whalen through the palace and into the garden. "I will place guards at the four entrances to the garden," he said, looking at Alex to make sure that was acceptable. "If you should require anything, one of the guards will get it for you."

"Thank you," Alex answered absently, and walked into the garden alone. His mind was too full for anything but the memory of the crying dragon.

Alex didn't notice Whalen and Timold leave; he just walked. When he came to a wall he turned and walked in a new direction. He didn't keep track of how many times he paced through the garden. After a long time, he sat down on a bench near the center of the garden and cupped his head in his hands.

The crying dragon filled his mind, a dragon whose voice had been taken. It was so evil that Alex had trouble believing it was true, but he knew that it was. Whatever Jabez had done other than this, whomever he had hurt, no matter how many people he had put in danger, none of it was as evil as stealing the voice of the dragon. It was like stealing a piece of the dragon's soul. Killing a dragon was sometimes necessary—Alex had killed an evil dragon on his very first adventure. Making a bargain with a dragon was possible. He had befriended the ancient dragon Salinor on the Isle of Bones. But to take a dragon's voice away and enslave it was cruel, wicked, and hateful. It was like leaving a wounded animal to suffer. It was an evil like nothing Alex had ever faced before.

Alex sat in the garden until late into the night, his mind replaying what he had seen in the valley. The dragon had been ashamed about what had happened, but it was more than shame that made it cry. The dragon was in pain; its very soul had been torn in pieces by evil.

The dragon cried. And Alex, alone in the garden, cried as well.

CHAPTER FIFTEEN
THE SEA ELVES

Alex was still sitting in the garden when the gray light of morning crept over the horizon. A chill ran through him, but not because of the cold air. Someone else had entered the garden—in spite of Timold's guards at the entrances. Alex didn't look up; he knew who the visitor was, but he wasn't sure why she was there.

"I am surprised that Timold's guards let you pass," Alex said without lifting his head.

The person stopped short in obvious surprise. There was silence for a moment, and then she replied. "Guards often see only what they are watching for."

"And it is hard to see what does not wish to be seen," Alex said, finally looking up. "But why do you come here in secret? What is it that you want from me?"

The person standing before him wore a dark cloak with a hood. "To understand," she answered.

"Understand? What could I teach an elf such as yourself?"

Again the figure paused in surprise. Then she took a small step forward. "We know Vankin's name, and the man you travel with looks like Vankin, but we do not see his magic.

220

Your name is new to us, we see even less about you than
Vankin. You both carry staffs, you survived a storm that should
have destroyed your small boat, and you came with the mage
wind in your sail. We see many things. We see that you carry
a great sword from the ancient people. We see that you have
come at a time and to a place where you are needed most. We
see all this, but we do not see who or what you are, and we do
not understand."

"And yet you hide yourselves among these men," Alex said.
"Your magic tries to hide you from all who might see."

"We hide because we must. We hide because of who we
once were and what we have become. We hide because of
shame," the elf said. "You hide, but not because of shame."

"And you do not trust what you cannot see," Alex said.

"Trust must be earned."

"Trust is a two-way street. If I tell you what you wish to
know and show you what you wish to see, will you also tell me
about yourself and your people?"

"If you speak truly, I will tell you all that I can. I cannot
tell you all, though, for I do not know everything you may
wish to ask."

"It will be enough." Alex sat up straight. "You cannot see
what I am because I do not wish to be seen. My magic is hidden from most because to show my magic in this land would
warn my enemy of my approach. I do not wish the evil in
Conmar to know I am here, so I remain hidden. I do not wish
that same evil to find my friend Vankin, so I hide him as well."

"There is wisdom in what you say, but I must doubt your
words," the elf said. "Magic knows magic, power knows power.

From a distance, perhaps you could hide your magic from another, but given the distance between us, I do not think that is possible."

"It is possible, but few know how to master it," Alex said. "I can show you. It is not hard, but I will need something from you first."

"And what is that?" the elf asked skeptically.

"The smallest seed of trust—your name," Alex replied.

The elf stood in silence for a few minutes, considering Alex's words. The silence grew between the two of them as the sun slowly rose over the garden walls. A bird started to sing nearby, and finally the elf answered.

"Very well. I see no hidden meaning in your words, no trap, and any possible danger is to myself alone. My name is Aliia—Aliia of the sea elves."

"Then look, Aliia of the sea elves. Look at me and see what you wish to know."

Alex concentrated so that his magic would be revealed only to Aliia and no other. Slowly he peeled back the layers of his magic that hid him from the world, the unexpected layers that his dragon magic made possible. He would allow Aliia to see his wizard's powers, but no more. His powers as dragon lord, and his dragon self would remain hidden.

Aliia's sharp intake of breath told Alex that he had been successful. He did nothing for a moment, and then he skillfully hid himself once more. Aliia seemed unable to speak, too surprised by what she had seen to even move.

"I have never seen a wizard's magic before," Aliia stammered. "I did not know that it was so great. You have so much more magic than we elves. I . . . I had been told, but having never seen such magic . . ."

"I understand," Alex said when Aliia seemed unable to go on. "Do you trust me now?"

"I trust you, and I will tell my people that they may trust you as well," Aliia said.

"Thank you. Now, please, will you tell me why you hide? What shame do your people carry? I do not understand why you hide even among the humans that you seem to trust."

Aliia sat on the bench next to Alex. "What do you know of the sea elves?"

Alex shook his head. "Not much. Rumors and old stories, mostly."

"That is not so strange," she said, nodding. "We are known only to a few, and those few we trust do not speak of us to outsiders." She hesitated a moment, then said, "And because I trust you, I will not hide from you."

Aliia reached up and pulled back her hood, revealing as beautiful a face as Alex had ever seen. She shook her head once, allowing her long jet-black hair to fall freely over her shoulders. She looked at Alex with piercing gray eyes. Alex was stunned. He had thought sea elves might have hidden themselves because they were disfigured in some way, or bore some kind of mark of their shame. Looking at Aliia, Alex knew that he had been completely wrong.

"The shame of the sea elves is an ancient one," Aliia said, smiling slightly. "So first you must know who we once were."

"You were not always sea elves?" Alex asked.

"Long ago, almost before the memory of men and dwarves,

my people were known as dark elves," Aliia answered. "We loved the earth and the riches that could be found deep underground. We loved the things we could make from metals and stone and gems. We created many things of great splendor; we made the finest weapons and armor; and we found many secrets of magic that perhaps we should not have found." Aliia paused for a moment as if lost in memories of an ancient time. "Only the oldest of my people know the whole story. None of the sea elves now living were alive when evil came upon the dark elves, when creatures of evil hunted and destroyed my people. What none but my people know—and perhaps the eldest of our relations in the known lands—is that the greatest evil and the greatest destruction was summoned by the dark elves themselves."

"How can that be?" Alex asked. "I have never heard of an elf turning to evil."

"Some have turned to evil, but I speak of something else," Aliia continued. "The greatest evil came because the high lords and ladies of my people thought they had learned enough. They thought they were wise and that they could control all the known lands. They believed that they could stop all evil everywhere. They thought they could change the land to suit their own needs and desires—and that they could control even the most powerful of creatures with their magic. They believed that they could tame dragons, griffins, and other creatures, making them pets or even slaves."

"They were seeking for more power than they should have," Alex said.

"Yes, and they would not stop," Aliia said. "When they

failed to tame and enslave the most powerful of creatures, their pride led them to do greater evil. I do not know what they did, though some say that they summoned up shadows to serve them. They gave solid forms to things that should have remained formless. Some say they gave life to other things, but whatever they did, their creations eventually turned against them. It was their own creations that caused the greatest destruction among my people, as well as the destruction of many who were our friends."

"That is the greatest shame of the sea elves," Alex said. "The destruction of those you once called friends."

"It is," Aliia answered weakly. "For trying to take more power than we should have, for thinking we were wiser than the makers and the guardians, and for causing so much destruction, we are shamed and cursed."

"Cursed?" Alex asked.

"We are cursed to live our lives at sea, away from the land we love so much," Aliia said. "We have only small towns in hidden places where we build our ships, but nothing more. Our magic was once the source of our pride, and it is now weakened and tied to the sea. The farther from the sea we travel, the weaker our magic becomes. In the lands we once called home, our magic is nearly nonexistent. So it shall be until the time of change, when *darloch est messer* comes, and the nameless dragon with him."

"*Darloch est messer*," Alex repeated, remembering the words he had read in the graveyard so long ago. "When will this master of dragons come? When will the nameless dragon appear?"

"You know these words?" Aliia replied, a slightly surprised

look on her face. "It is said that in a time when all the lands are in danger, when darkness threatens to take control and wipe away all that is good, *darloch est messer* will come and break the power of darkness. Then there will be a great change in the lands, and the curse of the sea elves will be removed."

"What more do you know about *darloch est messer?*" Alex asked.

Aliia shook her head. "Only what I have said. Why is this so important to you?"

"I've seen those words before," Alex said slowly. "The time of danger may not be so far away. *Darloch est messer* is a piece of a puzzle I do not understand, but I know that I need to figure it out."

"Why do you say the time of danger may not be far?" Aliia pressed.

"Because the evil of Conmar is only a part of the evil that I'm hunting," Alex answered. "There is a group called the Brotherhood, and they are seeking to gain control over all the known lands."

"We have seen many evils come and go," Aliia said. "Why should this evil be different than those before it?"

"Because the Brotherhood has been working their evil for a very long time. Because they are careful, hiding themselves, and taking their time. Most wizards do not even believe they exist. They do not believe that such a group could go unknown for so long."

"Pride—their pride blinds them to the truth."

"In part. The Brotherhood is powerful as well as patient. They have been at work for hundreds—maybe even thousands—of years, and when one of their plans fails, they simply move on to the next."

"I can try to find out more about the legend of *darloch est messer*," Aliia said. "It will not be easy, as only the elders of my people know the whole story and they are reluctant to speak of such things."

"Please try," Alex said.

"I will do what I can," Aliia promised. "May I ask something of you?"

"Ask what you will," Alex said.

"I will ask that you not speak of what I have said to anyone. Not Vankin, not another wizard, not even another elf. The shame and the story of the sea elves should not be shared."

"As you wish," Alex answered, touching his staff to his forehead, the sign of a wizard's vow.

"Then we should go," Aliia said, getting to her feet.

"Go?"

"There are many troubles in this land, and the kingdoms to the north have called on Darthon for aid. He will need the advice of wizards. It is time for plans to be made."

"Is Darthon recovered?" Alex asked.

"Darthon has rested, and though he is still weak he will want to speak to you and Vankin," Aliia said.

Alex stood up and stretched the soreness out of his body.

Aliia pulled the hood over her head, but she did not move from the bench. "Go to the east entrance. The guard will guide you back into the palace."

"And you?"

"I will make my own way," Aliia answered. "I must speak

with my people. I will share with them what you have told me
and shown me. We may meet again later, when Darthon calls
his council."

———•••———

Alex opened the door to a large sitting room and found
Whalen next to the fire in deep thought. The old wizard
looked up when Alex entered, then he jumped to his feet and
moved toward Alex.

"I'm glad you're here at last," Whalen said in a lowered
voice. "Tell me what happened between you and Darthon. You
mentioned a dragon?"

Alex nodded. "Jabez has indeed enslaved a dragon, and he
forced the dragon to entrap Darthon's mind and soul. I was
able to free Darthon and send him back to his body."

"And the dragon?" Whalen asked.

"I wasn't able to free the dragon, at least not yet," Alex said,
frowning. "But I have vowed to release him from Jabez's evil."
He set his jaw and looked at Whalen. "It is a vow I intend to
keep."

Whalen put his hand on Alex's shoulder and squeezed.
"And I will help you keep that vow in whatever way you need
me to."

"Thank you, my friend," Alex said. "Now, has there been
any trouble since last night?"

"No. Our hosts have been kind enough, and they have
provided everything we might hope for." Whalen looked at
the door and then back to Alex. "We've been invited to join

Darthon for the midday meal, but you and I must speak before then. These men of Westland are not a talkative lot, and I've discovered almost nothing that might help us defeat Jabez. Then there's the question of the elves. I'm sure you've realized that the hooded figures we've seen here are elves."

"Yes, they are sea elves," Alex said.

"Sea elves," Whalen repeated in wonder. "That explains why the elves in Darthon's room have said nothing to me."

"They can't tell you're a wizard," Alex explained. "I've hidden you too well, my friend, and the elves can't see your magic. I think that scares them."

"Yes, it would," Whalen said. He paused, then frowned. "How do you know all this, Alex?"

"One of the sea elves, a maiden, came and talked with me this morning," Alex said. "Though I'm not sure the rest of her people will be happy that she did."

"Probably not," Whalen agreed. "What did you tell her— this elf maid, who may have defied her elders to speak with you?"

"I let her see my wizard powers," Alex replied. "I explained why we are hidden, and planted a few seeds of trust. She's going to talk with her people, and let them know they can trust us. I hope that the rest of these sea elves will be friendlier to us."

"Dangerous," Whalen said. "While I don't believe any elf would work for Jabez or the Brotherhood, what you have done could be dangerous to our mission here."

"Perhaps, but danger is part of this game we play," Alex agreed. "Since I saved Darthon from the dragon's trap, he should be willing to grant us passage through his land. But I have the feeling that we might need the help of the sea elves to finish things here in Jarro. It would be very helpful if they trusted us."

"Yes, I imagine you are right," Whalen said.

"Now, I don't suppose you know where can I take a bath?" Alex asked. He gestured to his clothes, which were the same ones he'd been wearing while they had been at sea. They were dry, but stained with salt and they smelled of old fish and seaweed.

Whalen gave a slight laugh and showed Alex around the rooms that had been prepared for them. Apart from the large sitting room, there were two bedrooms, each with a smaller sitting room attached to it, and a fair-sized bathroom with running hot and cold water. Alex was pleased to see that the bathroom also contained a massive brass tub.

Alex spent much longer in the bath than he really needed to. The size of the tub allowed him to stretch out and relax, and the hot water and steam helped ease the tension and soreness in his body. He couldn't remember the last time he had felt so clean. The only thing missing was food. As he left the bathroom, his stomach growled loudly, reminding him that even wizards needed to eat. He and Whalen hadn't eaten much while fighting the storm at sea, and he'd had nothing at all since arriving the day before. He quickly dressed, and then laid his sword and his magic bag on the bed, as was customary for guests in most places, and went to find Whalen.

As he entered the main sitting room, a knock came at the door. A guard had come to escort them to Lord Darthon. Alex noted that the guard was courteous when asking them to

follow him, but, like the other guards he'd met, this man did
not try to talk with them at all. For some reason the silence
and standoffishness of the guards troubled Alex. He knew that
they were unsure of Whalen's and his motives, and, as wizards
were not common, not sure how to talk to them, but it seemed
odd that they didn't even try.

"Leave your staff," Whalen whispered. "It will be safe
enough, and we don't want to frighten these people."

Alex leaned his staff next to the fireplace, and then he and
Whalen followed their guide through the palace. Alex looked
closely at everything he could see as they walked. He noted
the rich decorations in the rooms they went by, the thick rugs,
colorful tapestries, and comfortable furniture. Most of all he
noticed how much gold was used as decoration. There were
trinkets of different kinds on the tables, golden lamps hanging
from the walls and ceiling, and gold-crusted armor and weapons all over the place. If nothing else, Darthon's kingdom was
a wealthy one.

"My lords," the guard finally said, opening a door and
bowing.

The room they entered was not a large hall or room, it
was more like a family dining room, with a round table in the
middle and ten or twelve chairs along the table's rim. The far
wall of the room was made up of windows that were open, letting in both air and sunlight. Darthon was seated at the table,
Timold beside him. Places were set for both Alex and Whalen,
but no one else, which surprised Alex. He had assumed there
would be more people who had questions about how and why
he and Whalen had come here.

"Ah, my friends," Darthon said, standing up and leaning on the table for support. "I hope that I may call you friends. You have done me a great service."

"Lord Darthon," Alex said, bowing slightly. He was pleased to see that the color had returned to Darthon's face.

"We are at your service," Whalen said, also bowing.

"Please, sit," Darthon said, waving his hand at the table. "Timold, ring for the servers. We will eat and talk, if that's agreeable to you."

"We did not expect to dine so privately," Whalen said, taking his seat. "I'm sure that many of your lords will have questions for us."

"Oh, I'm sure they do," Darthon said with a chuckle. "But their questions will have to wait. I am still king, and my questions come first. I may not keep many secrets from my lords, but as most of my questions are of a private nature, I thought this would be best."

"A private nature?" Whalen asked.

"Ah, here is the food," Darthon said. "Not the common fare of a midday meal, but not a great feast either. I hope you see something you like."

The servers entered, and what they brought both looked and smelled wonderful. There was bread and cheese, roasted meat that Alex thought was venison, fish, some type of roasted bird, and several platters of vegetables. Alex's stomach growled again, and he was glad the servers were making enough noise to cover it. The table was quickly laid and the servers departed before Darthon spoke again.

"As I mentioned, my questions for you are of a private

nature," Darthon said. "My sickness, for lack of a better word, is a private matter to me. What were you told about it?"

"Only that you had been sick for several weeks, and had been lying senseless in bed for ten days," Whalen replied.

"Yes, weeks of sickness that was not sickness," said Darthon. "I was plagued by dreams, nightmares. I could get no rest at all. Then, one night, I became trapped in the nightmare. I was lost, unable to wake or find my way home."

"It was an evil spell," Alex said, "sent from Conmar to keep you and your people in check, and then to destroy you."

"Keep us in check?" Timold asked.

"Darthon was unable to speak, to command. Your people had no leader," Alex said.

"Yes, I see," Timold said. "We could take care of our own kingdom, but . . ."

"But there were calls from our friends and allies to the north, seeking our aid," Darthon said. "Without my word, my people were unable to send assistance."

"That was what the lord of Conmar wanted," Whalen said. "To delay you, to keep you from sending aid to those in need."

"But then you came into my dream," Darthon said, looking at Alex. "You told me that my people needed me. You reminded me of Valora."

"Yes," Alex said. "Remembering your people and your home was all you really needed to find your way back."

"It was a terrible place," Darthon said, some of the color draining from his face. "A place so empty and desolate."

"Do not think of that now," Alex said. "Such dreams are best left in the shadows and forgotten, if possible."

"Yes, of course," Darthon said. "I will try to forget the dream, but I will not forget the debt I owe you, Master Taylor, for coming to my aid."

"I am glad that I could help," Alex said.

"Now for another matter, which is also very close to me," Darthon said. "I am told that you claim my nephew Joshua as a friend. That you met him during your travels in Eastland and you were companions until you reached Midland."

"Yes, that is true," Alex said. "I am troubled to hear that Joshua is missing. Do you suspect he could be a hostage of the lord of Conmar?"

"The lord of Conmar would not be so bold as to openly say he is holding Joshua hostage," Timold said.

"No, not so bold as that—not yet, at any rate," Darthon agreed. "Still, he hints that Joshua may be among the hostages. He says that he will check, and if Joshua is there he will review his case and try to get him released."

"Case? Released? I don't understand," Alex said. "Has some law been broken?"

"No law that we are bound to obey," Timold said angrily.

"A ploy," Whalen said. "Jabez no doubt pretends to have some legal claim on his prisoners so he can hold them without actually calling them what they are—hostages."

"And he can also deny holding anyone as he never makes a real claim stating what crime they have committed," Darthon said. "If he made a claim he would also have to name a punishment or a price to set the person free. He has been doing this for some time, and I have to wonder how many people of Westland he holds in his dungeons."

"Something will have to be done about that," Alex said.

"In time," Whalen said.

"Yes, in time," Darthon agreed. "But first, will you tell me the story of how you met Joshua and about your travels together? I have not seen my nephew in almost two years, and to be honest, he is more a son than a nephew to me."

"Of course," Alex said.

So Alex told the story of how he and Joshua had met, and how they'd escaped the men sent by the lord of Conmar to capture Joshua. He told the story up to the point when they'd met Whalen in the city of Shinmar. Whalen then told of their voyage across the sea and the encounter with the sea serpent, being sure to give Joshua credit for his courage in fighting the monster.

"Joshua was unaware that we are wizards," Whalen explained. "We have been in hiding since coming to this land. When we parted, he was going to make his way home by the fastest route possible. If we had known . . ."

"You might have been able to protect him," Darthon finished. "Though I see that you did keep him safe for a time, and I am grateful for that. I also see that I have been a poor host, keeping you talking and leaving you no time to eat."

"We've managed to eat a fair amount," Whalen replied with a smile, looking at Alex, who had his mouth full.

"You have given me some comfort, and that is a gift in such troubled times," Darthon said. "Now, I should rest. The healers don't like that I'm up and about so much already."

"You need to move around to get your strength back," Alex said.

"So I tell them, but they have their own ways," Darthon said. "You've seen some of them? Our friends, the ones who tried to heal me before you came?"

"The sea elves," Alex said. "Yes, we've seen them."

"We do not name them so openly," Darthon said. "We normally just say 'our friends.' They don't like to be talked about—or have outsiders know about them."

"And we are outsiders," Whalen said.

"Yes," Darthon said. "I will tell you plainly that they have expressed some doubt about you two."

"Their doubts may be less now than they were before," Alex said. "But if their doubts remain, we will find some way to answer them."

"Good. Very good," Darthon said. "I may not know much about wizards or magic, but I do know about men. I can see in your faces and hear in your words that you are good men. I don't know what troubles our friends, but I, at least, am willing to trust you."

Darthon stood to leave, and Timold was quick to help him. Alex and Whalen stood and bowed slightly as a sign of respect.

"Tomorrow . . ." Timold said softly.

"What? Oh, yes," Darthon said. "Tomorrow I will call a council of my lords. I would be pleased if both of you would attend as well. There are many things to be discussed, and plans to be made."

"As you wish," Whalen answered.

Darthon left with Timold, and a guard escorted Alex and Whalen back to their room.

Alex's mind was full of thoughts. Darthon trusted them,

but the sea elves had doubts. Alex thought that some of the sea elves would trust them once Aliia had a chance to explain what he'd told her, but he couldn't be sure. The sea elves had been hidden for many years, taking little or no part in the greater matters of the lands they lived in. They would not trust quickly, and he didn't think they would be willing to come out of hiding.

"Not what I expected," Whalen said when he and Alex were back in their rooms. "I suppose we'll have to wait until tomorrow to see where we stand."

"I don't know what to expect anymore," Alex replied. "I think Darthon will let us pass freely through his lands, but our quest has become something more. It's no longer just about you and I reaching Conmar and facing Jabez. Most of Westland is at war, and we have to help them. It wasn't part of our plan, but we can't leave them to fight alone."

"It wasn't part of *my* plan, you mean," Whalen said. "You've learned a great deal, my friend, and you are right. We can't leave them to fight alone, not now, and not against the Brotherhood."

Whalen fell silent as he took a seat beside the fire. Alex stood for a moment and then picked up his staff. He wanted to say something, but he didn't know what to say or how to say it.

"Tomorrow," Whalen finally said. "We will make new plans tomorrow."

CHAPTER SIXTEEN

WAR COUNCIL

A s tired as he was, Alex had trouble sleeping that night. His mind kept going over the plan that Whalen had made for them when they first came to Jarro. It was a simple plan, easy to follow—and it wasn't going to work. The plan had been too sketchy, and things had changed more than Alex had expected. Somewhere in his half sleep, Alex heard his own voice speaking to him.

"Whalen made a simple plan because he knew it would change," his own voice said, almost laughing as it spoke. "Just because you couldn't see that things would change doesn't mean that Whalen couldn't."

Alex's sleep was filled with strange dreams that he couldn't see clearly, and when he woke, the images and memories slipped away from him. Awake, his mind was instantly filled with questions that he couldn't answer. How big was Jabez's army? How many hostages did he have in his dungeons? Where was the Axe of Sundering hidden? If Jabez had made a dragon a slave, what other creatures might he have under his control? He had seen those wolf creatures in Midland. How many of them did Jabez have, and how would he use them here in Westland?

There was so much to do, too much that was unknown, and no time to waste.

Finally, in the hours before sunrise, Alex fell into a light sleep. His mind slipped into a dream that was so real that he wasn't sure that he was dreaming. He stood on the shore of a vast underground lake, but it wasn't pitch-dark as it should have been. The rocks in the cave seemed to glow with a pale green light, making the water look inky black.

Something in his dream pulled him toward the water, but he resisted. He could see his breath puff like clouds from his mouth, and he was certain that the water of the lake would be deadly cold. This was not a lake for swimming—not if you wanted to stay alive. His dream still pulled at him, forcing him to step to the edge of the water.

His hand reached out and touched the still water. Pain shot up his arm and he jerked back, but his dream dragged him forward. Fighting with all his strength, Alex clawed at the rocky beach, trying to crawl away from the lake, but nothing he did seemed to work. He was being dragged into the cold, cold water. He was sure he would die.

He heard a splash as his body fell into the water, and with a gasp, Alex woke up. He had fallen out of his bed, his legs tangled in his blankets. He looked around wildly, but he was in his bedroom, and everything was dry. Pulling his legs free of the blanket, Alex stood up and looked down at his right hand. It was dry just like everything else, but the icy cold pain lingered.

He stretched his fingers to work some blood into them, and at the back of his mind his O'Gash whispered to him.

"The lake is the key. That is where you will find what you seek. But will you pay the price to claim it?"

Alex sat on the edge of his bed, rubbing warmth and life back into his hand. He trusted his O'Gash, but he didn't like what it told him. The icy cold lake scared him, and he had no idea what price he would have to pay if he ever found his way there.

Unwilling to risk another nightmare, Alex got dressed. He made his way to the large sitting room that he shared with Whalen and piled logs in the cold fireplace. With a wave of his hand, he ignited the logs. He sat down close to the fire, holding his still-cold right hand out to the heat.

I slept on my arm, Alex told himself. *It's just gone numb, that's why it's cold.*

He knew that wasn't true—somehow it was his nightmare that had caused his arm to ache with cold, but in the predawn darkness the thought made him feel better. He flexed his fingers, and even though he didn't want to, he thought about the lake in his dream.

An underground lake that was deadly cold would be a good place to hide the Axe of Sundering. Nobody would willingly go into such a lake, so the Axe wouldn't be found by accident. If Jabez hid the Axe there, however, he must have some way of recovering it. If Jabez was forced to leave Conmar Castle, he certainly wouldn't leave the Axe behind. Could he hide it at the bottom of a lake without having a way to get it if he needed it? He wouldn't dare leave any clue to where the Axe was, so how?

Alex thought for a long time, but he didn't find any answers. It was possible that Jabez had some servant or slave who could go into the lake and get the Axe for him. But, no, that didn't seem likely. Anyone holding the Axe was a threat to Jabez; the dark wizard wouldn't trust anyone with it. So, if not a slave, then who? Or, maybe . . . what?

About two hours later, Whalen came into the room. He looked stern, as if he'd already spent a great deal of time thinking about things he didn't like. When he saw Alex, the look on his face changed to concern.

"Trouble sleeping?" Whalen asked, putting more wood on the fire.

"Too many thoughts and dreams," Alex replied. "Though nothing that won't find its own answer, in time."

"I imagine we'll get some answers today, though I can't guess what those answers might be," Whalen said. "Still, no sense worrying about it until we know how things stand."

Alex nodded, and remained silent.

Whalen went to the table and took several papers and scrolls out of his magic bag. He shuffled through them, occasionally muttering to himself.

An hour later, servants appeared, bringing Alex and Whalen breakfast. Whalen moved his papers to a chair, and the table was quickly filled with all kinds of food. The servant, while polite, said very little. Alex got up from his chair beside the fire and joined Whalen at the table.

"Are you finished thinking yet?" Whalen asked as he filled his own plate.

"Thinking and yet not thinking at all," Alex answered. "My mind is too full and completely empty at the same time."

"Well, let it be empty for now. I suspect it will be full again before this day is done."

"Do you think anything will be decided on today? Matters of war can often take a lot of time and even more discussion before anything is decided."

"True, but I think the decisions, or most of them, are already made. Darthon and his people will go to war, I'm sure of that. As to *where* they go to war—well, I hope that decision has not yet been made."

"Why?"

"The attack against Darthon came from Conmar. Some, maybe even most, of Darthon's lords will want revenge for that. Conmar also holds the hostages—including Joshua— and Darthon will want to free them, if he can. We will need to guide him away from anything so foolish as an assault on Conmar Castle."

"Would it be foolish? Maybe a direct assault would be best."

"Without knowing the size of Jabez's army, I don't think going straight to Conmar is a good plan. Apart from his army, Jabez is a wizard—a dark wizard, yes, but he still has a great deal of power and who knows how many magical friends as well."

"Without more information, we can hardly move at all," Alex said with a sigh.

"Oh, we can move," Whalen said, biting into a sausage. "We just want to make sure our first move is not also our last."

Alex let the conversation drop and concentrated on his breakfast. Whalen was right—of course they could move. Jabez probably expected them to move, but maybe not so soon. If he still believed that Darthon was trapped in the dragon's spell, then he wouldn't expect the southern kingdom to move until Darthon was dead and a new king appointed, which could take a long time, depending on if Darthon had any heirs. If they moved when Jabez didn't expect them to, they might be able to surprise the army of Conmar.

As Alex was pushing away his plate, a knock came at the door. Whalen, who had finished his breakfast and was back to studying his papers, got up and answered it. A group of seven soldiers stood outside. Six of the soldiers stood against the wall, three to either side, and the seventh in front of the door.

"Masters," the soldier in front began, "Lord Darthon calls you to his council, if you will please come with us."

"As Lord Darthon wishes," Whalen answered, picking up his staff and turning slightly toward Alex.

Alex understood what Whalen meant. Today, they were not simply guests, but wizards, and they would carry their staffs to show who and what they were. Alex quickly went to his room and retrieved his staff, and then he and Whalen followed the soldier. As they moved through the door, two of the soldiers turned to follow directly behind their guide. The remaining four men waited for Alex and Whalen to pass by, and then they turned and followed behind them.

"Ceremony," Whalen said quietly to Alex.

Alex didn't reply. Ceremony was an important part of a peaceful kingdom, and as this was Darthon's kingdom, he made the rules. They followed their guide through the palace, finally stopping outside a pair of massive wood and metal doors. Many people were crowded in front of the doors, but they moved aside for the men leading Alex and Whalen.

To Alex's surprise, they did not enter a hall or meeting room, but walked into the open air of a garden. Darthon sat in a massive stone chair, backed by several soldiers and flanked by Timold on his right, and a man Alex didn't recognize on his left. There were two empty seats to the right of Timold, obviously meant for Whalen and himself.

The remaining space was taken up with chairs set up in a half-circle, facing Darthon. Important-looking men, clearly Darthon's lords, occupied most of the chairs. Standing behind the lords were about twenty men dressed like travelers, all wearing weapons.

Alex also saw a small group of twelve people standing off to the side. They were all hooded, and Alex knew instantly they were sea elves.

He also saw eight dwarves in full battle armor. Two of the dwarves had removed their helmets and were sitting down, but they all looked more than a little grumpy.

"I didn't know there were dwarves in Jarro," Alex whispered to Whalen.

"Not many that I know of. They live in the far north," Whalen whispered back.

Darthon rose from his stone chair. "Ah, my friends, now that we are all here, we may begin."

"'Bout time too," one of the dwarves grumbled, none too quietly.

"We all know the reason for this meeting," Darthon went on as if he hadn't heard. "The question is not *if* we should go to war against Conmar. The question is *where* do we make our stand. And *when*."

"My lord," Timold said, rising to his feet. "Our armies have been preparing for some time. We are ready to face the battle whenever and wherever you command."

"My lord." The man to Darthon's left also rose to his feet. "May I speak?"

"Yes, Lord Belford. What course do you suggest?" Darthon asked.

"We should take the battle to Conmar," Lord Belford answered. "Conmar has assaulted you directly, and such an attack must be answered. Conmar is also where our hostages are being held, and we must attempt to rescue them, if we can."

"The mountain passes will be hard, if not impossible, to cross this time of year," Timold answered. "Our armies in the east could march to Conmar easily, but they are too few in number, and we have no way to supply them."

"The way over the mountains may be closed, but the roads to the north are open," one of the travelers said, standing up. "Both the middle and northern kingdoms are under attack, and they call for your aid. You know that for nearly a year there has been trouble in the northern kingdom, and even more trouble in the kingdom of the dwarves. What you may not know, Lord Darthon, is that a great army from Conmar crossed the mountains before the snows came to attack the middle kingdom as well. Already they have destroyed much, and your allies in the north need your help to drive them off."

"Not just crossed the mountains," the oldest looking dwarf there said. "Conmar has worse evil working for it than you think. My people are holding off a horde of goblins in the far north. I've no doubt that the foul creatures have tunneled under the mountains and are bringing supplies to the armies of Conmar in the west."

"Have calls for aid been sent to Midland?" Darthon asked.

"Some, but we've no way to know if they arrived," Timold answered. "Even if they have arrived, it will be two or perhaps three months before ships can sail from Midland."

"A fact well known by Conmar," Lord Belford said.

"Karill, do you have any advice? What do your elders say? Will your people come to our aid in this time of need?" Darthon asked, looking at the sea elves.

"We have had little to do with the affairs of men for many years," the tallest elf answered. "A direct assault on Conmar seems impossible, but most or even all the army of Conmar is already on the western side of the mountains. It would be foolish to let them remain here, and worse than foolish to let them return to the east."

"Aye, and what will the sea elves do to stop them?" the old dwarf asked. "Will your people come on land and fight, or will you sail away and leave the poor mortals to their fate?"

Alex noted the dwarf's half-hopeful, half-angry tone. Dwarves were not always friendly with elves, and the old dwarf's words were a kind of challenge. At a different time, they might have led to a fight on the spot. But the sea elves, it seemed, were not so easily angered as other elves that Alex knew.

"Lord Grimgold, we know well your feelings toward our people," Karill answered slowly. "We cannot blame you for what you feel, but you do not know our history. At this time, I cannot say if my people will come in force. The elders of my people are debating the matter even now, though I think that some will come to your aid no matter what the elders say."

"Debate," the dwarf scoffed, shaking his head. "If they talk long enough, this war will be over and there'll be nothing for your people to do but look at the bones."

"Enough," Darthon said sharply. "We have heard from most, but not from all. Master Vankin, Master Taylor. It is said that wizards have wisdom that other men lack. What advice do you offer, now that you see how things stand?"

"A difficult question to be sure," Whalen said, getting to his feet. "Our original quest in coming here was to deal with the man you know as the lord of Conmar. We know him as Jabez. For Master Taylor and I, stopping him must remain our primary goal. We did not expect war to begin so soon, and it appears that our plans must change to meet the current situation. The kingdoms to the north need aid; the armies of Conmar must not be allowed to destroy them. For myself, I think that my path lies north."

"If you go north and reveal yourself to Jabez, he will send everything he can to destroy you," Alex said quickly. "The kingdoms to the north need aid, yes, but Jabez must be dealt with. So long as he remains in command of his armies, there is no hope for a lasting victory. With Jabez destroyed, his armies will become less of a threat. We must also consider the hostages that Jabez holds. We cannot abandon them to death, or worse."

"You are right," Whalen replied with a slight smile. "Yet to win this fight we must take risks, we must all do what we can. It is a risk, but what I can do is go north. I would advise you, Lord Darthon, to send your armies there as well. We will face the armies of Conmar together, even if our victories will be short-lived. We cannot win a complete victory while Jabez remains unchecked, but we can hold off his armies, at least for a time."

"Then we will go north," Alex said.

"Oh no, my young friend," Whalen said. "*You* must continue to Conmar Castle, that is your risk. If we can distract Jabez with our battle to the north, then it will be easier for you to find the Axe of Sundering and stop Jabez once and for all."

"Alone?" Alex asked. He trusted Whalen, but he wasn't sure this was the best plan. It was a terrible risk, but what other plan was there? Jabez had to be stopped. His armies had to be stopped. Perhaps splitting up was the only way to accomplish both things and have any hope of victory.

"Distraction and deception are fine plans," Grimgold said. "But Jabez is also a wizard. He will know where you are, Master Vankin, and he will surely detect young Master Taylor long before he approaches Conmar Castle."

"No, he won't," said Whalen. "We are hidden from him, at least for the time being. Jabez knows that I am in Jarro, but he does not know exactly where I am. He will only be able to find me when I set my magic loose against his army."

"And Master Taylor?" Timold asked.

"I am unknown to Jabez," Alex said. "He does not know I am in this land, and he will not know who or what I am until I reveal myself to him."

"You are certain of this?" Darthon asked.

"Ask Karill," said Alex. "Elves are better at seeing magic than either men or dwarves. Tell them, Karill, what do you see when you look at Whalen and myself?"

"I see two men, and no magic at all," Karill answered slowly. "I have some doubt that a wizard would see as I do, but he might. I would not have believed that magic could be so completely hidden, but it seems to be so."

"Very well," Darthon said after a pause. "I will think on all that has been said. We will meet again after the midday meal. I will announce my decision then."

Everyone stood as Darthon left the open area. Alex watched him go, and then turned his attention to those that remained. Grimgold and the other dwarves stood in a group, speaking quietly. The men from Darthon's kingdom broke into small groups, mixing with the men from the kingdoms of the north. Most of the sea elves had left, but Karill remained standing in the shade of a tree, watching Alex and Whalen.

"That went as well as could be expected," Whalen said.

"Do you think Darthon will go north?" Alex asked.

"He doesn't really have much choice," Whalen answered. "With the passes over the mountains closed, he must either go north or do nothing until spring comes. And he does not seem like a man who likes to do nothing but wait."

"With the passes closed, I may have a hard time getting to Conmar myself," Alex said.

"I doubt that." Whalen chuckled. "You can use your magic practically right in front of me and I can't see it. I feel sure that you can use whatever magic you need to in order to get to Conmar, and Jabez won't be aware of it."

"For myself, yes, I can work any magic that is needed," Alex said. "I have a feeling, however, that I won't be going to Conmar alone."

"Why is that?" Whalen asked.

"Because once I reach Conmar, I will be trying to rescue any hostages that are there," Alex answered. "If they are still alive, I doubt they will be in any condition to run away on their own. Darthon will think of that, and he will want to send men with me to help with their escape."

"Probably," Whalen agreed. "Still, you can use magic on your companions—hide them as you've hidden me."

"To travel there, yes. But once I go to face Jabez, I'm not sure what protection I can offer them."

"When you face Jabez, he will be too worried about you to even think of the escaped hostages."

"He will, but we don't know who or what else might be there helping him."

"Yes, I understand. I'm sorry to say it, but the men and hostages will have to fend for themselves. Once you have freed them, they will have to find their way home without you. You have to find the Axe of Sundering, and I have no idea how long that might take."

"And if you are captured while I'm searching?"

"I am not so easy to capture as that. I'll be able to buy you some time at the very least."

"Remember my vision. . . the Orion stones. If he has them and can use one of them . . ."

"I'll be careful," Whalen promised. "And it's no good worrying about all the 'what ifs' and 'who mights' and such. We could plan for every possible thing that Jabez might do or have or throw against us, but if we did, we'd never get anything done. Instead of spending our time trying to guess all the answers, I suggest we concentrate on something more important."

"And what might that be?"

"The midday meal, of course."

———— ••• ————

Food was brought into the meeting area, and several small tables were set up for the council guests. The meal was another good one, though a surprisingly quiet affair. Groups around the tables spoke in low voices to one another, and very few people moved between tables. Alex and Whalen found themselves alone at a table set to one side. Alex wanted to be friendly and get to know Darthon's people, but it seemed that no one else felt that way.

"May I join you?" Karill asked quietly.

"Of course," Whalen replied.

Alex looked up from his plate as the elf approached.

"Most of the men here fear us," Karill said mildly as he pushed back his hood so they could see his face. "And you have seen for yourselves how the dwarves feel about my people."

"You can hardly blame them," Alex said. "Your people are separated from the world of men for the most part. The troubles between elves and dwarves are ancient, and I do not see them changing soon."

"We are separate," Karill agreed. "One might say that we are cut off from the world, though I wish it was not so."

"I know little of your people," Whalen said. "Mostly stories and rumors. Tell me, Karill, do you think your people will aid the men and dwarves of Westland? Will they come to the land and do battle with this evil?"

"You did not tell him?" Karill asked, looking at Alex.

"It was not my place. I made a wizard's vow to not share what Aliia told me," Alex said. "Not even with my friend."

"I see," Karill said, nodding. "To answer your question, Master Vankin, some elves will fight, I am sure of that. The elders may not like it, but some will come. Though not enough, I fear, to change the tide of battle."

"The young will come," Alex said. "Those who don't understand why the elders want to remain cut off from the world."

"Yes, mostly the young, but others as well," Karill said. "Times change, and many of my people feel that we should be more connected than we are."

None of them spoke for a time, each one lost in his own thoughts. Alex's thoughts were filled with questions about the sea elves. He wanted to know why they tried so hard to hide themselves. It seemed like madness to cut themselves off from the world simply because of their past. They were part of the world whether they liked it or not, and hiding themselves away would do no one any good at all.

"Darthon will return soon with his decision," Karill said, breaking the silence. "He will go north. To war."

"You know Darthon better than we do," Whalen said.

"I have known him since he was a boy, as I knew his father and his father's father," Karill answered. "He is a good man. He trusts when others might doubt. He will go north because his allies there call him, but his heart will go west with Master Taylor."

"West, to Joshua and the other hostages," Alex said.

"He cares for all his people, as a true king must," Karill said. "But if he were not king and responsible for all, he would burn all of Jarro to save Joshua from the evil clutches of Jabez."

"Then Joshua must be saved," Alex replied.

Their conversation was cut short as Darthon returned to the council area. He looked tired, and Alex thought he might be pushing himself too hard.

"My friends," Darthon said when the crowd grew quiet. "It seems that war is upon us, and we have no time to waste. The armies of the southern kingdom will march north as soon as possible. Ships and supplies will be made ready and move as soon as the winds of Jarro allow them to sail north."

There was a general cheer for Darthon's decision, but it was not a joyful cheer. Everyone on the council knew that this war would be a long and hard one, and even with Darthon joining the other kingdoms of Westland against Conmar, they were unsure of what the future might hold.

"Master Taylor," Darthon continued, "you will travel west,

to the seat of our enemy's power. All our hopes rest on you, and I would not send you there without others to help you on the road and once you get there."

"Lord Darthon, a small group of men would be welcome," Alex replied. "I do not know the paths of this land, and once the hostages are rescued, they will need assistance to make their escape."

"A small company then, no more than twenty men," Darthon said. "Is there anything else I can do to aid you in your quest?"

Alex thought for a moment. "The passes over the mountains will be difficult for men, maybe impossible for horses. Is there some other way we can travel? Can we not sail around the southern end of Westland and then go north to Conmar?"

Darthon turned slightly to look at Karill, and there seemed to be some unspoken communication between them.

Darthon looked back at Alex, but it was Karill that spoke.

"The seas to the south are dangerous at all times, and in winter most dangerous of all," said Karill. "To sail south and then north would be a slower path than you think. I cannot imagine you making that journey in less than two months."

"And how long before your armies join the battle in the north?" Whalen asked Darthon.

"Once we set out, we can reach the middle kingdom in two, maybe three weeks," Darthon answered.

"Too long," Alex said. "It seems that every path leading to Conmar will take too long."

"There is another way," a soft voice said from behind Alex.

"Aliia, no," Karill said sternly. "That path is not open. To take that road courts folly and invites death."

"He asked for a faster way, not a safer way," Aliia replied. "The road through the black lands is the only other path. I will guide Master Taylor to his goal."

"You will not," Karill said fiercely. "I forbid you to even think about such madness."

"My fate is not in your hands, Karill," Aliia answered defiantly. "This is my destiny, and I will follow it, whatever the cost."

"What is this path?" Alex asked. "What are the black lands?"

"A terrible place—a place no one goes to, not anymore," Darthon answered. "Those who have gone there never return."

"It was once the home of my people," Aliia said.

"I understand," Alex said, remembering what Aliia had told him in the garden about the history of her people. "I would like some time to consider this. How long before the armies move north?"

"Four days," Timold replied.

"And how long would it take us to travel through the black lands and reach Conmar?"

"Seven or eight days, if you can get through the black lands at all," Karill said. "After that, ten days to two weeks to the castle of Conmar."

"Very good. I will try to find some other way, but in the end, if there is no other option, I will travel through the black lands to Conmar," Alex said.

"Find another way," Karill said quietly, leaning close to Alex. "By all we hold dear, find another way."

The council was concluded, and the lords of the southern kingdom departed to deal with the business of war. The dwarves and men from the north had their own preparations to make. Grimgold approached Darthon as the groups were leaving and spoke quietly with him. Whalen watched everything but said nothing, and Alex didn't know what to say. He had to find a way to move himself and twenty men west as fast as possible, and he didn't know how he was going to do it without daring the deadly black lands.

"Master Taylor, may I ask something of you?" Karill whispered in Alex's ear.

"You wish me to refuse Aliia," Alex said. "If I take this road across the black lands, you wish me to forbid her to come with me."

"I do, but that is not what I want to ask you now," Karill said.

"What then? How may I be of service to you?" Alex asked.

"Tonight the elders of my people will hold a council of their own," Karill said. "As you may guess, our people are scattered across the seas of this world, but we have ways—magical ways—to speak to each other in times of need. Tonight we will talk about all that has happened, about what might happen to Westland and Jarro. Will you come and speak with them? After our council, you can ask about *darloch est messer*. You might be able to learn something that will help you."

"Aliia told you about my interest?" Alex asked.

"She told us all that passed between you," Karill said. "I

cannot tell you more than she did about this ancient legend, but the council can. Will you come?"

"Yes," Alex said. "I will come."

———✦———

"It's total madness, you know, this path through the black lands," Whalen said later that afternoon when they were alone in their rooms. "No one can say what evil is there, but it's clear that both men and elves are terrified of the place."

"Maybe they fear the unknown," Alex said.

"Yes, and maybe there's something worse than you can imagine waiting there," Whalen shot back. "When you rescued Skeld and the other adventurers from Karmus in Nezza, didn't you transform into a bird while they were inside your magic bag? Couldn't you do something similar now, and fly over the mountains?"

"Maybe," Alex said. "But that is a lot of magic. When I transformed with Skeld and the others in my magic bag, there were only a few of them, and no horses. And it was only for a short flight. Hiding twenty men and twenty horses while I transform into a bird and while still protecting you from Jabez and while hiding my own magic would be difficult. There are other problems as well."

"Like what?"

"What if we run into a storm over the mountains and I can't fly? How long will it take to cross the mountains as a bird? Do I change back and forth every day? The men and horses can't stay in my magic bag for the whole journey. You know how dangerous transformations can be for a wizard, how much more dangerous might it be for men and horses?"

Whalen sighed, his shoulders slumping in defeat and agreement. "But the black lands sound too dangerous to even consider."

"How can you say that when we know almost nothing about them?" Alex asked. "They do have something in their favor, though it is a small point. It might, however, be the small point we need to win this fight."

"What is that?"

"They are the last place Jabez will be looking," Alex said, smiling.

Whalen frowned, thinking. "You're probably right. I'm sure he knows about the black lands, but Jabez cares nothing for his men. So, if he is unwilling to send his own army there because he knows they will be destroyed, then we should take that as a warning."

"Does he know, or is that just what he believes?" Alex asked.

"I heard what Karill said, Alex. We need to find another way—though I don't have any idea what that might be."

CHAPTER SEVENTEEN

LEGENDS

I t was late and the palace halls were mostly empty. Alex had told Whalen what he was doing and where he was going, and Whalen had simply nodded his understanding and said nothing. Now, Alex followed Karill out of the palace and into the streets of Valora. They went downhill, toward the harbor, and Alex understood why. The magic of the sea elves was tied to the open sea, and they would need all the power they could summon to communicate with their elders who were scattered across the oceans of Jarro.

"This way," Karill said, leading Alex away from the docks.

They walked along the shoreline for a mile. When they came to the city wall, Karill produced a silver key which he slipped between two stones. There was a soft click, and a section of the ground and lower wall moved aside, revealing a stairway leading down, though not directly through the wall. Alex found himself in a passageway, expertly carved but poorly lit.

"My people built this when we first landed here," Karill said. "It was so long ago that only the king and a few of his lords know that it is here, and they would be hard pressed to find it without a guide."

The passage was straight and had a gentle downward slope. They walked in silence for another mile and then the passage started sloping up. Alex wondered where they could be, because by his reckoning they were moving eastward. After climbing a long set of stairs, they came out of a stone arch and into an open, bowl-like area. The top of the chamber was open to the sky, and Alex could see the stars high above him. He could hear the gentle waves slapping against rocks, but looking around, he could see nothing but stone.

"We are surrounded by water here," Karill said. "From the deck of a ship, this place looks like a small stony island. It is a place for ships to steer well clear of."

Alex nodded his understanding and took a closer look at his surroundings. The hollowed-out space was like a small amphitheater with stone benches carved along the walls. The wooden chairs in front of him were already filled with sea elves, their hoods removed and their faces revealed. Set in front of the elves were nine silver stands, each one supporting what looked like a very large and finely cut crystal.

Alex followed Karill to the front of the group of sea elves and took the seat that Karill offered him.

"We are ready," Karill said to Alex. "You don't need to do anything. The elders will appear shortly."

"How?" Alex asked.

"Ancient magic that we have protected for a long time," Karill said. "Each of the crystals has a twin, which is held by one of the elders. When they will it, their likenesses will appear, and they will be able to see and hear all that happens here."

Alex waited and watched. For a time, it seemed that nothing was happening, but he soon noticed that each of the crystals in front of him began to glow with a dim light. The magic of the crystals was very different than Alex imagined it would be. The lords of the sea elves did not appear above the crystals as he thought they would, nor were they the semitransparent figures he'd imagined. Instead, each of the crystals, along with the silver stands, vanished from sight, and in their places sat very real and solid-looking elf lords.

As soon as all of the lords had appeared, the elf in the center spoke. His voice was musical and strangely sad, and while the words that he spoke were not exactly the same as the elvin language Alex knew, he was still able to follow what was being said. Alex thought that maybe he should say something because the elves appeared to think he could not understand them.

"Good, he's agreed to come," the sea lord from the middle crystal commented. "We were not sure that he would."

"That he would dare," another lord to Alex's left added.

A spark of anger flared inside Alex. He knew that the elves had doubts and that they had lived in fear for many years, but the part of him that was a dragon did not take kindly to the comment about his not daring to come here.

"He appears to be all that he claims," Karill said.

"Things are seldom what they appear to be," one of the lords to Alex's right answered.

"And sometimes things are *more* than they appear to be," Alex said in perfect elvin. "I have dared to do many things in my short life, and I hope to do more. What, may I ask, have you dared to do in your long lifetimes?"

The elf lords fell silent. Some seemed surprised that Alex spoke their language, while others frowned in anger that he had challenged them so directly.

"Forgive our doubts," the elf lord at the center said after a pause. "We have not been introduced. I am Navar, the eldest remaining of my people in Jarro." He gestured to the elf on Alex's right. "This is Sarach, my advisor. I can see you are angry about our doubts, and perhaps at our fear as well. We have lived in fear for a long time. Too long, I think."

"We must protect ourselves," Sarach said.

"To hide in fear is not the best path to protection," another of the elf lords commented.

"Enough," Navar interrupted. "We have debated for a long time, and we have not agreed on a path. That is not the reason for this meeting. Master Taylor, we know what you have shown to Aliia. She may never have seen a true wizard, but what she tells us reassures us that you are what you say you are. We asked you here to offer you what we can. We will share with you the legends of the distant past, if you think they can help you in your quest."

"Thank you, my lords. I am grateful for your help," Alex answered. "To be honest, I wish to hear more about the black lands before we speak of *darloch est messer*. Tell me, if you can, what is there? What is it that you and all others fear in that place?"

"The black lands," Navar replied slowly. "A path I would advise against, and yet . . ." The elf fell silent as if lost in memory or deep thought. After a moment he shook himself, glanced quickly at the other elf lords, and then settled his gaze on Alex. "Aliia told you what she knows, and I will tell you more. In ancient times, our people sought for more power than was wise. They wished for things that were not meant to be. In their pride they used magic that they did not truly understand, and that was our ruin. They gave more life to things than they should have, and worse, they gave solid form to shadows."

"More life?" Alex asked.

"Perhaps those are the wrong words," Navar answered. "They could not truly give more life, but they made things more *alive*. For example, they gave plants the ability to move from place to place, when nature decreed they should remain. This was a small thing to them, and perhaps no greater evil would have come if they had stopped there. Sadly, they did not stop. They learned to give form to shadows, allowing them to move freely on their own. When the shadows remained below ground, working in the mines, things were fine."

"Wait," said Alex. "To give shadows form requires no great magic, and there is no evil in such an act."

"Perhaps not," said Navar. "The ancient dark elves, how-ever, wished for something more than mindless shadows that could do little for them. They wanted servants—slaves, to be honest—who could work without being constantly controlled. They tried their magic on many things, but in the end they de-cided that the best slaves, the most useful, would be something like themselves. So they gave their own shadows solid forms, and set them to work in the mines.

"As I said, if they had remained in the mines, below ground and away from the sun, things might have been fine. The shadows, however, had been given the ability to think for themselves—almost as living beings. They were beautiful creatures in the beginning, pale, silver-gray shadows in the forms of elves. But with their ability to think came emotions and desires, something their creators had not considered. The shadows longed for freedom outside of the mines and the sunlight they had never seen. So they came up out of the mines, into the world, and then . . ."

"They could not remain in the sunlight," Alex said when Navar seemed unable to continue. "Direct sunlight would undo the magic that gave them form."

"It did not *undo* the magic, it changed it," said Navar. "The light of the sun twisted the shadows the elves had created, distorting their forms, changing them into monsters. Seeing what they had become, they turned against those who had created them. They hate the elves, and they hate anything that reminds them of what they once looked like. Men and even dwarves are not safe from their hate or their desire for vengeance."

"They still remain?" Alex asked. "They did not fade away when those who made them died or faded?"

"Many of the remaining dark elves have faded, and many more have sailed to the undying lands in the west," Navar answered. "Or at least they tried to sail west. We have some doubts if they could reach the undying lands, leaving their evil alive behind them. As far as we know, the shadows remain in the black lands, but none of our people have gone there for many ages of men."

"And this happened to all the dark elves in all the known lands?" Alex asked.

"Yes," Navar said. "They did not see their folly until the practice had spread to all of our people. Now, those of us who remain must pay the price for their mistake." He gestured to the other elves in the room. "Our price is paid by a life tied to the sea."

Alex didn't say anything for a minute. He considered everything he'd been told and what he already knew about giving shadows a solid form. To create thinking creatures, living beings from shadows, would require some very powerful magic. That the creatures had remained for so long even after their creators had vanished was hard for him to believe. No magic that he knew of would remain for so long, unless something, or someone, renewed the magic from time to time.

The Brotherhood? Alex wondered. Could the Brotherhood be connected to these shadows? Has the group existed for so long, unnoticed?

"You believe that in time this curse will end," Alex finally said. "Tell me, if you will, how you think the curse will end."

"That brings us back to the legend of *darloch est messer,*" Navar replied. "Simply put, it is believed that in a time of darkness, when evil threatens all the known lands, the master of dragons will come. This master will fight the evil with the aid of a nameless dragon, and if he can defeat it with his dragon ally, a great time of renewal will follow. Many wrongs of the past will fade away, and better times for all the known lands will follow."

"And if they fail?" Alex asked.

"Then evil will rise and darkness will consume the known lands," Navar answered. "I, and many of my people, believe that failure would mean our end. It would be the end for many good things to be sure."

"I don't suppose the legend says when all this is going to happen," Alex said.

"Legends cannot be marked on a calendar," Navar replied. "We must hope that the master of dragons and his nameless ally will come soon. For now, we hope, and we wait."

"'Nameless ally,'" Alex repeated softly to himself. "All dragons have names, even if the names they go by are not their true names."

Navar held up his hands in helpless surrender. "I can only tell you the words of the legend, and they say only that a nameless dragon will come and aid the master of dragons."

"Very well," Alex said, his mind trying to see how the pieces fit together and failing. "I thank you for telling me what you have, though I feel I have more questions than answers."

"Answers are always harder to find than questions," Navar said.

"Press them to join this battle," Alex's O'Gash suddenly whispered. *"As a sign of good will, show them what you are—your wizard powers, the fact that you are a dragon lord—everything except your dragon side. Show them, and ask them to fight."*

Alex hesitated, but he knew his O'Gash was right. If the men and dwarves of Westland were going to have any real chance to win the coming war, they would need help from the sea elves.

"As a sign of good faith, I will show you what many of you wish to see," Alex said, as he stood up. He moved forward to stand between the elf lords and the elves seated behind him. "As I did for Aliia, I ask you: See me for what I am."

Alex bowed his head for a moment, concentrating on how much he would reveal. Then he looked up at the stars of Jarro and a surprisingly strong feeling of hope filled him. Somehow he knew that he would reach Conmar Castle and that he would defeat Jabez and his evil. He did not know how he would get there, and he could not see how he would win, he simply knew that he would.

Alex uncovered his magic for all the sea elves to see, and this time he did not hide his power as a dragon lord. There were a few gasps of surprise, but mostly there was a stunned silence. He didn't think many of them had ever seen a true wizard, and he knew none of them had ever seen a dragon lord. He stood for several minutes, allowing the elves see his true power, sure that none of them would reveal his secret to Jabez.

"You spoke truly," Navar managed to say. "Some things are more than they appear to be, as we now see that you are. I do not recognize all of the magic I see in you, as some of it seems very strange."

"That is the magic of a dragon lord," Alex said, returning to his seat. "I am a dragon lord, named such by a lord of dragons and the eldest of that race in all the known lands."

The elf lords didn't say anything for a time, but Alex could see they were talking to each other. Something in their magic allowed them to speak together while preventing Alex from hearing their words. After a few minutes of debate, Navar broke the silence.

"If you are a dragon lord, then are you not also the master of dragons that the legend speaks of?" Navar asked.

"I do not know," Alex said. "To my mind, dragons have no masters, except possibly the ancient dragon of whom I spoke. That is why this legend is so puzzling to me. I would not claim to be a master of dragons, though I believe that any dragon I faced would speak to me before attacking."

"Clearly you know more of dragons than we do," Navar said thoughtfully. "You have shown us your power and have been honest and true with us. Is there something we may do for you? Ask of us what you will. For myself and those of my house, we will try to do whatever you may ask."

"I would ask that you come to the aid of your friends here in Westland," Alex said. "The war that they are facing will be a hard one, and I am not sure that they can win it alone."

"As a united race, we have not meddled in the affairs of mortals for ages," Sarach said quickly. "To do so now would expose our people to the evil in this and other lands."

"Tell me, Sarach, do you think your people are safe because you do not meddle? Do you think they are safe because evil does not know you exist?" Alex asked. "Stories of the sea elves are told in many lands, and the evil facing us all surely knows where your people are. It may not see you as a threat because you do not meddle, but sooner or later the evil will come looking for you."

"Perhaps," Sarach replied. "But that is simply more reason

to remain hidden. Provoking evil seems a foolish course to follow."

"Yes, that may be," Alex agreed. "Yet I ask that you answer one question: What would you call an elf, or a man, or even a dwarf, who would not help when a friend was in dire need?"

"You would shame us further and call us cowards," Sarach answered angrily.

"Your word, not mine," Alex said. "If the title fits, you must live with it."

"Wizards are known for their cunning ways and their ability to twist words. What will you say to those of our people who will die if we join this battle? You know as we all do that many will die. What words do you have for them?" Sarach asked.

"Yes," Alex said sadly. "Many will die in the coming fight. Such is the price of life, even for the ageless elves. Those who die, however, will die with honor. They will die without the shame that your people have lived with for so long."

"Enough of this," Navar said loudly. "This is a choice that every elf must make individually. And for me, and the members of my house who wish it, I will join Lord Darthon in this war. If the other houses wish to join us, they will be welcome. If they wish to remain hidden, as Master Taylor said, you must live with the title that fits."

Karill stood and bowed to Navar. "I will tell Lord Darthon of your decision, my lord."

"Thank you," Alex said to Navar. "I know joining this war will be a sacrifice for your people, but I know we will not be able to defeat this evil without your help."

Navar nodded his head to Alex. "Perhaps we can begin to help you right now. There is one more thing you should know about the black lands, though I cannot say how true it might be or if it is simply legend."

"Something more about the black lands?" Alex asked.

"There are old stories about our ancient home," Navar explained. "They say that at certain times, strange lights appear in the night. Some say that the lights are the shadow's magic, used to mislead travelers and cause them to become lost forever in the darkness. Others say that the lights are the lost souls of those who have died, those who created the shadows in the first place and who are unable to leave the black lands until the shadows they created are undone. Whatever version of the story is true, I urge you to avoid the lights if you see them. All the stories say that the lights bring madness or even death to any who get too close to them."

"Thank you for this information, Lord Navar," said Alex. "It will be helpful when I cross the black lands."

"You still think the path through the black lands is the best way to travel? Even knowing all that you do?" Navar asked with concern.

"It seems the only path open to me," Alex answered. "I wish it was not. It will be a dangerous journey, and I would rather face that danger alone instead of taking others with me into such a place."

"Then take only those who choose to go of their own free will," Navar said, "those who will be most likely to withstand any evil you may meet."

"I hope that we all may withstand the evil," Alex replied. "Thank you again for what you have shared with me."

"I wish you luck in your quest, and I hope to meet you face to face one day very soon," said Navar.

"A hope that I share," Alex answered, standing and bowing slightly.

All of the sea elves stood and bowed to their lords until their images faded and vanished.

Without a word Karill turned and motioned for Alex to follow him. They remained silent until they were almost back to the city walls.

"I would not have you think badly of Sarach," Karill said. "He is not the fearful sea elf that he appears to be in council."

"I do not think badly of any elf," Alex replied. "I understand that he is only trying to protect his people."

"Not in the way you are thinking," Karill said. "It is Sarach's job in council to take a stand for the old ways, to uphold the traditions of my people. His own true feelings are very different. I think, if he had his way, we would be far more involved with what happens in the land of Jarro than we have been for many lifetimes of men."

"So he really wants to help, even though it means going to war, even though he knows many of your people will die?" Alex asked.

"Death is not always to be feared," Karill answered. "Most of my people believe that to die in a good cause is better than to live forever in hiding. Few of my people, however, would say such a thing out loud. We have been in hiding for a very long time, and old ways are not easy to change."

"Let us hope that the change will not prove too costly for your people," Alex said.

"Yes, let us hope," Karill agreed.

"The elves are going to fight?" Whalen asked.

Alex had found the old wizard sitting next to the fire in their rooms, waiting for his return. He had a worried look on his face, and a huge pile of papers scattered on the floor around him.

"Some of them, at least," Alex said. "Maybe even most of them."

"How did you manage that?"

Alex quickly told Whalen about what had happened during the council of the sea elves. When he finished, Whalen leaned back in his chair.

"You have done well, Alex. With the sea elves on our side, our chances of winning this fight without destroying most of Westland will be better, but . . ."

"I know, I know," Alex said. "Nothing will really matter if I can't get into Conmar, find the Axe of Sundering, and finish Jabez."

"Yes, and I've been trying to find something that will help with that," Whalen said, waving his hand at the papers around him.

"A magical way to find the Axe?" Alex asked hopefully.

"No, nothing as simple as that," Whalen said, shaking his head. "I doubt that Jabez would use any great magic to hide the Axe as that would simply act as a sign to anyone who knows how to look. Don't forget, the Axe is a magical weapon as well and any magic used on the Axe may react in unexpected ways."

"What are you looking for, then?"

"A way for you to get to Conmar without traveling through the black lands," Whalen answered. "Given what Navar told you about the dangers in the black lands, I feel even more strongly that you should avoid them."

"Yes, there will be danger traveling in the black lands, but the magic the sea elves used there is not necessarily evil. At least, it's not the same evil that we are trying to defeat at Conmar."

"The magic the elves used may not have been evil, at least not directly, but it was powerful, and it has caused a great deal of evil to follow."

"Most of that evil has been done to the sea elves," Alex said.

"Hardly," Whalen said. "Oh, I know the sea elves have suffered because of what they did, but what about the shadows?"

"The shadows?"

"They were given life," Whalen said. "Maybe not life as you and I know it, but life just the same. The shadows could think and feel and make their own decisions. What they were not given was a choice in what they would become. They were also not given an end, a way to die and become simply shadows once more. That, to my mind, is a greater evil than anything the sea elves have had to live with."

"I hadn't thought of it that way," Alex admitted.

"You should," Whalen said. "If you must travel through the black lands, you should look at things from all angles."

"It seems like there is always something more to think about," Alex said with a yawn.

"Yes, there is," Whalen agreed. "So, when you think you've thought of everything, you can be sure you are wrong."

Alex said good night to Whalen and went to his bedroom. He wasn't really tired, but he wanted to be alone to think. He took off his boots, stretched out on top of his bed, and looked up at the dark ceiling of his room. He thought about his main enemy, Jabez.

Jabez would know something about the black lands, but how much? If he thought no one could travel through the black lands, then he wouldn't worry about guarding them. It was a chance, maybe the only chance that Alex would have to get close to Conmar Castle as quickly as he needed to without being seen. Unfortunately, traveling through the black lands sounded like a way to vanish and never be seen again. Was it a risk worth taking? Could he gamble his life on it? What about the lives of the twenty men who would be joining him?

Alex tried to think of what he would do if he were in Jabez's place, which was difficult because he wasn't sure how much Jabez knew about the black lands or about the sea elves. But Alex knew that Jabez was worried about his ability to retain control of Westland. He had wanted to keep Darthon and the southern kingdom out of the fight for as long as possible. Perhaps Jabez was moving sooner than he had planned to— perhaps something was forcing him to try to take control before he was really ready.

"The Brotherhood must be pushing him," Alex's O'Gash whispered.

Why? Alex asked, and then thought through the answers.

The Brotherhood took their time; they were patient. They had taken hundreds of years in their attempt to conquer Nezza. Had their failure in Nezza changed their plans here in Jarro? Did the Brotherhood have some deadline for taking control of all the known lands?

Questions that Alex couldn't possibly answer began to pile up in his mind until it was hard to think clearly about anything. Slowly he forced himself to clear his mind, to refocus on the one problem he had to solve immediately. How could he reach the castle of Conmar quickly? Traveling through the black lands was the fastest way, but was it the right thing to do?

After a short time, Alex let his mind empty and tried to sleep. The next few days would be busy ones, and he would need to be ready. He would find out soon enough if his decision to travel through the black lands was a good one or not.

CHAPTER EIGHTEEN
THE BLACK LANDS

Three days after his meeting with the sea elves, Alex headed south, leading a group of nineteen away from Valora. They would follow the edge of the mountains, trying to remain unseen by any of Jabez's spies that might be in the area.

Whalen and the men of Darthon's armies would be moving north the next day, but Alex wanted to leave while the weather was still clear. He was sad and worried when he said good-bye to Whalen, but knew that dividing their focus at this point might be the key to destroying Jabez and the evil he had unleashed.

"You will see Whalen again soon," Alex's O'Gash whispered, which made Alex feel better.

Alex and his small group had traveled for several miles before the sky darkened with storm clouds. Alex could smell the rain before it started to fall, and the sound of it dripping from the trees calmed his mind. The rain didn't care about the evil of Conmar, and it didn't care about the war in Westland. The seasons went on, unchanged, and that fact gave Alex hope.

In two or three days, if the rain cleared up, they would

reach the southernmost pass over the mountains. Alex had promised Whalen that if the way over the mountains was clear he would travel that way. But if snow blocked their way, then Alex would lead the group further south and through the black lands.

Alex didn't look back at the group he was leading, but his mind called up each of their faces, seventeen men whom Alex had chosen from the more than two hundred of Darthon's army who had volunteered. He had taken Navar's advice and had not let Lord Darthon order anyone to go with him, but the number of men willing to go had made things difficult for Alex. He had chosen just seventeen, and now he hoped that he had chosen well.

Alongside the men was Dogmar Longdrink, a dwarf who had also volunteered to go with Alex. Grimgold had reminded Alex that there were almost sure to be dwarves held captive in the dungeons of Conmar as well as men, and seeing the face of another dwarf would make any rescued dwarves more trusting and possibly more helpful as well.

The final member of the group was someone Alex had not wanted to bring along. Aliia, who was riding just behind him, had insisted on coming. Alex didn't like the idea at all, and Karill had begged Alex not to allow her to go. Aliia had insisted, however, and declared that if Alex wouldn't take her as part of the company then she would follow behind them on her own. Alex had tried to reason with her, and when that didn't work he had asked why she should come. Aliia would not give any reason why, she simply said that she would stay with the company wherever it might go.

Alex turned his thoughts from his fellow travelers and concentrated on the trail before him. Aliia rode up beside him.

"You are still set on this path?" she asked. She kept her hood up, not only to keep the rain away, but to hide her face from the other travelers.

"I am," Alex answered without looking at the sea elf. "It is not too late for you to turn back."

Aliia shook her head. "How far do you think we will travel today?"

"A few more miles before the sun sets," Alex said slowly, not really wanting to talk. "The sun will be down in an hour or two—we'll make camp before we lose the light."

"There is a small cave up ahead that might be a good place for camp," Aliia said.

Alex looked at her. "You've traveled this way before?"

Aliia smiled. "Though we live our lives on the sea, we have not forgotten the land we once loved."

"I know the black lands were once your home. I wish I could have seen them as they once were."

"I wish that too," Aliia said. "The black lands are a strange place, a place where you always feel that you are being watched."

"By the shadows?"

"And the lights that linger there."

Alex didn't ask any more questions. It was clear that Aliia had been close to the black lands. It was also clear that her people had seen things that were both frightening and painful to remember.

They continued to travel through the rain until the dim

light from the setting sun lit up the tops of the trees. Aliia motioned to Alex and led him away from the trail they had been
following. They moved into the woods, riding around a large
boulder. The boulder was much larger than it first appeared to
be, and behind it Alex found a deep cave with an overhang that
could be used as a shelter from the rain. The spot had been
used many times, and Alex was grateful that Aliia had guided
them here.

"We will rest here for the night," Alex said to his men. "We
are safe here from weather and any prying eyes that might be
looking for us."

Some of Alex's men settled onto the dry ground while others tended to the horses. Dogmar gathered kindling to start a
fire, mumbling to himself. Alex was glad there was enough real
wood in the cave that they could use for a fire. He didn't want
to use his magic; he needed to conserve his energy so he would
be ready for whatever lay ahead.

While Dogmar and two of the men fixed a meal for the
group, Aliia came to sit beside Alex.

"Were you able to learn what you needed to know about
darloch est messer?" she asked.

"I know more now than I did," Alex said. "But not everything I wish to know. I still do not know if it means 'master of
dragons' or 'destroyer of dragons.'"

"Is there a difference?" Aliia asked.

Alex nodded. "I believe there is, and I believe the difference might matter more than I might guess . . . I need to think
about it some more."

Aliia tucked her hands under her cloak. "I used to dream about dragons, you know."

"You did?" Alex asked.

"When I was young. I always dreamed the same dream about a dragon," Aliia went on, talking more to herself than to Alex. "I thought it meant that I would meet a dragon one day."

"A strange dream for an elf maid to have," Alex said.

"I still believe it, sometimes . . . at least a little." She looked at Alex. "Have you ever met a dragon?"

Alex thought about Slathbog the Red; Salinor, hidden on the Isle of Bones; and the golden dragon he'd seen in Darthon's mind. Lastly he thought of his own second true form as a true silver dragon, and he simply smiled and said, "I have."

Aliia sighed. "Then perhaps the dream of a little elf maid might come true."

As the group settled in for the night, Alex found a comfortable spot to lie down, then closed his eyes and tried to clear his thoughts. He didn't expect to run into any trouble, at least not yet, and as he listened to the sounds of men around him, Dogmar grumbling about having to sit next to Aliia, and the rain falling outside, Alex fell asleep.

It was near dawn when Alex woke, but the sky was darker than it had been the day before. The rain was still falling, but it was a colder rain than before, and it would probably turn to snow before the day was over. Alex put his blankets away and took a heavy cloak from his magic bag.

"Winter is closing in on us," Alex commented, wrapping his cloak around his shoulders.

"Winter comes early in Westland," Aliia answered. "We should eat and move on. If we move swiftly, we can reach the black lands before the weather becomes too cold."

Alex nodded his agreement and helped Dogmar gather wood to make a fire to cook their breakfast. Aliia remained hidden in her cloak, lost in her own thoughts. Alex looked at her from time to time, wondering what she might be thinking.

A few hours after breaking camp, the rain changed to wet and heavy snow. Though the winter storm made traveling difficult, Alex knew the bad weather would also make it harder for Jabez's spies to see them as they traveled.

He and his friends pushed forward through the snow and the growing cold without stopping. The sky grew thick with thunderclouds, and the wind blew harder as the day went on. In the early afternoon the storm grew so wild that it was difficult to make any headway. The ground was slick with mud and snow, and it had grown so dark that it was hard to tell which direction they were going. Alex thought about magically pushing the storm away, but decided against it. It would take some powerful magic to push this storm away, and so close to Conmar, Jabez was sure to notice.

An hour later, Dogmar rode up next to Alex. "We should try to find some shelter," he yelled over the wind.

"I doubt there's a dry spot to be found," Alex yelled back.

Dogmar nodded. "If you are thinking of crossing the mountain passes, we'll have to turn to the west soon."

Alex had promised Whalen that he would first try to use

the mountain pass, and for a moment he hesitated. "The storm is too bad, and there is too much snow," he finally said. "We'll never make it over the mountain pass."

Dogmar brushed snow from his beard. "We'll follow where you lead, Master Taylor. But are you sure you want to attempt crossing the black lands?"

Alex looked at Dogmar, then at Aliia, then at the other men who had volunteered to come with him. "We have no other choice," he said. "We have to save the hostages, and I must face Jabez. Otherwise Darthon's army—our friends—and all our hopes will fail."

Dogmar nodded and rode back to his place in line.

"You are a good leader," Aliia said. "The men trust you."

Alex squinted up at the endless storm. "I hope they still do once we enter the black lands."

There was no shelter on the trail, so they rode on into the night. When the storm finally ended it was almost dawn, and the horses and men were too tired to go much further.

"We are almost there," Aliia said. "Almost to the black lands."

Alex nodded his understanding, too exhausted to say anything. He simply followed Aliia's lead as she turned off the path.

"Careful," she said. "The way through the woods will be slippery after the rain and snow."

Alex followed Aliia into the woods. They rode for almost a mile before Aliia stopped at the bottom of what looked like a cliff. She got off her horse and stepped close to the rock wall. Alex dismounted and joined her.

Aliia spoke an elvin word and the rock face slid back, revealing the dark opening of a tunnel.

"A well-hidden door," Alex commented.

"And one that has not been opened in many years," Aliia said, a note of fear in her voice. "I wish we did not have to open it now."

"Will it lead us to the black lands?" Alex asked.

Aliia nodded. "The other end opens on the northern edge of the black lands. It is almost dawn. We can shelter here for now. Tomorrow night we will be in the black lands."

Alex nodded his understanding and helped to set up their camp. They all needed to rest, and he knew that traveling through this dark tunnel would be harder for them all than the storm of the previous night.

After a quick but warming meal, the men settled into their blankets to get some much needed sleep. Alex stood for a time, looking at the tunnel that would lead them to the black lands. The darkness was forbidding, but darkness was the last thing Alex was worried about. So much about the black lands was still unknown, and he wasn't sure that he could protect all of these men from the unknown dangers ahead of them.

"You should rest," Aliia said quietly as she stepped up beside him.

"How long will it take to pass through this tunnel?" Alex asked.

"Half a day," Aliia answered. "Or half a night. Rest now, you will need all your strength when we reach the black lands."

Alex turned to look at Aliia, giving her what he hoped was a reassuring smile. He walked away without speaking, finding a place to rest, leaning against the roots of an ancient tree. He let his body rest while his mind continued to spin with questions. Slowly his mind emptied of questions, and without really falling asleep, he rested.

From under his mostly closed eyelids, Alex watched the camp and the men who were trying to sleep. None of the men were sleeping well, and most would jerk awake from time to time, glancing at the dark opening they had to enter, and then rolling over to try to sleep once more. Only Dogmar appeared to be sleeping well, and Alex wasn't surprised. A dwarf would have no fear of traveling underground.

Alex also kept an eye on Aliia. She hid her fear well, but he could tell that she was terrified. For long periods of time she would stare at the dark tunnel, as if seeing what was waiting for them all at the far end. A slight shiver would shake her from head to toe, and then she would turn to look at Alex. It seemed, at least to Alex, that his presence there gave Aliia strength and the will to go forward. He wondered once more why she had insisted on making this journey, and once more he found no answer.

Late in the afternoon, Alex got up and put away his blankets. He didn't wake any of the others, but quietly started gathering wood for the fire. Aliia, being an elf and not needing to sleep, had kept the fire burning. She soon joined Alex, helping to gather wood without speaking, but Alex knew what she was thinking.

"Let them sleep a little longer, if they can," Alex said in a low voice. "This might be their last chance to rest for a few days."

It wasn't long before the men were up and moving around. A large hot meal was prepared, though the men didn't eat as much as they could have. When the meal was being cleared away, Alex stood to address the men.

"It is time," Alex said, looking at the faces around him. "We now must travel through darkness into the black lands. I must ask you all to search your hearts and decide if you will move forward with me, or turn back and ride with your people to war in the north. Once we pass through this magical doorway, it will close, and there will be no turning back for any of us. So if you have any doubts, if your hearts tell you to find another path, then I ask that you turn back now. No man will ever speak against any of you for the choice you make now, but for myself, I must go forward into darkness."

The men all nodded their understanding, but none of them spoke. After a few moments of silence, a man named Robert Thorson, who had been one of King Darthon's guards, stepped forward and spoke.

"We shall follow wherever you lead, and pay whatever price we must to save our people and our land from evil."

"Thank you," Alex said, bowing to the company. "Thank you all."

Aliia now moved forward toward the tunnel opening, but Alex stopped her by raising his arm.

"What is it?" she asked.

"I will go first. We don't know what dangers might be waiting in the darkness."

Alex summoned several weir lights and the small glowing orbs hovered around his head.

"What . . . what are these strange lights?" Aliia asked nervously.

"They are called weir lights," Alex answered, surprised by Aliia's reaction. "They will go where I command them to, and remain as long as I need them."

"Send them away," Aliia said, her voice shaking slightly. "They look too much like the lights here in the black lands. I would rather take my chances in the darkness than have these lights close by."

Alex nodded and didn't ask any questions. With a wave of his hand the weir lights vanished, and once again the two of them faced the pitch-black darkness of the tunnel.

"You must think me foolish, being afraid of your small lights," Aliia said after a moment.

"Not foolish," said Alex. "I think you are worried about what might lay ahead of us in the black lands."

"Perhaps we could light some torches," Aliia said several minutes later, the nervousness gone from her voice.

"I doubt we could find anything dry enough to burn," Alex said.

Alex knew what kinds of things lived in dark caves, and he didn't want to lead his men into unwanted trouble. For a few moments Alex stood looking into the darkness, thinking about what he could do.

His magic sword, Moon Slayer, glowed blue in the moonlight, but that glow wouldn't be bright enough to help him now. He could, of course, ignite the end of his staff into a brilliant light, but that would help only the men at the front of the company, leaving those at the back in darkness. This was an unexpected problem, and though it wouldn't end his adventure, it needed to be solved.

The horses behind him shuffled and stamped impatiently, waiting to move forward. They didn't like the cold or the wet any more than the men did. Alex looked over to where his horse was standing beside Aliia's horse.

"I have an idea," he said.

He approached his horse and held out his hand. The animal sniffed his fingers, and didn't move away. Alex ran his hand over the horse's nose and up toward the top of its head. He needed to make sure he didn't use too much magic, but a little bit would still go unnoticed by Jabez. Whispering a few words, he patted the horse's head, right between its eyes, and then slowly drew his hand up and away, pinching his fingers as he went, as if pulling on an unseen thread.

A thin, spiraled horn rose out of the horse's forehead that glowed with a clear, white light.

Aliia gasped.

"Don't worry," Alex said. "It is made of magic, and won't do the horse any harm. This will allow us to have light while we pass through the tunnel."

Once the horn was about a foot long, Alex stopped and said a few more words.

The horse tossed its head, but seemed unconcerned about the horn or the light coming from it.

"Good boy," Alex said, running his hand down the horse's neck and patting its shoulder. He moved from horse to horse, repeating the spell, until all twenty horses had glowing spiral horns rising from their foreheads.

"I have never seen . . ." Aliia started and stopped.

"Are there no unicorns here in Jarro?" Alex asked.

She shook her head. "Perhaps they exist in other lands, but not here. They are beautiful. How is it done?"

"Horses are brave and loyal creatures, and they have strong hearts. I simply asked them if they would share their inner light with us for a time." He remembered his first horse, Shahree, who had been killed in the Lost Mountains. Her name had meant "great heart," and she had been a true friend to him. He still missed her. "The horns should give us enough light to make our way through the tunnel safely."

Aliia looked at Alex and then bowed her head. "I knew you were a wizard, but I did not know you had such power."

"Sometimes the strongest magic comes from asking for help," Alex said, swinging into his saddle. He smiled down at Aliia and started into the tunnel, the light from his horse's new horn leading the way.

The group followed Alex into the tunnel, and when the magical door closed behind them, it made no sound. The tunnel was expertly made, and large enough for riders to pass through easily. There were a few twists and turns as the path descended into the mountains, but nothing more.

Time underground seemed to drag on and on, but the light from the horses helped the men keep their nerve. The fact that the air in the tunnel was fresh, and that there were no cobwebs or even dust to be seen surprised Alex, but he didn't say anything. After about four hours of riding, the tunnel began to slope upward, and before long the rock walls and ceiling of the tunnel vanished. They were now riding along a stone path that led them through a dense pine forest.

When they reached the edge of the forest, Alex stopped and looked up. The stars were shining above them, and a cold winter breeze blew across his face. Ahead of him, down a small hill, Alex got his first look at the black lands.

"We will stop here," Alex said. He turned to look at the men following him. "Prepare a light meal and rest a little if you can. Then we must go into the black lands."

The men dismounted and went to work building a fire and preparing a meal. Dogmar stretched his back and ran his hand down his beard. He looked out into the black lands, sniffed the air with an unhappy look on his face, and then turned to help with the meal.

Alex dismounted and ran his hand down his horse's forehead and rubbed his nose. The horn slowly vanished under his touch. "Thank you, my friend," he said.

His horse nickered softly in reply.

Alex did the same with all the other horses, removing the magical horns and thanking the animals for their help. When he was finished, he went to see what there was to eat, leaving his worries about what lay ahead of them at the back of his mind. Whatever dangers there were would come soon enough.

Aliia sat down beside him as they ate, and he smiled at her. Alex could sense her fear, and he was amazed by her willpower, a power that allowed her to move forward no matter what. He reached out and took her hand, giving it a gentle squeeze, hoping to let her know that everything would be alright. He wasn't really sure that everything would be alright, but he wanted to do something, anything, to help his friend.

The wind was blowing harder as they finished eating, but the sky remained clear. Alex wondered if another storm was coming, but it didn't really matter. Storm or no storm, the black lands were waiting for them.

"Onward, then," Alex said as he led his horse to the edge of the forest.

Aliia was already standing there with her horse, but she didn't move when Alex spoke. Alex looked back at the men following him, then back to Aliia, but she didn't move at all. It seemed as if she was frozen in place.

"What is it?" he asked.

Aliia pointed into the black lands. "The lights. Look at the lights."

Alex looked to where she was pointing and saw hundreds of lights winking off and on in the distance. They were small, like his weir lights, but even from where he was standing, Alex could feel their magical power.

Alex looked away from the lights, studying the land he and his friends would have to cross. At first, it seemed that everything was normal except for the strange lights, but he slowly began to see how not normal everything was. For the first time, Alex understood why the area they had to travel through was called "the black lands."

Shadows lay thick on the ground, somehow even darker than the night. No moonlight or starlight reflected off the ground or anything else, yet it seemed to Alex that the ground rippled like water was moving over it, or maybe just beneath it. It made him dizzy to look at it directly, so he looked at the lights again, but that wasn't much better.

The lights moved randomly, at different speeds and in different directions. Just when he thought he could see a pattern to their movements, the lights would shift or disappear unexpectedly. New lights, or perhaps the old ones, would suddenly appear in places where no lights had been, and for some reason Alex thought that they were searching for something.

"It's worse than I expected," Aliia said.

"What do you mean?" Alex asked.

"There are more lights than I thought there would be, and they are moving faster."

"Do you think they sense our presence?"

"I don't know," Aliia answered, sounding worried.

"We must cross," Alex said. "We have come too far, and we have no other choice."

"I know, but I am afraid."

The men had gathered around Alex and Aliia. The reflection of the lights danced in their eyes, and they swayed on their feet as if half asleep and still dreaming. A couple of the men shuffled forward, trying to move toward the lights.

"Stay back!" Alex ordered.

He pulled the men back toward the forest, away from the lights, afraid that his friends would suddenly rush forward. Speaking a few words, he put a spell of protection on the group, and then he turned his attention back to the lights.

They were beautiful to look at, and their power seemed to call out to him. Alex resisted the call. Standing perfectly still, he let his mind reach out toward the lights, searching for the source of the magic that created and controlled them. As he suspected, there was nothing there for his mind to find. Still, the lights seemed to call out to him.

He wasn't sure how long he stood there staring at the lights, searching with his magic, and thinking. He heard Aliia say something, but the words were distant and unclear. She spoke again, and slowly, her words made sense to him.

"Alex, come back to us. We need you."

He turned to look at the sea elf, surprised to see tears in her eyes. He blinked, and she smiled in relief.

"What happened?" Alex asked. "Why are you worried?"

"I thought we had lost you to the lights."

Alex shook his head. "No, I was trying to understand them, and the magic that makes them, but I am too far away. If I can get closer, I think . . ." He looked at his men. "Enough of this, we should leave. Now."

"The lights?" one man asked.

"I will deal with them if I must," Alex said.

The man shook his head. "I know I said I'd follow you, and I want to help rescue the hostages, but if we go down there, I don't think we'll make it out alive." A few other men muttered their agreement.

"Let's at least wait until dawn," Aliia said. "The lights are less powerful during the day."

"That's exactly why we must leave now," Alex said. "I sense something, and I'm not sure what. What I do know is that we must hurry, or something far worse than lights may find us."

"What?" Dogmar asked.

"I don't know," Alex admitted. "And I really don't want to

find out if I can help it. We've all come too far to turn back now. To remain here means death, or worse. Forward is the only choice we have."

The strange lights continued to move in the distance, and Alex climbed on his horse and started toward them. The others followed without a word.

He knew it was risky to approach the lights in the middle of the night when they were at their strongest, but it was also when they were most visible. He hoped it would be easier to avoid the lights if he could see where they were rather than trying to weave his way through them during the day, when the sunlight would render them all but invisible.

As they rode forward, Alex motioned for Dogmar to ride up beside him. The dwarf came forward with a puzzled look on his face, but didn't ask any questions.

"I have a favor to ask of you," Alex said quietly, in dwarfish.

"You need only ask," Dogmar answered.

"We haven't known each other long," Alex went on. "I can see, however, that you are a dwarf to be trusted in all things. I do not ask this lightly, and I know your feelings about the elves, but . . ."

"But?" Dogmar prodded.

"I want you to promise me that you will stay close to Lady Aliia," Alex said. "I want you to stay close and to keep her safe, no matter what happens."

"You fear something?" Dogmar asked. "You fear that you cannot keep her safe?"

"Nothing I can name," Alex answered slowly. "I just feel

that she should have some extra protection, perhaps even protection from herself."

Dogmar looked troubled as he ran his hand down his beard, but then his eyes brightened and a slight smile crossed his lips.

"Because you ask this as a friend, and do not command me as leader or wizard, I will promise to stay close to Lady Aliia and keep her safe," Dogmar answered. "I will keep this promise until you and only you—or death—release me from it."

"Thank you," Alex said, smiling at Dogmar. "And let us hope that death has nothing to say in this matter."

Dogmar gave a grunting laugh, and then returned to his place behind Alex.

As they moved forward, the disorientation Alex had felt on the hilltop returned, stronger now that they were actually in the black lands. The ground rolled and pitched like the deck of a ship in a storm, and the lights moved faster as Alex and the others moved closer to them. Alex thought that he could just hear the hum and buzz of them as they whizzed past.

"Stay close," he ordered his men. "And stay alert. Don't touch the lights, and don't let them touch you. If you see one coming close, get out of its way."

"Should we draw our weapons?" one of the men asked.

Alex looked at Aliia, who shook her head slightly.

"No," Alex answered. "We don't know how the lights will react to sword or steel. Perhaps if we approach carefully, the lights will let us pass."

Alex took a deep breath and urged his horse forward. The path was dirt now, not the well-made stone it had been on the hilltop. It didn't take Alex long to realize that the rippling was just an illusion, a trick of the eye caused by the shadows that the lights created. He moved forward with more confidence, but still cautious of the lights.

Alex tried to stay calm, hoping that the lights would leave them alone if they moved slowly and with care. Almost immediately, however, a swarm of lights came rushing in their direction.

"Watch out!" Alex yelled, ducking as the lights darted over his head.

The men closed ranks, changing from one or two riders following in a line behind Alex to a close group. Alex wasn't sure which was the better approach. Single-file might make it easier to avoid the lights, but riding together meant they could try to protect each other.

More lights flashed and swooped toward the group. A man screamed and nearly fell off his horse trying to get out of the way.

"Steady!" Alex called. "Keep moving forward."

The air seemed to hum around them, and the darkness had a weight to it. The lights continued to buzz and flicker, but Alex noticed that more and more of them were clustering around Aliia than any of the others. It looked as if the men at the back of the group were traveling without any lights bothering them at all.

Alex frowned. Aliia was a sea elf. The lights must be able to sense her, and for whatever reason they were drawn to her.

Aliia crouched low over her horse's neck, trying to keep track of the lights flashing above her, but there were too many.

Her horse stamped and quivered, and Dogmar moved to the outside of the group in an attempt to shield her. Alex was afraid that some of the horses might bolt, scattering the company across the black lands.

"Quickly, surround Lady Aliia," Alex shouted. "We must protect her. The lights are targeting her more than the rest of us. If we surround her, they might leave the rest of us alone."

The men obeyed, drawing their horses into a tight circle with Aliia in the center. She was still terrified, but at least the lights were no longer appearing right over her head.

Alex could still hear the hum of the lights as they dove and spun around the company. He thought he could hear words in the darkness, but if so, he couldn't understand what they were saying.

"Keep moving forward," Alex ordered.

"We'll never make it," one of the men shouted.

"Yes, we will," Alex shouted back. "Just stay together, and keep moving."

The horses snorted in fear, and the circular formation began to break apart as the men on the outside of the ring had to move in order to dodge the swooping lights.

"Hold steady!" Alex called.

One ball of light, larger than the others, suddenly appeared right in front of one of the horses. The animal reared back, and the man on its back fell off, landing on the ground with a loud and painful-sounding thud.

As soon as he hit the ground, the man was surrounded by lights, some large, some small, but all of them flickering madly and swooping closer and closer to him.

Alex spun his horse around, rushing forward to help, but he was too late. He bent low in his saddle, reaching out to pull the man to his feet, but before he could help the man, one of the balls of light struck the man's chest.

An inhuman scream ripped through the darkness, and something darker than the shadows around them spread like oil across the man's body. The blackness grew, swallowing the man slowly, bit by bit.

Alex watched in horror as the darkness covered the man, and he simply vanished into the night. All that was left were the echoes of his scream, and a ball of light that suddenly winked out.

"Alex?" Aliia whispered. "What happened? What should we do?"

Alex looked around at the swirling lights. "Close formation," he ordered. "Get as close to each other as you can."

The remaining men obeyed without question, though Alex could see how afraid they were.

Alex joined the group, his horse pressed up against the others. He stood up in his stirrups and reached his hand into the air. A half a dozen balls of light immediately flew toward his hand, as if it were a beacon of some kind.

"Alex, no!" Aliia screamed.

Alex gathered his magic and lifted his staff into the air. A ring of silver light expanded from the head of his staff, expanding outward to cover the company. When it had grown large enough to cover the entire group, the edges of it dropped downward to the ground. Alex had enclosed the company in a shimmering dome of light, a dome that he hoped would protect them.

The balls of light hit the dome softly at first, like a gentle rain, but they could not break through. Not being able to get through the dome seemed to anger the lights, and soon they were crashing wildly into the silver dome, perhaps trying to break it, but the dome held firm.

Alex sat back down in his saddle and rubbed his eyes with his hand. He had not wanted to use so much magic, but he didn't have a choice. If Jabez was watching the black lands, he would almost certainly have noticed, but Alex had to protect the men who had chosen to follow him.

"What . . . what have you done?" Aliia asked.

"The lights!" one of the men said. "The lights touched Dongul and he disappeared."

Alex nodded. "I am sorry for that, but we're safe, at least for now."

"How long will the dome hold?" the man asked nervously.

"As long as I wish it to," Alex answered. "But it can't travel with us. It's fixed in this one place."

"So we either stay here, safe and protected but unable to move, or we take our chances with the lights?" Dogmar commented, shaking his head. "I don't much like either of those options."

"There is a third option," Alex said. He looked through the dome at the lights. They were gathering into larger and larger groups, and to Alex it looked like they were starting to take a more solid shape.

"No, Alex, you can't go out there," Aliia said, suddenly seeing what Alex saw. "It's . . . it's far too dangerous. You can't . . ."

"I have to," Alex said calmly. "We can't stay here, and we can't move forward. Maybe I can drive them away, or maybe I can strike some deal with them."

Alex dismounted and patted his horse's neck. He turned to face the curve of the dome and took a deep breath. He tried to remember everything Navar had told him about the dark elves, the shadows they created, and the lights of the black lands. It wasn't much, but it was all he had. Navar had thought that the lights were either the magic of the shadows the dark elves had created, or they were the lost souls of those who were somehow tied to this place. Now that he had seen the lights for himself, Alex wondered if both stories might hold some truth.

"It will be alright," Alex said. "Stay inside the dome. Don't try to follow me."

He put his palm against the inside of the dome, which felt as solid as glass but as soft as water, and pushed. The silver light bulged outward, and Alex stepped forward. Walking through the wall of light was like walking through ice-cold water, but after the first few steps he was outside the dome, alone in the black lands with the lights.

The humming noise had grown louder, and the whispers he had heard before sounded more like words than before. Alex still couldn't understand what the words were, but he knew they were words, ancient words that had long been forgotten.

Moving forward, away from the dome, he called into the darkness. "I am Alexander Taylor, wizard and warrior. I ask for safe passage through this land for myself and my friends."

If the lights heard him or understood what he said, they gave no sign. The largest group of lights had gathered together into a shape about as tall and as wide as a man, and that figure floated closer to Alex.

"We seek to destroy a great evil beyond these lands," Alex continued.

The figure was close enough to touch Alex, but it paused. The shape remained in place, hanging in the air. The outline of the figure was all light, but the inside was all dark, darker than the blackest night Alex had ever seen.

The whispered words that had been teasing Alex finally formed into a word that he recognized. "Evil?"

"Yes," Alex said.

"Show us," the figure hissed.

Alex felt the pull of magic against his mind, and he was moving toward the lights before he knew it. He heard Aliia screaming behind him, but it didn't matter. All Alex knew was he had to communicate with this figure of light and darkness if he or any of his company were going to survive. Slowly, Alex stretched his hand out to touch the darkness.

The man-shaped figure reached out as well, and the two hands met. Alex felt a cold chill run up his arm, and there was a moment of total silence. The lights stopped moving and flickering. He felt magic all around him, and Alex suddenly realized that he now he could see what stood in the darkness surrounded by light.

Navar had said that the light of the sun had twisted the shadows into monsters, and Alex wasn't sure what else he could call the creature that stood in front of him.

This shadowy figure was as tall as an elf, but its skin was a mottled-gray and slightly yellow-green in color. Where eyes, nose, and mouth should have been were pits of swirling darkness, and the long fingers of the creature were twisted and curled like claws.

A sudden and unreasoning fear took hold of Alex, and he reached for his sword, Moon Slayer. He tried with all his strength to pull his magic sword from its sheath, but the sword wouldn't move. Moon Slayer was a powerful sword, forged long ago by dark elves. With his fear melting away, Alex suddenly wondered if the sword knew that these creatures had been created by the dark elves, and was now refusing to be part of the pain its creators had caused.

"You cannot destroy us," the creature said. "Not at this time."

Alex let go his sword and faced the creature that stood in front of him.

"Show us this evil you fight," the creature whispered. It stepped closer and touched Alex on the forehead.

The magic engulfed him once more, and in his mind, everything he knew about Jabez, the Axe of Sundering, and the war coming to Westland rushed by. It felt like one jumbled mess, but somehow he knew the creature understood everything as well as he did himself. The pressure on his forehead increased, and suddenly everything he knew or suspected about the Brotherhood also flooded into his mind.

The creature of shadow paused, and then Alex heard a sizzling sound, like cold water hitting a hot pan, and he was thrown backward. He hit the wall of the dome and slid to the ground. He groaned at the impact and pressed his hands to his head. His entire body ached, but his head most of all.

Under the light of the dome, Alex could see the terrified look on Aliia's face. It was clear that she didn't know what to do, and at the same time she desperately wanted to do something, anything to help. Her eyes searched Alex's face, begging for some explanation of what had just happened.

He wished he could explain, but he wasn't really sure what had happened.

"We grant you safe passage, Alexander Taylor, wizard and warrior," the creature hissed.

"I thank you—" Alex started to say, but the creature cut him off.

"For a price," the creature went on.

Alex got to his feet and brushed himself off. "What price do you ask?"

The creature pointed a clawed finger at Alex's heart, and then moved past him to point at Aliia.

Aliia's face went white with fear and she shook her head. Dogmar moved in front of her, pushing her away from the dome's edge. The look on the dwarf's face was easy to read: "You'll have to go through me first."

Alex moved to stand between the creature and the dome. "I cannot pay that price."

"She is a sea elf. We can smell her. She must come with us." The black pits swirled faster in the creature's empty eyes.

"No," Alex said firmly.

"She is one of those who created us, who twisted us and

left us here to suffer through the ages. She is a sea elf. She must pay the price."

"It was not her doing. She is innocent."

"All are guilty!" the creature roared. "All must be destroyed!"

"No," Alex said again, his temper and his voice rising. "I warn you, if you ask this again, it will be *you and the other shadows that are destroyed*." He recognized the heat building in his chest as the power of the dragon, and he felt his skin hardening as it had when he'd fought the wolf creatures in Midland. He knew that if he unleashed his power now, it would scour the black lands clean. He couldn't do that, not now, or Jabez would be sure to flee. He didn't want to destroy these shadows of the dark elves, because he felt pity for them. He remembered Whalen's words about how they hadn't had a choice in what they had become. He thought about how long these creatures had suffered, never able to find an end. There had to be another way. He calmed himself, and out of habit his hand rested on Moon Slayer's hilt. Suddenly, he knew what he had to do and say.

As if the sword knew what he was thinking, the blade slid out of its sheath, free now when before it had been stuck.

Alex let the point of the sword drop to the ground in a gesture of peace. "I will give you this sword," he said, "to hold in good faith while we cross the black lands."

The creature seemed to take a step back as it looked at the blade, and the runes written in the language of the dark elves shone in the darkness as if they were made of white fire.

"We know of this blade and its power," the shadow hissed.

"Then you know that I will return to claim it, once I have defeated the evil that is spreading across Jarro and the other known lands."

The creature hesitated.

"You have seen my thoughts. You know that I believe the Brotherhood is working to keep you trapped here, in this half-life. If I am free to destroy the evil in Jarro, I will also strike a blow against the Brotherhood. And when the Brotherhood falls, you and your kind will be free."

"Free?" the creature whispered.

"To become what you once were, to find a lasting peace."

The lights pulsed around the figure, as if the creature was thinking. "And the sea elf?" it asked.

"She travels with me. Unharmed."

"And if you fail?"

"Then *I* will return in his stead," Aliia's voice said softly from just behind Alex. "And I will pay whatever price you name."

He turned in surprise. Aliia had somehow passed through the wall of the dome. Behind her, locked inside the dome, Dogmar was trying madly to follow her. Aliia pulled her cloak tightly around her shoulders, but her back was straight as she faced the shadow.

Alex was impressed by her courage, and her offer. "Are you sure?" he asked in a low voice.

She nodded once. "I know you will not fail, Alex," she answered in an equally low voice.

The creature reached out, taking Moon Slayer from Alex's hand. "We accept your offer," it said. "We will guard Moon

Slayer until such time as one or the other of you returns to claim it."

"And we are granted safe passage through the black lands," Alex said.

The creature bowed its head. "Agreed."

"I thank you, then," Alex said, bowing slightly.

The creature of light and shadow flashed once more, more brilliantly than the sun, and then winked out. One by one, all of the lights winked out until finally Alex and Aliia stood alone in the darkness while the rest of the company remained inside Alex's silver dome.

Aliia turned to Alex. "I feared for a moment that all hope was lost."

"No, hope is never lost," Alex said. "It can seem far away sometimes, but there is always hope."

"When you touched the lights . . ." Aliia started and then paused, her voice shaking with fear and wonder. "You . . . you touched the lights and did not lose yourself in them. How is that possible?"

Alex didn't know how to answer except to tell Aliia the truth, the whole truth.

"I was not lost because I am not just anyone."

"You are a wizard, a dragon lord," Aliia said before Alex could finish.

"I am both of those things and more," Alex said, taking a deep breath. "I am also a dragon, and it seems that your dreams have come true."

CHAPTER NINETEEN

THE CASTLE OF CONMAR

For seven more days Alex and his companions rode across the black lands, but they never saw any sign of the shadow creatures or the strange lights. Though they all continued to feel that they were being watched, their fear had mostly vanished. The weather continued to be unpredictable; one day it would rain, the next day snow, and then sunshine and warm breezes the day after that.

Their traveling was easy enough as the road was a good one. This left Alex with time to think, and his mind was full with worries about Whalen and Darthon's army. How far had they gotten on the road to war? Had they run into trouble? Did Jabez already know they were marching to attack his armies? Who was Jabez watching and where would he strike next? Were they all too late to help? Was he already too late to stop Jabez?

Aliia rode next to Alex as they moved north, and Dogmar always rode just behind her. After Alex had told Aliia that he was a dragon, he had sworn her to secrecy. It was not something he wanted just anyone to know. She asked a few questions when they were alone, but when Alex was reluctant to talk about it she let the matter drop. She stopped asking questions, but Alex noticed that she would watch him, turning away whenever he looked at her, smiling slightly to herself.

Once they had left the black lands behind them, Alex knew it would take another ten days or two weeks to reach the castle of Conmar. He wished they could travel faster, but he was already pushing the group as fast as they could manage. Every night when they stopped, the men were a little slower to make camp, and a little slower to prepare their evening meal.

As they moved closer and closer to Conmar, Alex started to hope that the stormy weather would return. The bright sunlight was nice, but it made the company far too visible as they moved across the grasslands. Alex tried to keep them hidden, moving behind hills and the few small clusters of trees that dotted the land, but he knew that anyone watching the lands would soon spot them.

Late one afternoon Alex called a halt. Something had caught his attention, but he wasn't sure what it was. He knew they needed to be careful so close to Conmar, and he wanted to take a good look at the area before moving forward. He climbed off his horse, told everyone else to stay where they were and rest if they could, and then moved ahead on foot by himself.

He climbed the hill to the left of the group, and found a spot between two boulders that allowed him to look north and west. His eyes searched the land, but there was nothing to see. The grasslands appeared to be empty, but Alex knew they were not. Jabez would have spies, maybe even guards posted to watch these lands so close to his home.

Alex shifted slightly and looked toward the north once more. There were no buildings to be seen, no smoke rising from fires, and no roads breaking the rugged landscape. None of that was as troubling as the fact that there were also no animals to be seen, and no birds to be heard. The land was empty, but Alex wasn't sure why it was so empty.

A movement to the north caught his eye. It was distant and unclear at first, and it continued to move. Whatever it was, Alex noticed that the sunlight was flashing randomly off of the moving object.

He sat stone still and watched. The hills to the north suddenly came alive, but what Alex saw didn't encourage him. An army was on the move, climbing up the low hills and making their way to the mountains. It was clear that they were moving toward one of the high mountain passes, which they were apparently hoping to cross even with the snow that had already fallen. The elves and men of Darthon's army would be hard pressed if this army found its way over the mountains.

Alex sat watching as the army passed, wondering what he should—or could—do. The most important thing was to destroy Jabez, but he thought there must be something more he could do for his friends. As the last of the army vanished into the hills, Alex made up his mind. His thoughts changed as he made himself think more like a dragon, and as the dragon inside of him woke, he worked his magic. The magic was powerful, but he was acting as a dragon would, and he believed that this magic would go unnoticed by Jabez.

He waited and watched for a few more minutes to make sure that Jabez's army had all gone by. Then he set his magic loose, summoning a massive storm from the west. When Alex started back down the hill, the wind was already picking up, and clouds were gathering in the west. The storm he had summoned would begin that night, but it wouldn't reach its full power for a day or two. Alex guessed that Jabez's army would be high up in the mountains when the full force of his storm hit them. By then it would be too late for the army to retreat, and impossible for them to move forward. They would be trapped.

Alex led the company into the growing darkness, moving slowly from shadow to shadow. The castle of Conmar was only a day or so away. He was sure of that, and he didn't want to be seen now that he was so close. Jabez's attention would be on the east where his war was raging. He would be hoping for a quick victory, but also troubled by Whalen's sudden appearance.

The feeling had come to Alex about a week ago as he was riding through the rain. At the time he hadn't really noticed it, but as the feeling grew he realized what it was. Whalen had used his magic, breaking the spell of hiding that Alex had put on him. Jabez would know exactly where Whalen was, and possibly what he was up to. What troubled Alex was that Whalen had used his magic so soon, and that there was nothing he could do to help the ancient wizard.

They made camp for the night several hours after darkness fell. Alex let the company sleep for as long as he could, but they were on their way again before dawn. As they rode, he worked to keep his mind focused, holding off the excitement and worries that were growing inside of him. The storm he had summoned had grown stronger, and was already pressing against the mountains. The dark clouds and rain left the land in a twilight gray, and it was hard to see very far in any direction.

Slowly, Alex and his men worked their way up one more hill, but Alex motioned for the men to stop before they reached the top of the hill. He continued forward until he could see just over the hill, and then he stopped as well. To the north, across a wide valley and up an ancient looking hill, stood the castle of Conmar.

The castle was built to overlook the surrounding country, but while the hill gently sloped downward from the front, the back of the castle stood at the top of a cliff that dropped into the sea.

Jabez had been careful in choosing his home. There were dozens of tents and wooden shacks set up around the castle, and groups of guards were making their way around the castle walls. As he watched, Alex saw that the guards on the ground weren't the only guards Jabez had. Several large winged creatures were flying around the towers of the castle, but it was almost impossible to see what they were in the rain. Finally, after several minutes of watching, one of the winged creatures flew far enough away from the castle for Alex to see it clearly.

"Gargoyles," Alex whispered.

He counted at least a dozen of the stone monsters circling around the castle. This was going to be more difficult than he had thought. Even though he had never seen one before, Alex knew about gargoyles and just how dangerous an enemy they could be.

Slipping back down the southern side of the hill, Alex led the company west toward the sea.

"What is our plan, Alex?" Dogmar asked.

"The castle is well guarded," Alex said. "I don't see a way of getting close without being seen."

"Then how do we get in?" Dogmar asked.

"I'd like to take a closer look at the cliffs at the back of the castle," Alex said thoughtfully.

"The cliffs?" Dogmar shook his head. "Dwarfs are not known for climbing, and we don't have the tools or the time to tunnel our way in."

Alex smiled. "We won't be tunneling. First let's find a safe place to set up camp. Once that's taken care of, I'll slip away and have a look at the cliffs."

"I don't like it, but we have to find a way in," Dogmar said, mostly to himself. "I hope there is a way—apart from assaulting the main gate, that is."

When night fell, Alex slipped away and walked carefully toward the beach. He was careful to watch for any guards, but it seemed Jabez wasn't worried about the beach. Alex did keep an eye open for gargoyles. He wasn't sure how good their eyesight was, but it wouldn't do to be spotted now. When he finally reached the base of the cliff, Alex looked up, trying to see if there were any cracks or openings that might allow him to get into the castle.

High above him, maybe two hundred feet up, he could see a stream of water that looked like it was coming out of the cliff face. The storm was still growing, but it wasn't raining hard enough to create the stream that was falling from the cliff. Where was the water coming from? Alex guessed that this was a drain for the castle, and if he was right, he and his company might be able to slip into the castle without being noticed.

Checking to make sure he was alone, Alex quickly changed into a small bird. Flying was difficult, as the winds from the storm pounded against the cliff face. When he finally reached the source of the water he found an opening. The opening was roughly carved, but it was large enough for a man to walk through, and it appeared to stretch deeper under the castle.

The only problem was that the opening was covered with bars. As a small bird, Alex could dart between the bars easily, but no one else could. He thought about it, and then he flew between the bars and into the tunnel, transforming back to his human form. As soon as he changed he noticed the terrible smell. The tunnel wasn't so much a simple drain—it was the outlet for the castle's sewer system.

Alex tried not to breathe too deeply as he looked around. There was plenty of room, and Alex moved forward a short way, hoping that this tunnel would lead him to the dungeons and the hostages.

Alex didn't have to go far before he found what he was looking for. He had summoned a dim weir light to guide him, and sixty feet or so into the tunnel he found an ancient stone door. The door was cut a few inches above the floor so water and other debris could pass under it. Pushing against the door, Alex found that it was locked from the other side. He reached out with his magic, and finding nothing and no one on the other side of the door, he let that same magic unlock the door. The ancient hinges creaked loudly as he pushed the door open. Alex waited for several minutes to make sure that the noise had not been heard. When he was satisfied, he stepped through the door and closed it behind him.

It was almost too quiet, and the sudden lack of noise made Alex nervous. His ears strained to hear any sound, but the only noise was the dripping of water. Slowly he moved forward, and soon the tunnel walls ended and he found himself in a large, mostly open space.

He had been right: the tunnel did lead to the dungeons. Ten cells that he could see in the dim light lined each side of the room. Looking closer, he found that one hostage was sleeping inside each cell. In the cell closest to him on the left he saw his friend Joshua. He took a step toward the cell door, intending to open it and save Joshua while he had the chance, but the sudden sound of approaching footsteps stopped him.

The guards were coming back. Alex wanted to stay and rescue the hostages, but this wasn't the time. He knew that if he saved Joshua and the others now, Jabez would know about it. He wouldn't have time to find the Axe of Sundering, and his real quest at Conmar Castle would fail. He needed his men to take care of the hostages while he dealt with Jabez.

Alex didn't like it, but he knew he had to wait. He gave Joshua a last look, and then hurried back through the stone door and magically locked it from the outside.

Alex returned to the bars, and without thinking he reached for Moon Slayer. Not finding the sword at his side, he remembered he had given it to the shadows in the black lands. Instead, he pulled out his dagger. Mr. Blackburn had said the steel was some of the strongest he'd ever made. It was time to see if that was true.

Alex had put his own magic into this blade, and it wasn't long before the blade found a groove and began to cut. He cut through the bars, creating an opening large enough for a person to crawl through. He left the last two bars, one on either side, standing. Reaching into his magic bag, he pulled out several lengths of rope. Tying one end to one of the remaining bars, he tossed the other end of the first rope out and down the cliff face. It was long enough to reach the ground. He did the same with a second rope, attaching it to the opposite bar.

After double-checking his work, Alex looked out of the cave's opening. The storm was growing stronger by the minute; he could see lightning not too far away. Climbing the cliff at night and in a storm would be dangerous, but it was the best plan he had. He took a moment to look around, and from this high vantage point, he could see a handful of boats on the beach to the north. It gave him an idea.

He transformed into a bird again and flew most of the way back to camp before returning to his own form.

"What did you find, Alex?" Dogmar asked as soon as he saw Alex.

"A way in," Alex answered.

He called the company together, and magically ignited a small and oddly dim fire. The magical fire was very warm, but Alex knew that it could not be seen by anyone that was more than twenty feet away.

"There is an opening in the cliff face. It will be hard and dangerous to climb to, but it will lead us directly to the hostages," Alex said, when the others had settled around him.

"Did you see the hostages? Are they alive?" Aliia asked.

"Yes, I saw some of them, and yes, they are alive," Alex

answered. "But if we are going to rescue them, it has to be to-night, while the storm lasts."

"At night?" one of the men said. "In this storm?"

"I hope the storm and the darkness will work in our favor." Alex picked up a stick and drew an outline of the castle in the dirt. "We must make our climb at night so the guards won't see us. While Jabez may not be worried about an attack from the sea, his guard still patrols the walls on that side of the castle. We will be harder to see at night and under the cover of a storm."

"And how are we supposed to climb the cliffs?" Dogmar asked.

"I left climbing ropes for us to use. That should help."

Dogmar looked relieved and nodded his head.

Alex looked around the circle at his men. "Not everyone is coming into the castle."

"Why not?" asked Aliia.

He smiled at her. "Because some of them will be helping you."

"Me? What do you need me to do?"

"We need to get the hostages to safety as soon as possible. They have been held prisoner for some time, and they look weak. They won't make it far without our help. I saw some boats on the beach north of where we'll climb. Aliia, I need you and most of the men to take those boats. The rest of us will get the hostages out of the dungeon and into the boats, then you can all sail swiftly to the south."

"And you?" she asked.

Alex shook his head. "You know that I must confront Jabez—and I must do it alone."

"A wizards' battle is no place for dwarf or man," Dogmar said grumpily. "Still, if a few of us went with you, it might help the odds."

"Thank you, my friend, but the odds are what they are," Alex replied. "Besides, I need you all to rescue the hostages. They need your help more than I will."

Dogmar ran his hand down his beard, an unhappy look on his face. After a minute he reluctantly nodded his agreement.

Alex looked up at the sky. "We have a few hours before we need to go. I suggest everyone try to rest. We have much to do before the night is over."

———•••———

Alex didn't sleep, but he let his body rest while his mind continued to work. The wind had picked up, and the trees around them creaked and groaned. He was trying to picture what the inside of the castle would look like. Where would Jabez be? Where was the golden dragon he'd promised to save? Where was the Axe of Sundering hidden?

When it was time, Alex woke the others. They made their way down to the beach following the path Alex had taken earlier. Alex chose six men along with Dogmar to help him rescue the hostages. The rest went with Aliia to help her take the boats.

"We won't have much time," he warned everyone. "Once the hostages make it to the beach, they'll need to get into the boats as fast as they can. Can you help them, Aliia?"

Aliia nodded. "On the water my magic is stronger than on

land. The boats will be ready, and I will care for the hostages. I promise."

Alex gave her a nod of understanding and a quick smile.

The ropes Alex had left earlier were still in place, and he pulled on the end of one of them, testing it. The rope held firm, and he noted that the rope, now wet, was easier to grip than when it had been dry. He started climbing, one of his men holding the end of the rope to keep it tight. Dogmar pushed his way forward and started up the second rope.

It was hard to see in the darkness, and the rain lashed at the cliff, making the rocks slippery. Alex kept climbing, pausing now and then to wipe the rain out of his eyes. Thunder rumbled behind him, and lightning flashed, throwing light onto the cliffs.

Alex was about halfway to the stone tunnel when he heard a different kind of rumbling. It was lower than the thunder, and more rhythmic. The wind against his back felt closer and more directed than the gusts he'd been fighting. He wondered what was happening and turned to look over his shoulder when a giant stone claw punched into the cliff wall right next to him.

The gargoyle screeched and pulled its claw back, taking a chunk of rock from the wall with it. The man climbing the rope below Alex shouted in fear. The gargoyle swooped close once more, and Alex felt the rope slide in his hands. Alex tightened his grip, and watched every move the gargoyle made.

Another gargoyle appeared out of the darkness, and then a third. Their shrieks sounded like rocks being split apart, and the beat of their wings was deafening. The gargoyles flew closer and closer to Alex and the men on the ropes. They repeatedly hit the cliff with their claws, knocking stones down onto Alex and the others. It was only a matter of time before a gargoyle would try to pluck one of them off the rope.

Alex didn't have many options. He couldn't draw a sword because he had to keep both hands on the rope, and what good would a sword do? His staff was safely stored in his magic bag, and there was no time to retrieve it, and hanging on the rope he couldn't use it anyway.

"What do we do?" the man below Alex shouted.

"Hold on," Alex shouted. "All of you, hold on." He climbed up a few feet and found a place to brace himself against the cliff. He looked at the black storm clouds filled with lightning and rain. He had to use magic, but he had to be careful as well. He forced himself to think like a dragon, knowing it would shield his magic from Jabez. He reached out to the storm with his magic, summoning the power that was already there.

"Close your eyes!" he shouted. "Look away!"

He didn't have time to see if the men obeyed him or not. A lightning bolt ripped through the darkness, slamming into the gargoyle closest to him. An explosion of stone hit the cliff where the monster had been, showering down on Alex and the others like broken glass.

The two remaining gargoyles moved backwards, away from the cliff. They hovered in the air for a moment, unsure about what had just happened.

A second bolt of lightning came racing out of the clouds, and again Alex used his magic to direct it. This time the flash of light was as bright as the sun and the explosion was deafening. A second gargoyle was gone, leaving nothing but falling stone where it had been. The third gargoyle now realized that it was in danger, that the storm might destroy it as it had its two companions.

The last gargoyle moved away, flying higher against the wind, hoping to reach the safety of the castle. Alex couldn't let the monster escape—his plans would be ruined if it reported what it had seen and what had happened to the others. As the gargoyle moved away it was harder for Alex to see, harder for him to hit with a lightning bolt, but he had to stop it.

Focusing all his thought, Alex called down a third bolt of lightning, but this one was different. Half a dozen threads of lightning reached down from the clouds, like blue-white fingers searching for something. As the gargoyle raced to the castle wall the fingers found what they were searching for. The threads of light closed around the monster, the crackling of raw energy filled the air, and a sudden explosion shook the cliff where Alex was hanging.

Alex looked down and counted his men. They were all there. No one had been taken by a gargoyle or lost to the storm. He let out a sigh of relief.

The climb was a difficult one, but everyone made it. Once they were all inside the tunnel, Alex led the way to the stone door that would let them into the dungeons. Pushing the door open, Alex led the group quietly up the tunnel and to the dungeon. Alex peeked out of the tunnel to see if any guards were in the room. There were two guards, men, playing cards at a table by the far wall. Alex gathered a thread of his magic and quietly whispered "Sleep" in their direction.

After a moment, the first guard yawned and laid down his cards. The second guard rubbed his eyes.

Alex added a little more magic to his spell, and spoke again. "Sleep."

This time, both guards slumped in their chairs, their heads falling backward. One guard started to snore softly.

Alex moved out of the tunnel and into the dungeon, his men close behind. He moved quietly to the sleeping guards and unhooked the key ring from the first guard's belt.

He didn't need the keys to open the cells, but once he had them he went to Joshua's cell and unlocked it first. The gate swung open with a loud squeak, but the sleeping guards didn't move.

Alex gave the keyring to Dogmar. "Unlock the others."

The dwarf did as he was told, and Alex entered Joshua's cell.

"Joshua," he said softly.

Joshua was asleep on a low dirty cot, his face turned to the wall. Alex touched his friend's shoulder to wake him up. Joshua flinched at the contact, and rolled over to face Alex. His face was dirty and looked much thinner than it had before. His eyes were red and bloodshot, and he had grown a beard since the last time Alex had seen him.

"Alex?" he whispered, his voice cracking from disuse. "How did you get here?"

"It's a long story," Alex said. "And one best saved for another time. Hurry. My friends and I are here to rescue you."

Joshua tried to push himself up from the cot, but only made it partway. Alex had to catch him before he fell back on the bed. "I don't know what's wrong with me," he said.

"Don't try to speak," Alex said. "Save your strength. You'll need it for the climb down to the beach."

"No," Joshua said, clutching at Alex's arm. "No, this is important. Jabez—"

"He doesn't know we are here." Alex helped Joshua stand up, but his friend swayed on his feet. His skin felt cold to the touch.

"Jabez did something to me," Joshua said as if Alex hadn't spoken.

Alex frowned. "What did he do?"

"He kept asking me to tell him about someone named Whalen. I told him I didn't know anyone of that name, but he wouldn't believe me. He asked me again and again, he wanted to know what plans this Whalen person was making. He did things to me—he was inside my mind."

"It doesn't matter now, that ordeal is over," Alex said softly, using his magic to calm Joshua and to lend him some strength.

Slowly he helped Joshua toward the stone door. Dogmar had finished opening all the other cells, and he and the men were helping the other hostages. Many of the hostages had beards like Joshua, and their clothes were in tatters. It was clear that they had been in the dungeon for a long time, but they all seemed stronger than Joshua.

Once they had gotten everyone to the opening in the cliff, Dogmar pulled Alex slightly away from the group.

"None of them are strong enough to climb down on their own," Dogmar whispered. "They'll fall off the ropes long before they reach the bottom."

"I have more rope; we'll rig a sling and lower them," said Alex.

It only took a few minutes for Dogmar to work a rope into a sling, and while he did that two of the men climbed down the cliff to help the hostages once they were down. Alex, Dogmar, and the other rescuers lowered the hostages, sometimes two at a time, down to the beach. Joshua was the last one to be put in the sling, and before he was lowered Alex sent two more of his men down the ropes.

"When you're all in the boats, tell Aliia to use the mage wind to speed you south," Alex said to Dogmar. "I'll make sure that Jabez doesn't notice."

"You . . . you're not coming with us?" Joshua asked.

Alex shook his head. "I can't. I need to stop Jabez, and I must do it alone."

"But he's a wizard," Joshua said. "A powerful wizard."

Alex smiled. "So am I."

Alex helped Joshua into the sling, and then helped him climb out of the tunnel. As he and the others slowly lowered Joshua to the beach, Alex turned slightly to look at Dogmar.

"Joshua may need more help than the others," Alex said. "Warn Lady Aliia not to try and break any spells she might see. They will break once I destroy Jabez."

"As you wish," Dogmar answered. "Are you sure you don't need my help?"

"No, my friend—as I said, I must do this alone."

Dogmar nodded his understanding and then he and the remaining men started down the ropes. Alex turned and returned to the dungeons, closing and locking the stone door behind him. He was alone except for the two sleeping guards.

He didn't want to leave by the main door of the dungeon; it would be too risky. He thought there would be more guards there and he couldn't keep putting guards to sleep. He looked around the room, remembering stories he'd read and other castles he'd been in. This was a solid dungeon, and the stones fit together without leaving any gaps. As he studied the dungeon, Alex saw one stone in the ceiling that seemed to be a different color than the rest. It was in the corner near to where the guards were sleeping.

Alex walked over to the guards and climbed onto their table. Reaching up, he touched the stone. The stone moved as he applied pressure to it, and he was able to push it to one side. This was exactly what he'd been thinking of—a secret passage. He didn't know where the secret passageway would lead him, but at least it would be away from the dungeon. If he was really lucky, it would take him somewhere useful.

Alex gripped the edges of the open hole and pulled himself into the ceiling.

The guards were still asleep as he replaced the stone and started off into the unknown.

Chapter Twenty
The Secret Passageway

Alex soon found himself in a long hallway that was only broken by short sets of stairs that always went up. It was clear that this passage would lead him into the castle. At the top of a long spiral staircase, the passage suddenly split into several other passageways, and Alex was certain that each one led to a hidden door somewhere inside the castle. He quickly checked the first few passageways, but one led to the kitchen, and another led to a room where guards were sleeping. He went back to the main passageway, sure that if he followed it there would be other paths to follow.

Careful not to make any noise, Alex made his way through the secret passages. The feel of dust under his feet reassured him that Jabez had not discovered these passageways, and that for the time being he was safe. As he moved deeper into the castle, he paused to listen and look through spyholes that he found hidden in the castle walls. He saw a few gargoyles inside the castle as well as men and goblins. He listened to everything he heard, but as he suspected, nothing he heard had anything to do with the Axe of Sundering.

Eventually, one of the spyholes Alex checked revealed what

had to be the throne room. Alex paused for a moment, and then quickly moved along the passage to find a new spyhole, one that would give him a better view of the throne room. This was his chance to see Jabez and possibly find out what he was up to. Jabez's plans were in full motion now, and it made sense that Jabez would command his armies from the ancient throne room of Conmar.

Alex found a spyhole that let him see most of the room, and as quietly as he could he leaned closer to learn as much as he could. The room he looked into was dimly lit, but there was enough light for Alex to see most of what was going on. More important, he could hear what was being said, and what he heard gave him hope. Jabez might let something slip that would help him with his quest.

"An army of elves has attacked our southern army," a cold voice was saying. "They appeared without warning, and have destroyed most of our supplies."

"More supplies are already moving across the mountains," a voice that had to be Jabez's replied. "You'll have all you need to continue the battle."

"The elves do not stand and fight like the men," the cold voice whined. "They hit us and run away, and we don't have enough warriors to chase them."

"Enough of your excuses!" Jabez shouted. "I've sent more supplies and more warriors with them. You will push on to the coast and destroy the cities of men. When that task is done, you can push south and destroy the troublesome elves."

"It would be better to destroy the elves first," a sly goblin voice commented. "They are cunning, and leaving them free to attack us is dangerous."

"Silence!" Jabez snapped. "I have considered the elves and what they might do. They are an inconvenience, nothing more. Once the cities of men are destroyed, we will hunt the few elves that remain in Westland."

It was clear from Jabez's tone that the discussion was over, and that he wouldn't listen to any suggestions about changing the plans he'd made. Alex thought that Jabez was being foolish, because he knew the elves would do more than just cause trouble.

"Now, what word from the north?" Jabez asked.

"Our armies continue to advance," a large goblin answered. "The men of the north fight hard, but our numbers are too great for them."

"Your numbers are being cut down too quickly," said Jabez, his anger growing as he spoke. "My gargoyle servants have reported your losses to me. You lose ten warriors for every human you cut down."

"The losses mean nothing," the goblin answered with a growl. "We have more than enough warriors to complete our mission."

"What about after that mission is over?" Jabez asked, rising from the throne where he'd been sitting. "What about after Westland is ours and it is time for us to move on to Midland?"

"There are always more warriors to be found," the goblin answered, fear creeping into its voice.

"No, there are not!" Jabez shouted. He slammed his staff against the floor and a blast of red light shot out of the top.

Jabez's spell hit the goblin like a giant fist. The goblin was thrown backwards, landing hard and sliding across the stone floor. It cried out in pain, but none of the other goblins in the room moved to help it. Jabez stood watching the goblin, and Alex could see him clearly in the torchlight. A look of evil joy covered Jabez's face, and he cast a second spell that crushed the goblin into the floor.

"Tell his second-in-command that he is the leader now," said Jabez as he returned to his throne. "And tell him that he'd better not waste my army, or he will face a worse punishment than his former leader."

There was a mumble of acceptance from those gathered around the throne. It was clear that all of these creatures both feared and hated Jabez. It was also clear that they would not fight against him. They wanted the power that Jabez offered them, and they were happy to do whatever Jabez ordered—for at least as long as they were winning.

Alex watched for several more minutes, but nothing was said that might help him find the Axe of Sundering. He didn't expect Jabez to openly mention the Axe, but maybe he would mention a treasure room or the underground lake. Alex replaced the spyhole cover and moved away from the throne room. He had one idea about where the Axe might be, but it would be difficult and dangerous to check. He was sure Jabez would have plenty of guards stationed outside the treasure room of Conmar, if he could find it.

Alex waited by the hidden doorway, listening as the guards moved up and down the hallway beyond the door. It was important to know how often the guards passed by so he could sneak into the castle proper without anyone noticing. He wasn't exactly sure where the treasure room was, but he could sense the presence of a dragon. If his guess was right, this would be the golden dragon he'd seen in Darthon's dream. It made sense that the dragon would be in or at least near the treasure room, as that would probably be the only place large enough to keep a dragon. Of course there would be other guards between here and the treasure room, but Alex thought he could slip past them without being noticed.

After a few hours of waiting and listening, Alex slowly pulled open the hidden doorway that he'd been waiting behind. It had been several minutes since the last set of guards had passed, and he knew it would be some time before more guards came his way. The castle was dark, the only light coming from torches placed every twenty or thirty feet along the passageway. Alex wiped away the dust that his shoes left on the stone floor. He didn't want to leave any clues that he had been in the castle, or how he'd gotten there.

Certain that the secret passage was safe, Alex started off as fast as he dared. He made his way down three levels without meeting anyone or anything, and he was starting to wonder where all the guards were. He was on his way to a fourth stairway when he heard heavy footsteps coming toward him.

Alex looked for a place to hide, but there wasn't one in the long hallway. With no other option, Alex pushed open the closest door and jumped into the room beyond it. He looked wildly around to make sure the room was empty, and then stood next to the mostly closed door, watching the hallway outside.

The footsteps came closer and closer, until Alex could see

a massive gargoyle stop just outside the door he was hiding behind.

The gargoyle looked from one side of the hallway to the other, sniffing the air as if it smelled something it wasn't sure about. Alex held his breath, afraid that the gargoyle would start checking the doors along the hallway. For a minute the gargoyle stood perfectly still, taking a long, deep breath. Alex tensed his muscles, ready for the worst, but the gargoyle simply snorted, and started moving down the hallway as if nothing was wrong.

Alex waited a few minutes to make sure the stone monster had gone, and then slipped back into the hallway. He hurried on, desperate to reach the lower parts of the castle where he would be less likely to run into anything dangerous. As he quietly rushed along one of the lower halls, he knew he had made a mistake.

"Well, well, well—what have we here?"

Jabez. Alex spun toward the voice and cursed himself for being so stupid. He should have checked more closely, making sure the hall was empty before entering it. He allowed his desire for speed to blind him, and now he would have to face Jabez without the Axe of Sundering, and without any real hope of destroying him.

"Ah, the young warrior my uncle brought with him," Jabez commented with a wicked smile. "I congratulate you on getting this far. My uncle must have put quite a spell on you so that you could slip past my guards."

"Your uncle is a great wizard," said Alex, drawing his scimitar as he spoke. He wished he had Moon Slayer in his hand, but he would have to make do without it.

"Ha," Jabez laughed, spitting on the floor. "My uncle is an old fool, and it seems his powers are not as great as they once were. There was a time he would have come here himself to face me, and not sent some hireling to do his dirty work for him."

"A hireling that slipped past your guards, and even now holds your fate in his hands," Alex replied.

"Surely you don't believe that," said Jabez, laughing again. "My fool of an uncle must have told you that your weapons would be useless against me. Did he really let you believe a mere sword could hurt me? What did he promise you? What have you sold your life for?"

Alex didn't say anything as he felt Jabez's spell wash over him. Jabez was using magic to probe his mind, looking for reasons and clues about Whalen's plans. Alex could have blocked his mind from the spell if he'd wanted to, but that would mean giving himself away and letting Jabez know that he was also a wizard. Instead, he hid parts of his mind from Jabez, only letting him see what he wanted him to see. At the same time, Alex tried to find his own way into Jabez's mind, hoping to find the hiding place of the Axe of Sundering.

"You are brave to come here alone," Jabez said calmly. "I'm sure my uncle planned things well, allowing himself a way out once you reached Westland. Still, I value bravery, even when it is misplaced."

"What do you mean?" Alex asked, holding back the rage that was building inside of him.

"My uncle has sent you here to die. That much must be clear, even to you," Jabez answered with a sneer. "I can always use good men. Give up this foolish quest of yours and join me.

I could use a man like you, and I am always generous to those who serve me well."

Alex knew that his words were a lie. As soon as he discovered what he wanted to know, Jabez would kill him, just as he had killed the goblin leader in the throne room. Alex held back, showing Jabez more of what he wanted to see while continuing to prying into Jabez's deepest thoughts. He was close to the answer he needed, but he didn't understand what he saw in Jabez's mind.

"Join me," Jabez said again, moving closer to Alex as he spoke. "Give up your foolish quest and serve me. It is the only way you can save your friends. It is the only way you can save the elf maid Aliia."

Alex was shocked that Jabez knew about Aliia. He was shaken by how deeply Jabez had been able to look into his mind without his knowing. Anger rose up like a serpent inside Alex, and he acted without thinking. In one sweeping move he stepped forward, striking out at his enemy. Alex felt the edge cut into Jabez's side, his dragon magic adding power to the blow.

Jabez looked stunned, shocked—and for a moment, afraid.

Then Alex felt Jabez's magic push him back, fire and ice filling his right arm. He fell, his scimitar dropping to the stone floor and ringing loudly as it hit.

Jabez staggered away from Alex, clutching at his side.

Alex struggled back to his feet, his right arm numb with cold and pain. His head was spinning as if he'd been hit on the chin. The two of them looked at each other for a long moment in silence, and then they both moved. Alex ran forward, scooping up his scimitar with his left hand. Jabez staggered back into the chamber, calling loudly for his guards to come.

Alex could tell that Jabez was enhancing his voice with magic. Soon, every guard in Conmar would be rushing to this hall, and Alex had only one chance. He had to reach the treasure rooms of Conmar. From there he might be able to find some way to escape.

Alex ran as fast as he could, his right arm swinging uselessly as he went. He ran down another set of stairs and down the long tunnels, heading for what he hoped would be the treasure room. He struggled to get his scimitar back in its scabbard, and focused on a source of magic he could feel and almost smell.

He came upon another long set of stairs and paused. There was a dragon waiting for him at the bottom of the stairs; he had been right to follow his instincts.

As Alex ran into the treasure chamber, the dragon moved back, a puzzled look on its face. Alex skidded to a stop. He recognized the golden dragon that had attacked Darthon's mind, and was relieved that it wasn't an unknown dragon. The dragon was still enslaved by Jabez's magic, unable to speak or even make a sound. Alex had promised to break the curse and return the dragon's voice, but he could already hear Jabez's guards racing down the tunnel behind him. There was no time, and he still couldn't let Jabez know that he was a wizard.

"I can't free you yet," Alex said, his eyes moving around the treasure room as he spoke. "Once I destroy the wizard who has done this to you, then his spell will be broken and you will be free."

The dragon looked sad, but nodded its understanding of Alex's words.

"Will you help me?" Alex asked, his eyes meeting the golden dragon's gaze.

The dragon nodded, and for a moment, Alex could see into the dragon's mind. He saw a pathway leading away from the treasure room and down to an underground lake. A shimmer of magical light glowed in the center of the lake. Alex understood perfectly where he needed to go and why. He also knew that the dragon would do whatever he asked it to.

Alex started to move toward his hope for escape, but before he could look away from the dragon, a vision flashed into his mind. Buried on the other side of a stack of treasure was an old iron box. Alex immediately recognized it from the vision he had had in the cave of dreams when he and Whalen had been traveling with the caravan.

Alex blinked his eyes, breaking his connection with the dragon, and hurried to the spot the dragon had shown him. He found the iron box and lifted the lid. Inside was one of the Orion stones he had seen in his vision. It glowed like a pearl in sunlight, and Alex could sense the magic surrounding it. He quickly lifted the stone out of the box, but hesitated before putting it into his magic bag. He didn't know how the magic of the stone would react to the magic of his bag, but he couldn't leave it behind. The Orion stone was too powerful, and he didn't want Jabez to be able to use it as a weapon against him. Alex slipped the stone into his shirt pocket instead.

"Thank you, my friend. If you can, give me time to reach the end of this tunnel," said Alex as he moved to the smaller opening on the far side of the treasure room. "When Jabez's guards enter this room, breathe fire down the tunnel after me. I will leave an image of myself to burn in the flames. Then I will be free to destroy your enemy and mine."

Once more the dragon nodded, and Alex ran for the tunnel. He didn't have a lot of time, but he thought he would be able to work the magic he needed without Jabez noticing. The fact that the dragon was so close would help, because Jabez would not be able to detect Alex's magic with so much dragon magic in the room.

Halfway between the treasure chamber and the far end of the tunnel, Alex stopped. He focused his thoughts on a large boulder that was lying next to the wall, and worked his magic. The boulder changed into a body that was almost an exact duplicate of himself. It was dressed the same as Alex was, and even had a magic bag and a scimitar, both of which looked like his own.

Weakened by his injured arm, Alex stumbled to the end of the tunnel where the path ended in a large half circle. The beginnings of a stairway remained attached to the right side of the platform, but there were only five worn and broken steps, and then nothing. He was stuck. There was no way down to the underground lake, and no way for him to go back.

As the light of dragon fire filled the tunnel behind him, Alex did the only thing he could do. He jumped. He felt the heat as a giant ball of flame passed over him, and then the cold rush of air as he fell. The icy black water tried to rip Alex's breath away from him when he hit the surface of the lake. He managed to hold his breath as he sank into darkness. His right arm throbbed painfully as he tried to swim, and his lungs burned from a lack of air.

Swimming as hard as he could with only one arm, Alex forced himself down toward the bottom of the lake. The air had almost entirely left his lungs before he reached his goal. He struggled to move a large rock and then forced his magic bag under it. Struggling with the straps, he managed to pull the bag close to his face and, with his last breath, he whispered the password.

Without a sound Alex vanished into his bag—wounded and cold, but alive and undefeated.

It took several hours before Alex felt ready to leave the safety of his magic bag. His right arm was still numb and he had trouble holding anything, but the pain was mostly gone. Alex took a deep breath and then reluctantly spoke the magic password that would release him from his magic bag and return him to the icy water of the lake.

The water of the underground lake was so cold it burned, and with some difficulty he retrieved his magic bag from beneath the rock. Wrapping the straps of the bag around his numb right hand, Alex pushed off the bottom of the lake, swimming as hard as he could for the surface.

Alex gasped for breath as he broke the surface of the water. He let himself float for a moment to let his eyes adjust to the darkness and get a sense of direction. He conjured a single faint weir light, just to make sure he was alone.

Alex swam to the edge of the lake and pulled himself out of the water. He rested on the rocky beach for a few minutes, catching his breath and trying to warm up. Far above him was the platform he had jumped from. Magic was the only way he could get back onto the platform, and he was sure Jabez wouldn't notice—he probably wasn't even looking for magic now. He concentrated, and rose from the surface of the lake to the platform.

Alex could see the glow of the dragon in the treasure room, and the stones of the tunnel he'd run down were still warm from the dragon's fire. He started back down the tunnel, noticing that the body he had left behind was gone. Jabez's guards must have carried it away, probably to prove that the warrior had not escaped them.

As Alex entered the treasure room, the light coming from the dragon increased. He smiled and moved further into the room. The dragon watched Alex as he moved, waiting patiently to hear what Alex had to say. For several seconds Alex didn't say anything, and when he did speak to the dragon, he did not use his voice.

I am grateful for your help, Alex said, his thoughts entering the dragon's mind. *I am in your debt, and I will do everything I can to break the curse Jabez has put on you.*

The dragon nodded its understanding but was unable to reply. Alex sat down on a pile of gold coins and let his mind move closer to the dragon's. He wanted to know how the dragon had gotten here, and how Jabez had managed to steal its voice. As he opened his mind, the dragon was able to show him the answers to his questions, and the more Alex saw, the more he understood. For a long time, Alex sat in the treasure room, sharing thoughts with the dragon, until he came to the question he needed to answer most.

Where is the Axe of Sundering? Alex thought, his own mind recalling what he'd seen in Jabez's thoughts. *I need it if I'm going to end this evil.*

The dragon did not show Alex an answer in its thoughts, but instead, it turned its head and looked at the tunnel leading to the underground lake. Alex looked at the opening as well, and then at the dragon. He didn't understand what the dragon was trying to tell him, and then suddenly he realized what the dragon was saying without words.

The Axe was not hidden in the treasure room, and it was not guarded as Alex thought it would be. Jabez had put the Axe in the one place he thought it would be safe, the one place that no warrior would ever be able to reach it. With a laugh, Alex stood up and bowed to the dragon.

When Alex moved toward the tunnel, however, the dragon shifted as if to stop him from leaving. The dragon looked around the treasure room and then at Alex.

You want me to take all of this? Alex asked.

The dragon nodded its head.

If Jabez returns before I have the Axe, or if I fail to destroy him, he will be angry with you for giving his treasure away, Alex said.

A light flashed in the dragon's eyes as Alex spoke, and its meaning was all too clear. If Jabez should discover the loss of his treasure he might try to destroy the dragon, which would be one way for the dragon to escape its prison.

Very well, Alex said. *I will take this, and hope that Jabez never returns to this room.*

It only took a few seconds for Alex to move all of Jabez's treasure into his own magic bag. With that task completed, Alex looked at the dragon once more. The look on the dragon's face told Alex all he needed to know, and once again he bowed to the dragon.

You will be free, I promise, Alex said as he turned to go.

Without looking back, Alex moved down the tunnel toward the underground lake. This time there was no hurry; he wasn't being chased. Now there was only one thing he needed to think about, and that was getting the Axe of Sundering out of the icy lake. Alex had seen the lake in Jabez's mind, but he hadn't recognized it for what it was, not until the dragon had given him the answer he needed. The spark of magic he'd seen in the lake wasn't Jabez's doing, and it wasn't the dragon's, either. The magic came from the Axe of Sundering, and no dark magic could ever hide it.

Standing at the edge of the platform, Alex looked out into the darkness. He had seen the magic Jabez had used to hide the Axe when he'd look into Jabez's mind. Now he used that same magic to call the Axe back. There was no need to worry about Jabez noticing this magic, because it wasn't his magic. He was using the magic of the Axe of Sundering itself.

After several minutes of staring into the darkness, Alex saw what he was looking for. A faint glimmer, like a distant star, appeared above the waters of the lake. Slowly the glimmer grew brighter as the Axe moved toward Alex and finally hung motionless in the air in front of him.

CHAPTER TWENTY-ONE

THE AXE OF SUNDERING

The Axe of Sundering floated just out of reach, waiting for Alex to take it. For a moment he hesitated, dazzled by the beauty of the deadly weapon in front of him. Without thinking, Alex lifted his right arm, reaching out for the axe with his numb hand. The axe moved away, as if it did not wish to be touched. Alex felt a wave of magic wash over him, magic that came from the axe. It was searching his mind, testing his power, and deciding if he would be the one to wield it.

Alex couldn't take his eyes off the axe as he stood waiting. Slowly words formed in his mind, words he had heard before.

"Will you pay the price? Will you give up all that you are to wield this weapon?"

Alex's mind spun wildly. Did he really have to give up everything he was? Could he only wield the axe if he gave up being an adventurer, a wizard, a dragon lord? Did the magic of the axe want him to give up being a dragon? Alex didn't know if he could give it all up, he wasn't sure it would be possible to meet the price the axe was asking. His mind raced through all his adventures, everything he had done, and all that he still hoped to do.

The Axe of Sundering didn't move as Alex thought. Suddenly his thoughts shifted to the evil that was being done by Jabez and the Brotherhood. If he failed to win the axe, all of Westland—all of Jarro—would fall into evil. If he didn't win the axe, the Brotherhood would soon take over all the known lands.

Alex moved his hand toward the axe, his mind made up. *Yes*, he thought. *I will give up everything to stop this evil.*

The Axe of Sundering moved down and forward, and when it touched his hand, the numbness vanished. Magical warmth flowed through him. The axe had chosen, but Alex wasn't sure what would happen next. He pulled his arm back, looking at the magical markings on the axe. Now that it was in his hand, Alex realized what was so special about this weapon.

"Made by magic," Alex whispered.

Unlike Moon Slayer, which had been made by hand and then had magic added to it, the Axe of Sundering had been made completely by magic. No hammer had ever worked the metal of this weapon, and no stone or file could ever make an edge as impossibly sharp. The Axe of Sundering was much more than just a weapon.

"You have paid the price, and yet remain yourself," a voice that Alex had never heard said inside his head. *"To freely offer all is payment enough."*

A sense of joy filled Alex as he shifted the axe from hand to hand. The balance was perfect, and as he swung the weapon, the axe felt more like a part of him, not just a weapon in his hands. The axe was small and light enough for him to use with one hand, yet large enough for him to use both hands if he needed to. There was powerful magic in the axe, magic that was both the same and different than the magic of Moon Slayer. Alex knew that the axe would help him in battle just as Moon Slayer did, but it would also help him in other ways. It would take time for him to understand this new power, but at the moment, time was something Alex did not have.

He had to find Jabez and end his evil. Alex hoped more than anything that he was not already too late to help his friends.

Alex slid the axe into his belt and returned to the treasure room. He bowed to the golden dragon as he passed, but he didn't have time to stop.

Surprising Jabez could mean the difference between success and failure.

He made his way back up the many flights of stairs and through the hallways until he was close to the throne room. He knew he would need all his strength in the fight that was coming. Even with the Axe of Sundering, it would not be an easy battle.

He reached for the throne room door, but then he paused. His sudden appearance would certainly surprise Jabez, but if there were guards or even servants in the room Jabez might escape. The dark wizard would certainly recognize the Axe of Sundering in Alex's hand, and the fact that Alex had it might scare him into running.

He forced his mind to focus, tried to think like a dragon, and became invisible.

As quietly as he could, Alex opened the door and stepped

into the throne room. He closed the door behind him, looking to see what dangers might be waiting for him. The room was empty, and that didn't seem right. He had expected Jabez to be here, giving orders or listening to reports of the war he had started. The fact that the room was empty brought new worries to Alex's mind.

A sudden rustle of movement made Alex jump, his right hand grasping the axe in his belt. The massive doors to the room opened wide as Alex moved out of the way, and a pair of gargoyles entered, carrying a wooden chest between them. A dozen goblin soldiers marched close behind the gargoyles, and walking in the middle of the goblins was Whalen Vankin.

Alex was stunned. Somehow Jabez had managed to locate Whalen, capture him, and then bring him to Conmar.

Whalen looked like he had been badly beaten. His clothes were dirty and torn, and he walked with a limp. A dirty bandage, stained with blood, was wrapped around his head. One of the goblins pushed Whalen forward, and he stumbled as he entered the throne room.

Alex wanted to rush forward and free his friend. He wanted to cut down the goblins that were gathered around Whalen, laughing their evil laughter. He wanted to use the Axe of Sundering to hack the gargoyles into pieces, but he knew he couldn't. He had to wait. He moved into the shadows at one side of the room, rage flowing through him. Jabez would be coming soon, and it was Jabez that he had to destroy.

The wait was a short one. Jabez came limping into the room, a pained look on his face as he climbed the steps to the stone throne. It took a few seconds for Jabez to turn and sit down. It was clear that he was suffering from the wound Alex had given him.

Alex moved closer, his hand ready to pull the Axe of Sundering out of his belt, but he did not act.

"You don't seem pleased to see me, uncle," Jabez said, a nasty grin spreading over his face.

"Why would I be pleased to see you?" Whalen asked. "You've broken your oath as a true wizard, you've brought war and suffering to Jarro, and you've dishonored my name."

"The dishonor you brought upon yourself," Jabez said with a sneer. "You always thought that I would be like you. You tried to make me into a copy of yourself, but I was too clever for that. You and your do-good attitude, always using your powers to help others because you claimed it was the right thing to do. Look where all of your good deeds have gotten you."

"I see you've learned nothing," Whalen said. "I tried to teach you the correct path and you refused to learn."

"Hah!" Jabez laughed, his face turning red with anger. "You tried to teach me the fool's path. What I've learned is that the gratitude of the poor and helpless is meaningless. All that really matters in this world is wealth and power."

"You are a fool," Whalen replied.

"A fool?" Jabez yelled back and started to laugh. He laughed so hard that he suddenly grimaced in pain from the wound in his side. "Let me show you who the real fool is."

Jabez snapped his fingers and the gargoyles came forward carrying their wooden chest. They placed the chest at the bottom of the stair that led to the throne, and then stepped away. Jabez's face was full of hunger as he looked down at the chest.

"Leave us," Jabez said, waving away the goblins and gargoyles. "There is little need to fear the great Whalen Vankin now."

The goblins all laughed as they turned and left the room, followed closely by the gargoyles. Jabez didn't say anything more until the throne room doors were closed, but his eyes remained fixed on Whalen. Alex used the time to move closer to Whalen, thinking that he might have to defend his friend from a sudden attack.

"I'm sure you think your plans will find success," Jabez began, his voice calmer than it had been. "You've always been so cunning, uncle, but this time your plans have all come to nothing."

"You're beginning to bore me," Whalen said, sounding much braver than he looked.

"Oh, you find me boring, do you?" Jabez laughed. "Then let me tell you about your foolishness. Let me show you how your plans have failed. Let me explain how I will be the greatest wizard in this land and all the other known lands as well. Your council of wizards will bow before me."

"They will never bow to you," Whalen said, the anger clear in his voice.

"Just as you would never bow," Jabez snapped back.

Jabez slowly waked down the stairs, holding his staff for support. Once he was steady, he swung his staff out, striking the wooden chest. The wood crumbled away like dust, replaced by a stone pillar. On top of the pillar was a single stone that shimmered with a silver light—an Orion stone.

Alex touched his pocket, reassuring himself that the other Orion stone was still safe in his possession.

"Yes, uncle, here is the secret that you did not expect," said Jabez, his eyes moving from the stone to Whalen once more. "The Orion stones that you thought had been destroyed. You and your foolish council thought the secret of their making was lost forever. Yet two of these wonderful stones were given to me, and now they will be part of your greatest and final defeat."

"The stones may not work the way you wish them to," Whalen said. "Use them if you will; they will do you little good."

"I thought that's what you would say." Jabez laughed.

He picked up the shimmering stone and walked closer to Whalen. He held the glowing stone tightly in his hand, and then pressed it against Whalen's chest, right over his heart.

Whalen screamed, his eyes clenched tight.

Alex stepped forward, his hand on the axe at his belt, but again, he had to force himself to stop and wait.

Jabez had a cruel smile on his face as he pushed the stone harder against Whalen's chest. A bright white light surrounded the two wizards and the Orion stone. Slowly, the light began to be absorbed by the stone until it was gone.

Whalen slumped to the ground with a groan. Jabez lifted the stone high in the air. It now glowed with an inner golden light.

"Now you are powerless. This stone holds your magic—magic that will soon be mine."

"My magic will never be yours," said Whalen, weak but still defiant.

"Oh, but it will," Jabez replied, a hungry look on his face. "I know how the stones work as well as you do, uncle. I know that once you are dead I will be able to absorb all the magical power this stone holds."

"Then kill me and be done with it," Whalen snapped.

"Kill you? Oh, it won't be as quick and easy as that," Jabez said. "First I must show you how foolish you've been. Before you die you will hear how your warrior was destroyed, how your well laid plans have come to nothing."

"I don't believe you," Whalen said, his voice sounding desperate.

"Oh, but you will believe," Jabez answered.

Alex moved slowly and quietly to stand just behind Whalen.

"I knew you'd deny everything," Jabez said, moving closer. "You never admit your mistakes, do you? Bringing the sea elves into the battle—a minor inconvenience. Sending your young warrior to try and kill me—foolishness."

"I don't know what you're talking about," Whalen answered.

"Lies!" Jabez yelled, swinging his staff and hitting Whalen in the stomach. "Lies and deceit from the most *honest* of all wizards!"

Alex had to stop himself from reaching out to catch Whalen, had to stop himself from taking the invisible axe at his side and attacking Jabez on the spot. He didn't know why he had to wait, but he knew there was a reason to wait. Some reason that was more important than his own desire to destroy the evil wizard in front of him.

"I suppose you didn't send the warrior," Jabez said, pacing back and forth in front of Whalen. "Yes, your young adventurer friend was here. He foolishly used a regular blade against me, and not the Axe of Sundering."

Jabez turned and climbed back to the stone throne, bending over to pick up something from behind the giant chair. "Here is the proof of your failure," said Jabez, turning to face Whalen once more. "Your warrior has caused me a great deal of pain, as you can tell, but it cost him his life."

Jabez threw a blackened sword and a badly burnt magic bag down on the floor in front of Whalen. They were the items Alex had created to go with the false image of himself, and he was more than a little pleased that Jabez believed they were real.

"Your mighty warrior ran into a little pet of mine," Jabez said, sounding almost gleeful. "So you see, uncle, all of your plans have come—and will come—to nothing."

When Alex saw the pained and troubled look on Whalen's face, he realized that part of Whalen believed what Jabez was saying. Unable to stop himself, he reached out and touched Whalen's shoulder. Leaning close, and in a whisper that only Whalen could possibly hear, he spoke.

"I am here."

Whalen looked surprised for a moment, but Jabez took the

look as one of defeat. He laughed at Whalen, who was still kneeling in front of him.

Alex thought fast, trying to find a way to free Whalen and at the same time destroy Jabez. His thoughts returned to what Whalen had told him about the Orion stones and about how they were used to steal another wizard's magic. What was it that Whalen had told him?

"You'd better be sure I'm dead before you crush the stone holding my power. If I'm even barely alive, my powers will return to me, and I will destroy you," Whalen said, rising to his feet.

Whalen's words told Alex what he needed to know, the reason why he was waiting to attack.

"Oh, you'll be dead," Jabez said with a wicked grin. "You'll beg for death first, but you will be very dead before I crush the stone."

Alex knew what he had to do. He moved without making a sound, stepping around Whalen and walking to the pillar where the glowing Orion stone sat. With great care, Alex drew the Axe of Sundering from his belt. Carefully he positioned the hammer-like back of the axe over the stone.

"You seem so sure of yourself," said Whalen. "Even now, you do not realize the danger you are in."

"Danger?" Jabez asked. "What danger? I've captured you and destroyed the warrior you sent to try and kill me. My armies are sweeping across Westland, and it is only a matter of time before I have destroyed the humans and elves that stand against me."

Whalen started to laugh as he forced himself to stand

straight. He continued to laugh as he looked Jabez in the eye. Jabez sunk back into his throne in fear. Even when Whalen was powerless and wounded, Jabez was afraid of him.

"Your evil has reached its end!" Whalen shouted.

Alex raised the Axe of Sundering over his head, and with all his strength, he brought the blunt end of the axe down on the Orion stone. There was a blinding flash of red-gold light, followed by a thunderous explosion. Alex staggered back a step. The light flowed like water, sweeping over and past Alex. Quickly the glowing, water-like magic gathered around Whalen's body. The wizard immediately stood up straighter, strength and light coming back to his face.

Jabez looked from Whalen to Alex, who brought up the axe, ready to attack now that his invisibility spell had been broken.

"You!" Jabez said in a shocked whisper. "It can't be. You were destroyed by the dragon. This cannot be."

"The dragon fire did not touch me," Alex said, moving toward Jabez. "The dragon you keep as a slave did as I asked. Now it is time to repay the dragon's kindness."

Jabez jumped to his feet, but stood frozen in fear for a moment, and then moved faster than Alex expected. A bolt of lightning shot from Jabez's staff, aimed for Alex's heart. Alex blocked the bolt with the Axe of Sundering without thinking. The lightning bolt bounced off the axe, hitting the ceiling above Alex and causing several blocks of stone to fall. Alex stepped to one side so the stones did not hit him. He shifted the axe and moved closer to Jabez.

Jabez lunged forward, his hand reaching out, ready to cast

a spell. Alex swung his axe, catching the tips of Jabez's out-stretched fingers and slicing them from his hand. Jabez pulled his hand away, screaming in pain and anger. A look of fear and unspeakable hate crossed his face as he started to work a new spell.

Alex moved, swinging the axe as he went, but Jabez leaped out of the way. Spinning around, Alex continued to follow him, even as he felt Jabez's spell growing around him. Alex's own magic was working as well, forming a protective shield around him as he moved. He swung the axe at Jabez again, making a wide spinning move as he did so. Jabez's magic hit Alex on the shoulder as he spun, causing him to rotate fur-ther than he'd planned and slam into the wall. Jabez was quick to take advantage of Alex's disorientation. He rushed forward with his staff, transforming it into a spear with a flaming tip. Alex ducked and rolled away, the spear tip following him as it gouged a line in the stone wall.

Suddenly a magical eagle dove from the ceiling with its claws aimed at Jabez's face.

Alex looked at Whalen, who was whispering the words to a spell.

Jabez pulled back, throwing his left arm over his head to protect himself. His right hand came up, catching the magical bird by the neck. As the bird vanished, Jabez let loose another spell, sending a curse along the magical thread that connected Whalen to his creation.

Alex acted without thinking. His dragon magic caught the thread of Whalen's magic, blocking Jabez's spell like a bead on a wire. The curse hung in the air, and then Alex forced it back along the thread toward Jabez. Alex's magic snapped the thread of Whalen's magic, and Jabez sent his curse into the wall, where it exploded and sprayed the room with bits of stone.

"I see you are more than just a warrior," Jabez snarled.

"Much more," Alex answered, his voice sounding more like a dragon than a man.

Jabez didn't wait for Alex to attack. Faster than Alex thought possible, Jabez sent a curse at him, a second curse toward Whalen, and a third curse at him again. Whalen didn't move; he didn't seem to be doing anything at all. Alex, however, was more dragon than wizard now. A combination of his wizard magic and his dragon magic reached out and caught all three curses at the same time. They bounced away from him and from Whalen, speeding back at Jabez, who was ready and slapped all three spells back at Alex.

Alex reacted faster than he normally would have. At the moment he was a dragon in a man's body, and there was no need to think. The curses bounced back and forth between Jabez and himself, moving faster and faster as they went. Alex acted on instinct, and he added a fourth and then a fifth spell to the deadly game.

"Enough!" Jabez screamed in frustration.

Jabez threw himself to the side, and all five spells slammed into the wall behind him, exploding like a bomb and shaking the entire castle. A large section of the wall collapsed into the room, filling the air with dust and smoke. Alex tried to keep track of where Jabez was, but it was almost impossible.

"Duck!" Alex's O'Gash screamed inside his head. *"Five feet behind you, two to your right."*

Alex ducked and spun, swinging the Axe of Sundering in a wide arc. Jabez's staff whistled through empty air where Alex's head had been, but the axe found its mark.

Jabez screamed and staggered backward, his free hand holding a deep gash across his stomach.

Alex closed in on his enemy. Jabez held up his staff to block Alex's next blow, but it did no good against the Axe of Sundering. There was a flash of greenish-yellow light as the axe cut Jabez's staff in two. Jabez looked terrified, as Alex moved closer still.

"You may have won this battle, but we shall win the war," Jabez yelled, throwing what was left of his staff at Alex. "Your victory will cost you dearly. I'll take you both with me in defeat, and most of Westland as well."

"Do your worst," Alex answered, raising the axe for a final strike.

Alex heard Jabez working a spell and he heard Whalen shouting something behind him, but he didn't understand either of them. It was the time to end this evil. With all the strength he had, Alex brought down the Axe of Sundering. When the silver blade hit Jabez in the chest, Alex saw the shocked, surprised look on Jabez's face.

Suddenly, a shimmering halo of light surrounded Jabez's body, and Alex saw that each thin beam of light was like a thread connected to and stretching out behind Jabez. Alex remembered that Whalen had told him that Jabez's magic kept him connected to all the people he had done magic for, tying his life force to theirs down through the generations.

One by one, the threads of light snapped, each one

vanishing with a small popping sound. The ends of the threads still connected to Jabez turned from gold to black and then were absorbed back into Jabez's body. The links to Jabez's victims were broken. The Axe of Sundering had done its work.

Alex pulled the axe free of Jabez's body, which crumpled into a heap of ash on the ground. Alex turned to check on Whalen, but he never completed his turn.

A wave of darkness covered him, and a thundering pain washed through his head. For a moment Alex thought that the castle of Conmar had collapsed on him, as pain beyond any he had ever known surged though his body. He felt the Axe of Sundering slip from his hand, felt the cold stone floor beneath him as he fell, and then everything went black.

CHAPTER TWENTY-TWO

A PRISON OF ICE

"Alexander Taylor," a weak, fearful sounding voice said. "I didn't think to see you again so soon, and I'm sure you didn't think you'd see me."

Alex could feel the cold stone floor under him, and he pushed himself up and carefully shook his head. His ears felt like they had been stuffed with cotton, and his mouth was dry. Everything he could see was in shadow except for a single beam of light coming from a window high above him. The light hit the edge of the Axe of Sundering, making it shine in the darkness.

Alex looked around to see who had spoken to him, but as far as he could tell, he was alone.

"Who . . . who are you?" he asked.

The weak voice gave a nervous giggle that was quickly cut off.

Alex picked up the axe, and with some difficulty got to his feet.

"Where am I?" he demanded.

"Where you belong," the voice hissed back at him. "In prison."

A shadow moved away from the far wall and limped toward him. It waved its arm, and the light from the window flared white. Alex shielded his eyes from the sudden brightness. As his eyes adjusted he looked around, trying to find answers.

Three of the walls around him were smooth, made of stone, and had a strange pearl-like color, but the fourth wall was made of gray-black bars. On the other side of the bars stood a man who Alex recognized now that he'd moved into the light. He was an old man with gray hair, wearing a long black robe that reached to the ground.

"Magnus," Alex said. "I'm surprised the Brotherhood didn't get rid of you after your failure in Nezza."

Another fearful giggle escaped the old man.

"The Brotherhood protects its own. I have been waiting for this day since we last met, *Master* Taylor." He sneered the word, making it sound like an insult.

"I defeated you once before, and I will defeat you again. You and the Brotherhood."

"The Brotherhood is more powerful than you can possibly imagine. Do you honestly believe that you—alone—can do what no one else has been able to do in more than two thousand years?"

Alex gripped the handle of the Axe of Sundering more tightly.

"If I have to."

"So brave, so proud, and so foolish." Magnus took step toward Alex's cell, and Alex saw that Magnus's left leg and foot were made out of the same grey-black metal as the bars of his cell.

"I see you've recovered from your injury," Alex said, nodding toward Magnus's leg.

"This? Oh, yes. A gift from my master, Gaylan. Forged by magic and stronger than true silver. The same magical metal makes up the bars of your cell—and the walls . . . well, I'll let you find out about the walls on your own."

"How did I get here?" Alex asked.

"Jabez was connected to many magical people. At one time he was a member of the Brotherhood. We've been keeping a close eye on Jabez since he turned traitor. When you managed to break his magical connections with the Axe of Sundering, we knew exactly what was happening and where we could find you. Gaylan opened a portal, and we brought you and Whalen Vankin here. Just as our master planned."

"It was a trap?" Alex asked.

Magnus shook his head. "No, it was an opportunity. One we had hoped for, planned for, and then seized when the moment arrived."

"What do you want, then?" Alex asked.

Magnus lifted his shoulder in a small shrug. "You must have figured that out by now. You've seen what the Brotherhood has been working toward. Surely you are not blind."

"You want to control the known lands," Alex said quietly. "You want power."

"We already have power," Magnus answered, laughing at Alex's answer. "Far more power than you dare guess. Now we will reach beyond the known lands, and you will help us achieve our goals. With you and your pretty little axe, we have the final pieces we need to win a complete victory."

"Whatever it is you're planning," Alex said, "I will stop you."

Magnus lifted his eyebrows. "How?"

Alex let loose his magic, sending a spell of destruction at Magnus and the bars that stood between them. The spell raced forward, but it never got even as far as the cell bars. The magic turned, divided, and melted into the stone walls and ceiling of his cell. Magnus stood, smiling wickedly at Alex, completely unafraid.

"Excellent," Magnus said. "Now you learn the real power of your cell. The walls are made as the Orion stones were made. Your magic is now locked into these walls, and slowly, so very slowly, every drop of your magic will be sucked away."

"You will never take my power!" Alex shouted, as he rushed forward and grabbed the bars of his cell. The bars burned his hands as if they were red hot, and he jerked back in pain.

Magnus laughed. "Looks like you need some time to cool off and consider things. Save what little strength you can, wizard. Gaylan will be along shortly, and if you play your part in our plans, he might just let you live."

Magnus waved his arm again and the prison fell back into shadow. When Alex's eyes had adjusted to the darkness, Magnus was gone.

Alex sat down on the cot that was at the back of his cell. He'd let the Axe of Sundering fall when he'd rushed the bars, and it lay on the floor in front of him. The weak light that filtered into the room made the axe appear to glow. Alex flexed his burned hands, trying to get rid of the pain. The heat from the bars hadn't done any real damage to his hands, but it hurt all the same.

Leaning back against the wall, he took a good look at his surroundings for the first time. There was nothing there to help him, or at least nothing he could see. The axe might help, but Magnus had said the gray-black bars were stronger than true silver, and Alex wasn't sure if he dared damaging the axe on them. He could actually feel his magic slipping slowly away and there was nothing he could do about it. A way out was what he needed, but all that he could think was *Where is Whalen?* Magnus had said that the Brotherhood had brought both Alex and Whalen here. He had to be close. Alex reached out with his magic to see if he could find Whalen, but the walls of his cell absorbed everything. He shouted for Whalen and thought he might have heard a weak groaning nearby, but he couldn't be sure. He slumped against the wall, his mind racing, trying to make sense of what had happened and seeking a way to escape.

None of his thoughts gave Alex much hope, and slowly his mind slipped into a dark blankness, where no clear thinking could take place.

———•••———

"All is not lost," Alex's O'Gash reassured him. *"There is always a way out, even if you don't see it at first."*

The stone felt cold behind Alex's back, slowly leaching away his body heat. The tips of his fingers and toes began to tingle.

Alex hated waiting. He would much rather be doing something—anything—than sitting and waiting for someone else to make the first move. He forced himself to his feet and began to pace around the small cell. The motion helped bring warmth back to his hands and feet, and it was only then that he realized how cold the entire cell had become. He exhaled, surprised to see his breath cloud in front of his face.

The shimmering bars appeared to have been coated with a layer of frost, and the stone walls were as slick as ice.

What was happening? Was it a trick of the Brotherhood? An attack of some kind?

Alex increased his pacing, hoping the extra movement would help keep the cold at bay, but the temperature was dropping too fast. The floor grew slippery under his feet, and the air around him crystalized into small snowflakes.

He moved to stand as close to the bars as he could. Ice had begun to build up between the bars, nearly closing in the one open wall to his cell.

"Whalen!" Alex called, his voice shaking with the cold. "Whalen, where are you?"

Alex knew that if he didn't do something fast, he would freeze to death.

Magnus had told him to "cool off"—he must have cast a spell. But how did you fight *cold?*

With heat, Alex thought.

He returned to the cot and held his hand over the bare mattress. "Inferno," he said, remembering the first spell he had ever learned.

Nothing happened.

Alex's heart dropped. It was the simplest spell he knew, one that required the least amount of magic. And if he couldn't even make that one work, what hope did he have to work any other kind of magic?

"The magic is still inside you," Alex's O'Gash said. *"Even if you can't feel it or access it. It is a part of you."*

Alex folded his outstretched hand into a fist. His O'Gash was right. His magic wasn't something that could be taken away by someone else. It was a part of him as much as his bones or his blood or his mind. It was part of what made him who he was. Alex picked up the Axe of Sundering, placed the head of it on the ground between his feet, and gripped the handle with both hands. If the axe could be used to sever connections to magic, maybe it could also be used to make connections to magic.

Alex closed his eyes and turned his thoughts inward, searching for that spark of magic that no spell or wizard or member of the Brotherhood could extinguish.

He remembered the fire of excitement he'd felt when he'd first seen the sign in Mr. Clutter's shop, calling him on an adventure.

He remembered the blaze of anticipation when he'd been measured for his weapons and learned he could be a warrior *and* a wizard.

He remembered the heat that emanated off Slathbog's body when Alex looked the dragon in the eye.

He remembered the magical fire that filled him when he wielded Moon Slayer in battle, the burning sands of Nezza under his feet, the heat of dwarven forges, and the purifying beauty of the Oracle of the White Tower.

He concentrated on those memories, reliving them one by one, until the handle of the axe grew warm beneath his hands.

He pushed further into his mind. He remembered the intensity of his emotions: his anger at facing down enemies who threatened the innocent people he tried to protect; his determination to uphold his honor, no matter the situation; his belief that good would always overcome evil.

He grit his teeth and reached for his deepest self, his truest self.

Dragonfire roared to life inside of him. Visions of the dragons he'd met filled his mind, Salinor leading the way, and he remembered that he was also a dragon.

My brother, Salinor said in his mind.

Alex's body trembled with the force traveling through it. Heat poured off of him in waves, driving back the cold that had threatened to overwhelm him. The magic he had sought rushed back into him, filling him completely.

He would never let it go again.

He would never let the Brotherhood defeat him.

Alex opened his eyes. Steam rose from the floor where the axe rested. The weapon glowed with a bright silver-blue light. Alex braced himself, then lifted the blazing Axe of Sundering up, swinging it over his shoulder. He took two steps toward the frozen bars and, with a roar that began deep in his belly, Alex brought the axe around with all his strength.

The white-hot blade cut through the magical metal bars

as if they were made of wax, the ice melting at the axe's fiery touch.

Quickly, Alex carved a hole large enough for him to walk through. Once freed from his prison, he moved swiftly down a long hallway. There was only one other cell door, and when he looked inside, he saw his friend. With three quick strokes of the Axe, Alex was inside the cell and by Whalen's side.

Whalen's prison wasn't cold like Alex's had been, but Whalen remained motionless. The only clue that he was still alive was that his chest was barely rising and falling.

"Whalen," Alex whispered. "Wake up." He reached out and touched the wizard's shoulder.

The moment Alex made contact, Whalen sat upright on the cot, eyes wide open, gasping for breath.

Alex took a step back in surprise.

Whalen turned to him. "Alex? What are you doing here?" He looked around in confusion. "Where are we?"

"In the grip of the Brotherhood," Alex answered. "But not for long. Can you walk?"

"I think so." Whalen stood up with Alex's help, and then squinted and held his hand in front of his eyes to block out the light shining from the Axe of Sundering. "How are you doing that?"

"I'll explain later," Alex said. "We have to go. Now."

Alex slung Whalen's arm over his shoulder and helped the old wizard from the prison cell. Together they stumbled down the hallway, past a dozen other cells—all empty—and through a dark wooden door. They emerged into what appeared to be the common area of the Golden Swan back in Telous.

Alex stumbled to a stop in surprise. He helped Whalen sit down at a nearby table before he took a closer look at the room they had entered.

The room was nearly an exact replica of the building he knew so well. Tables and chairs were placed around the room, though in the real Golden Swan they would be filled with adventurers gathering to talk and drink. Here, there was no one but Alex and Whalen. The room even had the same white walls, large windows, and emerald trim around the shutters—but instead of the image of a swan with emerald eyes hanging over the back bar there was a creature with three heads and six arms and a jaw opened wide as if to devour everything in its path.

Alex felt a chill run down his spine at the sight of it.

"The Gezbeth," Whalen said, his eyes fixed on the image of the creature. "The symbol of the Brotherhood. It is as I feared."

"What is it?" Alex asked.

"I fear we have arrived at the headquarters of the Brotherhood itself. We are in the very belly of the beast, Alex." Whalen's voice was low. He tapped his fingers on the table and frowned. "Something's wrong. I don't feel like myself." Whalen closed his eyes for a moment, and when he opened them again, his face was gray. "It's impossible," he whispered. "My magic . . ." He opened and closed his hands as if he could grasp something that had already been taken away. "I felt it return to me when you broke the Orion stone, but now . . . the Brotherhood. . . . They haven't taken my magic, but they have blocked me from using it."

"They did that to me as well," Alex said. "Or they tried to, at least."

Whalen nodded to the Axe of Sundering Alex had slipped into his belt. It was still bright, but not blazing like the sun. "You broke the spell? How?"

Alex rested his hand on the top of the axe. "I am Alexander Taylor, adventurer, wizard, and dragon lord." He smiled at Whalen. "And you trained me well."

Whalen offered him a weak smile. "I am not sure how much I had to do with it."

"Nonsense. You have been an amazing teacher—and friend." Alex sat in the chair opposite Whalen. "What is our next step? What do we do now?"

"I believe I can answer that," a voice said from behind them.

Alex and Whalen both turned. Alex half-rose from his seat, his hand on the axe at his side.

A man stood at the doorway. He was tall, and might have been considered handsome if not for the scar that ran down nearly the entire left side of his face. The wound bisected his left eye, leaving it milky white and cold. His right eye was dark and filled with cunning. He met Alex's gaze with a smile.

"Gaylan," Alex said. He had seen the man's face before in a vision. "Head of the Brotherhood."

CHAPTER TWENTY-THREE

THE BROTHERHOOD

G aylan bowed. "I am pleased to finally make your acquaintance, Master Taylor. Master Vankin." Magnus stood behind Gaylan, his hands tucked into his robes, a cruel smile on his face.

"What do you want?" Alex demanded. "Why have you brought us here?"

"Rest easy, Master Taylor," Gaylan said. "I want nothing more than to talk. For now." He strolled into the room, his black robes sweeping over the tops of his boots. Magnus trailed behind him like a dog. "I have wanted to talk to you for some time, now, so I was quite pleased when Magnus told me you both were in the dungeons below. I was less pleased when I ventured downstairs to find you both gone." He flicked his hand in the air and Magnus stopped immediately. "Magnus here assured me his spell would keep you contained, but, well . . . clearly he was mistaken." Gaylan dropped his hand back to his side, and Magnus crumpled at the same time. He hit the floor with a thud, blood dribbling from his nose.

"Master, please," he begged. "I—"

Gaylan made another gesture, and Magnus's words choked

off into silence. A horrified expression crossed his face, and he put his hands to his throat as if he could force his words to emerge.

"I am not interested in your excuses," Gaylan said to Magnus. "Nor your failures."

Alex could feel the power radiating off Gaylan. He had faced many powerful creatures and wizards in the past, but Gaylan was something more. An aura of age and assurance surrounded him. Alex suspected Gaylan had not been defied by anyone in a long time.

Gaylan reached the table where Alex and Whalen were and sat down. "Please, gentlemen. Let us be civilized while we still can."

Alex returned to his seat, slowly moving his hand away from the axe at his belt. Whalen looked between Alex and Gaylan with a worried expression on his face.

"Now, I believe your question was regarding your next step, yes?" Gaylan asked. He placed his hands flat on the table. They were strong hands, but unscarred. Alex wondered if Gaylan had ever handled a weapon before, been in battle, or if he had always relied on his magic to do the work for him. If so, then perhaps Alex could use that to his advantage.

"I'm thinking my next step is going to be to kill you," Alex said.

"Then you would fail," Gaylan snapped. His gaze locked on to Alex and didn't let him go. After a moment of tense silence, Gaylan's face relaxed into a smile, though the expression didn't reach his one good eye. "I suspect that would be a new experience for you, am I right, Master Taylor?"

"What do you mean?" Alex asked.

"I mean that considering all the adventures you have been on, you very rarely have faced a challenge that has defeated you."

"I worked hard—" Alex began.

"—and you found much success, yes, I know. But I believe one can take the measure of a man by examining his failures more than his successes."

"I thought you weren't interested in hearing about failures," Alex said.

Gaylan waved away Alex's words. "I'm not interested in *his*"—he pointed to Magnus, still silently quivering on the floor—"but I am *very* interested in yours. Not only have you failed to stop the Brotherhood on multiple occasions, but you still fail to understand what is truly going on here." He shook his head. "Did you really think that these adventures of yours had no other purpose except to provide you with the opportunity to defeat monsters, gather treasure, and uphold some silly notion about honor?"

"Do not joke about honor—" Alex began, hotly.

Gaylan laughed. "And there is that temper I've heard so much about. I wondered when it would appear."

Alex clenched his jaw and tried to get his anger back under control. He needed to stay calm and level-headed. He could see that this battle with Gaylan would be won with words and not weapons, at least not yet.

"Honor is more important than treasure," Alex said, quoting one of the first truths he had learned about in the *Adventurers Handbook*.

"No, *power* is more important than treasure." The scar along Gaylan's face twisted as he spat out the words. "I would think that you, of all people, would understand that. But once again, you have failed."

Alex opened his mouth, but Whalen put his hand on his arm and spoke instead. "You know we are powerful—we escaped from your prison. And we know you are powerful—we saw what you did to Magnus. You wanted to speak like civilized gentlemen, Gaylan, so dispense with the games."

"Master Vankin, I am surprised that you would lie to me." Gaylan clucked deep in his throat. "Claiming to be part of a *we* when we all know that *you* are blocked from accessing your magic. You are useless. And *you* did not escape from my prison." He pointed at Alex. "*He* did. He is the one who managed to summon his magic despite the wards placed on the cell and the spells that should have entrapped him. How did you do that, by the way? I'm honestly curious."

Alex kept his mouth shut.

"Ah, I see . . . silence is to be your strategy," Gaylan said. He leaned back in his chair. "A wise move. Very well. Then, if you would please follow me."

Gaylan stood up from the table and walked toward the tall windows along the far wall. He didn't look back, as if he expected Alex and Whalen to follow without question.

Alex glanced at Whalen, then, after a moment, they both joined Gaylan at the windows.

Gaylan threw open the shutters and spread his arms wide as if embracing the view.

On the other side of the glass lay a shifting kaleidoscope of colors. It made Alex dizzy at first, but the more he looked at it and studied it, he saw that what he had thought were just colors and shapes were actually small images of places, each one exquisitely detailed. Some places he recognized immediately: Mr. Clutter's shop. The Oracle's White Tower. The Tower of the Moon. Albrek's Tomb. He also saw images that looked to be bird's-eye views of Alusia, Vargland, Norsland, Thraxon, Nezza, Varlo. Other images flashed before his eyes, but they weren't of places he recognized.

"The known lands," Whalen murmured, standing beside Alex. "All of them. But how—? Why?"

"Gateway magic," Gaylan said. "You have only just begun to discover it, but I have had centuries to perfect its use." He reached out his hand, close enough to touch one of the swirling pictures, but he pulled back at the last moment. "One touch, and I am instantly transported exactly where I want to go."

"That is how you and the other members of the Brotherhood can travel through the known lands so quickly," Whalen said.

"And without much notice," Gaylan said. "It's beautiful. I designed the system myself."

"If only we had known what to look for," Whalen said, "we might have discovered your headquarters earlier."

Gaylan laughed. "I very much doubt that."

"Why do you say that?" Alex asked.

"Because this place," Gaylan gestured to the building they stood in, "does not exist anywhere in the known lands.

It is impossible to find unless you are a sworn member of the Brotherhood."

"If it doesn't exist in the known lands, then where does it exist?" Alex asked.

Gaylan nodded. "You are finally starting to ask the right kinds of questions, Master Taylor. It exists in a place *between* the known lands. A reality that is next door to the worlds that you know. By anchoring this place to the actual Golden Swan, I am able to eavesdrop on the adventurers who come and go from that place, learn the news of the different lands, keep an eye on my enemies, and evaluate who might be beneficial to my plans. You would be amazed at the amount of information I have been able to acquire without ever having to step foot out of this place."

He turned on his heel and headed for the windows on the opposite side of the room. He left the shutters open behind him.

Alex was tempted to grab Whalen's arm, touch one of the pictures, and escape while Gaylan's back was to him. He had even extended his hand toward Whalen when Gaylan spoke without looking around.

"I wouldn't do that, if I were you. Seeing as how you're not part of the Brotherhood, the gateway magic would split your soul into tiny fragments and scatter them to the winds. You would be lost before you ever arrived at your chosen destination."

Alex and Whalen exchanged a look. Alex lowered his hand.

"Now this," Gaylan said, "this is my favorite view of all."

This time when he opened the shutters, he did so reverently, as if what was on the other side was something so precious that it required the utmost protection.

Alex approached cautiously. The view was remarkably unimpressive. The perspective was as if they were standing on a hill, and the land that spread out behind the window was barren of life, the sand a soft gray color. Nothing moved. Alex could imagine the silence from that place seeping through the window and into the room.

He took a step closer. In the distance, though, was something that Alex thought he recognized: a low stone wall stretching from horizon to horizon.

"A wall?" he whispered.

"*The* wall," Gaylan corrected. "The wall between life and death. I believe you've been there a time or two yourself."

Alex swallowed. "You created a gateway portal to the *wall?*" He didn't want to believe it. He couldn't. "You're insane."

"I'm a visionary," Gaylan said. "I did not rise to be the head of the Brotherhood by having small aspirations."

"Traveling to the wall like this . . ." Alex shook his head. Every bone in his body screamed in protest at what he was seeing. "It is an abomination."

"Which is why I've never done it," Gaylan said.

"What?" Alex turned to look at him in surprise.

"Oh, the portal isn't for me to travel there. It is for someone *there* to travel *here.*" Gaylan's smile stretched across his face, pulling his scar out of alignment. A strange silvery sheen appeared in his blind left eye.

"But the amount of magic it would take to make that

possible . . ." Whalen shook his head. "It is beyond the ability of any one man."

"Precisely," Gaylan said, carefully closing the shutters.

Alex breathed a sigh of relief at not having to see the gray lands and the wall. He remembered all too well the pull of the wall, the desire he had to cross over into the shadowlands. He would have been lost there once had his elf friend Calysto not pulled him back.

"Where did you get the power?" Whalen asked quietly, not looking at Gaylan. "How are you harnessing it?"

Gaylan regarded Whalen for a long moment, then turned his attention to Alex. "What do you think our purpose is? The Brotherhood, I mean."

"To sow unrest in the known lands. To wage war and rule over them," Alex answered. He and Whalen had spoken many times about their theories regarding the Brotherhood.

Gaylan shook his head. "Again, you disappoint me, Master Taylor. Such narrow vision. Such small goals." He sighed. "Yes, controlling the known lands is important—even necessary—and the power we gain from that is certainly worthy of our time. But our goals in the known lands are not merely to sow unrest. We are looking for very special people to help with our very special project." He nodded toward the closed shutters behind him.

"Wizards," Alex guessed.

"Not just wizards, though they are high on our list. We search for magical people of all kinds, of all abilities and talents. We find them, we bring them here, and we, well, *persuade* them to relinquish their magic to us."

"The Orion stones," Alex said, feeling numb. "You were using the Orion stones."

"They really were quite handy," Gaylan said. "When Jabez stole them from me, it slowed us down considerably."

"He stole them from you?" Alex asked.

"Jabez had once been my most faithful servant," Gaylan said. "I trusted him like my own son." He stopped and then looked at Whalen. "Oh, but then he was originally *your* family, was he not? I should have known that he'd one day turn on me just as he turned on you. It seems neither of us could teach him the concept of loyalty." Gaylan reached out and gripped Alex's shoulder. "I must thank you for killing him."

Alex knocked away Gaylan's hand. "I didn't kill him for you."

"Are you sure about that?"

"What are you saying?" Whalen asked. His face had gone pale.

"You and Jabez were linked, mentally, because you were both wizards. But for many years, he hid himself from you. And then one day, that link was restored and you began to realize how evil he had truly become. It was almost as if he was challenging you to come find him. Does any of this sound familiar?"

It did to Alex. Whalen had told him those same details in what seemed another lifetime.

"That was you?" Whalen asked.

Gaylan smiled coldly. "Again you failed to properly estimate my powers. By then, Jabez had stolen the Orion stones and had hidden the Axe of Sundering from me. I needed them back. I didn't have time to do it myself, so I enlisted your help." He gestured to Alex and Whalen. "However unwittingly it was offered. And now I have everything I need to complete my spell and split open the wall."

"You're going to destroy the wall?" Alex asked in disbelief.

"Of course. The Axe of Sundering is the only object powerful enough to break the barrier between life and death. And the wall must be split asunder. How else will my true master finally return from beyond the shadowlands and assume control of *all* lands—known and unknown? How else will those of the Brotherhood achieve the immortality we were promised?"

"You're wrong, Gaylan," Alex said. "The Orion stones were destroyed along with Jabez, and the Axe has chosen me as its master. It will not work for you."

"But it will work for *you*," he said. "And that is all I need. Well, that, and the impressive amount of magic you can wield even when pitted against my own. I'm looking forward to adding your power to mine. And once I have your power, the Axe of Sundering will obey *my* command." He reached out his hand. A dark black shadow gathered around his fingers. Small flashes of lightning streaked through the blackness. "Now, this will not hurt at all."

At the last moment, Whalen roared and pushed Alex out of the way. Alex hit the ground hard. He felt something in his side snap, and an intense pain shot through his chest.

Gaylan's hand, already so close to Alex's forehead, touched Whalen's head instead.

Whalen screamed and the blackness spread down over his body, covering him completely. A flash of lightning lit up the room, temporarily blinding Alex. When he could see again, there was only a black smudge on the floor where the wizard had been.

Whalen was gone.

CHAPTER TWENTY-FOUR

BEYOND THE WALL

Gaylan cursed.

"Where is he?" Alex gasped. He tried to get to his feet, but the pain in his side kept him on his knees. "What did you do to Whalen?"

Gaylan clenched his jaw in anger. "The old fool. The spell is intended to absorb magical power, but if there is no power to absorb—or if the magic is blocked—then the spell kills. He is beyond my reach now."

Alex's blood ran cold. "You killed him? He's dead?" He couldn't imagine a world without Whalen Vankin. It was impossible.

Gaylan shrugged. "His selfless act to save you is merely a minor setback to my plan. I still have you—and the axe." He turned toward Alex and flexed his fingers again.

Alex's breath pulled at the pain in his side. Sweat ran down his face. He couldn't let Gaylan touch him. "My power is my own. No one will ever take it from me." He scrabbled away from Gaylan, crawling along the floor.

Alex needed his magic, his broken ribs were slowing him down too much, but the moment he turned his thoughts inward, he heard a clear sound, like the tolling of a bell, and Whalen's voice ringing out, repeating the same two words over and over.

Find me. Find me.

Alex gripped the axe at his belt, and the contact with the magical weapon only seemed to strengthen the connection. The sound of Whalen's voice rumbled through Alex's mind and body.

Gaylan continued to advance toward Alex, unstoppable as the tide.

Whalen? Alex asked in his mind. *Where are you?*

I'm here. I'm here.

The sound seemed to occupy a physical presence inside Alex's mind. He looked up at Gaylan's scarred and cruel face, but what he saw was an image of a single golden thread shimmering in the air. Alex realized that his connection to Whalen was still intact, master to apprentice.

The back of Alex's head hit the wall. He had crawled across the floor to the other side of the room, trying to get away, but now there was nowhere for him to go. He was trapped.

Gaylan crouched at Alex's side. His long fingers rested on his knees. "You should be honored, you know," he said. "Not everyone is offered such an opportunity to serve the Brotherhood."

"I will never serve you," Alex spat out between clenched teeth. "I'd die first."

Gaylan raised his eyebrows. "If you insist . . ." He lifted his hand and smiled.

Alex's eyes darted between the dark shadow gathering

around Gaylan's hand and the golden thread that only he could see. He knew his link to Whalen was mental, but perhaps, with some effort, it could be physical as well. He didn't know if it would work, but he had to try. He would only have one chance to get it right. If he missed, and Gaylan didn't, then Alex's power would be drained and the Axe would be used in the service of the darkest evil Alex could imagine.

He took a deep breath, hissing at the pain in his side, and concentrated all his magic and power and will into a single point—the end of the golden thread.

Hold on, Whalen. He sent his thoughts ahead of him. *I am coming.*

Then he grabbed the golden thread and held on.

He felt a sudden lurch deep in his belly, and his breath was knocked out of his lungs. His bones burned and his blood began to boil. He screamed, but he couldn't hear himself scream.

Alex opened his eyes in time to see the confused look on Gaylan's face. Gaylan's hand had not yet reached Alex's skin.

Alex? Whalen's voice reached him one last time. *Alex!*

He held on as the golden thread pulled him away from Gaylan and everything around him disappeared.

Alex woke in darkness. He knew that he was awake because of the pain. It felt as if he'd fallen down a long flight of stairs, hitting every step on his way down. He tried to sit up but the pain was too much, and he slumped back to the ground once more.

Where am I? he thought. *How did I get here?*

Even thinking hurt, but now that the questions had started there was no way to stop them. He tried again to get up and failed. All at once his body moved without his even thinking about it. He scrambled to his knees, looking around wildly. He knew he was trying to find someone, but who?

"Vankin," Alex said softly.

Yes, Whalen Vankin should have been close by, but why? Who was Whalen Vankin? Why should he be close? Alex tried and failed to find a face in his mind, the face that went with the name Whalen Vankin. His failure troubled him. His mind wandered for a time, going completely blank, and then a new question came: an important, urgent question that he had to answer.

Who am I?

For a moment the question didn't make sense. He thought about the answer for a long time, slowly forming the words in his mind before speaking.

"I am Alexander Taylor, adventurer, wizard, dragon lord, and . . ."

"Say it again," a voice inside his head demanded.

"I am Alexander Taylor, adventurer, wizard, dragon lord . . ."

"Again, louder," said the voice.

"I am," Alex started but stopped as a new pain ripped through his brain.

"Again," the voice demanded.

"I am Alexander Taylor, adventurer, wizard, and dragon . . ."

"Again, again, again," the voice screamed over the growing pain.

"I am Alexander Taylor, adventurer and, and . . ."

The words came slower and the pain in his head pounded like a giant hammer every time he spoke them. Alex didn't know why, but he had to keep repeating the words.

"I am Alexander Taylor, adventurer, wizard, dragon . . ."

Each time he said the words the pain grew. It felt like pieces of his brain were being torn away, and he put his hands on his head to try and protect himself from the pain. He continued to try to say the words, all of the words, but with each attempt he knew that something was forgotten, something was lost.

"I am Alexander Taylor . . . I am Alexander . . . I am Alex . . . I am . . ."

His mouth continued to move but there was no more sound coming out. The pain was so bad that he hardly noticed when he fell back to the ground and curled himself into a ball. Darkness closed in around him once more. When he woke again all of this would be forgotten, but there would still be one question to answer.

⋆

Out of the darkness came light, and with the light came pain. The pain was terrible, but it seemed to be fading. He moved slowly, unsure of himself and unsure of everything around him. His eyes felt out of focus, and the small lights above him were dim and seemed to be winking off and on. He reached out for them, trying to touch them or capture them in his hand, but he could not. His pain wasn't as bad when he put his arms down, and it was easier to breathe as well. For a long time, he stood looking up at the little lights, trying to remember what they were and why they were there, but he couldn't remember.

Eventually he noticed that the strange little lights above him were going out and staying out, but things were becoming clearer. He looked around and faced a blindingly bright light that appeared from nowhere. It confused and comforted him at the same time. He struggled toward this new light, and it grew brighter as he moved. He thought he must be getting closer to the light, because it was getting warmer. Everything he could see had changed, from darkness to gray and then to brilliant colors. The colors all had names, but he couldn't remember what they were.

Staggering forward, too weak and worn to worry about forgotten names, he watched the bright light climb into the sky. It was warm, and it would have filled him with hope, but he had forgotten what hope was. All that he knew was he had to keep moving, moving to where the light had come from. He tried to think of why he needed to move but there was no answer, there was only a desperate need to keep going.

As the light moved higher into the sky he stopped looking at it. He touched his side once, trying to force more air into his lungs. The searing pain forced him to his knees, and it was a long while before he could get up and move forward once more. He avoided touching his side as much as he could after that, holding his arm across his chest to prevent it bumping him and bringing back the pain.

As the bright light was sinking behind him he rested for a moment, looking into the bag he was carrying. It was empty, but he felt that there should be something there, if only he could remember what it was. This bag was important, but he couldn't remember why. The bag didn't matter. It was light enough to carry, and its straps helped him to keep his arm from bumping his side.

Times of darkness and light passed almost unnoticed. His only thought was to keep moving; moving to where the bright light had first appeared. The dark times were worse than when the bright light was above him. There were noises in the darkness, noises of things moving around him that he could not see. They were like ghosts in his mind, reminding him of things he had forgotten and could not remember.

Finally, after what felt like forever, he reached his end. Unable to struggle forward another step, he leaned against a large object that grew out of the ground. He was finished, and whatever force had driven him to move forward for so long was gone. There was nothing now, nothing but to sit and wait for darkness to cover him. Perhaps the darkness would take away his pain, and he could finally rest.

"Are you real?"

Alex felt someone poke him in the shoulder, pulling him from the dark fog that had filled his mind.

"You *are* real! How did you get here?"

Alex blinked and looked around. He was leaning against a stone wall that rose up from the ground behind him. In front of him was a vast expanse of rolling hills and plains. Crouching next to him was a young man in leather armor, his face shadowed by the hood of the cloak he wore.

"Where am I?" Alex asked. His mouth felt sticky, and his body ached, as if he had walked a long way in a short amount of time.

"You're beyond the wall," the man said.

"The wall?" Alex repeated.

"Between the living and the dead," the man said. "Which is impossible because I think you're still alive. How did you manage that?"

"I'm looking for someone," Alex managed. The pain in his side was still there, but it had lessened to a dull throb instead of a sharp stab.

"Who?" the man asked.

"I—I don't remember," Alex admitted. "Wait, you said we were beyond the wall?"

The man nodded and extended his hand to help Alex to his feet. "I've been here a long time, and I've seen a lot of people come here. But never anyone like you. What's your name?"

"I—I don't remember," Alex said again. "Who are you?"

"Zain Blackridge." He said it as though he expected Alex to have heard of him. He pushed back his hood, revealing a young face with blue eyes and blond hair. When Alex shook his head, without recognition, Zain's friendly expression hardened a little.

"I'm sorry," Alex said. "I'm still trying to get my bearings."

Zain folded his arms across his chest and looked Alex up and down. His gaze seemed to linger for a brief second on the

Axe of Sundering. "You said you were looking for someone. Might that someone be a wizard?"

A memory rushed into Alex's mind. "Yes! A wizard. Exactly." But he still couldn't conjure up a face to go with the memory. Was the wizard young, old? He didn't know. He just felt that he would recognize him when he saw him.

"I suspected as much," Zain said. "He must be someone pretty important—and powerful—to have you come looking for him in the shadowlands."

"He's the most powerful wizard who ever lived," Alex said without thinking.

The friendly smile returned to Zain's face. "That's good to know. Can I ask—what are your plans? For when you find him?"

"I need to help him," Alex said. "I came here to help him. To bring him back, if I can."

Zain's smile grew. "You sound like a good friend to have when trouble shows up."

Alex's memory was still shattered, but it felt like a voice was murmuring to him, low, in the back of his mind, and urging caution. Perhaps even distrust.

"You know, since I know this place probably better than anyone else, I could help you look for your friend," Zain said.

"Be careful," the voice in Alex's head said again. It sounded familiar, but Alex didn't know from where.

"How long have you been here?" Alex asked.

Zain shrugged. "Longer than I would have liked. When we find your friend, maybe you could help me too?"

"Help you? How?" Alex took a step back from Zain.

Zain licked his lips and looked down at the axe. "You know how to use that?"

Alex touched the axe and hesitated.

"Can I see it?" Zain stepped closer to Alex. "The workmanship looks incredible."

A rush of wind blew past Alex, materializing into an old man in worn wizard's robes. "Stop, Alex!" the wizard said. "Step away from him."

Alex obeyed without question. Memories flooded his mind like a wildfire burning away dry grass. He put his hand to his forehead. "Whalen?" he gasped.

"Stay out of this, old man," Zain snarled, all traces of friendliness gone from his face. "This is none of your business."

"Actually, it is." Whalen glanced at Alex. "Send him away, Alex. Now!"

Alex shook his head. "I don't know how—" He could feel a well of power inside of him, but he couldn't remember how to use it.

Whalen took his hand and the golden thread that had connected them once before appeared again. "I know the spell. You have the power. Now, banish him!"

Unknown words filled Alex's mind and he spoke them automatically. The power obeyed his command, shooting out of his fingertips like a tornado. It swallowed Zain in a cloud of dust and carried him away.

Whalen released Alex's hand and pulled him into an embrace. "It's good to see you. I'm glad you got my message. I wasn't sure it would work. Gaylan didn't touch you, did he?"

"No, well, I don't think so. Are you dead?" Alex asked. Whalen felt real, but so much in this place was not what it appeared to be.

"Yes, but it doesn't matter," Whalen said. "We don't have much time. He'll be back soon."

"Who was that man? Zain?"

"He is the dark wizard Gaylan hopes to free from death. He is the original founder of the Brotherhood, and if we don't stop him, evil will overtake the known world."

"But he is dead. He cannot cross the wall. Nothing can."

"He could if the wall was broken." Whalen looked at the axe at Alex's belt. "If it was Sundered."

Realization dawned on Alex. "This was Gaylan's plan. To use the Axe so Zain could break free of death and return to the land of the living."

"Yes," Whalen said.

Alex looked at the wall beside him. The top only reached to his waist. Over it, he could see the gray lands and the rolling hills that were familiar to him from his previous trips to the wall . . . though he had never been on this side of the wall before.

"Zain must not put his hands on the axe," Whalen said. "The wall must be protected. It must remain unbroken."

"And the dead must stay on this side of the wall," Alex whispered.

Whalen put his hand on Alex's shoulder. "Yes. I know you want to help me, but you cannot bring me back to the land of the living without opening the way for Zain to follow. That must never happen. He must stay here."

"I can't leave you here," Alex said. "You can't be dead!"

"It is too late for me," Whalen said. "If I had been able to access my magic, perhaps I could have stopped Gaylan another way, but at the time, I didn't have any other choice. Dying to save you was one of the best things I have ever done with my life. I am an old man; I have lived a good life. You still have things you need to do. Adventures to go on. Knowledge to gain. People to help. Go now. Take the Axe far away from here, defeat Gaylan, and never come back here. It is the only way."

"I won't leave you," Alex said.

"You must."

"How am I even supposed to return to the other side of the wall?" Alex asked. "Climb over the top? I can't use the Axe."

"No, you must return the same way you arrived. By using your dragon magic."

Alex nodded. His memories had returned and he knew the spell that would take him back to Gaylan.

"I am so proud of you, Alex. You are a fierce warrior and a powerful wizard, but most of all, you are a good man."

Alex embraced Whalen. "Thank you," he said. "I will never forget you."

A gust of wind blew past the two wizards and Alex looked up. Zain had returned with a storm of his own. Power rolled off him in waves. Anger had turned his blue eyes to ice, and his cloak billowed behind him like a dark shadow.

"Give me the Axe!" Zain thundered. He strode toward Alex, his hand outstretched.

Alex pushed Whalen behind him to protect him. "Never!" Alex shouted back.

"You dare to deny me, you worthless, pitiful, embarrassing excuse for a wizard?" Zain gestured wide with his arm and a bolt of lightning shot out of the clear sky and scorched the ground inches in front of Alex's feet. "You think you can defeat me? You can't kill me—I'm already dead!"

Alex held his ground. He kept his hand on the Axe, determined to keep it from Zain no matter what.

"We have all the time in the world here," Zain said. "Eventually, you will wither and die of old age, and I will still be as you see me." Zain circled Alex, his footprints lined with fire. "I suppose I could simply wait and then take the Axe from your cold corpse, but I've never had much use for patience."

Alex moved in a circle as well, always keeping his eyes on Zain.

"I fear I cannot help you," Whalen murmured to Alex. "Without my power . . . And if I stay here, I know you will try to protect me and that will distract you from this battle that you must not lose."

"Whalen—" Alex began, but then he felt a gust of wind behind him and knew that Whalen had vanished, moving away to a safer place.

"Do you know how long I have worked and waited for this moment?" Zain said.

"You'll have to wait even longer," Alex said. He worked a spell and a ball of ice flew from his fingers, heading straight for Zain's chest.

Zain's body suddenly became transparent, like he was a ghost, and the ice flew through Zain's body, crashing against the stone wall and shattering on impact.

Zain laughed. "As I said: pitiful." He returned to his more solid form and summoned a cloud of green gas that enveloped Alex. "And useless."

Alex coughed and gasped as the toxic gas filled his mouth and lungs. His eyes burned. He summoned a rain shower and the gas evaporated with a hiss as the water washed it away.

"Better," Zain said. "What else can you do, I wonder?"

Alex's mind raced. Zain was dead, and any weapon or spell he crafted to attack his body wouldn't work; the ice ball had proven that.

Alex changed tactics. He drew on his magic and created an illusion of himself, multiplying copies of himself until there were a dozen identical versions of Alex holding a dozen identical versions of the Axe. The illusions raced around Zain in a circle, trying to disorient the wizard. When they stopped, Alex had his back to the stone wall. He held his breath, hoping that his trick would work.

Zain shook his head. "As if I could be fooled by something so primitive as an illusion spell. The dead can see more clearly than the living. I know exactly which one is the real you." His eyes suddenly glowed red and he swung his arm in an overhand throw as if releasing a dagger. But instead of a steel blade, he threw a shaft of red light, sharpened to a point.

It pierced Alex's shoulder, pinning him to the wall. Alex slumped against the shaft of light; it was the only thing holding him upright. The illusions around him vanished as if they had never existed.

Zain dusted his hands together as if wiping away a layer of dirt. "There is nothing you can do to stop me, so why don't you just give me the Axe and all of this can be over. You can die and be with your friend Whalen. And I can return to claim the power that is rightfully mine."

Alex struggled to pull the shaft of light out of his shoulder, but it was wedged tightly into the wall. He couldn't pull it loose.

Zain stood in front of Alex and smiled. "Gaylan began as my apprentice two thousand years ago. You've seen his power. You know what he can do. I am far older and so much more powerful. You will fail, and I will win. Accept it."

Alex released his grip on the shaft of red light and pulled the Axe from his belt in nearly the same motion. He held it across his chest, blade glowing with a fierce, inner light. Zain was too close for Alex to manage a proper swing, but all Alex needed to do was get the edge of the weapon as close to Zain as possible.

Before Alex could move, Zain lunged forward and wrapped his hands around Alex's wrists.

Alex struggled to maintain control of the Axe, but Zain had better footing, better positioning, and better leverage. Alex was still pinned to the wall. There was nowhere he could go.

Slowly, Zain pushed forward, twisting Alex's wrists until he feared they might break.

Sweat beaded on Alex's forehead. He could feel himself losing ground. The pain in his side was overwhelming, and with one arm pinned to the wall, he was not strong enough. He gritted his teeth and redoubled his efforts.

Zain bared his teeth in a grimace and leaned more of his

weight forward. He pushed Alex's arms up as far as they would go until the Axe was past Alex's chest and head.

Slowly, so slowly, Zain forced the blade of the Axe of Sundering toward the edge of the wall.

Alex gathered all his strength and roared with one last effort to stop Zain.

But it wasn't enough.

Zain drove the Axe of Sundering into the stones at the top of the wall.

A tremor ran down the shaft of the axe. The weapon quivered in Alex's hands, and then a blast of white light exploded from the Axe. The earth rumbled beneath Alex. Zain took a step back, triumph in his eyes.

The shaft of red light vanished, and Alex slumped to the ground. He twisted on his knees and saw a crack splitting the wall from top to bottom where the Axe blade touched the wall.

"No," Alex whispered through numb lips. He looked around, hoping to see Whalen, hoping there was something he could do to stop what was happening.

The crack widened and spread as the stones surrounding it began to crumble to dust.

Zain began to laugh madly.

Out of the corner of his eye, Alex saw a dark cloud began to gather. He thought Zain had summoned another storm, but as it drew closer, he saw that the darkness was filled with spirits of the dead. They were pushing forward, racing forward, each one eager to be the first one through the crack in the wall.

"No," Alex shouted, but his voice was lost in the roar of the oncoming wave of the dead. "Stop!"

If the spirits heard him, they ignored him.

Zain caught Alex's eye, inclined his head in a nod, and then he stepped through the crack in the wall and was gone.

Chapter Twenty-Five
A New Name

Alex groaned. How could he have failed so terribly? He had been rash and foolish and angry, and now the wall was broken, Zain was free, and the Brotherhood would soon be in complete control of the known lands. This was not what he had intended, not what he had promised to do, but everything had happened so fast and he had been all alone. On his other adventures, he'd often had his friends with him to help him fight the battles or solve the problems. But this time the burden sat squarely on his shoulders.

He rubbed the sweat from his eyes with his good arm. The one that had been pierced by the shaft of red light hung limp by his side. He coughed, the motion tugging at his broken ribs, and blood filled his mouth. He spat it out and shook his head.

He had failed. There would be no calling back the spirits of the dead. There was no way to mend the wall. He had unleashed a terrible fate into the world of the living.

He was not fit to be a warrior or a wizard, and worst of all, he didn't feel fit to claim the title of dragon lord. All his training and experience and knowledge had not helped him in the moment when it mattered the most. A single decision—to try to use the Axe of Sundering, even knowing the danger it carried—and all the good he had done had been turned to evil.

"I cannot make this right," he muttered. "I don't know how."

"I have never known you to be a liar, Alex. Not even to yourself," a deep voice said nearby.

Alex lifted his head and his mouth dropped open in surprise. Salinor stood on the other side of the wall, his true-silver scales shining against the softer gray landscape behind him. He drew himself up to his full height, towering over Alex, who was still crouched by the wall, and snapped open his wings with a sound like a thunderclap.

"Salinor?" Alex asked weakly. "How did you get here? You were hidden away on the Isle of Bones."

"A dragon may go wherever he is needed, and at this time, I am needed here." He folded his great wings back against his powerful body. He snaked his head down to Alex's eye level. "I am here to help you."

"No one can help me," Alex muttered. "I have failed you. I have failed Whalen. I have failed myself. I destroyed the wall!" He pointed at the cracked stones around his feet. "I let Zain back into the world."

"You know I have no love for Zain or Gaylan or the Brotherhood, but Zain did say one thing that was true."

"That he will reclaim his power and rule the known lands?" Alex asked bitterly.

"No. *That* he will never do. Not as long as there is a

true-silver dragon drawing breath. Never, so long as the guardians remain."

"What then? What did he say that was true?"

"That you can take the measure of a man from his failures better than from his successes."

Alex gestured to the empty shadowlands around him. "Then take my measure, Salinor, because I find I have come up short."

Salinor shook his head. "Everyone fails at some point. It is what you do next that matters."

Alex rubbed his hand through his hair. "There is nothing I can do."

Salinor remained silent. The moment stretched out between them. Then he said, with a kind curiosity, "Do you truly believe that?"

Alex bowed his head. He thought back over his adventures. He had defeated trolls, bandits, and goblins. He had befriended elves, dwarfs, and oracles. He had helped his friends with their problems, sometimes even saving their lives. Even when a situation had seemed hopeless, he had always found a solution. He had been in dark places before and had always managed to find his way to the light.

"Is this really so different?" Salinor asked as if reading Alex's thoughts. "Your adventures—your choices—have led you to become a man of honor. What would an honorable man do now?"

"He would not give up," Alex said quietly. "No matter what."

Salinor nodded solemnly. "Will you give up? Now—when the need is so great?"

Alex reached out to grasp the stone wall. He used it for support as he pulled himself to his feet. He was broken and bloody, but he lifted his eyes to meet Salinor's piercing gaze. "No. I will *never* give up."

Salinor threw back his head and roared in triumph. The silver sheen to his scales grew brighter and brighter until Alex had to shield his eyes from the glare.

"Alexander Taylor," Salinor said, his voice deep and his tone formal, "you have proven yourself more than a man. More than a wizard, even more than a dragon lord. You are a true-silver dragon and now it is time for you to accept your destiny."

Alex swayed on his feet, but he forced himself to remain upright. "What must I do?"

"True-silver dragons are guardians—of people, places, ideals. We guard the world and protect it from evil in whatever form it takes."

"And I am to be one of these guardians? How?"

"You always had the potential to be a guardian, but it was your choices, your successes and your failures, that brought you to this point. At this moment, you are a nameless dragon. If you are willing to take your true dragon name and accept your role as a guardian, you can mend the wall and set things right."

"I can fix my mistake?" Alex asked, hope filling his heart.

Salinor nodded. "It will not be easy. But yes, it can be done."

"Then I accept," Alex said. "Tell me my dragon name,

and I will do whatever I must to stop Zain, Gaylan, and the Brotherhood."

"I cannot tell you your dragon name," Salinor said. "You must find it within yourself. It is powerful and personal. When you find it, you must keep it a secret because those who know your true dragon name would then have some power over you."

"I understand," Alex said. He remembered when Salinor had entrusted him with his true name and the feeling of power that had swept through him. "How will I know when I have found my true name?"

"You will know," Salinor said.

Alex nodded and closed his eyes. He reached deep into himself, looking for the path that would lead him to his true dragon name.

⟶ ⟵

Alex stood on a path that led through a dark wood. He knew he hadn't really gone anywhere, that his body was still standing by the wall between life and death, and that what he was seeing was only an illusion, a kind of vision that would help him find what he needed.

Quickly, now, Salinor's voice said in his head. *Stay true.*

Alex stepped forward and the trees around him seemed to draw closer, forcing him to stay in the center of the path and narrowing his choices. He walked faster until he was almost running. The path rolled out in front of him, leading him deeper and deeper into the forest. The tall trunks that lined the path rose up and over his head, the branches tangling together and turning it into a tunnel. Still Alex pressed on. He could sense the urgency. He needed to find the name.

He had no other choice but to go forward. He followed the tunnel as it twisted and turned until it eventually led him to a small clearing. A bonfire with true-silver flames burned in the center of the clearing.

Alex stepped forward, his eyes fixed on the fire. He had reached the deepest part of himself, a secret and private place. He looked around. The tunnel had closed behind him. He was alone in the clearing. A great peace settled over him. He couldn't feel his wounds any more. He had shed his doubts and fears and all that was left was a calm confidence that he was doing the right thing.

"I am Alexander Taylor," he said to the flames.

They flared at the sound of his voice.

"I am a true-silver dragon, and I have come to accept my destiny as a guardian of the good."

The flames sparked and twisted.

"I have come to claim my true name."

The silver flames spread out in thin tendrils along the ground, moving and twisting as though drawn by an invisible hand. They blazed with a white-hot light and then faded in a flash until only a line of coals remained of the bonfire. The glowing lines spelled out a name on the ground.

Alex took a step back.

"Invictus," he whispered.

As soon as the name passed his lips, he felt power like he had never known before surge through him. It mended his broken ribs and healed his wounds. It filled him with a light so tangible he wondered why it wasn't seeping through his skin. His true name echoed inside of him, melding into his bones and muscles. He was whole.

Without a thought, he transformed into his truest self: a giant, true-silver dragon. His claws gouged great trenches into the ground beneath him. His tail broke through the tunnel behind him. His wings snapped open and he launched himself into the air. His roar shattered the sky.

———◦•◦———

Alex opened his eyes, surprised to see he was eye-to-eye with Salinor. He thought his transformation had been part of the vision quest, but now he saw he had changed in reality as well. In his true-silver dragon form, he was nearly as tall and as large as Salinor, the most ancient of all dragons.

Salinor bowed his head. *Welcome, brother,* he said in Alex's mind.

Salinor, Alex replied. *I would have lost myself today if you had not shown me the truth. Long ago, you trusted me enough to share your name with me. I wish to do the same.*

It is not necessary—

It is, Alex said. *My name is Invictus.*

Salinor bowed his head again. *I am honored to meet you, Invictus, darloch est messer.* He spread his wings and his shadow fell over Alex. *I name you guardian of the wall between the living and the dead.*

Alex's breath left him in a rush. *You want me to guard the wall? Even after I cracked it?*

It is because you cracked it that you are the only one who can restore it to wholeness. The power is within you. As guardian, you need only reach out and make whole what was broken.

Alex looked down at the crumbling section of the wall. It seemed such a small crack, but it had resulted in great damage. If he could fix it, he would. He had to.

But first, Salinor said, *you must return the evil that has escaped to the shadowlands, where it belongs.*

How?

Defeat Gaylan. Defeat Zain. Destroy the Brotherhood. Then you will be able to mend the wall.

Alex nodded. *I will not fail you, my brother.*

Alex gathered all his strength and his dragon magic and then sprang into the air, his wings spread wide. He soared over the wall and saw a black streak of ash marking the gray lands below him. Zain had left devastation in his wake, which made it easy for Alex to follow the path toward a distant hilltop, where a speck of light was twinkling like a fallen star.

As Alex drew closer, he saw that the light was actually coming through the open shutters leading into Gaylan's headquarters. He remembered the two large windows on either side of the room and that the one connected to the gray lands was only one-way. The glass separating the portal had been shattered, blown through by Zain as he crossed over. As Alex flew through the same portal, he transformed from his dragon form back into a man. He landed hard and rolled to his feet, one hand on the axe at his belt, the other stretched out in front of him, a defensive spell tingling in his fingertips.

The spell remained uncast.

The room appeared empty, although Alex knew it was not. Gaylan and Zain had to be hiding somewhere. Shards of glass from the broken portal lay scatted across the floor of the main room. Alex took a step forward, careful not to step on any of the glass. He didn't want the sound of a crack to alert his enemies of his arrival. A door near the back of the room was ajar, and Alex made his way toward it.

He positioned himself near the entrance, but didn't enter.

"My lord," Alex heard Gaylan say. "I am at your service."

"You have done well," Zain said. "The Brotherhood has flourished under your leadership and care."

"Thank you, my lord," Gaylan said. "I am honored by your trust in me."

Alex tightened his grip on the axe. Anger rose up in his chest. Gaylan had killed Whalen. Zain had plans to destroy the world. The Brotherhood had brought nothing but misery and evil to the known lands. Every bit of power that Alex possessed screamed at him to rush into the room and put an end to this once and for all. But he waited. He knew from experience that it wasn't always wise to be led by his anger. It appeared he still had the element of surprise on his side. That was an advantage worth holding on to.

"There is still one more service you can render for me," Zain said. His voice sounded strange to Alex's ear. It was thin and whispery, as though Zain was merely a shadow of his former self.

Alex moved closer to the door and peered through the opening. He was careful not to reveal himself to the men inside the room.

Gaylan knelt on the floor, his robes spread around him like a black puddle of oil. Zain hovered in front of him. Alex blinked, and looked again. Yes, Zain was actually hovering. When Alex had confronted Zain on the other side of the wall, Zain had appeared solid. He had fought and attacked like a real person, but the Zain on this side of the wall was more ghost than man. The edges of his body were fuzzy and indistinct. He seemed to drift on a breeze that Alex couldn't feel. The faint light in the room shone through him.

"How may I serve you, my lord?" Gaylan asked, bowing his head. "Ask, and I will obey."

"My soul has escaped death, but my body has long since turned to dust. Without a new one, I am not nearly as powerful as I need to be."

Gaylan looked up at Zain. "My lord?"

"You are young and strong. You are powerful in your own right. Together, we would be unstoppable."

Alex's anger turned white-hot. Everything about this felt wrong to Alex. Dangerously wrong. He had to put a stop to it. Now.

"Wait!" Alex's O'Gash said with sudden clarity.

Alex looked down at the axe in his hand. He had grown accustomed to its weight and to its power. He felt connected to it in the same way he felt connected to Moon Slayer and to his staff. It was a part of him, and as he felt the power in the axe surge into his body, his mind cleared and a plan began to form itself in his mind.

"I understand, my lord," Gaylan said. He threw back his head and opened his arms wide.

Zain's eyes glittered and a cold smile crossed his face. He nodded and then his ghostly form swooped down and melted into Gaylan's body.

Gaylan screamed and his body shook. He fell forward, bracing himself against the floor with his hands. His head dropped, and Alex saw blood trickling from his mouth.

"My lord?" Gaylan's voice rasped in his throat.

"I am here." Zain's voice emerged from Gaylan's mouth.

Alex shuddered. He had never seen anything like this on any of his previous adventures, and there was a terrible wrongness to it that made the hair on the back of his neck stand up.

"Sleep now," Zain said. "I will summon you if I need you, but for now, I must learn how to control this new body of mine."

Gaylan's head bobbed as if he were a puppet on a string, and then his eyes rolled back in his head. When they cleared, they were glowing red, just as they had been when Zain and Alex had fought.

Now! Alex's O'Gash yelled, and Alex burst into the room.

Zain turned his head in surprise. "You!" he spat. "You can't be here! You should be rotting on the other side of the wall."

"So should you," Alex said. He summoned his newfound power as a true-silver dragon guardian and channeled it all into the Axe of Sundering.

CHAPTER TWENTY-SIX

AN HONORABLE MAN

The weapon responded immediately, bursting with a white light. A low hum filled the room as energy crackled from the blade's edge.

Zain lifted his hand and pointed it at Alex, but Alex was faster.

He gestured with his free hand, curling his fingers into a fist and then using his magic to throw Zain back against the wall.

The dark wizard hit the wood with a thud, and then fell to his knees on the floor. He looked up at Alex, his red eyes glowing brighter than before. He pulled his lips back in a snarl. "You are a persistent little fly, but my patience with you has worn thin."

Alex took a step forward, his hand still pointing at Zain, keeping him pinned to the floor.

"You couldn't defeat me when I was a spirit on the other side of the wall. Now that I have Gaylan's body and have added Gaylan's power to my own, I am indestructible. No one can defeat me now."

Alex clenched his teeth and tightened his hold on Zain.

He could feel Zain using his own magic to test the limits of the binding spell. He was strong—stronger than Alex thought possible—but if Alex had learned anything during his adventures it was that honor and goodness were always stronger than evil.

"I'm not sure if I thanked you properly for breaking the wall for me," Zain said. The veins in his neck throbbed with the dark wizard's efforts to find a weak spot in Alex's spell. "With the spirits of the dead now free, I will be able to add them to the Brotherhood, and my army—my power—will grow."

Alex took another step forward. The Axe still blazed in his hand, and the power it contained both anchored him and strengthened him. The plan Alex had in mind would work; he was sure of it.

"You are nothing," Zain spat. "You are nobody, and I will crush you beneath my boot heel."

Alex finally spoke one simple word: "No."

The red light flickered in Zain's eyes and an expression of uncertainty crossed his face.

"You believe that because you are powerful that you will win," Alex said. He stood in front of Zain and looked down at the dark wizard on his knees. "You believe that because you want something that you should get it. You believe that because you hold yourself in such high esteem that you can force others to bow to your will."

Zain tried to scuttle away from Alex, but he couldn't move. His red eyes lost their glow and returned to a normal shade of blue.

Alex shook his head. "But let me tell you what I *know*. I know that power should be used for good. I know that an honorable man is willing to make sacrifices for others. And I know that helping others creates strong friendships and lasting loyalty."

Zain opened his mouth, but no words came out. His shoulders slumped as Alex tightened his spell around the dark wizard.

Alex locked the binding spell and then held the Axe of Sundering with both hands. "And I know that evil will *never* win so long as there are good men willing to stand up for what is right."

He felt a deep calm in the center of his being. He had faced many enemies and fought in many battles, but this fight was different. This one felt more important than all the others. The fate of the known lands hung in the balance, and Alex knew what he had to do.

One last time, he swung the glowing Axe of Sundering in a wide arc.

A loud crack sounded in the small room and Zain's head rolled to a stop at Alex's feet, his body falling to the ground.

Both the head and the body began to turn gray, then black, before they disintegrated into powder and ash. Even the wizard's robes were gone.

Gaylan's body had been destroyed. Zain's soul had been destroyed.

Alex had cut off the head of the snake that was the Brotherhood, and the evil it had spread across the known lands would now wither and die.

He slipped the Axe into his belt and bowed his head. Alex thought he would feel a sense of triumph at the victory, but he mostly felt sad inside. He was sad that Gaylan and Zain had spent so much of their lives and their energy pursuing power. He couldn't help but wonder what they might have been capable of if they had decided to be men of honor instead of men of evil.

The ground rumbled beneath Alex's feet. A crack appeared in the floor, zigzagging its way towards the door and up the walls. Dust and bits of plaster rained down from the ceiling. Alex looked around in alarm.

Gaylan's recreation of the Golden Swan began crumbling around the edges. Alex wondered if the actual tavern was experiencing the same damage. He hoped not. Alex ran back into the main room. The cracks in the floor and the walls continued to spread throughout the building.

Alex saw a pile of gray ash on the floor. It was where Magnus's body had fallen after Gaylan had punished him. Alex smiled grimly. It appeared he had been right in thinking that the power of the Brotherhood had been broken, and those who had served its evil purposes would suffer the same fate as Gaylan and Zain.

The building was collapsing around him. He had to find a way to escape. The two large windows on either side of the room trembled in their frames. The one leading to the shadowlands was already shattered and fractured, but the one holding all the gateway images of the known lands was still intact.

Just as Alex took a step toward it, the window exploded,

showering him with sharp shards of colored glass. He twisted away and put his hands up to protect his face and head. Some of the shards still cut into him and he felt small trickles of blood on his back and legs.

He looked up and his gaze was caught by the scene he saw through the window that connected the tavern to the shadowlands. Alex could see the silvery sheen of Salinor's scales in the distance. And next to the dragon was a long, flowing shadow pouring through the cracked wall. The spirits of the dead were returning to the shadowlands.

Alex smiled. Here was more evidence that the Brotherhood's evil had been broken.

It is time, Salinor's voice spoke in Alex's head. *Time to mend the wall.*

Alex nodded, even though he was alone in the room. He ran towards the window. Gaylan had said it was one-way only, but Gaylan had never anticipated the power of a guardian.

Alex jumped through the window and immediately transformed into his dragon form. He loved the feeling of freedom that came with the change. He pointed his snout toward the wall and beat his huge wings once, twice, three times—gaining speed with each downward thrust.

In no time at all, he had reached the wall and touched down next to Salinor, folding his wings against his body.

"You made swift work of the Brotherhood, I see," Salinor said.

"There was no time to waste," Alex answered. He looked over the wall. "Have all those who belong to the shadowlands found their way home?"

Salinor nodded. "I believe so."

"Then it is time for me to fix my mistake and mend the wall." He had reached his claw out to gather the scattered stones when Salinor spoke.

"A moment, if you please."

"What is it?"

Salinor nodded at a figure approaching the wall from the shadowlands. "Perhaps there is one last task for you to do."

Alex looked down and saw it was Whalen. "My friend," Alex said. "I am glad to see you are safe."

"Safe, yes," Whalen said. "And grateful that the shadowlands have been set to rights again."

"Whalen, I cannot thank you enough for everything you have done for me. I wish Gaylan had not . . ." Alex stopped, sadness filling his throat. "You sacrificed your life for me."

"I would do it again," Whalen said.

"You are a loyal and true friend," Alex said. "And a powerful force for good."

Whalen inclined his head. "I simply tried to do the right thing whenever I could."

"It's not fair—" Alex began, then stopped, an idea sparking in his mind. He looked from Whalen to Salinor. "Salinor, what exactly do my duties as guardian of the wall require from me?"

Salinor seemed to smile, as if he knew what Alex was thinking. "You must protect the wall from any and all evil that might seek to break it. You must preserve the balance of light and darkness, and protect those who serve the light. You must swiftly answer any summons from any of the other guardians who call for you and help them to the best of your abilities. You must fight for honor, loyalty, and goodness the rest of your days."

Alex nodded slowly. "I can accept those responsibilities." He smiled. "I learned how to do most of those on my adventures, after all."

Salinor laughed. "And I suspect you will learn even more on the adventures yet to come."

Alex tilted his head. "I thought being a guardian meant I couldn't go on any more adventures."

"Not at all. Being a guardian simply means you have more responsibilities," Salinor said. "But there is nothing stopping you from choosing to undertake another adventure."

Alex nodded. "I understand. And I am glad to know that I can still go on adventures. Though I think I will be taking a break from them for a while. I would like to spend some time learning how to be the best guardian I can be."

"I think that is wise," Salinor said. "Now, ask me what you really wish to know."

Alex looked back to Whalen. "As guardian of the wall, am I allowed to make an exception? If I feel it is warranted?"

"You are," Salinor said.

"And how might I make that happen? If I happened to find a soul worthy of granting access past the wall?"

Salinor grinned and looked down at Whalen. "You simply invite that soul to join you on this side of the wall."

Alex nodded and turned to Whalen. "Master Whalen Vankin, you are the noblest, strongest, best wizard I know. The known lands still need you. If you wish to continue fighting alongside me, I will grant you access to cross the wall."

Whalen stood up straight with pride. "I do wish it, Alex. I believe there is much more for you to do, and I would be honored to continue to be your mentor and your friend."

"Then cross the wall, Master Vankin." Alex gestured to the crack, glad for once that it was there.

Whalen nodded and made his way through the broken stones. When he crossed the barrier, his wispy, ghostly form solidified back into a solid, normal man. Whalen looked down at his body, flexing his fingers and stretching his legs. "I feel like a new man," he said with a laugh. "And my magic! It's back. I am whole again."

Alex smiled, glad his friend had returned.

"The wall?" Salinor prompted gently.

"Oh, yes," Alex said. He reached out his giant silver claws and scooped up the scattered and broken stones. He stacked them back into place on the wall's foundation and sent a surge of power through his dragon's leg and into his claws. The stones fused together, stronger than before. When he removed his claw, no hint of a crack remained.

Alex transformed back into his human form and turned to Whalen. "That's done."

"And done well," Whalen said.

Salinor nodded his approval. "Farewell, Master Taylor, Master Vankin," he said. "Until we meet again." The great dragon leaped into the air and flew away without another word.

Alex watched until Salinor was a mere silver speck in the sky. And then even that disappeared from his sight.

Whalen slapped him on the back and smiled. "I believe our work here is done, Master Taylor, wouldn't you agree?"

"For now," Alex said with a smile. "For now."

STORIES FOR ANOTHER TIME

Alex stood at the end of a stone dock in the harbor of Valora. The sun was just rising in the east, and a gentle breeze was blowing out to sea. He could feel when Whalen approached, but he didn't move or speak.

"Early or late?" Whalen asked.

"Early," Alex answered, knowing what Whalen meant. "A little more than two hours ago."

"Darthon and his people will be happy to see that you're back," said Whalen.

"Any word of Joshua and the other hostages?" Alex asked.

"They reached the city three days ago," Whalen answered. "Joshua's been asking about you—where you were and when you'd be back. He was very worried about you going off to the black lands alone. I think he's planned a mission to rescue you."

"There was no danger," Alex answered. "I made a vow to return to the black lands and I had to keep it. Besides, I needed to retrieve Moon Slayer."

"And?" Whalen pressed.

"The shadows are free at last," Alex said. "The sea elves are free to return to their ancient homes."

"And your other friend, the dragon Jabez had enslaved?"

"Flying south. It seems there are some fairly large islands there that the men of Jarro haven't yet discovered."

"Good, that's very good," Whalen said softly and fell silent.

The two wizards stood in silence, watching the sea until the sun was fully up. Dockworkers started to appear near the shore, and the city behind them began to wake.

"So," Whalen finally said. "What's next, then?"

"For you, or for me?" Alex questioned.

"For both of us, I suppose," said Whalen.

"I imagine you're ready to go home, at least for a time," said Alex.

"Yes, I am, even knowing what's coming."

"What's coming?"

"There will be a lot of questions, Alex. Wild rumors, nervous talk, fear even," Whalen said. "You've destroyed the Brotherhood, Alex. Powerful people all over the known lands have mysteriously vanished. People will want to know what happened."

"There may not be as many questions as you think," Alex said, rubbing his chin. "And I think that most if not all of the questions should remain unanswered."

"Unanswered? How would that help?"

Alex shrugged. "Powerful, well-known people have gone missing. What good could come from telling everyone that those who have gone missing were, in fact, evil?" Alex asked.

"The Brotherhood was hidden for a reason. People won't want to hear that the people they trusted were evil."

"No, I'm sure they don't want to hear that," Whalen agreed.

"The council of wizards will need to know the truth, even if they don't believe it, but other than that. . . . I just don't see any good coming from telling everyone what really happened," Alex said.

"You're right," Whalen said. "This adventure of ours should remain mostly secret."

"Good," Alex said. "Very good."

"When do we start for home?" Whalen asked.

"I'm not going home," Alex answered. "Not yet, anyway."

"Oh?"

"Jabez left many evils and scars in Westland and in Jarro. They need to be healed."

"Time will heal them, Alex. It isn't your task to undo all that Jabez did in this land," Whalen said.

"No, it's not my task, but sometimes healing needs a little help," said Alex. "I think the sea elves will also need some help."

"Yes, I think that's true," Whalen said, a faint smile crossing his face. "I know of at least one elf who would be happy to have you stay for a time."

"What?" Alex asked.

"I was just thinking, if you intend to stay in Jarro for a while, you might think of returning to Midland. Perhaps you could escort your friend Lupo to the oracle. I'm sure that would please him, and improve his chances of seeing the oracle," Whalen said.

"That would make Lupo happy, and it would give me a chance to explain why I had to lie to him. That would make me feel better, I think," Alex said.

"Yes, I'm sure that explaining things to Lupo would help you both," Whalen replied, running his hand across his beard.

"There is much to be done, here and in other lands. If the sea elves are to become dark elves once more, and if Westland and Jarro are to be at peace, well . . ."

"There is indeed much to do," Whalen said. "And many new adventures as well."

"Oh, I still plan to go on adventures," Alex said quickly. "I am an adventurer, after all."

"And going on adventures isn't an easy thing to give up," Whalen added. "Not even for an old man like me."

"You're not that old," Alex said, smiling at his friend.

Whalen laughed. "I hope I live long enough to hear the stories of your future adventures told."

"Stories for another time," Alex said as he and Whalen walked down the dock toward the city. "There will always be stories for another time."

Discussion Questions

1. At the beginning of the story, Whalen Vankin appears and asks Alex several questions to make sure of his identity. If you and a friend were in a similar situation, what questions would your friend ask you?

2. When Alex first meets Joshua, he senses almost immediately that he can be trusted. When you meet someone for the first time, are you usually more cautious or do you trust people from the beginning?

3. During their voyages together, Alex notices Whalen is distracted at times, and Alex is concerned that Whalen is trying too hard to make sure his magic is hidden from Jabez. Have you ever had a problem that you've tried to hide from your friends? Have you ever had a friend try to hide a problem from you? How did that turn out?

4. To join the caravan, Whalen and Alex pretend to be merchants. If you were in their place, what part of being a merchant in a caravan would be interesting to you? What part would be boring?

5. When Lupo first challenges Alex to practice sword fighting with him, he's confident that he's better than a merchant's

apprentice and is surprised by Alex's skill. What hidden talents or skills do you have? Are there specific skills that you wish you had?

6. In the cave of dreams, Alex sees several scenes that predict the future. If you were able to predict the future, would you rather see what would happen to you, to someone else, or to the world in general?

7. As a dragon lord, Alex has learned that dragons have a true name that holds great power, and so they only share it with those they absolutely trust. Does your given name have any significance? If you could pick another name to call yourself, what would it be?

8. After his battle with Zain, Alex finds himself facing the consequences of a true failure. What is his response? What should we do when we fail?

9. The Axe of Sundering is unique because it is made entirely by magic. If you had the power to create anything at all with magic, what would it be—and why?